The Ten-Day Forecast

The Ten-Day Forecast

Steven Hartman

iUniverse, Inc.
New York   Bloomington

The Ten-Day Forecast

This is a work of fiction. All of the characters, names, incidents, organizations, and dialogue in this novel are either the products of the author's imagination or are used fictitiously.

iUniverse books may be ordered through booksellers or by contacting:

iUniverse
1663 Liberty Drive
Bloomington, IN 47403
www.iuniverse.com
1-800-Authors (1-800-288-4677)

ISBN: 978-1-4401-5699-1 (pbk)
ISBN: 978-1-4401-5700-4 (ebk)

Printed in the United States of America

iUniverse rev. date: 8/20/2009

For Maggie

1

I think we remain virgins for quite some time. I mean, even after the first time, what do we really know? We stay babies for a long time and continue to grow, even when we are all grown up. I take great satisfaction knowing that I can always learn something new whether or not I'm an old dog. Virginity had always meant something else to me besides remaining celibate; the loss of virginity was saying goodbye to innocence, an ignorance that changes you from a blissful state into reality. You are thrust into a world that holds more responsibility and danger around every corner. There is a tree in everyone's life with a lot of cherries that need popping. With each loss you gain more education, you're more experienced. It's a new sensation of pleasure, pain, excitement, loss, happiness or realization.

I can't sleep tonight because tomorrow, at four in the afternoon, I'll share my last name with someone else. Linked bank accounts and a little less tax owed at the end of the season is what I have to look forward to, along with starting a family. I'm in love but my feet are cold. I don't know if I should take solace in the fact that Las Vegas odds give us a fifty-fifty chance of survival or if I should be scared of it. Does one out of every two people make the wrong decision? I've gambled once and lost, I must ask myself if the rate of success improves or is history destined to repeat itself?

As I pace this foreign, unfamiliar room alone, I can't help but think of how I got here. The women I loved and loathe; the ones I hurt and was hurt by. And the shower. I never cared too greatly for a shower that has been shared by hundreds, if not thousands, of people. The water pressure is too low. I wish we were getting married closer to home, but I can't complain with this as a second choice.

The first girl I ever loved was Lisa. She was nine and I was a blossoming eight and a half. Our eyes met on the first day of school. Her purple t-shirt with the flower in the middle made my Elementary heart go pitter-patter. It was also the one and only time I spread a sexually transmitted disease, one I wasn't even aware that I had. Lisa made sure the whole fourth grade class knew it too.

It started out as a bet at the beginning of October. Bradley Haneday, who stood as the tallest kid in class with his spiky blonde hair, wagered his chocolate milk against the big chocolate chip cookie my Mom packed in my lunch that day. I would have to go up to Lisa Soren and kiss her.

"Kiss her where?" I asked.

"I'll give you odds." Brad replied.

"What are odds?"

"My Dad says it when it's football season, like he has odds on the Cowboys. I guess it's a better deal. So, kiss her on the cheek and you get my chocolate milk. But kiss her on the lips and I'll give you a dollar."

Little did I know that this exact scenario would play out nearly twice a lifetime from now.

"Okay."

"Shake on it," Brad said holding out his hand. I took his hand and gave him a good hardy shake and then I started my monumental walk across the playground.

Lisa sat with her girlfriends talking about whatever eight-and-nine-year-old girls talk about. Truthfully I don't know, and honestly,

I didn't care then. My slow approach was not going to interrupt a Berlin Wall crumbling debate. My heart pounded and, this may or may not be accurate, but my hands were sweating too. Reminiscing about it still makes my hands sweat to this very day.

There were three others on the swings and their conversation broke as I got within ten feet. That is when I realized I had no game plan. I had no way to pull this kiss off. Granted I could get close but would probably be pushed away, falling on the dirt and followed by a glass-shattering screaming. My return walk to Brad would not consist of dignity and there would be no chocolate chip cookie upon my arrival.

"Hi Drew," Chelsea said softly. She was Lisa's best friend at the time and, one and a half years later, would end up being the first girl I ever danced with.

"Hi Chelsea," I replied. I rubbed my possibly sweaty palms on my jeans and looked in the general direction of Lisa. "Hey Lisa, can I tell you something?"

"Okay." The term bitch did not exist amongst my vocabulary until the spring of my sixth grade year but her tone of voice portrayed such a description. That was irrelevant; I had a bet to win. A cookie was on the line.

I went right up to her, still unable to look her directly in the eyes, took a deep breath, and with one swoop and, may I add, slyness, I plopped a quick one right on her lips. I triumphantly smiled as one chocolate milk and one dollar waited upon my return. I wish that was all I received.

"Ewwwwww!" Lisa started followed by her friends.

Once again, I lacked the words at the time, but "oh shit" seems like a good phrase.

Lisa hopped off the swing, arms flailing about.

"Cooties!" Her cries tripled by her friends. My face turning light red and increased in darkness for every second this continued. "Drew kissed me!"

My childhood STD transmitted, I pivoted away and rushed towards Brad. Chocolate milk and a dollar, I didn't think it was worth it. At age eight and six months I thought my life was over, I'll forever be known as the boy who gave Lisa cooties. My first love had gone bust. She won't marry me. We won't grow old together.

The rest of the school year is all a blur as what happens when you get older. Remembering becomes a useless chore and ends in forgotten memories and frustration. Occasionally, I'll pass a playground and the scene will replay in my mind; always the same result and the same feeling of my first rejection.

As the middle school years crawled on very little excitement happened. I had my crushes and the girls who once had chests similar to my own had begun to grow, unlike mine. Seventh grade started with most girls taller than I however, by the time I entered high school, I had all but caught up.

Everything with Brad was becoming a dare or a bet. He dared me one night to call Missy and tell her I liked her. He even held out the phone and, after dialing the numbers, said, "You tell her you have a crush on her or I say you want to touch her boobs". (Oh, how we naively teased those whose breasts grew only to realize a little later on in life that the one big difference was the biggest thing we craved.) I went for the latter. She had a boyfriend at the time and therefore my feeble attempts at a girlfriend failed once more. I was just glad to learn that Missy's house sat beyond my high school district lines. Knowing I would not see her in high school helped me overcome my humiliation easier.

Chelsea, Brad and I were the triangle of average high schoolers. Chelsea's ambition to be active in studying and reading books removed her from the Lisa Soren crowd. She was the first person I ever knew who voluntarily watched a documentary.

Brad at this point had taken on the role of band member playboy. His girlfriends came steadily throughout the freshman year or, as I readily pointed out during a heart-pounding game of "Madden", "he was getting some mad band ass". He neither flaunted his successes nor did he make a third wheel out of me. Whenever possible, Chelsea tagged along and the four of us roamed the mall, the arcade and the movies. The two girls always five steps ahead of us Gentlemen. It mattered little where we wanted to go; Chelsea and Clarinet Girl led us into shops that smelled of fruity soaps and lotions. Brad often dropped hints that I ought to "tap" Chelsea.

I wasn't exactly sure what tapping involved, I just knew it was something I wanted to try. I found myself staring more at Chelsea. Her chest. Her butt. Her eyes. Her smile. It all appealed to me. The sexual tension grew and often showed its lovely, ugly face when we asked each other for advice on how to pursue the crushes we had; that subtle "oh" or shift of the head that screamed silently, "But what about me? I like you too." A fourteen-year-old doubts and fears were always strong enough to push away the possibility of Chelsea and me getting together.

The summer between freshman and sophomore year Chelsea and I, Brad and now Drummer Girl, sat in Brad's backyard, his parents away for the weekend. We drank our pops, ate our chips and talked. Brad and Drummer Girl flirted, touching each other. His hand caressed her leg while her hand interlocked with his. I caught myself observing the display and felt my heart beat quickly and every so often skip. I wanted that and the girl I should be having it with sat not two feet away from me.

Brad asked Drummer Girl to come inside for a moment and she lovingly obliged. We knew they were headed for a heavy make out session which left Chelsea and I alone on a cool, clear, starlit night.

"So."

"So."

"It's a beautiful night," Chelsea said. Her face pointed toward the stars as her eyes looked in my direction. I knew this, for I was doing the same thing.

I was full on determined to find out the truth whether it was good or bad. Determination combined with curiosity and a scared shitless mentality dropped my hand from my lap onto the swing padding. Like cold molasses in January, I slowly moved my hand closer to hers. It must have been ten solid minutes before my fingers crept next to hers. I made contact. Pinky to pinky and she accepted.

Simultaneously we let out a chuckle and turned our heads toward each others as our hands slipped into one another's. Closer and closer to one another, I had no idea what to do or if I was going to be good at it. But in cases such as this a tiny voice in our head knows that you are welcome to advance forward and go for that kiss.

"Green light to go forth," the General guiding my conscience said and our lips touched, lightly at first but gaining intensity as our kissing turned into a full on make out. Over a year's worth of sexual energy and passion was escaping.

Something nervously was happening downstairs. I was becoming aroused and I feared that this may very well be a turn off for her. I shifted a bit and tried to conceal the impossible.

"Everything okay?" She inquired.

"Yeah, of course," I replied as I continued kissing her.

Our arms embraced one another's body. I made it to first base and it was perfect.

Brad informed me that he eagerly watched Chelsea and me, expelling a congratulatory quiet cheer at our expense, before rendezvousing with Drummer Girl on his twin bed. The next day we talked of our ventures. First we spoke of my incredible lip-locking experience and then he revealed his loss of virginity.

The rest of the summer flew by quickly and by Labor Day we were all back in school. Chelsea and I spent what seemed like every waking moment with one another. If we couldn't walk somewhere, our parents drove us, and if our parents weren't around, we bribed our siblings. My brother, David, had a less fulfilling summer. His started out fairly different from how mine did. He was starting college in the fall and his girlfriend of eighteen months had decided to break his heart. Perhaps what happened set the mood for the rest of his life. You can always look back at heartbreak and realize how necessary it was, but never after it happens.

David was an aspiring average Joe. His life, I felt, would excel him to mediocrity. Married a little too young. Kids a little too early. David got stuck in the dead end job that no one wants to do. Nine to five held little excitement for him and by his late twenties with a young son and incoming daughter; he was weighing in at two-twenty-five, not muscle, and rising. Needless to say, and in complete honesty, what once was a life filled with bad decisions was a life I aspired for.

At eighteen, David was a good looking young man on the road to Eastern Michigan University. He dealt with his break up by seeking out the comfort of friends and their pot. More often than not that summer David would be getting home as I was waking up. By the time I was out of the shower, he was asleep and usually remained in that state until four in the afternoon. I never mentioned this to my parents, they already knew, and when they debated over how to handle it, I sat in another room or nearby quietly eavesdropping relishing the fact that I was the good son. They worried as mothers and fathers often do with little control over the situation. They prayed it was a phase and hoped he would meet a girl who would kick him out of it.

David and I talked every once in a while. I held back Chelsea information as much as possible with respect for his broken heart. Conversations were often unclear and came back to the same topic.

"She's going to dump you, they all dump you. You know why? 'Cause they're all cheating whores." David had become quite cynical since his infamous break up. Half the time I would tease him about it.

"If she was such a cheating whore, why do you miss her?"

"Huh?" He darted back. Whenever he was stoned he couldn't make sense of anything that he didn't already know or anticipate. Telling him that Dad asked one of us to mow the lawn would have garnered a similar response. "They all want to leave something good to try something they think is better. That's never the case."

"What if the other person is better?"

"Huh?"

"Dad wants one of us to mow the lawn."

"I have to poop." Satisfied with that response he would head to the nearest bathroom and with a grin on his face, close the door, excited for his odor altering opportunity.

"I guess that means I'm mowing the lawn." There was no use debating. David was going to take care of his business and most likely fall asleep while doing it. My day was just starting and I was going to rake in fifteen dollars for lawn maintenance. "What should I do if Amy calls?"

"Tell her to go screw a donkey, that slut," David yelled through the door. I stood nearby for three more seconds for the follow up. "Wake me up if she does. Do you think she will?"

"Everyday is a new day," I replied philosophically.

"That it is." He said and let the gastro-pyrotechnics begin.

Back and forth. The blades roared with a cutting fury at a volume that dwarfed that of my headphones. Listening to anything but a lawnmower engine was impossible. All that existed were my thoughts, which I had to be careful about, because most of the time my mind wandered to Chelsea. I contemplated what she was doing at this very moment. I knew the answer. She was hunched over a register at the music store in the mall but my concern was what she was wearing. This produced the danger as I cared very little about her shoes and socks; it was her shirt, her bra, her pants, and her panties that interested me and it was at this point that I needed to find a different and less alluring topic to ponder. The neighbors of fourteen years and the first non-relatives to change my diaper probably did not want to see little-Drew-next-door's raging semi, and, bless their souls, I cared not to show them.

The future ahead was a mystery and I remember thinking about the very real possibility of spending the rest of my days on Earth fantasizing about girls, their clothes, and their nudity. Is this what men of today's society, and each one that preceded our own, dealt with every minute of every hour of every day? Yes, it sure was.

As human beings, especially immortal and infallible teenagers, we are prone to the ideas that the burdens of life are what happen to other people. They get into the car wrecks that make the nightly news, they died by mountain lion molestation in the wilderness, they get broken hearts, and as I twisted the lawn mower around for another lap across the yard, I reassured myself that heart breaks happen to David, not me.

Fifty minutes had passed by; the lawn was manicured. The morning summer sun had temperatures on the rise and I had developed a great sweat. I entered the air conditioned house and felt a chill run down both my arms. My two desires were lemonade and a shower in that order, but instead, when I strolled into the kitchen, David was sitting at the table looking physically tired but very mentally awake suffering from a female induced thousand-yard stare.

For as long as I could remember I prided myself on buckling down and being there for someone when they needed a shoulder. David required one. so as I pulled the lemonade off the top shelf of the refrigerator and grabbed a plastic cup from the cupboard, I inquired about his mental state.

"To have love, and to have lost," he started.

"She called didn't she?" I was young and ignorant and didn't know that the same tree that made me think of the park that Chelsea and I spent nearly two hours eating lunch at, playing on the swings and slides, and walking hands clasped together yesterday could make another man remember a joyful memory turned sour and bitter.

"It sneaks up on you. When you least expect it." David kept his head lowered, hurt and reminiscing. "All the good things you once had are gone."

"How exactly did taking a crap remind you of Amy?"

"We had sex in that shower a few times."

"I shower in that shower."

"Yeah, as is life. Don't worry, we let the water run for a while after."

"That sanitized it," I replied sarcastically inclined never to bathe in that bathroom for the rest of my time in this house.

"Do you love Amy? Or do you hate her? Ya know, for what she did." It was a strong question that couldn't be answered quickly. After someone puts you through hell, I needed to know if love evaporated or was it just too powerful to leave. David sat motionless staring into his hands.

"I love her. But I'm working on it." My brother struck back as hard as I hit catching me off balance. "This Chelsea girl, you love her?"

I stood at the kitchen counter for nearly a minute, my eyebrows curling inward, unable to drink my lemonade. The condensation dripping coolly amongst my left hand as my right hand balanced my body against the counter. I have never been in love and could not be sure of the exact emotional punch it could have, for love has the annoying tendency to sneak up on you when you least expect it without confirmation that the one you desire, desires you back.

"The possibility is there, I suppose. I don't know," I replied. David's eyes ascended upon my own and with a half smile as if to claim a checkmate, he chuckled a bit.

"You love her."

Fifteen-plus years on this planet and up until that point I had never been this scared. Three years of friendship and now one month of dating, being boyfriend and girlfriend, he was right. I felt an emotional assault fire upon my life, the risk of loving, the brick wall tumbling with the might of a San Francisco earthquake. Without my affirmation, my heart was exposed to all kinds of possibilities and I was overwhelmed and frightened.

"Should I tell her?" I asked my brother.

"You should, indeed, and if she doesn't love you back, you know what you do?"

My mouth gape wide open, I begged for his answer silently.

"You donkey punch her."

"Do what?"

I wanted to kick myself for falling for ritualistic sibling harassment. He just laughed prior to zoning out once more. His cheek rested in the palm of his hand. Surprisingly, this was one of his better days since the breakup. He lifted his leg slightly and expelled a gradual fart. It lasted a shattering ten seconds pulling him out of his trance. I stood at the counter, sipping my lemonade, and accepting it.

"I could go for some weed," he proclaimed and looked at me.

"Well, I don't have any."

"Ever try it?"

"No."

"Hmm, maybe I have some upstairs." David shot up from his chair and headed to his room.

By the time I finished my beverage and passed his open door, he was sound asleep.

Valentine's Day a few years before this time. I had no girlfriend at the time. I spent the night sitting on the couch watching a movie with my two best friends: Chelsea and Brad.

David walked down the stairs feeling like a million bucks but looking more like ninety-five dollars.

He held his arms wide and looked at the three of us. "I need a woman's opinion, so you three will be perfect. How do I look?"

"Salvation Army having a clearance sale?" Brad started.

"I think you need a few more dozen sprays of Dad's cologne," I added sarcastically.

"You look fine," Chelsea said. "I mean, I wouldn't make out with you, but there are plenty of desperate girls out there who might."

David laughed off the comments looking into the mantleplace mirror, fixing his collar.

"I look damn sexy."

"Where are you taking this girl?" Chelsea was a woman, hence, she required details.

"Amy and I? Well, we start off with a nice dinner and I got tickets to the local player's rendition of 'Streetcar Named Desire', which is her favorite play."

"Flowers?"

"Of course"

"That's actually pretty sweet," Chelsea said with a hint of jealousy in her voice.

"Yes, Chelsea, it sure is. Too bad neither of these two jokers would swing a night like that for you".

From this night on I would hear, see, and be forced to hang out with Amy. She was an aspiring actress, had the lead in nearly all the high school plays and, just like her performances, she was over-the-top and dramatic. She had plenty of yes-friends and she had David, who was always willing to let her spend all the time she needed with her lead actors practicing their lines.

There's a special lesson learned in relationships, something usually observed from the sidelines but still never truly grasped: Denial. David would have fought to the death any allegations towards Amy's infidelity because, he said, she would never cheat on him. "Not in a million years," David claimed.

Truth be told, I don't know how many guys, or girls for that matter, Amy had her way with in the eighteen month relationship, but I personally witnessed two. That was two David wouldn't believe when I told him and two weeks that he refused to talk to me for merely implying what my twisted little perverted mind thought it observed.

Sophomore year of high school started suddenly and deliberately and my brother was off to college where his pot smoking could expand, a place for his substance abuse to progress. Amy was a thing of the past as his future lay ahead at Eastern.

I strolled down the halls of high school awaiting everyone to approach, congratulate me on having found a girlfriend and then ask about Chelsea. Speaking of which, it had nearly been a week since I saw or spoke to her.

I played the role of stalker, riding my bike past her house, even getting my Mom to drive me to the mall where I could look into the music store. Each time I found no signs of her. A fellow employee by the name of Chris offered the advice that women do crazy shit for crazier reasons and just let her wait to come to me or call.

Neither had happened so on day one I stood by her locker tossing hellos to acquaintances. Brad stopped by and, knowing of my dilemma, shared his mellow words of support while offering dates with his girl band buddies.

One thing was certain, I had second, fifth, and sixth period with her, so unless she was in some horrible accident that I was not informed of or she became a high school drop out statistic, I would be able to see her.

English II rolled around and I sat quietly in the third row near the window and looked at everyone who came in. All the familiar faces of last year, some had grown a bit taller, some fatter, some thinner, most stayed exactly the same with the exception of tans. Curious on who I would be spending the next nine months in English with wasn't one of my greatest concerns. Where was Chelsea?

She arrived with the bell and spotted me sitting up straight and smiling at her. She forced a nervous smile across her lips and graciously took the chair in front of me. Holy hell her hair smelled lovely, I thought.

Knowing of my increasing concern and want for answers she turned her head towards me ever so slightly and whispered, "We need to talk, later".

I could only comply and stare at the back of her head. The bagel and cream cheese began swishing back and forth in my belly. Actually, it was more like my brain and heart decided to exalt revenge upon my stomach. The battle of acidic pains was on.

Concentrate? Impossible. Even though I mentally begged her every time the minute hand crossed the twelve, she didn't turn around. Every minute dragged and every second of every one of those minutes slowed to a crawl.

The introductory class ended and she finally made eye contact with me. My mouth opened slightly as if asking a dozen questions at once.

"Not yet, Drew," she said in a nervous and shaky tone. I knew that the class felt as long for her as it did for me, "after school. Will you walk home with me?"

I zombied my way to the next class not sure if this walk home was going to be good or bad. I feared a breaking up in the midst and losing my one true love. With shot nerves I could think of only the end of this relationship, the loss of a friend, and a farewell to my one and only. The horrors of staring at the back of Chelsea's head all through Mister Lewiston's English class along with fifth period Algebra and sixth period U.S. History, and suffer the daily reminders of what I no longer possessed stained the images of the blissful relationship I had conjured up. My ego and self-respect quivered in curiosity.

Only another four hours until I get my answers. Two-hundred-forty minutes of hope that I was over-exaggerating, that I feared the worst.

Fifth and sixth periods came and went with Chelsea making minimal eye contact. Her mind was traveling at lightning speeds and clouded with doubt. She wrestled her demons and went over a thousand times what she wanted to say to me and how to say it.

The two-thirty bell rang signaling the end of U.S. History and the end of the school day. We walked awkwardly out of class together and I did not dare reach for her hand although I desperately wanted to.

"Do you need to go by your locker?"

"No," she replied. We walked out the main doors, across the parking lot and onto the sidewalk in screaming silence. After a muted ten minutes I knew that I was the one to have to initiate a conversation. I peeked out the edge of my eyes at her, we made no eye contact, and hence, no opportunities to break the spell were going to be handed to me.

I wanted to ask what was wrong. I wanted to say that whatever was going to happen, we would remain friends. I wanted to beg and plea for her not to hurt me. I said–

"Are you going to break up with me?" It was one of the first times I was scared to hear the answer of a question I was proud to have the balls to ask. I laid it on the line opening the gates to an impending flood.

"What? No!" She blurted back forcefully. I nearly lost my balance. For the first time since this morning I was able to expel a big hulking breath of relief. The weight was lifted and I had to sit down. I chose the rail over the creek where children in a nearby field often lost soccer balls, footballs, and Frisbees, letting them float downstream to an undisclosed and faraway destination.

"Chelsea. Please, babe. What..." I couldn't finish the question because that sort of sentence had no end. The ellipses were invented for these specific purposes.

She stood in front of me but looked down the street in hopes of an answer that would conveniently come on a school bus or mini-van hurtling by at forty miles-per-hour.

"I love you, Drew," she said still looking away. It was almost as good as the first time I told her the same and she replied back verbatim.

"Chelsea, I love you too."

"I don't want to talk about it," Chelsea said. I could not impose and doing so would create a lack of selflessness. The courage took me so far and the fear stopped me from inquiring. Now was not the time to share what had happened, maybe when we were older, when dealing with whatever problem she had could be resolved amicably and without the dread I had built up inside myself. I smiled up at Chelsea and she accepted my gentle understanding. "Thank you, Drew", she said with a tiny smile. I stood up slowly as she came near, our arms wrapped around one another's body and, for the first time in eight days, we kissed. The resolution would be easier in the future, I told myself, after our past had slipped past us, the conversation would begin with the two words "remember" and "when".

"Remember when I didn't see or talk to you for a week? The week before school started?" I had all but forgotten that day from nearly three years ago by pushing it deep into my subconscious. I could suddenly recall it like yesterday.

Chelsea and I shared so much through high school; times of both genuine happiness and satisfaction. Every Thanksgiving and Christmas, in the summer I went with her to her grandparent's cottage on Lake Huron, she followed me to New York last year on New Year's Eve with my family. We've made love countless times and became comfortable around each other to the point we could discuss any and every thing, except that week.

I was eighteen and about to head out of state for college, Chelsea would remain in-state, but at this moment, I became the scared fifteen year old boy again.

"His name was Chris," she started. My eyes automatically closed and I hoped that when I re-opened them I would be in bed staring up at the ceiling, hearing the angry tones of the alarm clock. My heart dropped to my shoes and tears that I tried to hide found their way into my eyes. A lump grew to the size of a baseball in my throat. It took four words to physically and emotionally crush me. Thirty-four months of suspense ended with a punch to the face.

It was the summer between our freshman and sophomore year of high school. Chelsea was working part time at the music store at the mall. Not much happens in retail during the day time and co-workers begin to talk. Chris was three and a half years older than Chelsea and had been out of high school a few months. His career path was uncertain and the order was to get a job or get kicked out of his house. He couldn't afford rent, or the tires that lifted his truck even higher than necessary, but he used the latter in his games to get the girls he wanted.

Chris took a natural liking toward Chelsea. She was young, cute and innocent, her experiences were kissing one other guy and everything she had done with me up to this point. Chris offered advice and inquired about my resume of love which was fairly empty. Presented was his challenge and he pursued.

"He has no job and he has never kissed another girl?" Chris asked obnoxiously.

"That's right," Chelsea replied.

"How can you love him then? What does he give you?"

"He's my boyfriend."

"So?"

"What do you mean so?"

He ranted about how a fifteen year old virgin was no match for a man of his caliber. He told Chelsea that for someone as mature and beautiful as her, she deserved better. The general theme of his rants on love was how girls often had an ill sense of a fairy tale *amore* over what was reality. The lectures began to resonate and Chelsea became doubtful.

"He brings me flowers sometimes," she argued, "and he's sweet and a gentleman."

"Can he fight?"

"Why would he need to fight?"

"What if someone was provoking you two? How would he handle it?"

"I don't know really."

"I'd protect you, Chelsea. Against anything." He told her.

She knew what he was getting at and, although it repulsed her a bit, something about it still rang true. She told me how this slip up made her appreciate me more. I rose up the image of their tongues in each other's throats as well as other parts of the human anatomy. I began to feel sick to my stomach. Chelsea is a bright girl and for her to fall into this trap was both insulting and demoralizing to her intelligence.

The summer dragged on and day by day Chris fought her into submission until, that week before school started, she caved. They were closing the store together, she had finished with the receipts and he was working on inventory. She went into the back to say her goodbye. I didn't want to know details and she gratefully did not give them, but they had kissed. The kiss lead to something more. She assured me they didn't have sex but there just weren't enough assurances in the world to sway my belief.

Upon hearing this news and what we knew lay ahead in the coming months, our final conversation as boyfriend and girlfriend began. It was six days since graduation. Had I known this, I may have kissed her once more and taken in everything I would no longer feel. You don't know when that last kiss or last holding of a hand will take place. Ours had happened the previous night. I wondered if when her head was against the pillow she was rehearsing what she was going to say or had fallen into a slumber amid tears.

"You're a nice guy, Drew," she told me, "I'll always love you. I just don't think I can love you that way anymore."

It was not fair. Not to me. We were going to be thousands of miles apart come September but it could still work. We were going to grow apart and begin to find out who we really were, but I didn't know that. I wanted Chelsea. I wanted her touch. I wanted my hooded sweatshirt to smell like her because she wore it the previous night or she rested herself on me. Helplessness is scary, I loved her so much and I didn't want her to leave, but she was going to go and there was nothing I could do about it.

Three weeks out of high school and two weeks from the break up I found myself dining on fast food with Brad. I ate my cheeseburger in silence, head down wallowing in the misery that accompanied a love now lost. Brad did all the talking and found it necessary to discuss the post high school life. Brad had worked his way through the band girls boasting near fifteen spanning four years.

"I didn't bang 'em all," he claimed.

"I suspected not," I told him.

"Just a couple. Three, actually. I guess I'll have to find some new chicks this fall, huh?"

"Last I checked Michigan was a coed campus."

"And so is UCLA," he responded. He constantly pressed that what happened was for the best and moving on was the proper course of action. He didn't think he would talk to Chelsea anymore than I would. She had disappeared from our lives. Whenever I roamed the mall, I wondered if she would be shopping in the same area I was. If I went to the movies, would she just so happen to be going to the same theater at the same show time? I spent a lot of time either in the house or at work. I was employed full time at a video store and worried little about seeing her there. I assumed she didn't want to run into me anymore than I wanted to accidentally see her.

"Hey, look who just came in," Brad said nodding his head toward the door. In walked Lisa Soren and her crew. They were overly tanned, overly blonde, and dressed like jailbait. They spoke loudly and all at once. Occasionally one would escape the pack and place their order. The whole group sat nearby and dared not speak to us. They recognized Brad and I but we were fresh out of the trend that was high school and neither of us was worth their time.

Brad took a glance at them and turned his head toward me with a bright shining smile.

"What?" I dared to ask.

He looked down at my food. I had about five fries and a cookie. Brad was finished with the exception of his chocolate shake. He reached into his pocket and pulled out some money, tossing a one dollar bill onto the table. "I dare you, Drew, to go over there and kiss Lisa."

"You're not serious."

He kept smiling and continued, "I'll bet my chocolate shake against your cookie. And if you get her on the lips," he tapped the dollar, "I'll throw in that."

"Odds."

He smiled wider and nodded. "What do you have to lose? You're never gonna see the bitch ever again. You don't have a girlfriend..."

"Thanks for the reminder." It wasn't meant to be painful, but the comment stung.

"Sorry, dude. But you don't. And she has nice breasts."

I confirmed, "They are pretty nice."

"Come on, California Boy. Why don't you go pick up your balls where you left them back in the third grade?"

I thought about it. It weighed heavily in my mind for nearly ten seconds. The pros. The cons. This wasn't a playground and I knew nobody else in the place. If she flat out rejected me, Brad and I would laugh about it later. I picked up the one dollar and folded it nice and neat, putting it in my pocket.

"It was the fourth grade, Brad." I stood up, full of everything great that most men wished they had. The approach was similar, the closer I got to Lisa, the more my knees weakened and my heart began to race. I was standing at the edge of the table and all four girls looked up at me, I had no game plan, so I played the same card I did nine years ago.

"Hi Lisa," I started.

"Hi."

"Can I ask you something?"

She lifted an eyebrow and sighed annoyed. "What?"

I knelt down right next to her and got real close. I struggled a moment, not quite sure if it was part of my act or nerves. I couldn't look at her at first, but then my eyes lifted and met hers. Lisa's eyebrows were raised wondering why I was wasting her time.

"Ijustwantedtokissyou," I mumbled quietly, turning my head away.

"What?" She asked and leaned in closer.

I was Cary Grant as I raised my head and smiled, "I just wanted to kiss you...again." I moved in, placing my hand on the back of her head and bringing her in for a quick kiss. I felt her lips part slightly with the anticipation or even consideration that I may be slipping her a little tongue. I let go and stood up. She sat there, amongst her group, stunned. They all had open mouths and had no idea what to say. I backed away slowly; bumping into a table, then turned and strolled out the door. Brad grabbed his chocolate shake and my cookie and followed.

"Holy shit of all shits!" Brad screamed upon exiting. I was leaning against the wall.

"I'm gonna vomit. My stomach..." I rolled my finger like a constant whirlwind of nerves.

"Probably the cooties," he replied jokingly. "I can't believe you did that."

"You dared me, you bet me," I said beginning to smile.

"A lot different reaction than last time," he chuckled turning his attention back to the girls inside the restaurant. They all sat close, figuring out what just happened. "You're my hero."

My eyes were welling up. I kissed Lisa. She was the girl I had kissed before Chelsea, and now the first girl after. I subconsciously moved my hand toward my nose and sniffed. Just as I had suspected, her hair smelled just the same as Chelsea's.

"You alright, dude?" Brad was concerned, he threw punches every shot he could, but this time he knew to hold back. "Ya know Ryan is having a party. We should go get you drunk."

"Hi this is Chelsea, leave me a message and I'll get back to you when I can. Bye." A beep followed. I knew she wouldn't answer. Her phone would show my name and my phone number and at one-thirty in the morning she knew better than to answer.

"Chelsea, hi there, it's Drew. Hope you remember me." I shook my head, in stupidity. "Um, anyway, I just called because, well, we don't talk anymore and I miss you and, ya know, I kinda, sorta, still love you. I just want to hear your voice." Again, I twitched my head. "I'm sorry I've been drinking....shit."

I hung up the phone. I could only think that she wasn't answering because she was too busy having sex with someone else. The alcohol was slowly depressing my system and only creating undesirable thoughts. This was the first time I learned that alcohol plus ex-girlfriend's number equals a major disaster. Chelsea didn't call me back that night and it was a long time before we spoke again.

2

The air was cool coming in from the open window. I'm still wide awake and pacing my room. It has been an hour and I had spent most of it thinking about my younger years, the times when you're stupid and the times you never forget. They molded me into the person I have become and, standing here, hours before my marriage begins, I know that Chelsea played a major role in getting me to this point. Whether they are a Lisa or a Chelsea, you never get over your first love. I wish I could fully forget Chelsea.

I yawned but wasn't tired. I was looking at the coffee maker in the room and debating whether or not I should rip open the small sealed package. I weighed the pros and cons while staring down at the small four-cup glass pot. I would certainly be wider awake but would constantly need the caffeine entering my bloodstream throughout the day so I could remain alert all day not to mention that increasing my intake of coffee would equal frequenter trips to the bathroom. I pictured myself in the tuxedo that required a little taking out since the last time it was donned and hopping around on the altar doing the pee-pee dance with a urinal on my mind instead of my bride.

Middle school is the time you begin molding who you are mentally and emotionally, high school is honing these new found discoveries or changing based on what is considered popular and trendy if that's what you fall for. After high school is when life, as far as truly mattering, begins. Without the constant pressure of social norms you can focus on yourself, usually. My life really began to change at the start of college. I was a young eighteen and, depending on your experiences and choices, you are apt to change more in that one year than almost any year prior. At least that was partially my case. I threw away all known familiarities and guided myself onto a path that led me to this crossroad.

I opted against the coffee for the meantime and rested my head back on the pillow. The sun would soon rise slowly and steal the darkness from the night. I closed my eyes and tightened my stomach in a pain felt when loss is remembered. The one thing that could make this day even better was impossible and therefore I tried to accept the circumstances. I think of college and I chuckle while fighting back tears.

Smog and sunshine at its peak, I was now in Los Angeles. My parents didn't want me to go but I craved a climate that was nice and warm in a state far from my own. It had been a goal of mine to leave Michigan, but despite the migration to another world I will forever be a Michigander.

I had hoped my Mom and Dad would help this college freshman move into his first dorm room but they had work and could not afford to drive across the United States with me. Life in the middle class spared little such luxuries.

The halls were narrow and cramped with crying daughters, weeping mothers, and fathers holding back tears. I scooted past them all and entered room 303 carrying a bag on my back and a box in my arms. I tossed it on a bed, a small one of two that were built, along with two desks, for an optional extra charge.

"Yeah, here we go," a deep voice called out from the hallway. I turned my attention to the door and saw a family of four nestling inward. "Hey, man," the son said to me.

It was Mike, a black kid, my age and my first roommate. His father who was sweating heavily having carried an oversized box from the car and still wearing his sunglasses stepped past the others and dropped the cardboard square onto the ground. He rubbed his hands on his pants and held one out for me.

"Nice to meet you, young man. I'm Jerry." I shook his hand.

"Hi," I replied.

"This here is Mike," he pointed out the only other gentleman in the room besides me who was a bit nervous. We shook hands.

"I'm Drew."

"Nice to meet you, Drew," his Mom, Lorraine, said, "Where's your family?"

"They couldn't make it."

"Ya from here?" Jerry asked.

"L.A.? Nah, Detroit area."

"Well, I'll be," Jerry started enthusiastically, "Chicago. Two good ole Midwestern boys."

I smiled as an awkward silence fell upon the room. After a few seconds Jerry recommended we finish hauling boxes into the room. Mike came down to my car and helped and Jerry, with minimal help from Lorraine and the daughter, whose name I hadn't picked up, finished unloading their car.

Mike and I hit it off right away. I was a history major, he was heading into filmmaking. I found that I was asking more questions about the entertainment industry than he was about the early twentieth century but either way we were excited to explore and get lost in this giant metropolis we had moved to.

Mike's family hung around a few more days helping stock the room and even treating me to a couple of much appreciated dinners, however, word was going around of the first big party and Mike and I were eager to go. As Mike was saying his goodbyes to his family I roamed the campus observing all the girls I would get a shot at once the year began. There were a ton, mostly blonde, and I feared mostly out of my league. I suddenly felt as if I were surrounded by Lisa Soren and her gang of cell phone yammering ilk.

"Yo Drew!" Mike was screaming from up the hill rushing down to me. "They're gone!"

"Did you cry? Was it a quality Lifetime original moment?"

"My Mom cried, dude," he said.

"It happens, we really should find some party to go to, help ya get over this traumatic experience," I replied unenthusiastically. Our minds synced to the same remedy.

Mike put his arm around me as we headed into the dining hall. "I just think I know of a party going on this evening, young scholar." We chuckled a bit, "Ya know, Drew, this could be the beginning of a beautiful friendship," he concluded in a poor Humphrey Bogart impression.

Something about a garbage can filled with punch and all sorts of alcohol really introduces you to the college life. All over the world, parents pay for their children to go off and shine in the adventures of academia, to learn and grow, and in the fine print, the children add that within in this experience they shall get so drunk and belligerent that they would throw the fundamental basics of look before you cross the street out the window.

Mike and I stood near the side of the dangerously packed house watching as pretty eighteen year old girls danced provocatively on one end, continued to get smashed on the other and somewhere in the middle the guys pounced on any look their beer goggles thought they were getting.

"I went to a party like this back home a couple months ago," Mike hollered over the loud generic hip-hop, "It was," his eyes lifted upwards reminiscing, "Three injured, twelve arrested and something like fifteen thousand dollars in damage. It was a good one."

I was astonished, the only party I frequented involved loud music, minimal damage, usually a vase or glass cup, and one time there was one wounded when a table dance went south.

"And pot in the basement," Mike added, "but I don't think anything ever came of that".

We saw the possibilities that lay ahead for us. The suburbs lacked ethnicity; everyone knew the name of the one Indian kid in their class because there was really only one. The color palette was mostly white. Mike had noticed the collaboration of cultures and said that there was nothing like alcohol and youth to bring the world together. He also started a conversation with a hot blonde girl the moment I turned my head away. I did my best to hop into the pleasant 'where are you from' and 'what's your name', but I couldn't quite enter it before she was gone.

Mike turned to me and answered, "White flight". I inquired further. "New school, from tornado alley, I was probably the first negro she ever saw with the exception of MTV and the news".

"That sucks." I told him and he shrugged it off. "You cool with it?" He shifted his head toward me with an air of honest sympathy.

"There are plenty of fish. She doesn't know what she's missing," he responded. "Let her go slobber on some frat-boy wannabe's herpes laced knob."

"So, you're cool with it."

"Of course," he responded facetiously grinding his teeth.

"Did you get her name at least?"

"Brittany". We both laughed for the same reasons. I began to learn about it that night and saw it every time someone stepped into a room that Mike was in. He could profile and size up just about anyone he ever met with stunning accuracy. It was a gift and I bet he didn't ask Brittany where she was from, that he knew the moment he introduced himself, and that he should count down the seconds before she suddenly needed to find a bathroom.

Mike had grown up in a suburb west of Chicago; his father was an optometrist who desperately wanted his only son to follow into the medical profession. Unfortunately for Jerry, at the young age of six, Mike took the lead in the Elementary school rendition of "The Little Bugs". He was the protagonist ant. The acting bug never officially bit him but he performed for fun and spent his recesses playing four-square or drawing cartoons. Eventually, by the fifth grade, he was turning his cartoons into three pages or thirty square comic book style stories which he refuses to show anybody and swears he would find a gun and shoot down whoever may decide to display them. Mike's Mom, Lorraine, decided when her children were old enough and could take care of themselves after school she would get a job as a bank teller close to the house. Within a year she graciously accepted the opportunity to be promoted to new accounts. Her pay increased substantially and she was happier, always loving the idea of helping others save the one item most people don't conserve.

Mike's love for storytelling blossomed into countless short stories and three screenplays by the end of his senior year in high school. His scripts involved gruesome murders usually occurring in the first ten pages. Not a violent man, he claims he just enjoys finding wicked ways for his characters to die. I was noticing how he would stare off at a distant construction crane or metal fence with a smile having concocted a new way for the bad guy's henchman to bite the big one.

He wasn't a fan of being called an African-American. He liked black and whenever the situation came up with someone he never met, if I were around, I was introduced as his European American amigo. I just saw him as Mike, the bud who on a bored Thursday night recommended we order an extra cheese pizza, split a gallon of milk, invite our mutual friend Alex over, and let the lactose go to work. After that particular night Alex refused to come back to our room unless we were around girls and the next morning took a dark felt-tip marker to our door properly labeling our domicile "The Dutch Oven".

We lived the lives of little kids in grown up bodies. He left me notes on my bed saying, "I may or may not have farted on your pillow". My counterattack was calling his cell phone to make him aware that I may or may not have farted on the cell phone receiver. When it came to the ladies, he, more often than not, would have one of his socks on the door. If he had a date, I took a book when I left for the night knowing that I should wait at least until midnight to return. It was his hot date with a girl named Katie, who he knew since the first day of class that started my relationship with Abigail.

It could have been mistaken for two college coeds writhing back and forth in ecstasy, the head board pounding in rhythmic thrusts against the weak plaster wall. It was a washing machine on full spin, taking its passengers for the cleansing ride of their lives like children on a carnival gravitron.

Abigail sat on the university-provided couch with an Abnormal Psychology book flattened on her crossed legs, her left cheek resting on her knuckle. The realization of my presence startled the hell out of her.

"Holy shit!" She screeched. She wasn't from a small town, I could tell that right off the bat. Her eyes were green, like spring grass after the fourth much-needed rainfall off a dry winter. They were big and beautiful; I couldn't help stare at first. She'd heard a million times how pretty and breathtaking they were and I would be one million and one. When she giggled at herself from being lost in her textbook, the mere sound melted my foolish heart.

I asked her if she minded if I sat and she threw back the generic "it's a free country" line. So began the usual chit-chat progressing beyond our majors and college life into an argument about police corruption and a Rampart scandal; a local topic I knew very little about. Before I knew it, I had accepted an invitation to march in a protest outside the Federal Building on Wilshire Boulevard. Neither of us was much on protesting but we had never been and it was different than a dinner and a movie. Plus I would have accepted about any proposal she offered based solely on being in college and this possibly being my first major make-out. The possibility of a little action could drive men off cliffs in droves, I thought.

Her laundry finished its drying cycle and, with our date set, Abigail collected her clothing in a far too small basket, tossed her Psych book on top, crushing a green t-shirt and slightly stained jeans and said goodbye.

Abigail grew up in the San Fernando Valley, also known as Los Angeles' suburb. Her parents were an aspiring actress and an aspiring director. They met in college on a student film set and within eight months, the mother was pregnant. Her father, who subconsciously placed blame onto Abigail for ruining his career, became a car salesman for Hartland Motors in Canoga Park.

By the age of ten Abigail's father, nearly one-hundred pounds heavier than prior to her birth, and her mother, still trying to become that movie star, split. With her obsessively stunning physique, Abigail's mother went out picking up producers and agents; kissing them, going down on them, and/or sleeping with them under the false pretenses that her breaking role would be offered.

When the demoralizing circumstances fell short she brought Abigail into the picture. She disagreed with Mom's choices and voiced her constant complaints in a pre-adolescent whine. Eventually, her mother gave up hopes that her beautiful baby girl would make it in this town.

The Hollywood dream ended as most do: Failure.

"Dreams are what you do when you sleep," a mid-fifties and rather rotund producer told her after a quick blowjob, "some got talent, most don't." He escorted her to a cab and with his ensuing power looked her in the eyes and said, "Send me your headshot, kid, and I'll see what I can do".

Excited that her sexual exploits paid off, she sent one of her black and white one-thousand headshots for one-hundred dollars to the producer who opened the 8 ½ x 11 envelope clearly marked

"Do Not Bend" in front of his assistant. He held up the picture to the recently graduated twenty-three year old and stated, "See John, they blow you and think they have a chance, like it's their way in." He laughed as he strolled into his office hollering back, "If it comes to getting some hot young actress, tell them you're an associate producer with me".

Abigail was exotic and new. She told me what she wanted, never waiting for me to make a move.

"I think we should kiss," she said but she wasn't thinking. She knew. For a man like myself to hear those words was not only a welcome reassurance but also a gift.

Her lips were not familiar. They were not as full as I was used to. She bit my lower lip and pulled back. It was enjoyable, quickly becoming that new car that after a few drives around the block would become comfortable and make my first car obsolete.

—

When I was seven years old, my brother celebrated his tenth birthday receiving a wide array of toys from friends and family members. Meticulously sealed in cartoon wrapping paper were action figures with tiny weapons, helmets, and canteens. I took one that sat alone on the kitchen table and opened it. I brought life into this tiny creature pretending to be the man in the heat of battle or play out fantasies of foiling enemy attacks and saving the day.

My brother entered and with sudden pent up sibling aggression tackled me to the tiles. He wrestled the figure from my hands and I grabbed it. He was much bigger than I was but I was much quicker. His grasp was tight and both of us refused to let go. As our parents flew into the kitchen to see what the commotion was, the action figure broke; the little rubber band connecting the torso to the legs flew off into the sink.

I was jealous and wanted the present as my own. With enough

begging, my parents probably would have bought me one, in fact, afterwards, they re-bought one for David and I received a neatly packaged toy as well.

At seven years old I learned the meaning and consequences of jealousy. The very same emotion appeared at the beginning of the third week of my relationship with Abigail.

The class was English Literature and our latest assignment was a compare/contrast on themes in two of these books: "Fahrenheit 451", "1984", and "Brave New World". Six of us from class decided to create a study session to discuss each other's findings. Four of those in our group bare no relevance. It was I and Denise that mattered. She was easy to talk to and easy on the eyes. Sexual tension and flirtations grew as the evening wore on and talk of book burnings and totalitarianism turned to anecdotes about snowfalls, thunderstorms, and other wicked weathers of the east from where nearly all of us haled from.

Abigail made a surprise visit which I welcomed. The group perceived Abigail as "cold" or "bitchy". She was, in fact, cold and bitchy as well as un-talkative and she sprayed dirty glances to Denise. Weather turned to movies as Denise inquired about the allure of Marilyn Monroe.

"She was hot", someone said.

"She died before she lived up to her full potential, like James Dean or–".

"Chris Farley," I said jumping into the dead celebrity debate. The group chuckled, Denise louder than most, Abigail not at all. I said it as a joke but as the small laughter lowered we all realized I was probably right.

"Isn't this a book discussion?" Abigail retorted, "What does a fat dead Saturday Night Live alum have to do with Aldous Huxley?"

I turned my attention to Abigail, "we were just taking a little break from the depressing predictions of the future fascist state of our nation".

"Personally," Denise started, "I think Bradbury mistakenly

fell into a classic, he rushed Fahrenheit and typed it all in a library. You can't deny the genius of the Chippendale's skit".

We all laughed again, except Abigail who jumped up and stormed out of my room.

"She's nice," someone said sarcastically.

I swallowed my pride and excused myself from the group. Abigail wanted to be left alone but didn't. I was clueless about her problem and only found out the next day of her jealousy towards the other person in the room trying to steal her toy.

"There's no reason for you to be friends with her," she said during the argument, "there is always some semblance of sexual tension between guys and girls which is blatantly there. I know guys, Drew, and I don't want to find out that you've been screwing, let alone looking, at that whore. You have me, why do you need more girl-friends?"

Truth be told, we weren't friends. Acquaintances, maybe. Denise and I were classmates and probably would have become good friends; maybe even started dating in the inevitable post-Abigail days. If that would have happened, Abigail would have felt that she had been right all along. Coincidently, I only knew Denise for four more days. She dropped out and dropped all connections, dropped the boyfriend none of us knew she had until he came to us asking for her whereabouts and dropped off the face of the Earth.

On this night, I had no time for a fight; my English Lit paper was due by week's end.

"Katie good?" I asked. Mike's eyes stole a glance at a passing girl.

"Well, we're not boyfriend/girlfriend. We're not steady. We're not dating." Mike reported.

"Friends with benefits?"

"More like acquaintances with perks."

I acknowledged with a chuckle as I reached into my pocket to grab my ringing cell phone.

"Shit." I said as the display screen revealed Abigail's phone number.

"That's the fifth time she called," Mike made sure I was aware of the constant barrage of Beethoven's 'Fur Elise' in electronic tones, "five times in a half hour."

"Right, I know."

"Do you like her?" I shrugged my shoulders at the question. I wasn't really sure. She was definitely cute and she gave me the lovin', but we were only together now a total of four weeks and within that time, as October started, I noticed that Los Angeles was strangely getting warmer and Abigail was losing her appeal. She was attached, which, I explained to Mike, is not necessarily a bad thing, "but it doesn't feel as right when you aren't as attached to her," he said completing my thought.

I agreed. Relationship number two didn't sport the same chemistry as the initial one had. This would end in heartache as most do, but I had to face the challenge of being the breaker-upper. My role was the boss who had to take the employee who loved their office and the people around them and buck up the courage to tell them in not so many words, "Don't bother coming in on Monday".

"Sooner is better than later, Drew. You kids do the nasty sit-ups?"

"Nasty sit-ups?" I had to confirm I heard that metaphor correctly. "Do you mean did we partake in sexual relations?"

"Precisely."

"Yes."

"But you never had home court advantage, did you?"

"No. It was always her place. It's only been a couple times."

"Well," Mike said lifting his head high, pushing his shoulders back, "I can prep the Dutch Oven. That might make things easier for the talk."

"You're a true friend, Mike. I'll think about it."

With an ear-to-ear grin, Mike said, "I'll do it anyway, a practice run if you will."

Beethoven filled the air once again. I could take little more of this classic music piece. The ringtone and Abigail had to go.

I hesitantly answered. Abigail took off into a fit of anger before I could squeeze in an entire greeting. She was upset that I was not at the infamous Dutch Oven. She came over for a surprise visit and, after knocking for five minutes, suspected I was off with Mike chasing girls. Further proof was the previous missed calls in my phone.

"If it were just you and Mike then why didn't you answer?" Her voice shook from emotional lapses of anger and sadness, fear and denial. It echoed in the hallway outside room 303. I lacked the sack to tell her I didn't want to talk at this moment or any moment in the immediate future, but I was failing at creating a different excuse. My mumbles were only further accusing me of seeing someone else, which wasn't true, and before I could enter my defense Mike snatched the phone away.

"I've got some shit going on right now, Abi. Issues that need to be resolved so once my bro here and I work through it, he will call you back," he paused a moment, "I don't care, you stupid bitch." Mike tossed the phone back to me.

Frozen in sheer terror, I held the phone I barely caught and looked at Mike. "You're an asshole." My legs tightened, the adrenalin pumped gallons of blood through my heart getting fuller and fuller until it was on the brink of bursting. I was preparing my sprint to the dorms.

"Nah, I hung up before that last part."

I could now unclench my ass cheeks knowing that a fear-ridden unauthorized dropping wouldn't take place. As we continued walking I questioned how if Mike really did say that last sentence how much things might have been easier as far as letting Abigail go.

* * *

Love really is unpredictable. Sometimes it takes months to fall for someone, sometimes minutes. On the other side of the spectrum there is the sudden and gradual dislike of your partner. I didn't not like Abigail; I just didn't really like her. My perception of her had fallen to the side of more bad than good but I couldn't bring myself to tell her this or even build the nerve to feel it myself. I was hardwired to constantly ponder the chances of our relationship making a complete one-eighty and becoming great. I think we are all afraid of leaving something that is just okay on the off chance that it would become something better. There's an in-grown fear of not being able to find someone new and regretting such a decision, which is also the same fear of being alone. The other option is sticking it out and settling. The illusion is positive but you are just as likely to be alone in the company of someone else.

The phone rang twice before it was answered by a familiar sounding man. He had his energy and excitement, a big unseen smile. Brad was living it up at the University of Michigan, not yet declaring a major and roaming through a whole new set of band girls. We had slightly grown apart but that was more due to class loads and different scenes to experience. We were still great friends and, when we talked, it usually was a solid one-hour worth of jokes and stories.

"My dirty bitch," he started. "How's Cali? Bang any actresses?"

"No."

"Then why ya calling me?"

"Got a problem."

"We can work it out. Lay it on me."

I relayed my situation and he responded with "uh huh" and "um"s. My story seemed to come out more complicated than I had intended, but Brad assured me it was far from complex.

I was in the midst of a quagmire. I already knew what had to be done; my problem was how to execute the solution.

"Not a sprain, nor a fracture," Brad began poetically, "you

need a clean break. Better do it now, you don't want to hold off." The answer I've heard over and over.

I changed the subject. "You, uh, ever see Chelsea?" I shunned myself immediately for inquiring.

"As a matter of fact I ran into her a couple days ago."

"Yeah?"

"Yeah."

There was a pause that screamed from Brad telling me he held more information than he was willing to share.

"She asked about you." Again I remained silent, the strategy worked and he continued, "Basic stuff; wants to know you're okay. Understand that she stopped talking to us because of you. Not in a bad way, mind you, it's just easier getting over someone when you don't see them. You know, out of sight, out of mind."

"Brad, you never get over your first love. If you see her again, tell her I say hello. Will you do that for me?"

"Of course I will." There was a loud sigh twenty-three-hundred miles away and Brad went on, sounding exhausted and generally concerned about how the next bit of business was going to be received. "I think she was strung out when I saw her."

"Strung out? You mean like..."

"Is there another strung out?"

"Shit."

"Yeah." He agreed with me.

"Chelsea?" I wanted the confirmation.

"Breaks your heart, a girl like that," Brad said. We were two old men talking of a gal we once shared memories with. Chelsea was no longer the girl I went to high school with, nor the girl I loved. Time changed her. Time changes everyone.

Our conversation was cut off by a knock on my door. I clutched the phone between my shoulder and ear; head slightly cocked to one side and moved towards the other side of the room. A knock came a second time, a little louder, a littler angrier. I opened the door, Abigail stood in the hallway.

"Who are you talking to?"

"Brad," I responded.

"Is that her?" Brad's voice questioned through the receiver.

"Yeah," I reported back, "I should go."

"To the curb, my friend." Before I could spit out a salutation the length of the call started flashing signaling the end button pressed on the other side.

Abigail sat on my bed and looked at me, half smiling innocently. Perhaps she came over to watch me do my homework or to watch TV with me, I'm not really sure. I could feel blood rushing to my head, or maybe it was draining, I wasn't sure. Light-headed, nervous, and jittery I stood before Abigail. The time was 7:45. I could only suspect that I wasn't the only person in the world about to break up with their significant other, probably not the last before midnight passed us into tomorrow. I felt a little better that my approaching act wasn't the first performance, that there were other such actors in other cities acting out the same scene. Guilt thrust upon me again and my stomach acids danced inside my belly. I spilled my guts metaphorically; I told her I think we should see other people.

"See other people? See other people! You want to break up with me? Why?" Her face turned red with anger, or maybe sadness, possibly confusion.

I couldn't answer. My emotions were indescribable. Truth be told, I didn't want to break up with Abigail. It would have been easier to drag it on until we duke it out with words at raised volumes filled with names and adjectives we didn't really mean.

"Huh? I really like you, Drew, and you do this to me? I knew I shouldn't have gone out with a freshman. You're just a stupid little freshman straight out of high school. You're not stupid though, just inexperienced. Don't you think I'm cute?"

"Yeah."

Abigail stood up. There were tears in her eyes. She went for a second plan. If questioning mine and her judgment in people wasn't enough of an attack then she opted for tears on my shirt and the smell of her hair bouncing off my olfactory. Her small arms tightened a hopeful grip around my body and she buried her face in my chest. I nearly caved. I was beginning to think that maybe it was better to have somebody than nobody. I refused these impulse urges.

"Why don't you like me?" She pulled back, "I can't believe you're breaking up with me. There's another girl, isn't there?"

"No." I was honest. I was also a bit hungry. McDonald's sounded good.

"I'm a great girlfriend, right?"

"Yeah," I threw some hesitancy in there; I don't think she caught it.

"So there has to be another girl. You're cheating on me!" Plan C. Sadness and begging was now anger. "You're a real asshole."

"There isn't another girl."

"Bullshit. Who is she? It's that Denise bitch, isn't it?"

"Abigail. I'm being honest, there is not another girl."

"Ugh," she barked, annoyed. She was five feet away now with her arms crossed and her head slightly tilted. "Whatever." Abigail lowered her head and shook it in disappointment passing by me. As she opened the door, she turned towards me. I looked into her eyes, she into mine. "Bye." She was gone.

Holy Shit, I thought to myself. I was in shock. I reminisced about the last few moments but couldn't comprehend the situation. It was all a blur. A crock pot of evil stares and over exaggerated explosions of sighing air mixed with verbal lashings and questions unanswerable because honesty was not the best policy.

There was a soft knock on the door. It was Abigail.

"I'm sorry; you're not really an asshole. I was just...I'm gonna go." And she did. I closed the door and took a seat on my bed. I was still hungry but feared exiting the room. How could I face her again? It will be awkward and a bit scary at first. I'll look up and down the hallway, slowly take the stairs or have my heart jump if the elevator stops on her floor. In the commissary, I'll constantly raise my eyes from the food to see if she has entered or to check out if she is in line at the McDonald's, or Subway, or Taco Bell. Eventually we will move on to someone new and when I do she will be jealous and when she does, I'm sure I'll feel the same jealousy. Semesters come and go, winter will bring darker days. The sun will climb out of the desert and fall upon the ocean bringing new opportunities. The first rain since April was expected in two days, tomorrow, though, will probably be easier for me than it will be for Abigail.

My first collegiate girlfriend had come and gone, it lasted one-thirty-sixth the time of my previous relationship and I was the one who did the heart-breaking.

Halloween that year I spent on an eastbound airplane. My headset kept me company throughout the redeye flight; I couldn't sleep against the roar of the engine and the occasional tremor on my lip. My father woke me up that morning to say my grandfather suffered a fatal heart attack and passed away.

My trip home, for the first time since I left, would consist of four days with my tearful family and observing the small subtle difference from the last time I drove down the main road towards my old house. I planned an escape for half a day. Brad suggested I stop up at the University unless I was too busy with the family in which he would travel north.

"You don't have to marry her," I started, "I mean, come on, it just so happens seven and a half months after your anniversary your child will have a birthday. That's like obviously saying that either one: You were an accident; or two: It was a forced marriage because one: You were an accident."

"Got a better plan?" David asked. We sat alone in the dining room of my Uncle Rich and Aunt Meg's house. My brother and I attended the funeral of our grandfather not six hours ago and here we were, living proof that after death, life moves on. David had taken his two-year associates degree and started work at a coffee shop. His hair was ragged and he looked tired, although he didn't lack sleep. His mind constantly ran at full speed with the now most important decision of his life.

"When are you going to tell Mom and Dad?"

"She may not have it," David answered with a swig of his beer.

"Oh." I knew what he was talking about and his girlfriend would be the first person I would ever know who would actually go through with it, if she did.

"We...we might not keep it."

"A woman has a right to choose."

"Hey now, half that zygote is mine. It may be stuffed in her uterus but..." he looked over at me, "how about we leave politics out of this discussion."

I threw my hands up, I cared not to debate.

"I need a job. I need..." My brother had it hard; tomorrow wasn't looking much brighter for him either. He spurted out how there was so many unintended life circumstances that you only have so much control over. "I fear the next four years, Drew. I wake up every morning asking myself, what could happen next?"

David leaned back in his chair and rubbed his eyes with both hands. "I think I should get married."

Two days later I stood outside the red brick building in my black fall jacket zipped up most of the way. It was cool out and the fresh fifty degree air sent a little shiver down my arms. I could feel the sticky underarm sweat accumulating, turning my light green shirt a dark shade. All I could do was stare straight up.

Brad patted me on the back. He took me as far as he could; the rest was up to me. Like a best friend should, he gave me a little push and I tripped forward a few steps.

"What room?"

"Three-oh-three."

"Three-oh-three?" I laughed at the small coincidence.

"You don't have to go through this, dude."

"Some people sky dive," I said taking in a deep breath, "I visit drugged up ex-girlfriends." I feared she would be different than what I remembered. Her hair. Her smell. The way she looked at me. I don't want my perfect image of her to be ruined but I loved her too much to not offer help. An offer she may very well reject. I was here and I wanted to be here for her.

"A dollar and a chocolate milk?" Brad dared an encouraging dare.

"Not this time, Brad." I patted his shoulder with gratitude and walked toward the dormitory.

Time moved in slow motion but I found myself suddenly outside her door with no real recollection on how I got there. I had played scenarios in my head, every conversation we may or may not have. Was she there or would I have to explain myself to her roommate, her boyfriend, her girlfriend? Was she going to be stoned? Would she even remember me?

My hands clasped to the side of my jeans and I felt and eerily cool breeze steal the air around me and twitch four lone hairs on the side of my head. I closed my eyes and lifted my hand, index finger rolled back for a soft one white knuckle knock.

In a matter of seconds the door opened. She was skinnier but not in a healthy way. I noticed her arms were thinner too. She was Chelsea but not the Chelsea I knew. My first impression of her was rewired, sadden and uncomfortable. Her personality changed, as I'm sure mine had as well.

We both stood there staring at each other. Her gaze was of surprise mixed with the relief of familiarity. Her bottom lip trembled. I wanted to speak but lacked the power and perhaps the words. Despite all the change, this was, after all, Chelsea standing before me in a light pink shirt and a pony tail and with it a feeling of love returned.

She threw her arms around my neck and held tight. A sense of longing for what the past once held and the present remembered. The harder she squeezed the more both of us begged for time to reverse. My hands went beyond each other crossing her back. Her hair smelled like it always did, the scent that every woman knows but a man doesn't know where it comes from because they aren't permitted to know such things.

We remained speechless for what seemed like an hour just hugging and holding. My cheek rested right above her ear. When we finally separated we both had tears in our eyes.

"Drew. What are you doing here?"

"My grandfather died. I wanted to come up here to..." I had no answer, at least no acceptable or logical one. We would have been great together but we knew it wasn't going to happen. I had to return to Los Angeles and she wouldn't follow. Chelsea was my friend; I wanted to make sure everything was okay. That's why I was here, but I could not tell her.

"I'm a mess," she said, "I'm sorry". It wasn't an apology for her looks or her newly adapted lifestyle. Perhaps it was meant to be a courtesy for her actions a few months ago for not talking to me. I nodded. Time had healed that wound and needed no apology.

All we did was tell one another what we were up to and filled the silence with awkward glances to the floor and walls. I stayed for only ten minutes; our conversation never going beyond anything more than catching up.

"It was good to see you," she said with a smile. We hugged goodbye. I knew that Chelsea had become someone I just knew of and would remain "that high school sweetheart". She was part of the past and claimed no relevance in the present. We lied and promised to keep in touch.

The head wind was strong and pushed against the nose of the plane as we cruised at thirty-five-thousand feet. I sat on top of my floatation device, my back against a slightly tilted window seat. I rested my elbow against the window and my chin in my hand. I reflected. I pressed the rewind button, slowed through the parts I wanted to remember and fast forwarded through those I didn't wishing my memories could be sprayed onto a computer screen and deleted at will. I was in deep thought when we hit a patch of turbulence that knocked my chin off my hand. I shook my head out of a daze and looked around the airplane. The engines slowed a little bit and I worked through all the scenarios of the professional aircraft aviator's playbook. I thought to myself that we hit a rough patch of air and the pilot slowed things down to alleviate any major bumps. We were fine.

The safety belt light dinged on and I watched as an older man grasping the back of every chair made his way to his seat. He reminded me of my grandfather if for the only reason being that he had thin white hair, glasses and a vest. What had this man seen? What had my own grandfather witness? He never shared any advice with me and I contemplated what his message would have been if he left one behind.

"Women. They're nothing but trouble," he may have written in the pages of a journal he kept near his bedside knowing that once he closed his eyes for good someone else's would read his passage and, like everyone before him and most after, not follow the advice of an old and experienced man.

"Women. They are the best. Treat 'em well and they'll treat you the same," he could have said to me if I had visited just one more time. If I knew I were going to die and my number was up soon I may spill all the knowledge onto anyone's ears in hopes that a part of me would live on through their actions.

"Work is important. It'll make a man out of you. Family is important. It'll make a human being out of you." My grandfather might have told me that over a piece of dessert at Thanksgiving, one of those times where family members and friends scurry around the house doing what it is they decide to do on a cold Thursday night and two people are left on opposite sides of a table to share their thoughts on politics and current affairs. The elder inquiring about the younger's school activities, girls, and plans for the future. The younger talking and not listening back, refusing by subconscious desires to not learn about his elders; or maybe because they are not hardwired to ask the right questions.

It had been a long time since I shared a conversation with my grandfather. As I grew older he grew sicker and weaker. Our hospital visits were spent watching the nightly news and my mother hoped her father would gain enough strength to talk more. His eyes always half open and his mind in a daze. At one point, I stopped caring and as I watch this old man sit in his pre-assigned seat, I wish I hadn't. I'm just a kid. That's my excuse. It comes with life. Maybe it's our way of distancing ourselves from loss. I think of a couple on the brink of a break up and wonder if amongst some blurry gray line, they both emotionally went their separate ways but hung together just a little longer in hopes of crossing back into a happier place where they both feel they belong and only with each other because that is what feels safe and comfortable.

My fictitious takes with my grandfather continued in my head. I wanted his worldly advice and thought a part of him genetically passed on the knowledge he would have liked to share.

We made our final descent into Los Angeles and I felt happy to return. It didn't feel like home but I was glad to be back.

3

I'm worried. It's late. It's so late in fact that it's almost early. The faint rising sun is turning the black sky into a midnight blue. The small beam of light is pushing its way through the break in the dark curtains and pouring a white line across the ceiling along the wall and creeping towards the floor. I think about the altar and the rehearsal that went off without a hitch. Our ceremony is to be presided over by Father Timothy Krauss. My fears of no sleep are being replaced with images of myself in front of family and friends, my knees buckling under fatigue and my face planting squarely onto the marble floor. The back doors open to reveal a bride's tears as her big day is ruined by her soon-to-be husband's cracked open head bleeding over her maid-of-honor's shoes.

My nineteenth birthday. I'll never forget it.

It was right after Spring Break. Of course, it was right after. I had stayed in Los Angeles planning on Brad visiting me. He was my plan and there was no fallback but due to unforeseen circumstances, Brad left me with an entire university campus and nothing to do. He called a week prior to his supposed visit and broke the news that his father had suffered a heart attack. It wasn't fatal and his father would go on to live for many decades, but as Brad explained to me, "nothing is better at scaring the shit out of you than possibly losing someone like a parent". I understood but couldn't relate. I wasn't going to fuss because we weren't in hindsight. Brad would say he should have visited me and I shake it off saying if his father had died, it would've been better if he did so with you taking care of him, not hitting on stupid fake-and-bakes down at the Third Street Promenade.

My nineteenth birthday came and went. No one really took notice. I received phone calls from family and friends and a couple packages in the mail. Brad wished me a happy birthday and I responded with a general thank you and an inquiry on his father's condition. I was alone. It was really the first time in my life I felt this way which was an overwhelming feeling. I sat in my dorm room watching daytime TV, my Mom had just called and we talked for a few minutes. When she asked what my plans were I told her I had none which really sunk in when I hung up the phone. Nobody was here to celebrate with me, no one to tell a waitress that it was my birthday and they should sing and buy me a dessert. There was no girl to kiss or no guy to take me to a strip club.

I don't know what was on TV that day. I sat and stared straight at the box for at least an hour with idle thoughts that ran rampant bouncing from synapse to synapse until getting a fast food burger seemed to be not good enough for my day. I would get the biggest sized value meal and no one would see me more than for what I was; a kid ordering lunch.

It was Westwood on a late-March afternoon. Not too many people roamed this college village except a few businessmen and women from the nearby buildings. Doctors, nurses, X-ray technicians, janitors, anyone a hospital might employ could be seen at all hours dining on cheap and quick food or drinking a cup of coffee.

I approached the Burger King on the corner and avoided eye contact with the homeless man there. He was hunched over a bit with dirt marks over his brown toned jacket and gloves. His face hadn't been washed in a while. I felt bad but knew it was best to hold on to my own dollars than give them to him. Ever since Mike and I gave him a buck each, watched as many other people did the same, and finally stumbling home one night from a party saw this very same man passed out on the curb with an empty bottle of booze in hand, well ever since then I couldn't muster up the will to be charitable.

The line was short. Only one man in khakis and a tucked in light blue shirt stood in front of me. He wore his sunglasses and tilted his head back and forth at the value meals and single items. "Hi, welcome to Burger King," the lady behind the counter said politely.

"Yeah, a three," the man replied.

"What size would you like?"

The man now diverted his attention from the board to his wallet, picking out a five amongst his twenties. "The regular size".

They exchanged money and the man moved on. I stepped forward and gave my order, paid, and moved to the side to fill up my drink. As I scanned the restaurant for the perfect birthday meal seat, preferably a booth-type backing, I laid eyes upon a girl of unknown age in a white top and jeans, face downward to a book she had just started and thus had trouble keeping open while eating. She was pretty; and could have been between the ages of sixteen and twenty-six. It seems so hard to tell. I wanted to sit next to her and wouldn't have minded having her for my birthday.

"Fifty-seven!"

I looked about the restaurant, keeping her in my peripheral vision with what I could only imagine to be a goofy smile on my face and the illusion of a stiff neck. If she looked at me, I wanted to be smiling.

"FIFTY-SEVEN!"

She had reached a pivotal point on the page. Her hand was pressed firmly at the crease as a fry dripping ketchup was held with her thumb and index finger, her mouth slightly open. It was as if something grasped her attention and she was frozen, stuck in this world of words until—

"FIFTY…SEVEN…sir, is that you?"

The girl looked up from her book and I spun on my heels around towards the counter. I shyly looked down at my receipt and recognized that there were no other patrons waiting for their order.

"That's me," I said and took the tray. I slowly moved my way closer to the girl but I found myself inching toward a table. I sat down, opened up my burger in a wrapper and took a bite. My time here was limited. I had only so much of it to talk to this girl, get a number, maybe a date. I wished I brought something to read, a book or magazine, anything besides the paper place mat over the tray and the quirky fun facts on the side of the cup. I sipped my drink, ate a handful of fries and continued sitting in silence, never making direct eye contact with this girl, hoping she would look up at me, smile, and just throw out a line, any line.

Time moved and I finished a tasty birthday lunch. I twisted in my chair to take a glance at the menu; I felt I owed myself a tasty birthday dessert. It wasn't going to come with singing waitresses or dancing strippers, nor would it be free, it would just be something more to cram into my already expanded stomach.

The girl tossed a bookmark into the book and closed it. As she stood up and headed for the door, throwing her garbage away on the way out, I begged her to turn around and just give me some sign that I should pursue. Something. Anything. But she left. All the will power and telepathy you think you possess never seems to do the trick. Happy Birthday Drew. I guess a year older doesn't necessarily make you any more confident.

* * *

49

I spent part of Saturday crumbling up some of Mike's sheets and mashing up his pillow. This was in no way out of anger over anything he had ever done. A few hours later we stepped into room three-oh-three and he took a glance at his bed.

"Someone's been sleeping in my bed, Goldilocks," Mike said.

"Why do you assume such events have taken place?"

"Gee, I don't know," Mike responded holding out his hand towards his bed as if he were a model on a seventies game show displaying a new piece of furniture and then motioned to my neatly made bed.

"Oh yeah, I slept in your bed last night?"

"Dare I ask?"

"A bad case of gas. I was feeling kind of strange about it, ya know, like one of those farts might be expelled with a little extra and I thought it best to not sleep in my own bed."

"But you would've been wearing boxers or pajama bottoms, right? It would've 'leaked' onto those."

"Right, you are correct," I said counter-arguing, "that is why I opted to sleep naked...with one of your pillows between my legs...I'm not going to tell you which one though."

"Looks like I'll just have to burn them all along with the sheets."

"No need to do that." I reached over to my desk and grabbed four quarters I had laid out for this very occasion. I handed them to him. "For laundry".

"Yeah, I'm burning these, you can keep the dollar."

He tossed his suitcase on his bed and unzipped it.

"Got you something from Chicago," Mike said lifting his leg about a foot off the ground. It was a short burst; it could have been a zipper moving a couple of notches. "Chicago style pizza. Delivered right to your door."

We both started chuckling and that led to an uncontrollable laughter until the smell seeped within olfactory gland range. Mike wafted his hand around his nose laughing harder.

"Aww!" I buried the bottom half of my face into my shirt.

"Wait, wait..." he let another one rip, "someone answer that and see what that asshole wants."

I fell to the floor laughing and Mike bent over, tears in his eyes, and banging his head on the corner of the bed. My laugh turned silent as I had trouble breathing in and I started to cry.

I took one quick breath inward and claimed, "We should get out of here before the smell starts to stick to our clothes."

We sat at Starbucks. The weather was cooler than expected and Mike and I drank mochas as he shared stories about the Windy City.

"It changes. It all changes. Not big and dramatic like they tore down an entire neighborhood but places close, new places open, you don't see the douche bag football player at the mall with his "head" cheerleader. I went to my old high school and saw some girl I dated two years ago, she's a senior this year, and even she looked really young. Let me tell ya, Drew, if I drop out of college, if this is my one and only year here, I'm going to walk away with a very important lesson. Life moves on. I think that realization is better learned when you're younger. Granted I have no long term experience in the matter, I'm just thinking like a fifty year old man."

"Chelsea. Look at that. I know exactly what you mean."

"You ever talk to her?"

I shook my head. It's the first time I thought about her in a few days which resonated as strange in itself. "Man, I used to think about her all the time."

"So, let's create life lessons or experiences. A list of things that people know but don't know, ya know?"

"No. Okay yes. You mean like moving away and seeing how things change even whether you like it or not."

"Yes," Mike responded excitedly. "Or, you should get your heartbroken once and break someone else's heart once."

I looked away a moment, soaking in that theory and I nodded. "Yeah, 'cause both suck but you should go through both."

"I'm liking this." Mike stood up. "I'm gonna go pee." He walked into the coffee shop and I leaned back in my chair. Crossing my arms my mind wandered to a view of Chelsea the last time I saw her, her hair strangely thinner along with her body in general, I wondered if I altered her physical appearance subconsciously to what I wanted to remember and if she ever really changed at all. My daydream danced from Chelsea to Brad and a girl he used to date then skipped to the girl at Burger King. I should have said something, but I couldn't. What would I have said? That's the lesson we all should know and learn: How to talk to someone, or at least, how to strike up a conversation with a person. Easier for some. I was seriously wondering if I would go through life in the hopes of meeting women through contacts or mistakes.

Mike sat back down and shook me out of my little stroll from reality.

"What's on your mind?" He asked.

"What do you say to the woman you're going to marry?"

"I'm not engaged."

"I was reading this book about a few sailors in World War II and one guy says that this gal walked into the bar and he told his buds that she was the woman he was going to marry. How did he know? And how the hell do you go talk to her? What do you say? What's your opening line?"

"Hmm, I'd tell her I had a cheap bottle of wine and a ticket aboard a destroyer tomorrow and I don't know if I'm going to make it home."

"Pity sex."

"What's wrong with pity sex?"

"I'm not dissin' it. If it wasn't for pity sex I'd never get laid."

"Do you get laid anyway?" My face flushed a little bit and I looked around in hopes that my surrounding peers didn't hear Mike's comment. "I'm kidding, dude. Pity sex rocks," and then he leaned in close like he had a secret to share. A secret that would change history, bring down governments, and spark revolutions. "Hi."

"What?"

"That's the opening line. Girls don't want to be fed bullshit. I don't want to be fed bullshit. They don't want us coming up to them, staring at their tits hanging out of the low cut shirt they're wearing at some ten-dollar-a-drink club in West Hollywood and say 'I want to ride you like the Saddleranch bull'."

"They don't?"

"Well, some might."

"I think a lot do," I stated mocking Mike a little but expelling a deep fear I felt about women really being that skanky.

"You don't want those chicks. They're like the batter's box. Good for practice, but if ya spend too much time there you're apt to pull a muscle. And by muscle I mean get herpes." Mike leaned back and lifted his arms, ending the presentation. "Just say hi and go from there".

That next night I spoke with my brother, my tone implied not all at the university was going aces and his tone implied that the independent coffee store he worked at wasn't giving him the hours he wanted.

"I have a baby on the way, Drew. Less than two months." David told me as if my Mom hadn't given me an exact countdown every time we talked. Mothers really want grandkids whether or not their children could provide. Much to my mother's delight and my father's dismay, David and his girlfriend would be living at home.

"Something in me feels like I should head home." I stated, wanting to scream this to Mike or Brad or anyone who would care to listen.

"What are you talking about?"

"This whole Los Angeles thing isn't exactly my cup of tea."

"It's Los Angeles. It's way better than here. Trust me. It snowed last night, man. Beginning of April and it freakin' snows."

"I kind of miss that."

"Don't be retarded. You're just not getting laid, are you?"

"Well, no but I don't think that's the sole reason for me wanting to come back."

"Stay away from here, Drew. It ain't worth coming back, no matter how good it seems. Once you move out of your home it's never the same coming back. You're speaking to a man with experience in the matter."

"Or am I speaking to a man with the experience of moving back in because he can't afford to take care of his girlfriend and incoming baby?" I was a little hesitant on saying it, but it was more of an attack against his thoughts on me rather than my thoughts on him.

"That's what I mean," he shot back, "you come home and Mom and Dad are going to have two kids, a daughter-in-law, and eventually, a grandkid. This place isn't big enough for all of us. If you weren't there, what would you do?"

"I don't think college life is for me, David. I go to classes, come to my dorm room, study, party a bit, eat pizza, all that fun crap. Everyone else does it. I looked around my Psych class today and just didn't feel the same urge to reach the destination all my classmates seemed to be heading, ya know? What if I came back took some classes and worked?"

"I'm your brother and as such I'm going to throw out this very important bit of advice about asking for advice. The final decision is on you. You're asking me, someone who has an Associate's and working at Java Brew, for career and school advice, find someone else. Dad and Mom are from a different generation and have different work ethics. Make mistakes now while you can still change and most importantly, don't impregnate anyone, male or female." His theory and what I figured was the obvious circumstance was that I was burnt out. He said that once I came home for the summer I would be re-energized and, by September, excited to head back out of state.

When we hung up the phone that night I stood on my bed for a few minutes staring at the floor, then back up at Mike's computer, and then out the window. The door flung open and Mike stood there with a girl I had yet to meet. She was tall, almost as tall as Mike and her body was proportional which meant she was no skeleton and had a decent sized balcony which I felt myself purposely keeping in my vision. He had to say no words, I knew it was my time to get up and let the two do their thing. I still did my laundry in fear that Abigail would be there and sending myself there now to study was not a dare I wished to act on.

Mike looked into his girl's eyes, "you have class early tomorrow, right?"

"Yeah, eight o'clock," she responded.

I stood up and grabbed my bag and walked into the hall, Mike excused himself from the room and came out into the hall.

"Thanks, man."

"No problem, Mike."

"Give me a couple hours, if even that long."

"Just give me a call when all is clear."

Mike tapped my arm with a smile and spun back into the room.

It was about three weeks before the UCLA quarter came to a close, the campus shut down, and all the students began heading home. I was studying for finals and researching a pesky Intro to Western Civilization paper. I considered the library but everyone was too busy in their own little world and I prefer to be around a more chaotic environment, so I headed for coffee where I knew I would find a group of high school teenagers on their Spring Break chatting about celebrities and a few other students working on their papers.

I stood in line for a few moments and ordered the largest coffee I could. I dripped in a bit of cream and threw in one sugar, taking the wooden stirrer and mixing to create a lighter brown colored brew. All seats were taken, mostly singles buried in laptops and notebooks and then I saw her. The girl from Burger King. She was turning the page of the same book she was reading before, now closer to the end, and when she went for sip of her coffee had trouble keeping the book open. I smiled at noticing the similar pattern.

'Just say hi', I thought to myself and bee lined towards her table in the corner. I wrestled with the two scenarios of her either looking up at me and observing as I pinpointed her exact table and fought through pulled out chairs to reach her specific table and the other possibility of awkwardly having to clear my throat and pulling her out of the middle of the sentence to vie for her attention. I was a few feet away and she tilted her head up. It was perfect timing. Our eyes met and I smiled.

"Hi."

"Hi," she said, not friendly or cruel, but cautious.

"There aren't any tables available, so I was wondering if I could share yours." I was nervous and the guy behind the counter thirty feet away probably felt the tension.

"Sure," she said. I sighed a monstrous breath of relief. I put my coffee on the table and my bag on the floor. She looked back down at her book and continued reading. I sat not having exchanged any real words at all, not saying thanks or asking her name. As I slowly took my notebook out I thought anything spoken now would plainly interrupt her and therefore plainly kill any chance I had of getting to know her better, on top of which, she would never let another annoying boy share a table in an overcrowded coffee shop again.

I opened my notebook and began studying, changing from Intro to Western Civilization to Psychology 101, everything I was attempting to put into my brain wouldn't stick as I could only think how close I was to this cute girl who I had miraculously ran in to a second time and how I was going to let it slip away again. I kept lifting my head and looking out the window, hoping the split second I looked at her face, her eyes would be pointed in my direction. No interruptions and no annoyances. Each time ended in failure. The roar of the coffee bean grinder powdering down pellets of caffeine polluted the area with noise; the cross between a garbage disposal and a dentist drill and both of our attentions diverted to the inconvenience. When we shifted back to our respective priorities we smiled bashfully at one another. I cursed myself for not speaking at that moment but sold myself on the notion that shouting my name at this point over a coffee grinder was the equivalent to talking politics at a club in Hollywood.

"Would you mind watching my stuff for a minute?" She asked me. I brought my nose out of the wonderful world of Egos, Super Egos, and Ids and nodded.

"Sure." She got up and went straight for the bathroom. I assumed my smile wasn't creepy and my manners weren't a complete turn off because she entrusted me with her book and bag, but not her purse. The time is now, I thought to myself. It's do or die time and I could not expect a third run-in with this beautiful brunette. It's a small world but it's never small enough to run into the people you actually care to see. It's only a small world when you don't have the time to talk to someone or don't care to.

My eyes were back onto the page but still not comprehending anything I was reading. The id follows what Freud termed as the pleasure principle. It demands instant gratification of instincts without consideration of law, social custom, or the needs of others. I re-read those two sentences over and over again and three seconds later I could only tell you the words: Freud and pleasure.

Just say hi.

I over-thought the whole situation. What would she say and how would I respond? I wished I could go to Mike and have him open up his scriptwriting program and create a scene for me, one which played out on my terms and ended how I wanted it to. The harsh light shines upon Drew's slouched shoulders, the shadow of his neck and head spilling upon his Psychology book, he would write. Drew turns his head slowly towards the bathroom as the girl walks out, her hair blowing in slow motion as a light, convenient wind gust seeps into the room. The leading lady. I replaced Mike with God, a long white bearded man atop a cloud with the same scriptwriting software, directing the page of the story to my life.

She sat back down accidentally tapping her knee against the already partially off-balance table.

"Oops, sorry," she said. I don't even think I looked up, I grunted. The heavenly based writer made me grunt in a way that sounded as if I were annoyed by her presence and that a simple apology would mean nothing to me. I meant it to sound like the world would continue to rotate and there was no harm nor foul done.

My recovery time would have to be fast. I had seconds before she took my grunt personally and picked up her book with regret in allowing me to share her table, pack up and head out. The world became small. Very small. Too small. My heart raced as I was going to finally introduce myself, the wind blew calmly through the opened door and blew back this girl's hair. I caught her in my peripheral vision and my heart beat faster. It was a small world indeed and Abigail wanted coffee too.

She called me an asshole and thought I was cheating on her almost six months ago. Doing a back flip out of my chair and landing in perfect splits would have been easier than starting a conversation with a complete stranger seconds before an ex-girlfriend noticed me. With any luck she wouldn't remember who I was and if she did, would go about her business.

Suddenly, personally, it started to get considerably toasty and I falsely placed blame on the hot drink in front of me. I could feel the perspiration cracking from beneath my skin and glistening on my forehead. I was thankful for wearing two layers of shirts because the first one looked as if I popped water balloons under my arms.

"Hi."

There was no better coincidence in the history of coincidences. I was not sure why I said it, maybe it was a moment of pure delirium or an extra kick from the coffee but I lifted my head and said "hi". We smiled at each other and chuckled a bit because at the very same moment I spoke she did as well.

"That's pretty crazy," I said.

"Yeah, I can't believe that just happened."

It was the first time I could look at her directly without any awkwardness or need to turn my head quickly. It was the first time I saw her smile and the first time I heard her laugh.

"My name is–."

"Drew?" I closed my eyes slowly as I was suspended in disbelief. I turned my head and saw Abigail at the counter nearby tossing a packet of sugar into her coffee. She looked happy or surprised with her mouth slightly open and her head tilted a bit.

"Hey Abigail," I said back with nearly a crack in my voice.

"How are you?" She stepped closer. The one girl I wanted to have a conversation with sat on the other side of the table and approaching was the one that I let get away because I needed her to be away. I went months without thinking of her, roaming my building with the occasional skip in my heart when I feared she might see me and want to talk. I spent a long time avoiding this very scene, not because I didn't want to talk to her, but rather I was afraid of what might happen if I did.

"And who is this?" She asked her eyes darting to the girl with a hidden agenda under her breath, "your girlfriend?"

"Um, no, actually," I started, "we have yet to meet one another."

"But yet, here you are, sitting across from one another, sharing a cup of coffee and a table."

"We're just sharing a table. There weren't any available when I came in and she kindly let me sit here." I had to hide my eyes from this girl. Embarrassed on what I might read if I looked into her eyes; or what my eyes might be telling her. Even with Abigail I could only look at her faintly. I had nowhere to lay my eyes without fearing a wrong signal being broadcasted.

"And yet," Abigail said, one hand wrapped around her cardboard coffee cup and the other gliding through the air pointing out the few tables that became vacant within the last five minutes.

I nodded. Not wanting this conversation to continue any further. If only a friend of Abigail's could step into here and whisk her away, or a boyfriend, or the fire alarm goes off and we're all forced to evacuate.

My mystery girl remained quiet, looking at Abigail in amusement of the circumstances.

"Would you mind if I shared this table with you two? I wouldn't want to take up a table that seats four with just my lonesome."

"Um," I began.

"I'm just being silly with you Drew, I'm not going to sit here and block your attempts at trying to meet this beautiful girl who you so randomly chose to sit with."

"Excuse me," a man said, an annoyed senior mere weeks away from claiming one degree only to thrust himself upon the adventure of a master's. He sat next to us hoping for the peace one might achieve in the ambience of a coffee shop; a place where no specific dialogue is heard except when an ex-girlfriend haunts her ex-boyfriend. He slid out of his chair, around Abigail and grabbed his black backpack before strolling out the door. He cursed under his breath at having to endure the unsettling situation. I watched as he tossed his backpack onto an empty table outside the café and became jealous at his ability to exit the awkwardness.

"I'm meeting somebody here so, unfortunately, I do need a place to sit and I don't much feel like waiting in the middle of this place." Abigail plopped into the still warm chair at the table next to us.

I went on reading about the ego and the girl across the table from me lowered her head indulging in her novel. Again, the same sentence, over and over, reading but never registering. Again, I lose the girl but this time not at the expense of my own cowardice. Outside influences swept in at the most inopportune time.

The girl lifted her head and placed Abigail into her peripheral vision. Abigail pretended to look out the door moving her eyes toward me, toward my used textbook which I could not concentrate on. My eyes became heavy and I got warmer. I felt as if I had a fever for a week that was finally breaking, I no longer shivered, I sweat and stained.

Abigail stood up and walked back to the counter, not enough sweetness in her bitter coffee, I thought. She looked back at me and the girl and as Abigail turned away for just one brief second; the time it takes to throw a wooden stirrer into a trash bag the girl with her head in her book, lifted her eyes.

"My name is Claire," she whispered softly and hardly audible.

I smiled, still looking down at the ego and id and page number 277 and responded very quietly, "nice to meet you."

We both grinned like we told a joke in our third grade class about our third grade teacher and just as we thought she heard us, she continued writing the multiplication question of 4 X 3 on the board. We had successfully gotten away with the joke.

"Uh oh," Claire whispered as Abigail returned and sat within ear shot. She was looking through me, staring at me unintentionally but thinking about me. I looked up at Abigail and she knew she was caught, she held strong but I caught a glimpse of sadness as she turned back to the door. There was a part of her that wanted to sabotage the beginning of anything that wasn't me with her even though the time that was "Drew and Abigail" had long since passed. The pain may not have been the issue, it was the principle. If nothing else, it was my lack of acceptance that exacted revenge; a child that breaks their siblings toy because it simply wasn't theirs. I would not accept her back into my life and if she could bring hurt to me in a fraction of what I might have done to her, why not go for it?

I stared. The same way she looked at me, I looked back at her while her eyes were diverted. It was not in a longing way but I saw myself in her position. She was meeting someone, that was no lie, and there was no place to go. The challenges that are brought upon us, the ones that test our character, that make us bigger than anyone else for a brief moment, those are bigger than the ones I was studying for. I sat there knowing I couldn't talk to Claire. I couldn't ask where she was from or what she was reading. I couldn't. Out of respect for someone else's heart and treating others the way I would have wanted to be treated amongst the same circumstances. It wasn't fair for Abigail to have to witness it.

The door opened and Abigail stood up. She waved and rushed over to meet them. It didn't matter who.

"Can I call you sometime?" I asked Claire before she had a chance to put down her book and look at me again. A small, pleasing smile crept across her lips and she tore a small piece of paper out of my open notebook.

"Yes you can." She wrote her number and her name, Claire, as if I would forget it, as if I would ever forget it. "I'm going to take off, but...call me," she said shifting my notebook back with the torn off sheet inside. I closed the notebook and she closed her book. Claire rose out of her chair and smiled one last time as she walked away.

The id follows what Freud termed as the pleasure principle. It demands instant gratification of instincts without consideration of law, social custom, or the needs of others.

* * *

Mike. Brad. My brother, David. These were my friends. Not to say I hadn't gathered a few acquaintances along the road, but they aren't the ones I can actually spill my guts to and expect them to listen and offer secure and sound advice by knowing me and knowing about me and how I think.

It began to scare me. I saw others around me gathered around mass amounts of friends; going to the movies, eating at restaurants and talking bad about each other behind each other's backs. It frightened me to think that if I were to lose one of my best friends then I would have lost one-third of those I could count on. I wouldn't have thought this way if it weren't for my brother. I saw his life amounting to a wife in a forced marriage and a baby by accident. He had his family, no one else. His best pal Aaron had moved away and moved on, as did most of those from his high school. It happened over night, David would give Aaron a call and there wouldn't be a response for nearly a week. Aaron called and droned on and on about his great life in Arizona. The weather was warm and the girls at ASU were one of two things: drunk or really drunk.

"I'm gonna be big," Aaron would say, "I'll be one of the only millionaires at our high school reunion." Yet David wasn't too sure where these millions would come from or even the business ventures that his best friend was working on. Aaron became his material objects and phone calls turned to emails, those emails soon came less frequent and shorter until David opened up his email and, after two and a half weeks, Aaron responded with three sentences that had been "sent from his PDA".

David's world became half empty as he was overburdened with the good he could never see. He had a fiancée that cared for him, but he would stop off for a quick beer at an Irish tavern in the same parking lot of his coffee shop instead of going home to his future bride who sat quietly in the living room that David and I once set up our toys in. One drink turned to two and two turned into more. He borrowed the bar phone and called for his fiancée to pick him up. She always did and they sat in silence for the seven minute drive home. My Dad would drop him off at work the next morning, also in silence, and David slouched at the register taking the orders of business men on their cell phones, teenage girls on their cell phones, and proud soccer Moms on their cells phones.

"It's all a blur to me, I wish there was something more," he would say to me as reality struck him.

I finished my final paper. I took the last of my final exams. I had been dating Claire for almost three weeks. She was fun to be around when time permitted. She wasn't in school and cared not for the college experience. Her choices led her to a secretarial position in her father's office near Westwood Village. She loved books and her dream was to write professionally.

We sat in a movie theater one week before I was going to leave Los Angeles and shared a popcorn watching the pre-show slide show of local Dentists and Real Estate agencies vying for our attention but what really appealed to our senses were either the trivia or the restaurant that offered a free dessert when we brought in our movie ticket stub.

"I'm smart, you know, almost too smart for you." Claire said facetiously.

"Is that so," I said looking up at the screen, "then answer this, miss smarty pants, name three movies that starred both Jack Lemmon and Walter Matheau."

"Grumpy Old Men," she replied quickly. "The Odd Couple and," she hesitated, staring at me as not to get a glimpse of the answer on the approaching slide." The Fortune Cookie." She grabbed four kernels of popcorn and shoved them into her mouth with a smile, one nicking her lip and falling off her breasts into her lap.

I caught myself staring and quickly but not subtly back at the screen. "Damn. They need to change these slides, I asked you that trivia question two nights ago."

"Yeah, you did. But I'm still smarter than you."

The house lights dimmed.

"You don't have to act this way," I said.

"Shh." She lifted her index finger to her mouth, "movie's starting."

We chuckled a bit as the commercial for a movie ticket internet site played and before the thirty second spot was up, we were already kissing.

Our lips parted at the first movie preview and occasionally met during the film for a few moments. They were kisses that spoke loudly how much we wanted to be with one another yet short enough to let each other know that we were interested in the actual movie.

Two hours later we were leaving the theater into the cool night air.

"It's only a matter of time before this cold spell lightens up to warmer summer temperatures," Claire said.

"This is chilly to you? This is sixty degrees. It's a heat wave."

"Come here," she said as we stopped at the street corner to kiss one another romantically. I was beginning to fall for her but I was also a week away from leaving her. The light changed and we crossed the street with no agenda other than to walk up and down the boutique-shop streets with one another.

"What happens next week?" She asked blatantly.

"With me leaving?" I knew that's what she meant but I wanted to avoid this question for as long as I could, even if it meant a few seconds.

"Yeah."

"I can't stay in the dorms and Mike is heading back to Chicago which leaves me without a roommate to share an apartment with."

"What about Alex?"

"He's going back east too plus he's a little too weird. I don't think we would make good roommates. He brushes his teeth in the dorm room and spits it into the garbage."

Steven Hartman

"That's gross," Claire commented.

"Yeah, his roommate didn't care for it too much either. He forced himself into the first relationship he could squeeze into so he could avoid Alex."

"Oh."

"But he's cool though," I said defending my quasi-friend.

"What is it with all you east coast or Midwestern folks anyway? Always need a little adventure so you come to Los Angeles." Claire asked changing the subject.

"Are we getting on your nerves?"

"A little bit."

We kissed for another moment.

"Are we boyfriend and girlfriend?" It was the most serious question of the night and one she asked like inquiring where we were going for dinner.

"I like you," I told her.

"That's not an answer."

"It's the answer to the question that I hoped you were going to ask."

"Four months is a long time to be apart and I know you don't plan on coming out here during that time and I could only come to you for maybe a week."

"What do you want?"

"Don't answer my question with a question, especially one that puts the ball into my court. I asked you first."

I didn't respond for a few moments and she didn't insist. It was our vain attempt to spare each other's feelings.

"I just want to know what you want with us." She said shyly, refusing to let silence answer this difficult question.

After a few more moments of pondering I started to talk it out, playing the role of a patient in a therapist's office. "I know that it will be hard for us to be in a relationship over two thousand miles apart. It involves a commitment that neither one of us at our age may be able to make. But then I think about the time I was cheated on and how that happened with a girl who I was even closer to both emotionally and geographically." The light changed but neither of us moved. I looked into her eyes and put my hands at her waist sliding them slowly behind her back and thus moving her nearer and nearer to me. "Claire, I'm coming back in the fall and I want you to be here for me. I want you to be my girlfriend." I spoke firmly and direct, right from my heart. Her lips curved as she smiled; her eyes portrayed tears of relief and happiness. We kissed and held it, passionately.

"I was going to say that we should make out with as many people as possible between now and when you come back but I guess I can handle it your way as well," she said playfully.

We kissed again.

"I think we should kick Mike out of the room for a while. Make him sit in the laundry room and watch crappy and fuzzy network TV."

"I think that's an excellent idea," she said.

The moonlight bounced off the side of the brick wall and landed upon my computer desk and bed. Claire held on closely, her head on my bare upper chest and my arm around her.

"What are you thinking?" Claire asked. I chuckled through inner thoughts and briefly inquired why women loved asking that question. She didn't have an exact answer for it and claimed mental programming.

"I'm thinking about the tie on the door and how maybe we should take it down?"

"Not yet," Claire said, "I'm sure he can occupy himself for a few more minutes".

We kissed.

"Am I going to see you before you leave?" She gently caressed her index finger in a circular pattern in the middle of my chest.

"I don't know." I responded truthfully.

"I have that thing tomorrow."

"Oh right, that thing."

"Dinner with my sister's lame ass husband."

"An evening out with the brother-in-law." I motioned around my stomach in a twirling motion, "the jealous stirs about in my abdomen," I moved my hand lower, "heading slowly to my nether regions. It'll come out in a burning sensation when I pee."

"Oh you have the most romantic pillow talk. What if this is the last time we see each other?"

"I still have to walk you down and kiss you goodbye. Watch you get into your car and fumble with yours keys. Watch you drop them and bend down to pick them up accidentally either hitting your head on the steering wheel or the horn. And as you pull out of that parking spot...ERRR, you barely hit the approaching car."

"You would like that wouldn't you?"

"What I would like is for you to walk out of here naked so my last glimpse of you for four months is bare backside in the moonlight."

"Just stroll into the hallway."

"Mmhmm."

"With the florescent lighting, do you know the kind of hideous perception it would give my skin tone?"

I feigned interest, pretending to let my mind wander.

"I'm sorry, I was thinking about your ass. You were talking. Go on."

We kissed again.

"Look," I started poetically, "I'll take you down to your car and give you a nice kiss goodnight, holding you close as we both decide that it's best to part ways only to meet once again down the road of life. Your last vision of me will be one waving goodbye from the sidewalk and mine of you driving away, your brake lights burning red at the stop sign and then fading as you accelerate telling me that this really is goodbye but just temporarily."

That's what happened.

* * *

Mike and I were working on packing up the room. We had taken four boxes down to my car already and the room seemed halfway done.

"We've accumulated a lot of shit," Mike said.

"Seriously," I said lifting up a puppet in the shape of a nun with boxing gloves on, "I don't remember buying this and I don't think I've ever even used it."

"Never did anything kinky with it?"

"With the fighting nun?"

"Yes, with the fighting nun."

I put my hand inside the puppet and placed my fingers on the triggers for the nun to punch. I pressed down and the nun jabbed with the right hand.

"This may have actually come in hand." I pressed on the trigger a few more times, "get that 'hard to reach' spot."

"Am I interrupting something?" Mike and I looked at the open door and Claire stood there innocently. I tossed the nun into the cardboard box.

"No, we're just...what are you doing here?" I asked Claire. I stood with a smile that responded I was glad to see her. She stepped in and seemed nervous like a child walking into a room as her mother wrapped her Christmas present.

"I'll give you two a couple minutes," Mike said rushing out of the room.

"Mike," Claire yelled back. Mike stood in the hallway as a tie flew out of the room and into his chest. "Put that on the door, will ya?"

Mike, as speechless as I was, closed the door with a giant grin on his face.

I took Claire into my arms and we stared at each other.

"What are you doing here?" I asked like a lawyer already knowing the answer.

"I wanted to see you. I wanted to see you one last time."

4

"More coffee, sir?" The waiter asks. He's dressed in black pants and a bright white shirt buttoned all the way to his neck. A small black apron wraps around his waist, a booklet bulges outward, and a pot of coffee is presented towards me.

"Not yet, thank you," I reply.

"I'll take some more." The waiter tilts the pot and fills David's coffee cup. He sports a five o'clock shadow which he scratches upon thanking the waiter. The waiter nods and walks away.

"What's up?" David asks recognizing I've spent more time awake amid life's quandaries as opposed to being fast asleep and letting the subconscious squeeze the air out of my lungs as I dream I'm drowning.

"Been thinking. Thinking about life."

"Yeah?" He shoves a piece of white toast into his mouth and sips some coffee prior to chewing.

"Are you going to shave?" I ask him.

He nods and wipes his mouth. "Wanna talk about it?"

"You shaving? No thanks."

"No, you dumb shit. Whatever is on your mind."

"I'm just thinking about life, you know," I start. "Why am I here?"

"You're soon-to-be wife wanted to get married here."

"Remember Chelsea and Abigail and Rose? I've just been

reflecting. I keep telling myself that this is when life starts then I remember something later and tell myself that that was when life started."

"Life begins at conception," David responded with his mouth full smiling and winking, trying his best to ease a little comic relief into an overly hectic day. "Life happens, man. There's no beginning, you're always learning. You have to kind of think of it all in chapters."

"Yeah." I can see the clouds in the sky shifting slightly and noticeably. The sun peaks out for a moment to shine down upon the water and the ground in the distance, eventually it hides behind the thick clouds that keep moving in. I remember that summer and look at my brother. His band across his ring finger holding a fork in one hand stabbing into a breakfast steak. A knife saws off a chunk and he places it in his mouth. While partially chewing he gulps down another sip of coffee.

"How the hell do you not have digestion problems?"

His response is a mere shrug of the shoulders as he continues chomping on the breakfast steak.

"Dude!"

All I could do was blush with my hand on the wheel and another on a forty-four ounce gas station fountain cup. I was a million dollars that felt like a billion. As much as I absorbed the jealousy from my college roommate I also felt a little bit sad. I was sure going to miss Claire.

"I can't believe that happened." Mike screamed with wide eyes and an open mouth smile.

Mike's constant verbal disbelief in the final events of our freshman year of college lasted non-stop for nearly an hour and ended when he shook his head grinning and turning his attention to a clear freeway as the urban landscape of Los Angeles turned into the high desert.

"So, I've got an idea for a screenplay that I wanted to run by you," Mike said conveniently at the end of a CD.

"And you pick an undeclared history major to develop your little stories with?"

"You're unbiased..."

"Oh, I'm very biased."

"...you'll be honest..."

"Honesty always enhances a relationship," I added sarcastically.

"...and I'll actually value your opinion."

"Keep in mind that I can only be so honest, if I choose to think this is the worst idea since," I sipped a bit of the Coke, "since my purchasing of such a large beverage before embarking on a very open road then this will be an extremely long drive to Chicago."

"Good thing I'm in the stage of what we Hollywood types call development."

"Lay it on me."

"That's what she said." Mike put his hand up to his mouth like a seven year old who just accidentally swore in front of his parents for the first time.

"Yes. That is what she said," I took my eyes off the road and raised an eyebrow at Mike.

Mike laughed and I brought my eyes back onto the white lined double-lane freeway heading north. He couldn't find the right words to create the appropriate comeback and I basked in the few minutes of glory I created for myself before turning and asking him about this brilliant script idea.

"Ah, right. Well, it's a sci-fi kind of movie about aliens that came to earth like a thousand years ago. I figure North America wasn't too populated then and they could plant some shit in the ground and start a life. Well, flash forward to the present where, after ten centuries, they have made up a colony underground. Now, they're all technologically advanced and they want out. Their home planet spaceship forgot about them and now they come up from beneath the earth and wreak havoc. Where else would they just happen to dig up than Los Angeles?"

"A group of aliens pop out of the ground on Wilshire?" I asked, not sure if he was telling me a joke or if he was serious.

"Pretty much. It sounds totally goofy and stupid, I know it, but there are a lot of cool elements to it. Like an Adam and Eve thing where, here are the aliens that created a colony," he put his hands up and mimed quotation marks, "paradise and they leave paradise to enter..."

"Hell?"

"Yeah, Los Angeles."

"How many aliens?"

"You have to figure quite a few; I'm thinking like a thousand."

"They must not have much of a birth rate if for a thousand years all they have to show is a thousand folks."

"I see your point."

"Look, there are two ways you can go about doing this. At least I think there are," I wanted to give him advice and encourage his writing but on no good conscious could I tell him that this was not a movie I would search out show times for on a Saturday night. "One way is to tell me about the aliens, their life, how they survived and why they're coming up now and how they were never seen before."

"And two?"

"Blood thirsty zombie aliens that pop out for no reason and just start killing people. And where in Los Angeles is this taking place? If its south of the Ten Freeway then they better have technology on their side because they will certainly get shot."

"Maybe a place like Portland, Oregon instead."

I nodded in agreement. "They don't really have guns up there."

"And it's freakin' Portland."

"Yeah, if there's one place in this country that needs to be ransacked by psycho aliens from the underground, it's Portland. Maybe Concord, New Hampshire."

"Or Delaware. What does Delaware really have to offer?"

We simultaneously accepted the idea that the posh New England society was a great place to have possible mutant murdering aliens take over. I didn't care to discuss this idea on a serious level. There wasn't a way and I could only take jokes so far before Mike thought I was mocking him. Criticism is so hard to accept if it's an idea or opinion you cherish and want to see grow.

"Maybe a romantic comedy instead," Mike said.

"With aliens and humans?"

"No, that was kind of a dumb idea," he shrugged away and looked at the desert mountain and bare land pass us by. I remained quiet, not acknowledging.

"Sorry, dude," I said after five minutes of silence.

"For what?"

I didn't have an answer and felt I needed to provide one but lacked the courage.

"What do I know about movies, right? If you like it you should write it."

"Oh, the alien thing. Nah, the more I think about it the more it pretty much sucked. Might have worked fifty years ago when there were movies like 'Green Aliens from Planet Zero' or..."

"On the Waterfront?"

"Exactly, cheesy B-movies like 'On the Waterfront'."

"It might be a summer flick," I added in all seriousness. It was certainly an idea that could have a drinking game associated with it. That aspect piqued his interest again and we were back to talking plot and exploding flying saucers versus pimped-out Toyota Tercels.

There was only one thing I could think of to break the awkward air from the car; a bond that gentlemen share who when amongst friends could tear down the wall they may place in front of each other. I struggled for the answer but within ten minutes out of sheer will power and with some help from a breakfast burrito, I tilted my right leg up slightly and expelled some musty air and the noise of a balloon deflating. I smiled and flicked the window lock on. Mike clawed at the windows in a jesting manner and I slapped his hand away when he reached for the air conditioner. I gave it a few seconds before I unlocked the windows and gave him his breath of fresh air.

"Oh, you will rue the day." Mike stuck his head out of the window and took in a deep breath of dry desert air. We were on the same level again and back to being friends.

We didn't have much to say for quite some time and enjoyed the comfortable silence. A lowering gas gauge and hunger pangs took over and we began to look for our first official stop.

"I wish we were twenty-one," Mike said shoving a handful of fries in his mouth. The twinkling lights from penny, nickel, quarter and dollar slots smashed our optical senses as did the aroma of "casino", an indescribable smell of freshly cleaned dark carpet, cigarettes, and recycled oxygen pumped up to keep those who dared sit at the green felts' eyes open a little longer. We sat in a restaurant towards the back of a casino somewhere between Las Vegas and Laughlin, Nevada and stared down the Keno board. Our senses were on overload but our driver's license forbids us in taking part in some of the games we've played only on a computer or amongst friends.

"In two years, we need to come here," we both looked around the restaurant and out into the craps pit where we spotted an old man hunched over with a cigarette in his mouth, the ash nearly as long as the filter about to plummet to the pass line. The pit boss frowned and warned this man for the ump-teenth time to place the cigarette below the table. "Okay, not specifically here, but Las Vegas," Mike added.

I nodded as I took a gulp of my large-sized combo drink. "You got it. Roll some dice."

"Bang some hookers."

"Maybe." I said back. "Do you know how to roll dice?"

"I know how to bang hookers," Mike spouted out as two old

local ladies crept by our table. "Hi," Mike said to them hiding his shame. He segued nicely. "Speaking of getting the wax dipped, what's the full story with you and Claire?"

"I'm not exactly sure you could consider us boyfriend and girlfriend."

"Yes, we established that before, but that was before she wanted one last hurrah in the Dutch Oven. That's some pretty serious shit for her to come by and give you a goodbye..."

"Bull riding session?"

Mike clapped his hands. "Yes! You're on a role today, Drew."

"What can I tell you, Mike, I like her. I really didn't want to leave but people have plans. You have to go to Chicago and I can't afford a summer in some sublet in West LA. I hope she's there when I get back."

Mike empathized, "I hear ya, man. I'm jealous; I'm not going to lie. I would like that, well not exactly that. I could go for the non-four-month hiatus. You know what I mean?"

"I'm living what you mean," I stood up and popped the lid off my empty twenty-ounce cup. "It scares me that she might decide to move on," I told Mike without thinking that I doing the same had any slight possibility.

I walked over to the fountain machine and tapped my cup against the ice dispenser. My mind raced and I pulled the cup away allowing the few remaining cubes to fall into the drain. I filled up and walked back to our table. All I could see was Claire and how much I was beginning to fall for her and how frightened I really was that an entire season would pass before I could see her in a situation that didn't involve one of us meeting the other at the airport and having to share one of our parents' couches. Even then, we didn't have any set dates on when one would visit the other.

"Shall we go?" Mike asked.

"Let's go," I replied.

* * *

The thing about driving across the country is it can get very quiet, very fast. We were an hour on the road from our last stop when Mike dozed off, the side of his face smashed against the window.

It's a lonely country. If you aren't in a major populated area it could be damn near impossible to stumble across someone, anyone. I turned on the radio and allowed the automatic search to locate one of only five stations available in the remote location we were in. It stopped on a partially static country station. It was peaceful. I didn't know the song, or the lyrics, or the artist but I felt that when all you have are hazy mountains and the occasional distance signs, we were 283 miles from Salt Lake City, then this music works.

I looked over at Mike and pictured what it would be like to have Claire by my side on a cross-continent road trip. No doubt she would be asleep and I would have the same predicament of a serene and calming boredom, the exception being I would be able to slip my hand into hers and she would rotate into a position where she would lean closer.

The disc jockey cut into the last ten seconds of the song announcing the artist and told his audience that following this commercial break we could expect a weather and road conditions report. I reached for my cup and took the final sip of my Coke sucking up the remaining beverage mixed with air pockets that told anyone within ear shot that this drink was done.

I checked out my cell phone which lay quietly in the driver side door console. I hoped for a missed call but my ears never deceived me and no call came through. The time was 4:32pm. I had one signal bar. An American made truck sped past me on the left and I spotted a passenger jet in the distance many miles up.

I took back a thought on not being able to find someone out amongst the beige, barren rocks out here. If you travel long enough, and nowadays it wouldn't take too long, you're bound to spot a fellow traveler.

The dark, water-filled clouds poured down in the east. I was approaching rapidly and although they were headed in the same direction I was, I had more horsepower and would soon gain up on them. I was excited for the rain and smiled at the considerable chance that I would see lightning and hear thunder. Many move to southern California for the weather, and it is beautiful most of the time, but when you don't have an overcast day and a chance of precipitation on the horizon, then it's comparing good to bad when you have never experienced bad and the lack of comparison depreciates the good.

When we pulled into a suburban area of Salt Lake City, Mike had been awake for an hour and he had remained deep in thought with the exception of a comment on the music.

"This seems oddly appropriate."

The rain came down lightly. My gas gauge had been hovering between a quarter tank and empty.

It was my turn to fill up.

We found our motel: a La Quinta which sported two beds and the satisfaction of knowing that we weren't going to be shot or stabbed. My car would remain untouched and the windows would be unbroken at dawn's light.

My stomach turned at the thought of more fast food but our budgets didn't allow for a sit down meal and our forty-nine dollar a night penthouse on the second floor next to the ice machine didn't have the proper requirements needed for cooking. It was another round of burgers, fries, and drink preferably kept at the smallest combo size, however, we could never resist the thirty-nine cent upgrade.

"You want me to drive at all tomorrow?" Mike asked.

"We'll see. I'm doing fine on my own and we only went seven hundred miles."

Mike nodded.

"What's been on your mind?" I asked referring to his unusual tranquility.

"Just thinking."

"Want to share?"

Mike hesitated, but we were best friends so hesitations don't often exceed a few minutes. "My script idea. The alien thing. I know it's stupid but it's been the only thing I've been able to come up with. I think that's why I at least wanted to try to develop it more. I want to do something people will see, you know? I want that 'Written By' credit across the three-thousand screens," Mike said motioning his hand against an invisible backdrop, "but I want to do something good too. Popcorn flicks are fun and all but I want some artistic semblance to accompany my movie."

"Write something artsy-fartsy."

"Yeah, I don't know. I need the idea and then I can build it up from there."

"There's a ton of open road to think on out here, you may not believe me but I saw it, you were asleep, but it's there," I assured him.

There was silence as we hunched back into our own imaginations. My mouth opened and I never expected to say the words I said, "I think I want to change my major."

"To what?"

"I don't know."

"Well, you have plenty of time to think about it, it's not like you've taken anything other than general classes. What do you want to do if you don't want to study history?"

"That's the thing. I have absolutely no clue what I want to do and I know that a history major is pretty much useless unless you're going to be a history teacher."

"Denial," Mike started. "You're telling me you didn't know that the only jobs out there for history majors are teachers and museum tour guides? Come on, Drew."

He was right and it took seven hundred miles into a cross country trip and thousands of dollars in student loans to figure out that I might be wasting my time. I didn't want to teach. The six in the morning alarm and bratty kids who preferred, and usually did, sleep throughout the class didn't hold any appeal to me. All the twentieth century history classes I took in high school, which were three: Twentieth Century History, World War II and the Building of the Modern Day Democracy, and finally 1950 to the Present; I enjoyed immensely but sat next to note passers and nappers and any number of peers who opted to use the time to do their math homework. I didn't want to be the man in front of the class who was excited to tell everyone, students mostly there just to fulfill a requirement, that the turn of World War II in the Pacific Theater had been Midway and stare down at thirty blank faces that screamed "who gives a shit".

Mike didn't want to be the guy standing in front of cash register and talking to kids half his age about how at one point he met Kevin Costner at a bar in Hollywood and he had asked to read his script when in all actuality it was just a man who looked like Kevin Costner sitting seventeen rows away at an over priced movie theater.

We were scared of failure, only Mike knew what he would fail at, and I had no idea what I could fail at. At least not yet.

"Damn this whole thinking-about-life crap," Mike spurted out. "I can't believe I'm nineteen and this concerned about my future. I wonder if it's normal."

"I couldn't tell you, but based on what I've heard, life doesn't always go according to plan."

"So, I'm going through life worrying about shit."

"Uh huh," I took a bite of the cheeseburger that resembled nothing of the sign in which I ordered it from. "I think we grew up a lot this year," I said with a mouthful.

Mike shrugged it off, "New experiences and all that, I'm sure we grow about the same every year. This year's finals were junior year's SATs."

"Tomorrow's onion rings are today's fries," I said lifting a handful of fries, dipping them in ketchup and shoveling them into my mouth.

* * *

"I kind of miss you."

"You do, huh?" Her voice was a wonderful relief. It was distinctive and sexy. I could picture her in cloth shorts and a tank top laying on her bed and staring at the ceiling.

"Kind of. Don't be getting any sort of an ego now." I warned sarcastically.

"Ha ha, you want some."

"Maybe a little."

"You want to kiss me."

"Maybe a little. It's not like you don't want to do the same," I teased back.

"Mmm, good point."

There was a moment of silence between us.

"So, do you know when you might be coming back here?" She inquired for a date that fell on a calendar sooner rather than later but the short time I had been away brought very little time for considering the exact date of my return.

"I think school starts back up in mid-September so I'm thinking Labor Day. As far as another trip this summer, I don't know yet. What about you?"

"I don't know either."

"My brother is getting married in late July."

"That soon after the baby?"

"I don't think they are going all extravaganza blow-out party-of-the-century with their wedding. As far as I know it'll be a small ceremony with a few dozen people and maybe just a little party in the backyard. Either way, I'd kinda like you to be there."

"You just tell me a date and I'll discuss it with the father figure. Hopefully he will accept this little adventure."

"He doesn't want you traveling all the way out to Michigan to meet up with some guy you only were dating for a few weeks?"

"Not the highest on the list of things he wants his daughter to do, but there is one thing going for you?"

"And that is?"

"You make me happy and when I'm happy, my father is

happy, and he'd rather I have a Bruin as a boyfriend then my last boyfriend."

"Oh, we're talking exes now?" I feared not for my own stories, they seemed fairly normal. However, normalcy varies from person to person.

"I never brought up that one girl in the Starbucks; I know you broke her heart. Should I inquire?"

Silence.

"Thought so. You were nice. That's actually one of the things I liked about you right off the bat. You could've been all flirty with me, lord knows I would have liked it, but you played it cool out of kindness and once I saw you do that, well, I just had to talk to you further. I had to give you my phone number. Now Drew, I think I might have to ask about her."

I looked at my phone. My bars were low and the battery was hitting on empty.

"Maybe some other time? I need to plug in my phone."

"Oh, is it," she said flirtatiously, "so if I wanted to get all phone sexy with you, you would have to go as well?"

"Unfortunately yes. Well, I'd just throw up the warning about the battery and go as long as I could. I'd also hope Mike doesn't wake up and walk into the bathroom. That would make for an awkward car ride tomorrow."

"I'd prefer you to not crash and die tomorrow due to sleep deprivation or blue balls so goodnight, Drew."

I smiled.

"Good night, Claire."

I ended the phone call and looked at the screen. I thought it. Couldn't say it. Not even alone in a bathroom in a motel in Salt Lake City where no one would hear it. I didn't say it out loud but I wanted to tell her three little words that if spoken would appear to have been too soon.

5

I don't know how women do it. I think it's peer pressure because once most are married it seems that very few are happy. It's what they're supposed to do; they grow up, find a husband and live happily ever after. Some call this character Prince Charming, others call him Bob. I believe that this fairy tale is creating a false hope amongst the youth; a cruel joke that the previous generation wants their children to fall for. Then again, it works for some. Then again, here I am falling for it myself.

Someone is knocking on my door. I look through the peephole and can only see black. It's either somebody about to rob me or my father jokingly putting his hand over the hole. I take the risk and open the door. Dressed in khaki pants and a blue and white Hawaiian shirt he enters and gives me a hug.

"You look tired," he tells me and I shrug refusing to deny it. "Nerves?"

"It's nothing new. I was just thinking about how Claire and I met."

"Was all that the summer David and Nicole married?"

"Yeah."

"Christ," my Dad says taking a seat on the bed, "time just kind of melds together the older you get. More memories piling on..." he drifts off in a mumble as if recalling his thoughts is a difficult task. "Why are you thinking about that time?"

"I woke up at like three this morning and just started reviewing my life. You're right; it does all kind of mush into one long blurry memory. It seems like Chelsea breaking up with me was both yesterday and years ago." I look at my Dad who is staring at the remote control deciding which combination of two numbers would produce a news station on the television. He presses two buttons and a documentary on owls appears. Frustrated he begins flipping one by one.

"What are you doing here anyway?" I finally ask him.

"Your mother has started the getting ready process and since it will take me ten minutes, I'd figure there was no use sitting on the bed smelling perfumes and hair-styling equipment and make-up, plus the hair dryer will start blowing and making me turn the TV up to a ridiculous volume." He stops on a station with a commercial. "Is this CNN?"

"I don't know."

"Fox News?"

I shake my head.

"Screw it," he throws the remote onto the bed and looks up at me. "So, life reflection, I do that sometimes. Just remember that all your decisions will often times seem like the wrong ones and as much as it annoys you, you can't go back."

"So, bottom line, I could be entering the biggest disaster of my life right now but I shouldn't worry about it."

"Uh huh."

"Why do people get married?"

"To have babies." He came back quickly.

"If you analyze it does it really make a lot of sense? Here I am, going to be married in a few hours and I can't really figure out why. There is always some commitment thing that women like to press on you but what comes after this commitment, do you need to commit further?"

My Dad stood up off the bed and came close to me, putting his hands on my shoulders and looking me square in the eyes.

"Drew, I have no fucking clue. They want it so just do it."

"Just do it. So, your's and Mom's marriage can be summed up with a Nike slogan."

"Yes. Some are happy, most are not. We lucked out and we're happy. Come on, you know the story."

I nod as he lifts his hands off my shoulders. Although I am sure I am taller than my father by two inches it always seems as if he's looking down at me when he talks. Even if he is sitting down, he still feels above me. I guess that's what it's like. Even when I'm sixty and my Dad's decrepit and in a wheelchair, he will still be someone I am forced to look up to.

"Reason number two for being here," he started grabbing a magazine and walking towards the bathroom, "I have to drop the kids off at the pool".

It was my first night back that summer. Nicole sat at the end of the table eating waffles with syrup and a side of celery. Her stomach bulged out slightly under her shirt and I couldn't help but constantly have to divert my eyes away whenever she rose out of her seat or walked around with her hand on her stomach. Her curly blonde hair ran down past her shoulders. She remained quiet and when her fork wasn't passing soggy waffles into her mouth she was leaning back with one hand on her large belly.

The rest of us ate grilled cheeseburgers with unfrozen fries and canned corn. It was plain, tasty, and my first home cooked meal in a few months. I chowed it down.

"You've put on some weight," David told me with a mouth full of burger. One bit escaped and flew onto the side of his plate. He pressed it down with his index finger and put it back in his mouth. "Looks like a standard freshman fifteen to me."

I vainly peeked down at my body. I had gained some weight, probably more like twenty pounds, but I was never a big guy so the bad part was it actually showed and the good part was I could pass it off as it was without being too self-conscious.

"As long as Claire doesn't mind it much, right?" My Mom asked. "How is she?"

"She's fine," I responded, "I haven't talked to her yet."

"You really should give her a call. You don't want her to think you forgot about her."

"Or let her forget about you," my brother added.

"David." My Mom scowled him and Nicole smacked his arm.

"Oww," David rubbed his arm.

"They got that routine worked out pretty good," my Dad said. "It unfortunately works the other way too."

"Lou," Nicole said pointing her fork at my Dad and my Mom proceeded to smack him across the arm.

"It's good to have you home," my Mom told me smiling a motherly smile.

As we continued eating I looked around the kitchen/dining room. Nothing had really changed. David and Nicole's engagement photo was on the fridge and a new TV sat on the corner of the counter but there was a lot that felt different. There was a new guest at the table and she was not just a weekend guest. David and Nicole had been sleeping in David's room and turning my room into a nursery. My first few nights were going to be on the couch in the living room and being woken up when my Dad made breakfast in the morning before work. This first night I was feeling like a visitor in my own house and, in the morning, trying to fall back asleep with the smell of coffee molesting my nose.

I needed a room. I needed a bed. I needed to stop glancing over at my brother's fiancée's increasingly bloated stomach. I was getting slammed by random thoughts as I faked comfortable; eating my cheeseburger and drinking my pop. My room was now going to be the basement. My parents promised a new fold out bed as the old one from the mid-eighties had dark yellow foam oozing out of the ripped seams of the multi-shaded brown cushion. The TV felt twice as old and still had a dusty Super

Nintendo plugged in. I came home to a cold cellar that once was used as a play area and then for sleepovers.

My Mom inquired about Claire coming in for the wedding. I could only shrug my shoulders lethargically. I hoped she would, but hope isn't set in stone.

"It would be nice to meet her. Who knows, there might be wedding bells there too," my Mom said with teeth glowing white. I couldn't respond.

"We all have to get tricked eventually," David said. Nicole knuckle punched David's arm and he grabbed it in pain, "damn it, Nikki, you hit the bicep."

"I think it was justified," she said.

"I know the hit was justified but not the bicep. I have dead arm."

"Aww," Nikki rubbed his bicep a little. She felt guilty and proud. There was chemistry between them. For the first time I felt that their marriage and children, no matter how much of an accident it was, would hold out for a while. Mike had told me how a good friend of his from high school had a brother who married a girl when she got pregnant and nobody thought it would last more than a year. He concluded the story by looking at his watch and proclaiming that the wedding took place eight years ago. I stared at David and Nicole and the few seconds she spent rubbing his arm their eyes met and there was a connection, an energy, a love between just them that most people don't pick up on. Their smile crested a little more, their eyes spoke silent poetry back and forth.

After dinner, my father plopped down onto the couch with an easing groan. Over the years, as with so many aging humans, his stomach continued to grow. It wasn't the size of Nicole's and probably wouldn't get to that point for a few more years assuming he kept to the same diet. He sat slouched down a bit with his chin tucked in and hands, grasping the remote control, rested above his rising and sinking stomach.

"Hey Dad," I said entering the living room.

"Hey Drew. What's up?"

"Nothing," I said collapsing into the second much smaller couch. I'm sure there was a name that differentiated the two couches but I wasn't married and I didn't own a house, therefore, I recognized there was a difference but cared not to learn it. "You're in my bed."

"Oh," my Dad said looking on both sides of his body. "You're not going out tonight? Your first night back?"

"I called Brad. He's at dinner with his parents so after that."

My Dad nodded and continued watching the news. He shied away from network news recently and started watching more cable outlets. He said he could hear the local news on the radio in the mornings and on the way home from work, but cable news was broader and reached more than the metropolitan area, therefore, it had to be more interesting and less attention grabbing. "No 'what in your house could kill you as you sleep, after this commercial break' is on CNN because they are a general news outsourcing station. They do not need scare tactics," he would claim. It was also nice because I could interrupt him at any point and anything he missed he could catch in the next hour if he desired.

"How many friends do you have?"

My Dad turned his head toward me with a curious look. "Friends? What do you mean?"

"People you hang out with. You hang out with Uncle Marty and Gerald, but are they the only friends you have?"

"You make me sound like I have no friends," I couldn't tell if he was insulted. "It's not really about how many friends you have but who your friends are. I have great friendships with my brother and Gerald and whenever your mother and I go out we usually go with them, but I also have a lot of other friends from work. You just don't see them as much unless there is some event going on. They're friends around the office and we go out for drinks after work sometimes and we eat lunch together every day.

If I were to quit, you would probably hear about them more and hear about us going out with them more but sometimes spending eight-plus hours a day with co-workers is enough."

"Hmm," I understood and sympathized.

"When you're in school, high school or college, that is your life. You don't have a home life; a family life. You have the opportunity to party with your classmates. I can't go out and get drunk with Bill from the office across from mine. He has a four-year-old and it just doesn't fall into place."

I nodded and acknowledged. I still felt like there should be more people to call upon. In my nineteen years of existence I had very few people I could depend on; the main ones that came to mind were either in a different state or at dinner with his family.

"You want more friends?"

"Everyone needs variety here and there. I know some people from school that I could hang out with."

"Well, get a job."

"There's the fatherly advice I've been waiting for."

"When you have a child you'll incorporate that quote into your repertoire. Every parent needs to say that to their child at least once. You were a good kid so you were studying and not getting into trouble, worked part-time at the video store, mowed the lawn, shoveled the driveway, cleaned the garage; we could afford to keep you on allowance. Maybe it's time for another summer job."

I felt he was right, I felt sure he was. We turned and watched the news.

"By the way, mow the lawn tomorrow," my Dad threw in, partially feeling the need to officially end the conversation on a high, humorous note but mostly serious.

Back and forth. To and fro. I mowed the lawn. I hadn't even touched this loud beast of a machine in months but I could still handle it. Some things never leave you. It's like riding a bike, having sex, or wiping your ass. Men tend to not mind mowing the lawn and I liked doing it. At least I thought I did. It wasn't until I was five minutes into lugging a screaming motor across the grass with the sun beating down on my neck that I realized I missed the dorm life. No mowing lawns there. There was also no garbage day; just a chute that at any time of the day you could toss the trash down into a giant bin filled with bottles, papers, and possibly a few used condoms. That was much easier than placing bins on your driveway on a designated day, forgetting, and then running them over with your car. By one o'clock I was finished and showered and ready to head out. Brad rolled into the driveway and we were off to the mall. As we walked the capitalism-in-action plaza we felt old. This was such a good past time back when there was nothing to do and high school girls were attractive. Now they were attractive physically but their obnoxious laugh and disregard for anyone within ear shot was just a nuisance. A lot happens between eighteen and nineteen if you accept the opportunities. My long distance girlfriend was about the same age as me which makes her and I a couple of years, if not just only one year, older than these scantily clad prizes yet I found her much more appealing. They were "that drunk guy/girl" who is moderately funny if it's your friend and a bit embarrassing.

"I think that's Ellen's sister," Brad said staring one down.

"Who's that?"

"Just this one girl," he switched subjects fast. "There's a party tonight".

"Yeah, where at?"

"Jason Kilpatrick's house. I'm hearing it's like a one year reunion for the high school." Brad paused for a beat. "Chelsea will probably be there," he snuck in while keeping an eye on me to gauge my reaction.

"Oh," I tried playing it off like it wouldn't matter, but we both knew that it did.

"Where there's free booze and drugs, Chelsea will be there." It was cruel whether or not he wanted it to be. It was his attempt to make me feel better about a sobering situation while letting me know he had had plenty of opportunities throughout the school year to witness her downward spiral.

"I need a job. Any ideas?" I retorted in a desperate attempt for a topic change.

"You could be a waiter."

"Don't you need experience for that?"

"I'm sure the intense training programs at Red Robin will be more than satisfactory to make you an expert in the waiting business."

"I thought there was more to it in the serving industry than just saying 'what do you want'".

"Sometimes...sometimes, you need to put an order in. But that's, like, after three years of on the job training."

"You don't have to be an asshole."

"Oh, Drew," Brad said with a smile on his face, "if you become a waiter, you can guarantee I'm going to come in and harass you. You don't even know the meaning of the word asshole yet."

"Let's go to the book store so I can get an application and pick up a dictionary to find that true meaning of the word asshole."

"Maybe I'll apply too while we're there. I need to occupy some free time this summer with something constructive."

"Well, what happens if I get the job and you don't? Then we'll have that between us and whenever you look at me all you'll see is failure and misery and how you just weren't good enough to work at a bookstore," I said for a comedic jab.

Brad thought for a second. We stopped walking as he placed his hand to his chin, caressing as if carefully pondering the universe from Red Giants to the tiniest of atoms. "You're right, if they accept you and not me, it's only because they know they could control you more and thus, in me, they will see I am too good for such an establishment and realize my attempts at applying at their organization was merely an experiment in social standings."

"Or maybe I'm just cooler," I said with every intention to mock his ability to shoot big words off in a vain attempt to bring the other person down.

"Name. Andrew Meade. Address 46872 South Baybury St."

"Make sure when you get to the social security number you say that real loud so it echoes in this public arena."

I hadn't touched my food. I was drawn away towards the application.

"You'll probably land some hot book-reading ass."

"I have a girlfriend."

"Yeah, in Los Angeles. I don't know if you've checked the weather report, but it's supposed to rain tomorrow. Therefore, this cannot be Los Angeles."

"It rains in Los Angeles. Sometimes. Well, people turn on their sprinklers. That's like rain. You're not seeing anyone, right?" I asked.

"Nah, I was seeing that one chick I was telling you about but I figured it best to break it off at the end of the semester," Brad said.

"Bianca the cellist?"

"Julie the flutist," he confirmed.

"You loved her that much, huh?"

"Ya know what they say, if you love them, set them free. If they don't come back, it was never meant to be." He put a mouth full of a burrito into his mouth, "If they return, then get a restraining order."

"Sound advice. What should I put for previous employment?"

"Have you had previous employment?"

"Yes."

"Well then put that down."

"A year at a video store and nothing since. Won't that look bad?"

"Don't be such a butt. They'll probably swoon over your UCLA merits anyway."

"I wasn't aware I had UCLA merits," I said wondering if Brad was using the correct word usage.

"Merit. Attendance." Brad shrugged the difference shifting his eyes toward the two glass sliding doors at the end of the food court. He nodded and I turned in my seat to take a glance at the jailbait in an insanely short jean skirt walking in.

I mocked him: "She's alright."

"Claire must have a two-thousand mile short leash on your nuts. Eat your damn food before I start taking some."

"You touch my chips and you're a dead man, like knife to the genitalia dead man. I want to finish filling this out." I threatened.

Brad's eyes shifted towards a hot young girl, probably eighteen with no qualms to showing her cleavage underneath a white button shirt, the top two buttons undone. "I'd like to fill that out. I'm not sure when this mall turned into a whorehouse but I'm not going to write anything negative on a comment card."

I looked up. "Want me to tell her about your desires?" I asked as the girl walked closer.

"No."

"How's she going to know if you don't tell her and I don't tell her? Women can't read minds, they just think we can."

"Yeah, you'll really go up and say that to her." He said, not believing my threat.

"Sure," I hopped out of my seat and Brad jumped twice as fast to grab my shirt.

"Sit down," he chuckled nervously and thought I would've actually done it.

I looked over my shoulder and saw her at the yogurt stand. "I can tell her you'd like to treat her like a keg and tap that."

"Don't you have an application to fill out?"

"Or I can tell her that instead of getting that yogurt that my friend has a different kind of yogurt that's less calories and just as satisfying." Struck with a general shock of dismay over the comment he busted into a loud laughter that caused his head to fall flat onto his arm hiding his face from the world. His body shook as he tried to inhale any breath of air his lungs would permit. I smiled at the girl as she gave Brad a strange glance.

They looked older. Fatter. Skinnier. Balding. Bearded. Streaked. They were all part of my graduating class and as Brad and I entered Jason's house at a quarter-to-ten, the music was blasting, the drinks were flowing and cliques had reformed. The cheerleaders and the jocks did shots in the kitchen. The nerds were there, red party cups in their laps as they played video games on the fifty-inch flat screen. There was Melissa who sat next to me in Math and Luke who was my lab partner in Chemistry. Garrett was telling everyone how great his life had become, how he had met big businessmen and they were carrying him to the top, he was overdressed for an early summer underage slosh-fest. He was the only one passing out business cards. Sammy who was picked on at prom for bringing his cousin was now engaged to a twenty-two year old knock out doctor in training. Some struck gold and some just acted like they did. Most of us at this party were just finishing our freshman year and had nothing to boast but college experiences that all seemed to be similar. In one corner was Kathryn and in another corner avoiding all possible contact was Marcus her high school sweetheart. They broke up six months ago and the rumor going around the party was it wasn't a very clean, amicable parting.

Within a half an hour I was standing next to the staircase talking with two guys. We had hung out a few times throughout our K-12 careers, both Boris and Kyle came to my tenth birthday party and I went to Boris' Bar Mitzvah. Boris just concluded telling me about his Geology teacher and how it took him nearly two classes to realize that "Lie-meh" was "climate", the teacher's accent was so thick. They were excited to hear my adventurous tales of the West. Had I seen any celebrities? Did I go to the beach every day? They ogled over my run-in with the occasional TV star in a famous place like Santa Monica and a second sighting of a mid-nineties sitcom star at a grocery store buying a bottle of Southern Comfort and a frozen pizza.

"All I can tell you is either our high school was conservative or every girl becomes a bisexual once they hit the university level," Kyle chimed in, "seriously, how may parties did ya go to where chicks were just making out all over the place?"

As if the Gods had heard Kyle's statement as a request a roar of cheers bellowed from the other room and we all took notice. Lisa was kissing one of her friends, Andrea. Both sloppy drunk, they had fallen to the pressure of making a public scene. They parted lips and drank their respective alcoholic beverages. Kyle, Boris and I couldn't help look at each other in disbelief as well as agreement.

"That answers that," Kyle said.

Brad stumbled into the room with his shirt half off and a girl whose name I couldn't remember, I did remember she was Violin Girl.

"Look who I came across," Brad slurred, "it's Violin Girl."

Apparently Brad lacked the name as well but, as she was laughing and dropping her head onto Brad's shoulder, she didn't seem to notice or question it. Violin Girl's head was lowered and Brad looked at us grinning and nodding his head telling us he was so going to get laid tonight.

"I need more ah-ca-hall," Violin Girl spurted tipping her cup over and letting the final drops spill onto the steam cleaned carpet.

"Yeah, ya do," Brad said.

"Dude," Kyle tapped my arm and I turned to the direction he was pointing. Chelsea walked in. She still looked skinnier than I remembered and she wore a black tank top and black pants. Her hair was a different color too, still brown, just a darker shade. Behind her was Michelle, a seventy pound heavier version of Chelsea. I knew Michelle went to the same university as Chelsea but this was the first I was seeing them together as friends. Michelle was that outcast in our high school. She always dressed dark and stayed lonely; no one paid much attention to her because she was rebellious in a way that wasn't acceptable amongst her peers. We had an English class together and were in a group with two other for a discussion about a chapter in the Great Gatsby. I can't remember the actual assignment but I do remember that her two cents were usually condescending in regards to ours. She liked not being accepted by her classmates, it thrilled her and gave her something to make fun of when around her friends, wherever they were and at whatever schools they had attended. Now Chelsea was with her and my heart and stomach both tightened. I could feel the acids build and the blood flow faster. Further proof that you never get over the ones you love, especially the first ones; I had Claire thousands of miles away who I was beginning to care for deeply and I was ten feet from Chelsea and wanting to kiss her. I didn't want this washed out, jaded version of Chelsea to kiss, I wanted my original Chelsea.

She nodded at me with no expression, not even a courtesy smile, and went into another room.

"What the fuck happened?" Boris asked.

"Chelsea and Michelle hanging out? Gotta be lesbians." Kyle added.

I remained quiet, too cowardly to defend my ex-girlfriend's honor.

"I don't know if there's another explanation for it. They are one step away from wearing combat boots and cutting their hair," Boris continued.

I shook my head away from them. I didn't want to stand up for Chelsea, not at that moment, but I didn't want to encourage further insults. I took a sip from my cup.

* * *

The walk home wasn't long. Brad lived in the other direction and based on his and Violin Girl's activities I doubted that was going to be their destination. I pulled out my cell phone and clicked down to Claire's number. Three hours behind put her at about 10:30. It rang. Two times. Three times. Then it went to voice mail.

"Hey Claire, it's Drew. How's California? Just stumbling home from a party. Anyway, give me a call sometime and we can discuss you coming out here. I really think you should be around for this wedding." I stopped mid-thought and wondered if this was asking too much. If dating for a month and going into a long distance relationship made it okay for us to attend a wedding, especially my brother's, together, "or ya know, whenever. Talk to ya later."

I hung up and continued forward on the empty suburban street passing green lawn after green lawn. The sprinklers ran on one out of every three houses. Most everyone was asleep; the houses were dark. Occasionally a room would be lit by the blue glow of a television.

Her handshake was light and I dared not squeeze too tightly. I didn't want to come across with a weak handshake but broken fingers weren't the best way to start a job interview.

"So, you go to UCLA?" Tricia asked. She was only a few years older than I was but radiated the kind of stress a forty-year-old with three kids would have. She was supporting herself through school and was counting down the days until she could switch into her real career and out of bookstore management. Her downfall was her love for this job and the instances that she subconsciously let herself slip in school to maintain a good reputation with the corporate offices. She loved her job, but she hated loving it too.

"Yes."

"The weather out there is nice, isn't it? No rain. No snow."

"It gets cold sometimes, but it's pretty nice."

"Ever see a movie star?"

"I saw the one guy from Will and Grace once," I said trying to impress her but I suddenly lost the names and faces of the other celebrities I saw. "And a few other random ones," I added.

"Ooh, at a fancy restaurant?"

"No, he was at the same movie theater I was at."

"Oh wow, so you can say you saw a movie with him. What's his name?"

"I don't know his real name. I'm not good with actors' names"

She was slightly interested in knowing more and asked if I wanted to be an actor. To her disappointment I said no and told her I met plenty of people my freshman year who aspired for the Hollywood dream. She mentioned a friend who occasionally auditioned for Community Theater and was considering the big move west.

"So, why did you move out there?"

"I wanted to get away from this place for a while. I grew up here. Same house since I was four. Just wanted a change and UCLA is a great school and they have a decent history program."

"You're a history person."

"I like non-fiction material."

"Do you read a lot?"

"Not as much as I'd like to. Unless it was required reading, I didn't get a chance to pick up a book the whole year."

"Why apply here?"

"I like books. I like reading. I'm pretty sure I like people and bookstores have increased in popularity as a place to hang out and read. I'm all about that."

She chuckled.

"Look, I'm determined to do well here. It's a retail job, I know, but if I can't take a position like this seriously and try to gain experience and knowledge in helping everyday people then I might as well become a night guard at a high rise office complex," with a smile on my face and the words that Mike had script-written for me in my head I leaned in and said, "I want your store to be my second home this summer." I should've been an actor.

She hired me on the spot. Whether or not my dramatic speech made a difference I'll never know, they could've just needed to hire a bunch of kids for the summer. Either way, I started training on Thursday which was only two days away. I was to get there at ten in the morning and spend two hours filling out tax forms and reading a training manual. The sexual harassment paper I had to sign was the icing on the bureaucratic employment requirement cake and it took all I had to not laugh. I guess I shouldn't grab the breasts of the gal behind the Information Desk near the humor section, however, if I were to pull a stunt like that it would make sense to execute it near the self-help shelves so that way I could claim that it was an addiction which is why I was in "self-help" to begin with.

I had finally talked to Claire that night. I sat on the porch step for ten minutes, stood up, walked down the driveway, walked back, paced, and sat back down. The conversation lasted nearly two hours to the point where she had to warn me that if the line suddenly goes dead it's because her "low-battery" light was flashing. It did. Mid-sentence. Unfortunately that sentence was mine and I could have been rambling on for two minutes before I waited for a response, checked my cell phone, and saw that my ear had been pressed against the dimmed menu.

We had talked about everything from my new job to her adventure to Venice Beach and watching some foreign man, probably Indian, jump from a folding chair onto a pile of broken glass in which Claire and her friend offered the man a dollar for the show.

"He must have collected thirty dollars in the ten minutes we were standing around," she claimed. "He was so professional that the bottom of his feet must be calloused over to the point that he could walk across lava and only feel a slight itching sensation."

Then we talked travel dates. Claire had been excited when I asked her to attend my brother's wedding. She loved weddings and had been to two of her high school friends' already. She was only six months older than me and I had trouble picturing myself or anyone I knew getting married. Suddenly, like a wind gust punched me in the stomach, my mind flipped to a time in my senior year of high school when Brad, Chelsea and I were at the mall and I turned toward a jewelry store and saw that they were having a Columbus Day sale offering up to seventy percent off select rings. That night I contemplated, while sitting on my bed atop my dark green comforter, that I should hop up, rush to the mall and buy Chelsea a ring. I had indeed thought of marriage before and I had indeed envisioned myself standing at the end of a long aisle inside a church and watching my beautiful bride walk through the doors. Chelsea in her white dress and flowers in her hands becoming the center of the universe and this ring that I would have gotten at seventy percent off being the first step towards eternal bliss.

So much for childhood dreams.

Claire asked about Mike and I asked about her family.

The phone died after she promised to search for a flight the next day. I stood beneath the porch light and watched a moth skim the light and shy away from its heat, then circle around for another close encounter. Claire would soon be at this door. I stepped inside, went to my living room couch and plopped down onto my back holding the cell phone in one hand against my chest. I closed my eyes and fell asleep.

I dressed nicely. No tie and no shiny shoes though I was casual without being too normal and I stepped out the door to get into my car to take me to the big building housing thousands of books that will never be touched unless myself or one of my fellow employees needed to move it out of the way.

In the hours that followed I learned about shelving, displays, and idiot customers. I wasn't going on a register quite yet. They didn't say it but I was pretty sure they wanted to test out new employees on the floor and make sure they weren't about to go psycho and steal hundreds of dollars or take a lunch break and never come back.

Books from all different sections land in different sections across the store. I had found a self-help book in the history section and when I took that back I found a horror book beside the "Pregnancy for Dummies". There were CDs in finance, a DVD box set in reference, and a Styrofoam ice cream cup on top of the coffee table picture book "New England Flowers". Everyone stepped through the doors, the young and old, men and women, cliques and nerds and part of my job description was roaming the aisles asking if they needed assistance.

When lunchtime came I took off the shoelace name tag and walked three doors down to grab a burger, fries and drink. I sat down for my half hour which I had originally felt would go by quickly. Instead I was back inside the store ten minutes before I needed to clock back in. I sat quietly inside the break room until a multi-pierced, multi-tattooed girl stepped in to get a drink.

"You're new," she said rather fiercely.

"Yes, I am," I responded.

"How's your first day?"

"It's good."

"Not much of a talker, huh? You in high school or something?"

"Between my freshman and sophomore year of college."

She averted her eyes back to the giant canned soft drink machine and asked if I smoked. There was a condescending tone in her voice that disapproved of caving into life's social norms as if she didn't want a further education for the purposes of short-term financial freedom and because everyone else does it. She was judging me on whether or not I was judging her.

"Damn it," she replied when I told her that I didn't smoke, I was now a goodie-two-shoes in her eyes, "I left mine at home. I really don't feel like buying another pack."

"You're gonna have to buy one eventually, right?"

"I guess." She snapped open her caffeine infested beverage and chugged down half the can, I anticipated a very unladylike belch that never came. She wiped her mouth with the back of her hand. "How old are you?"

"Nineteen."

"You're such a baby. Shit, nineteen."

"How old are you?"

"Twenty-five."

"That's not old."

She shook it off and stood near the soda machine picking at something in one of her back teeth. She was cute but really skinny. Her arms were a little bony but I didn't peg her as heroine junkie. Then again, I've never witnessed firsthand what a heroine junkie would look like so my references based on R-rated gritty films may be skewed. She took another drink and continued thinking, really wanting that cigarette.

"Do you know anyone off hand who smokes?"

"I don't." I didn't. I had met Eddie the man who showed me all the joys of re-shelving and the manager Tricia who hired me and left me alone in the conference room while I filled out the necessary documents. Other than those two I was introduced to a variety of bookstore characters whose names I barely remembered. Eddie was cool but nearly twice my age and the others didn't seem to like him socially. He had reached that age where retail became a career but his lack of people skills prevented him from advancing; he remained positive and pitied.

I told her my name which seemed to come out as a segue away from any topic she may have been inquiring even though neither us were saying any words. I didn't know her name and she didn't know mine, if I was going to continue employment after a few hours then I might as well start letting people know who I am and begin learning who they are.

"My name is Page, which is spelled P-A-G-E and not P-A-I-G-E," she flipped over her badge, "customers love looking at my name tag and commenting how appropriate it is for me to work at a bookstore. I think of different ways I want to decapitate them for mentioning the irony," I assumed she was kidding. "I'm in the café and if they haven't told you yet the employees get a thirty-percent discount. You come over to me and I'll hook you up, charge you for something cheaper."

"I'll do that." Lunch time was over and I stood up with a slight groan. Five hours of standing on my feet and my legs were tiring. I hadn't been prepared for such a long stint but it came with the territory.

Upon exiting the break room I wished Page good luck on her search for a cigarette.

According to my watch the time was 4:43pm. As I was shoving books onto the shelf from the handcart I was tallying up the total amount of money I had made thus far. It neared forty-nine dollars which didn't seem like a whole lot. That was just gross; my net pay would be closer to forty dollars, maybe even lower. It hardly seemed fair, but across five days of work I would bank on over two-hundred-seventy-five dollars. Gross.

I grabbed the mystery/thriller and looked for its appropriate shelf placing. The author's names were off. Someone put a Bradley next to the Evers. I looked down the aisle one way, then the other way. I wasn't sure what I was looking for exactly, perhaps the culprit, the illiterate book reader or the lazy, maybe the thirteen year old who found it conveniently funny to switch books around for no other reason than to know that some nineteen-year-old making a few pennies above minimum wage would have to spend his time fixing the mess. I placed the Bradley in the proper last name alphabetical order and continued shelving.

"Hey, new guy," I heard someone say behind me. I spun around and the tall, dark haired man lowered his chin to get a better view at my name tag. "Drew. Is that short for Andrew?"

"Yeah," I responded.

"I'm Jon," he pointed to his name tag and moved is finger across the letters. "J-O-N. No H."

"Nice to meet you, Jon."

He approached the cart and grabbed a few books assuming my pleasantries were a general set of ingrained manners with no actual feelings of meeting him being nice.

"These are so lame. I weep for those who find entertainment amongst this drivel. What determined FBI agent can bring down the terrorist cell or serial killer before they claim another victim or attempt an assassination on one of this nation's leaders?"

"I've never really read them," I responded, slightly lying.

"All the cops have powerful names. Lieutenant Sword. Captain Striker. Special Agent Wolf. The villains are nearly as rotten." He started reading the back, "Veteran FBI agent Angel is on the hunt again for long time nemesis and ruthless murderer 'The Devil'." He tossed the book on the shelf. "How appropriate. What imbecile thinks any of this as quality?"

His conscious ploy to make those around him feel like a lower sub-species for not piecing together the meaning of words easily found in the English dictionary was unfortunately working on me. I was uncomfortable with any reply that lacked fancy words, especially on my first day. I looked at one of the books before placing it on the shelf. The CIA logo appeared under a murdered woman. The tagline on the cover was 'The Infamous Mole has Returned'. The price was $7.99; with my employee discount I could swing that down to $5.59. I looked at Jon as he grabbed a handful of similar titles and placed them face out on the shelf in front of the other books. The title bursting in big lettering. My Dad was that imbecile who occasionally sat in the backyard in the summers as the sun was setting late in the evening reading one of these books. Everyone has their definition of quality and I wasn't one to devalue someone's taste, at least not my father's.

"Airplane books," I said.

"I'm sorry?" Jon looked at me.

"These make great airplane books. Take one on board; they're easy to close, easy to pick up, easy to read."

Jon turned away as if the very idea of showing that you bought and read one of these socially poisonous materials in public was worse than farting at a funeral. I opted not to tell him that on more than one occasion my father passed a mystery/thriller to me and I leisurely read it pool-side or on an airplane, to go further and say I enjoyed them would have been suicide.

"What kind of books do you like?" I questioned.

"I've read most of the classics. Dostoevsky. LeCarre. Fitzgerald. The ones that have held true. Russian literature is both depressing and fascinating. You also have the contemporary works that are worth reading. Those are harder to come by based on our generation's ability to sweep whatever may be good under the rug in order to fall for the next big trend."

I didn't like Jon. He was an elitist. Whatever you did, he said he did something better and of higher quality. You see a new movie; he saw the latest and greatest art house film. You bought a new CD or like a new song, his favorite new song was a band you never heard of and a CD you can only buy at two places: their show or their website.

Call it ignorance or being thrust upon a situation that involved older and bitter twenty-something's whose lives took a detour on their planned life's road trip but I had a hard time believing that anybody I knew would turn out like Page, Jon, or even Eddie. They weren't bad people, just bad role models. I feared momentarily that I would become one of these three; the kid who had his goal dangling in front of him like a carrot within inches of a mule's nose but at some point you kicked off the rider and lost track of the carrot.

Maybe my first impressions were wrong. Maybe they were freer than those stuck under a fluorescent light in a cubicle. I was too inexperienced to know.

I left the bookstore that day with my head held high and my shoulders back. My first full day of work in which I helped people find what they were looking for, even if it was the bathroom, and met a few new characters that would enter the stage that was my life.

"You acquired a cigarette," I said to Page as I walked past her, her back leaning against the beige wall. She puffed out a lung full of smoke.

"Sometimes you've got to show a little skin to get what you need," I couldn't tell if she was joking. It was hot in a 'girl-you-don't-take-home-to-Mom' kind of way. She was serious.

"I wouldn't know," I replied. "See ya."

She didn't say anything back.

"Push! Push!" The nurse screamed as the doctor's sweat beaded across his cheek soaking up his face mask. Nicole let out an enormous cry as she pushed as hard as she could.

The floor in the waiting room was tiled like my high school. I think there is one generic tile that government-type buildings are required to have or maybe it's just easier to clean up vomit and blood. I wasn't sure how Nicole was doing or if she was screeching until her throat was sore as the doctor attempted to pull the watermelon out of the orange. My only reference was the network sitcoms that used one of the main characters having a baby as a major storyline in hopes to boost its dwindling ratings.

Another family consisting of a set of grandparents, a father, and what I believed was an aunt and uncle were overjoyed to welcome their baby into the world. They already had one who the grandmother held in her arms and made googly noises to while the others coddled. The little boy chewed on his toy and stared away spaced out and unaware of his current circumstances.

He would have a playmate soon, one who would vie for all the attention, and most likely get it. He didn't know what was in store and had no choice in the matter. His uncle took him from the grandmother's arms and started lifting and lowering him, the child was unimpressed.

I hopped off my seat and went down the hall to get a drink of water. As I passed the happy little family I wondered how much responsibility I would have to take part in as uncle. Would I have to lift him up and down? Baby-sit him on the off chance that Nicole and David wanted to go out for a night? Clean his ass when he craps in a diaper? I suddenly became less enthused about my baby niece or nephew arriving. He already took over my old room and changed the paint on the wall to a light blue color; my brother and soon-to-be-sister-in-law claimed they didn't know the sex of the child yet and powder blue works for a boy or, with a few pink and yellow flowers painted on the wall, would be great for a girl. I would have to fight for attention myself. I was the one who wouldn't be in any of the pictures because I would be the one having to take the pictures. I sighed and speculated how many times I would have to tell so-and-so to move in closer and to smile and try to get the little baby with the attention span of a stoned teenager to look at the camera. If I learned anything about reviewing my old pictures and any baby pictures, most of the time the baby doesn't smile. In fact, the majority of baby pictures consist of the little figure staring off to the side with either a sad look on his face that everyone interprets as cute; or a constipated one, which everyone interprets as cute as well. It was exciting at first until the sun started to rise in the distance and I became bored. I read every Time magazine and skimmed the pages of every National Geographic in the entire waiting room. When I came home from work there were no signs of life, just a scribbled-on piece of loose leaf paper hanging from the refrigerator door. Three hours prior David had rushed home from work to take Nicole to the hospital. I was told that it wasn't completely out of the question for me to be placed in this exact scenario and, as I grabbed a drink, I thought how lucky I was to not have the just-as-possible plan B occur; being woken up in the middle of the night to barking orders and screaming contractions from Nicole.

The first child was statistically going to take a ridiculous amount of hours to deliver which was why I was confronted by a note and not a cell phone call. I locked the front door, walked to my car and drove to Beaumont Hospital.

The sun was beginning to rise and I was approaching my tenth hour at the hospital. I was tired, I'm sure my deodorant had worn off, and my stomach rumbled partially from hunger and partially from having eaten a little too much vending machine junk food throughout the night.

I looked at the clock on my cell phone. The hours were beginning to blur together. I was half attempted to go into Nicole's room and yell at her to hurry up. Conversation ceased with my parents long ago. My Dad slumped in his chair, his mouth wide open and his breathing just under a snore. My Mom worked on a crossword puzzle.

Nicole's parents were somewhere. I wasn't sure exactly but their boredom seemed to get the best of them. I imagined them at a twenty-four hour restaurant a few blocks away stirring cream and sugar into their third cup of coffee; a conversation absent by shear fatigue and inconvenient annoyance. I flipped to an image of Nicole's father in a bathroom shaving; his first comment upon meeting us at the hospital was rubbing the two day stubble on his face and wishing he had brought a razor. At this hour, I figured everyone in that first picture with the newborn baby was going to look like they just drove all night through the bowels of hell.

I checked my cell phone again. Only a few moments had passed since the last time I pulled the device from my pocket, I think it's a habit officially thrust upon our generation; the constant need to see if anybody tried to reach us. No missed calls and no new text messages. I didn't expect anybody to call me this early in the morning, especially Claire. Jumping three hours back to west coast time and I was sure she was asleep in her bed dreaming about me. Well, I hoped she was dreaming about me but most likely it was something strange that if she tried to tell anybody it wouldn't make any sense to them for the sole reason that it was a dream.

My Dad, now awake, and my Mom excused themselves for a few minutes only to return and sit near me both groaning with the bending of their knees. They were tired too and my father plopped down near me leaning low in the chair. My Mom sat across from us and remained silent. The allure of this baby had worn off and my father mentioned how he wanted to go into the delivery room and tell Nicole to just pop it out already, that people have things they need to do.

"No shit," I responded.

At 7:58am on June 20, after a seventeen hour labor, Theodore Warren Meade was born. I was an uncle and a Godfather on the same day. I also had to be to work in two hours. My mother, father, David and I crowded around Nicole and looked at the tiny baby. Everything it did generated an "ohh" from somebody, mainly my mother and Nicole. David and I moved towards the back of the room and I congratulated him and inquired about the name they had chosen.

"It's not really a popular name."

"We didn't want popular, we wanted...not ordinary..." David struggled for the right words.

"Nothing helps define a childhood and adolescence like a name that sticks out and reminds people of their grandparents."

"Theodore Meade. I think it's strong. Presidential. Executive. How many Theodore's do you see on a name tag when you walk into a fast food restaurant?"

We both looked over to the family. David smiled proudly and nodded.

Nicole's parents entered and rushed to their child and grandchild's bedside.

"If this is the only thing I accomplish in life, then I think I may have just done something right." I looked up at my brother. We were nearly the same height but I still felt myself looking upwards at him as if this moment would define the change in his life. I grew jealous of his revelation as if I aspired for someone or something that would light the fuse under my ass. "We're going to have so many visitors," David added.

I looked at my cell phone and my time to hang around the hospital was wearing thin. I moved in closer to my nephew as he slept in his mother's arms. He looked like a Theodore, whatever they look like.

It was the first day of summer, technically speaking, and five weeks into my summer job. I drove to work with just a hot shower and a cup of coffee to my morning as well as the slowly diminishing joy that accompanied my brother's first born. I would have preferred more sleep but had to settle on what I got. I knew I was working with Angie, Page, and Bill on the floor so the day wasn't going to be a complete downer. They were my newly acquired acquaintances from work and although I had never hung out with them outside the bookstore I did find satisfaction in knowing they were on the schedule with similar hours as me. To add an extra stress to my day, Brad had told me of a party tonight and to keep my mind occupied at the traffic lights I calculated the hours of sleep I could possibly get between work and social life. Off of work at six-thirty, home by six-fifty, asleep by six-fifty-five and awake at eight-thirty. At least I had tomorrow off.

The party Brad and I were going to was another high school related gathering. I was likely to run into a good chunk of my graduating class and, as always, that included Chelsea. We lived only miles apart and were the best of friends and boyfriend/girlfriend for a good part of high school, I still had a phone number for her but I didn't know if it was right anymore. The closest association I had with her was whenever I needed to scroll down to Claire's name. On many occasions I would double-check to make sure I hadn't accidentally pressed the send button on Chelsea's number.

The truth behind never getting over your first love, especially if it lasts three years of your teenage years, is one hell of a fact. I didn't want to see her but couldn't help to think of how our conversations would go.

"Hi Drew."

"Hi Chelsea."

"How's your summer?"

"Good, yours?"

"Good. I've got a job."

"Oh yeah? I'm working back at the mall again. Same store."

"Really? Is that one asshole you cheated on me with still work there?"

That wouldn't be how the conversation would progress but your mind wreaks havoc when you think about the pain of yesterday. Throw on the fire a lack of a good night's sleep and decent meal, add the peak of a caffeine kick, and I was headed in the right direction for a loopy, off balanced day shift. I was stopped at a light right before the bookstore parking lot entrance and my heart was racing and my face grew warm. How could I still be upset over what Chelsea did? It was a long time before I had even found out about her and Chris, that asshole, and we had a few good chats between the break up and now. Sometimes you can't persuade your mind to move in the direction you want it to.

Angie couldn't take her eyes off of me; unfortunately it wasn't in a sexual way. I had the stubble of a nineteen year old who hadn't shaved in three days. My eyes were fairly non-existent because the lids were almost closed. I was clumsy and my breathing was labored. I could have been in a fight; the dark lumps under my eyes were only growing by the minute. I feared resting my chin upon my arms if I dared to lean. The day would turn into one long haze and tomorrow morning I'd wonder how I even made it through the previous day without causing major injury to myself or someone nearby. I was so tired that I could lie down on a cold meat locker floor with a cow's rib as a pillow and blissfully slumber for hours.

"You look like shit," Angie eventually said and I slowly raised my eyes to meet hers.

"Thanks."

"You look like you've been awake for a week straight," she added.

"Going on thirty hours, I think. What time is it?" My speech was soft and slurred. I spoke slowly. I told her my brother finally had the baby and I was at the hospital until an hour before I had to come into work. Angie became hyper in milliseconds like some switch in the female body gets flipped at the mention of a newborn. "Theodore Warren Meade."

"Sounds like a senator," she claimed and I nodded in agreement. "Senator Theodore Meade of Delaware."

"Some people are born to be great leaders. Others are just named that way."

Angie started chuckling in regards to my situation and implied that Tricia would probably let me go home under these circumstances. She raised her arms and exaggeratedly looked around the uninhabited store. There were the mellow sounds of an unrecognizable local band on the speakers filling in the silences between conversations. One lady and her son had entered the store, the first in fifteen minutes, and they were reading in the children's section, an illustrated hardcover with minimal amounts of words on her lap, her finger scanning each letter. The child too young to remember, the mother unable to forget such moments.

"It's your life, Drew. Kill yourself being tired but a nice, soft, pillowy bed awaits you at home. Just imagine collapsing onto a blanket and closing your eyes. Before you know it, you're awake again not realizing that you slept ten hours, unable to recall a dream. The warm comforting environment in the dark." She smiled and I only thought of two words to reply.

"Screw you."

"You have a girlfriend, Drew," she backed up and twirled allowing me to spy on all her curves. She was beautiful but didn't show it. She was older, more experienced and I couldn't help think of what her breasts would feel like in my hands. Kissing them. Touching them. "Too bad, all this could be yours," she flirted.

"Angie, I'm too tired. I don't have the energy to be turned on. You're going to have to go to a club and find some loser with spiked hair and a striped shirt to buy you a drink to love you quickly," I responded.

"Don't remind me. That's all I can find on the internet too."

"You need to raise your standards."

"They are raised."

"Maybe you need to go out with someone who has more to offer than an over-inflated ego, a giant truck or tiny car, and a small penis to match."

Angie sighed and turned away. There was no changing unless she wanted to change. I figured I hit the nail right on the head and she couldn't steer clear of how right I was and how much she wanted to find somebody with all the good qualities that no one at clubs could offer.

"Maybe you should go to the self-help section," I joked. She took it somewhat seriously and decided to head off into that section but was stopped instead by a second floating customer looking for a biography on a 1940's movie star named Cary Grant.

Within moments she came back stating a new problem now plaguing her morning. Jon had spotted her crossing the aisles between thrillers and humor on his way in and followed her to the front where I was stationed.

"Good morning, fellow bookworms," Jon spoke behind Angie, partially yelling to get her attention and speaking to me. "How goes the morning of this second day in the summer solstice?"

"Swell," Angie replied.

"Fantastic," I said sarcastically. Jon looked at me.

"Sweet merciful Jesus, did you get in a fight and left in the middle of the interstate before getting ran over by a truck?"

"Something like that," I said.

He shrugged. "My reason for bothering you two instead of helping the clientele was I noticed that I have this pesky shift on Saturday afternoon and as much as I would love to fulfill my duties at this exuberant display of capitalism, I have alternate intentions for my weekend day. Would either of you care to take hold of this prime opportunity?"

"A friend of mine's in a play."

"You are friends with an actress?" Jon asked. "Is she one of those high school play leads who aspires of Hollywood fame and glamour to only have it get slapped back in her face in the form of anorexia and a pornographic film? Or would she be the long lost starving artist who claims prominence on the stage?"

"She works at an insurance company and likes to act. So, hobby would be her reason. Either way, no, I can't pick up your shift."

"What about you, Drew? Do you have plans that don't entail 'Our Town' at the local theater house?"

"I have to sleep in late and watch TV. Maybe, ya know, take a nap at some point. It's turning out to be a full day and Sunday isn't looking too promising either." I responded facetiously.

"Don't be an oaf, Drew."

"Can you say please?"

"I can. And, for you, I may consider such useless add-ons to bolster the emotional human psyche. So, Mister Andrew Meade, would you be so kind to pick up my shift this Saturday? Please."

"Sure. I could use the extra spending cash."

"Wait until the bills start rolling in," Angie added.

"I've had a year at a university far, far away. Much further than Kalamazoo, I know all about bills."

"I appreciate your acceptance in my offer, I will inform Tricia." He turned to leave but put his finger into the air like the brilliant thought both stopped him in his track and he needed our attention to share it. "You know, please is a form of begging, which is why I don't often use the word. You should be quite gracious I stooped to that level for this eight hour extravaganza you're taking for me."

"I appreciate you begging for it," I said with a smile as he continued away.

"That guy's an asshole, why did you take his shift?" Angie asked.

"Gives me something to do on Saturday now plus with the new baby around and relatives visiting it gives me a chance to breathe."

"You come here to breathe?"

"When I drive, I breathe. When I come here I'm suffocating once again." Angie and I remained quiet for a few moments until my curiosity got the best of me, "You have a friend that's an actress, huh?"

"Yeah, we went to high school together and she likes to act but never wanted to do it professionally. It keeps her locally famous, I suppose, and it gives me and her friends a reason to do something besides go out drinking or seeing a movie. She's good. You should come to a show."

"I think that would be pretty cool. Not too many rush out to plays these days."

"Unlike when we were younger and frequented the theater circuit?"

"You know what I mean."

"Back in the 1980's when all there was to do on a Saturday evening was dress to the nines in our tuxedos and gowns and head over to old playhouse for the latest rendition of...a play."

"Yeah, yeah, yeah. You've made your point."

"Her show run is over Saturday, that's why I'm going. But they're pretty regular; I think they have another one starting in a couple weeks. I will keep you updated."

I was lying upon my couch in the dark basement. The house was quiet and I was embracing the final opportunities for comfortable silence. David, Nicole and the baby were at the hospital and my parents were upstairs also relishing in the lack of noise. I was on my back staring straight up at a ceiling I couldn't even see with my eyes wide open. I expected to be dead asleep by now dreaming of obscurities featuring friends and families surrounding me relaying advice in a code I could wake up and try to cipher; my subconscious telling me that I needed to confront fears or, most likely, that I shouldn't have rented the horror movie that I did the other night. Whatever I could have been dreaming of I certainly wasn't at this moment. I would have loved to experience a nightmare just to know that I did indeed rack up a few moments of rest.

I sighed loudly and became frustrated. I shifted to my stomach and wrapped my arms around a pillow squeezing it tight so the middle section would pop up and provide a comfortable head rest. That didn't work. The red digital clock three feet from my head was shining 7:17. I shot my body upward and stepped off the couch.

The basement door was cracked open a bit and I could hear the clinking of a fork against a plate. My father was sitting by himself over a small pile of spaghetti and the newspaper. He looked over to me as the door creaked open.

"I thought you were sleeping," he said.

"Couldn't fall asleep." I plopped down into a chair and looked down at the table, spacing out.

"You're officially an uncle," he told me as if reciting a fact in a newspaper article he was reading.

"So, I've seen. Is there anything I need to be doing?"

"I don't know. Be brotherly. That should cover it." I wasn't sure what it meant perhaps I should keep doing what I'm doing or I should consider it a warning behind the massive amounts of work required when you're part of a family unit. My father continued, "I've never had a grandson before so this is all new to me. I've had children and even then you kind of learn as you go." He put some spaghetti in his mouth.

I stood up, rubbed my eyes and warned my father the bathroom was going to be occupied in preparation for the night's events.

"Be responsible, okay?" I assured him that I would be. "Drew," he started, "this whole having a baby around now and, well, as far as anything in life, if there's one thing I've learned it's that you don't have control. You may think you have control, but you don't. Your brother is the perfect example. I'm sure one year ago he didn't think he would be holding his first born in his arms or trying to find a job that pays better than a coffee barista but you take life and maneuver around it. It's like a wave, you can't overpower it, you can only hop on a boat or a surfboard and ride it as best you can."

"Thanks, Dad. That's some solid fatherly advice." Although it didn't particularly have to do with me, I could tell my father had something to say and decided that his youngest son would be his outlet. I was proud to receive it.

"I do what I can. Are you working tomorrow?"

"Nope."

"Good. Mow the lawn."

I heard my phone buzzing from the top of the stairs and flew down to see Claire's name on the display.

"Claire."

"Hi, Drew," she said. I could hear cars roaring by in the background and she was breathing heavily.

"Where are you?"

"Walking to my car."

"You can slow down, you sound winded."

She explained that she was using the time between work and meeting her best friend at the Fox in Westwood to call me. I instantly recalled the few movies her and I had made out during at that very theater. I used the opportunity to tell her that I was officially an uncle, a responsibility I still hadn't fully comprehended.

"What's the first swear word you're going to teach him?"

"I'm thinking asshole," I responded confidently.

"So, what's his name?"

"Theodore Warren Meade."

"Sounds like a Congressman. A Republican congressman."

"Most have thought Senator, but close enough. They're all elected officials."

"It's not a name too common in the NBA."

"I'm excited for you to come out here." There was a pause. "Claire?" Still no answer. I checked my phone and saw that the time was still ascending and put the receiver back to my ear. "Hello?"

"Oh, sorry. That wasn't meant to sound like I was nervous about you being excited for me to see you. I'm excited to see you too. I haven't even been on a plane in over fifteen years, I'm a little uneasy about the whole, you know, taking off, soaring five miles above anything but air and clouds thing."

"Flying is easy. Just close your eyes and pretend you're on a freeway and the little bit of turbulence you feel is merely a pot hole or bump or random road thingy."

"Right, random road thingy."

There was silence again and I stood in the dark basement waiting for a response. I could hear her breathing and figured she was crossing a street or had lost her train of thought.

"I should go." She said. "Congrats again Uncle Andy."

"Uncle Drew works better for me."

"Well Drew, I do miss you. Have a good night, okay?"

"You too."

The ascending numbers stopped and flashed at the end of

the call, I closed the cell phone and tossed it onto the table. The only light emitting was my digital clock and the phone. I walked to the light switch and flipped it up. My eyes took a moment to adjust and I looked around the slightly messy corner of the basement I called home. I was still tired but there was no point in napping now.

When Brad and I arrived at the party, the sun was still shining in the distance. There would be another two hours of partial sunlight before it would be officially dark. There was music coming from the back of the house and we decided to skip the interior and followed the walkway through the fence into the backyard. The radio was blasting generic pop music; my fellow alums and a few I didn't recognize were swimming and bouncing around a beach ball. One guy would get it and smash it towards a buddy who unexpectedly got nailed in the side of the head. In turn he dove under water and darted towards his friend and a fight would ensue until one of the others called it quits or a third party member hit the ball at someone else.

It was the first time I saw many of the girls I wanted to see in swimsuits dressed in swimsuits and, lucky for everyone, they wore bikinis. Most were on the side of the pool with a party cup in hand filled with beer gossiping about lord knows what and played upset when one of the guys splashed water in their direction. We had a few greetings shouted towards us accompanied with the proper directions to the alcohol.

Brad and I stepped inside to a low key party where about twenty men and women were sitting around playing "asshole" at one table and beer pong at another. The gathering had yet to take off into a full fledge drunkfest but experience and common knowledge told us that whatever we wanted to accomplish should be done by midnight as anytime after that was a gamble as to when the cops were going to show up.

"Where's the smokey-smokey," a kid who was still in high

school, probably a brother or a friend of someone else at this party, yelled to his bud.

"Boris told me he'd be here by now," Brad said looking through the living room as we entered the kitchen. A sink full of ice and beer along with a counter with liquor and soda awaited all those who dare enter. "You think Chelsea is going to show?"

The question took me off guard but I had noticed this becoming a general topic at each party. I wondered if Brad was using my fear and occasional misery to compensate for something in his life. I also thought that maybe he enjoyed watching the downfall of somebody who broke up with me. "How would I know? I'm not her day planner." At the last party people assumed she had gone the ways of a lesbian which were a rumor that turned into a denial that fell to the side of not-a-chance. She spent half the night on her cell phone talking to her twenty-six year old boyfriend. His excuse for not showing up was that he had to work in the morning. Seven years is a big difference when you're our age. There are so many experiences and general life lessons you're supposed to learn between eighteen and twenty-six just as there are when you go from twelve to eighteen. I figure that once you hit twenty-six it would be okay to date someone who has garnered a few more years than you. If Chelsea were in her mid-twenties and dating someone in their thirties it would have been acceptable, but this twenty-something she had been dating just felt creepy.

"Maybe she'll bring her senior citizen boy toy with her this time."

"Are they accepting AARP cards to cover entry here?" I cracked back.

Within an hour the party size had doubled, the music was a little louder and the guests a little more inebriated. I was in the backyard dancing amongst my old classmates around the pool. One of the first important lessons learned in college is how to dance and not spill your beer. I opted for the beer bottle and not a cup which pushed me ahead of the game as far as most others were concerned.

In my immediate area was Boris who entered the party with a hello and one shot of tequila before shaking my hand taking a second shot and turning to shake Brad's hand. Melissa, my old Math neighbor was provocatively swinging her hips near me in a non-lethal way. I wouldn't hold her or touch her; I just let her thrust her ass around nearby. She knew I had a girlfriend and stayed at a friendly distance which was about five inches in this crowd. My eyes diverted toward the house where I could see Brad standing on one of the house's wooden benches with a couple of band mates but his attention was gazed towards me. We caught eyes and he motioned to his right. I looked and saw Chelsea. My heart skipped, dropped, and my stomach turned slightly upside down. I don't think my body language showed it too much and if it did, nobody noticed. I continued dancing and kept Chelsea within eyesight as she talked with former classmates. She eventually reached Brad and they began to talk. I was jealous and motioned to Boris and Melissa that I was heading out of the crowd.

"...it's a bit of a pain sometimes but the pay is okay," Chelsea followed Brad's eyes and turned around to see me.

"Hi Drew."

"Hi Chelsea."

"I was just telling Brad that he, and you, should stop by my work sometime." I could feel her desperate attempt to reconnect but there was no connection forming.

"Where are you working?"

"Mitchell's." It was a casual but nice restaurant nearby. The food was a little pricey but it worked splendidly for a first date or an evening out. It's not a place you would frequent unless you're a business person on lunch; otherwise, it's a good once-a-month treat-yourself-nice restaurant famous for steak. It was also in the same parking lot as where I worked and now gave me a good reason to constantly look out the window in search of Chelsea's car. I didn't mean to tell her how close our employment establishments were but revealed it immediately, idiotically.

"Really? Now I have a place to go on my breaks." Chelsea said with a smile.

"Me too." I smiled back thinking of the bookstore employee break room. "What else is new? We don't ever talk." I regretted the statement the second I said it, even before I said it. I was giving fuel to a grease fire that I had finally been able to tame.

"Well, I broke up with that one douche bag I was dating before."

"Grandpa?" Brad wanted to confirm.

"Yes, the twenty-six year old. Apparently he thought he could cheat on me, which, um, I let him." Brad winced in pity pain at Chelsea's demise. "Twice. And well, I broke up with him. At least I didn't get any diseases," she added.

"Good to hear," Brad said.

"He broke up with me." Chelsea said admitting defeat. I looked into her drink cup which was a very light brown; a mixture of a minimal amount of soda and a good amount of whiskey. The whiskey was a giveaway based on her breath.

"So, you're not dating anyone?" Brad asked. Chelsea shook her head. I looked at Chelsea and Brad who both broke eye contact for a moment during the awkward silence. I wasn't sure if Brad asked her the question for my expense or his. He had started dating someone recently which I knew wasn't serious and according to him wouldn't become anything more than dating. I couldn't help think that I was the third wheel they were trying to detach. Brad then hopped down from the bench and put his arm around me.

"Chelsea, Drew here needs a refill and that gives me just as good an excuse to get a refill myself. We'll be seeing you."

Brad and I walked away. I still had the unshakable feeling that something was amiss. I hoped it was just the alcohol talking but I found he was using my presence as a way to escape the allure and sexual tension that Chelsea was creating. I was optimistic and realistic, I was pessimistic too.

I didn't have a problem sleeping that night. I came home and fell face first onto my couch and stared down my alarm clock for the better part of a minute. It was a quarter after midnight and I reeked of alcohol and cigarette smoke. I thought about the benefits of brushing my teeth and washing up. I let out a nine second belch, closed my eyes, and didn't reopen them for nearly twelve hours.

The best part about sleeping in a basement is that it is underground. If there are any windows, they shine in the bare minimum of light. As I fluttered my eyes open with the taste of dehydration in my mouth I realized that in the dark I had no concept of time. My only thought was how quickly I needed a bathroom and how more ounces of alcohol than the FDA recommended had been floating in my body for the last half day and was begging to be let out.

I opened the basement door to the evil sunlight that sought out my eyeballs from ninety million miles away. I thrust myself back into darkness as I closed my eyes and used my memory to guide myself blindly towards the bathroom down the hall. It worked for the most part but I was still uncoordinated and rode the wall with my right shoulder part of the way.

Two minutes later I was back on the couch sitting straight up watching the television that remained off. I had a whole day to kill and no plans to fill in the empty spaces.

Absence makes the heart grow fonder. Out of sight, out of mind. I knew which one I applied towards Claire. I wondered which one she was applying towards me.

"Next time, I swear to God, I am driving here. Forget the plane." Mike stepped into the baggage claim area at Detroit Metro

Airport and I stood there waiting for him. He gave me a great big hug dropping his carry-on and small piece of luggage right beside us. "Oh, I missed you, Drew," he said acting a little too frisky with his hug and petting my hair. I became increasingly nervous. "I missed your touch, Drew, and your smell." He took a big whiff. "It smells like springtime in Montana."

I pushed him off me but he came near again.

"Don't you want people to know our feelings for one another? Are you embarrassed by what we have going on?" He giggled and picked up his carry-on. "This is it," he said looking down at his luggage, "let us go rape us some Detroit bitches."

We started to walk toward the exit dodging parents not paying attention to anything but their kids who wanted nothing more than to run around the open baggage claim and play while trying to determine which ramp their baggage was going to spill from.

"By rape you mean court some classy ladies and hope they touch our pee-pee areas, right?"

"I get the classy ladies and they will be courting this region right here," Mike shouted waving his hand in front of his crotch. I walked further ahead praying nobody heard him and hoping I didn't know anybody but he caught up. "You have a gal thousands of miles away," his hand circled my nether regions, "the only hand that touches this pee-pee area will be your own."

He tossed his suitcase and carry-on bag in the trunk and we headed for the highway.

"Delayed, dude. Okay, get to the airport an hour early, get delayed an hour, fly an hour, drive...how long's the drive?"

"Half-hour."

"I've decided that I'm coming back out here in August for shits and giggles and I'm bringing my own damn car. Spend that kind of money to save two hours? Not happening." He punched my shoulder. "So, what's new? How's work? How's life? How's the baby?"

I told him all was peaches back at the house and how

advantageous it was sleeping two floors beneath a crying baby. "I've racked up a buttload of minutes on my cell phone from David calling asking me to pick up diapers."

"The wedding is..."

"Three weeks from Saturday. Claire comes in the Thursday before."

"Midsummer Boinkfest." Mike motioned an ass smacking. "I'll expect no phone calls the entire time she's in town."

"You can guarantee that," I offered with a smile.

"But maybe I'll randomly call you in the evening just to see if I can interrupt your..." and Mike went back to the ass smacking motion, waving his arm dramatically back and forth. "Where are we headed first? I'm starving so the answer is food. What about the party you mentioned? I do get open free reign on every girl you went to high school with, right?"

"All except one."

"Fair. Am I going to be like the only negro there?"

"No, I wouldn't say the only one but you will be claiming a certain part of the percentage."

"The negro percentage?"

"Yes."

"Say it."

"That's alright."

"Damn it, Drew, say Negro percentage. Say it or I enter the party shouting about all your midnight homoerotic rendezvous' in West Hollywood. I'm the roommate, they're going to be asking me stuff about you and I'm good with creating creative situations."

I did my best to persuade him into thinking that most wouldn't care what he had to say but he was quick to remind me that everyone loves a scandal involving old classmates. His threats of fictitious tales were not something I was willing to gamble on.

"Negro percentage." I caved.

"There ya go. You're off the hook this time. I might throw

in a little ditty about how you tried spooning me on Valentine's Day." I didn't respond. "No? Fine, be that way." He was hyper and his mind raced from one topic to another. He turned the subject to working in his Dad's office and not being able to hit on the girls that came in for eye appointments because his father was constantly over his shoulder. "You'd be amazed how many random people can't see worth shit," he added. "Chelsea going to be there? I'm assuming she's the off limits one."

"I never know. This party won't be as big as the others so, your guess is as good mine." I paused. "And yes, she's off limits."

"Then I'm going to guess she will be there 'cause I like drama."

Hanging around Mike was good. I hadn't seen Brad too much recently, his summer employment destination landed him at a grocery store and I asked for a full time schedule at the bookstore. Our off-times didn't coincide as much as either of us would have liked and we were hanging out only once or twice a week. There were a few nights I would go out to eat or see a movie with my newly acquired work friends. Mike and I had a history though and being around someone like him, a good college bud, was what I needed.

Mike and I played video games, ate pizza, and tried to ignore the crying baby. I would occasionally take on the role of good uncle and hold Theodore so Nicole could just sit back and relax. Mike took an instant liking to Theodore and Theodore to Mike.

Nicole was currently a stay-at-home mother while David was finishing his last two weeks at the coffee shop. Through an internet service he found employment as a salesman riding a desk in a tiny padded cubicle on the third floor of an office building not too far from home. His hours were set up so that he would be going to work when most everyone else does and leaving with them as well turning a normal ten minute drive into a thirty-five minute commute.

"All I know is that there is paid training, I have to wear a tie, it's not illegal, and they pay pretty decent," David claimed at the dinner table one night trying to feed his child, "it's communications of some sort, there were multiple openings. They have medical after six months," he said trying to sell us on being a salesman.

At the party, the usual former people were there minus the jocks and cheerleaders. The host told us how he didn't need an out of control party with people he didn't like breaking things his parents treasured and treating the house like a gas station bathroom. With alcohol and underage drinkers, it definitely wasn't on its way to becoming an early night. I introduced Mike to Boris and Melissa who feigned interest for a while until they both needed more beer. Brad popped out from the kitchen and greeted us with handshakes. It wasn't alcohol but I could tell that a foreign substance had entered his body that he wasn't used to. My experience with recreational drugs were limited which was quite an accomplishment having attended a major university for a year. Although he stopped sophomore year of college, I had seen David stroll around the house in his underwear while stoned so I was used to it. I wasn't against other's participation but I never expected to see Brad like that. It was unsettling if only because it was unfamiliar.

Hours went by and the party got a little rowdier but still resembled some form of civility with the host constantly peeking out the windows to see if the neighbors were peeking out of their's. Rain began to fall and everyone moved indoors; most into the basement. Chelsea arrived solo at ten-thirty and presented herself to Mike. We talked a few moments and she requested a reason on why I hadn't visited her at Mitchell's in which I answered back wondering why she hadn't come into the bookstore. Truth be told she had on a handful of occasions. I often spotted her and ducked back into the stock room until I felt the coast was clear. She hadn't asked the employees if I was working and only assumed that I wasn't in that day or was fired and didn't tell her yet.

There was one time our paths crossed inside the bookstore. I was helping a customer with ordering one of the store's summer recommendations that apparently was doing its job as we were currently out of stock. I had wrapped up and Chelsea came over for a quick chat. I played as if I were helping her and took her back into the Literature department so Tricia wouldn't think I was messing around on the clock. By then, to my excitement, Chelsea only had a couple minutes. It was always situations like this, seeing her or knowing she was looking for me, that made me open up my cell phone and send Claire a quick message. It was a reassurance that I had moved on. Preferred avoidance on my terms was a key sign in my improvement as opposed to avoidance by fear from my heartbreak from only one year ago.

Mike was polite and when she proceeded to the alcohol he turned to me and told me how he couldn't understand what there was between us. Our personalities not only didn't match, he explained, but we just didn't seem right for one another.

"I guess at one time maybe, but you two make about as much sense as genital herpes on a nun. Opposites attract, I suppose."

"We used to be good for each other," I defended, "we're just different now." It had struck me that Chelsea wasn't the only one to have changed, I was becoming different too. New experiences with new people in new cities switched my personality daily and, unnoticeable to me, over the course of a year could make me unrecognizable if I subconsciously allowed it.

"They say we change personalities entirely every seven years," Mike said.

"Is that from the department of random statistics?" I responded sarcastically.

"Alright fine." He then stated philosophically, "the only thing constant is change." He bowed his head completing his thought.

The hours passed by and Mike and I boozed it up to the

point where any further would be problematic for a walk home and unlucky for a few house's bushes. That was, unfortunately, not the same for a few other guests one of which was Kathryn who darted past me in the hallway and just about missed the bathroom toilet. In fact, it was about half and half. I dared to enter the half open door leading into the bathroom. Kathryn was hunched over the toilet and as if on cue to my stage entrance she yakked one more time.

"I threw up in my hair," she said lifting her face partially out of the bowl but still looked down in a strange curiosity to hazily figure out what she had thrown up.

"The porcelain God thanks you for your generous donation," I said. Kathryn tilted her head towards me, she looked like hell. I braved the smell and walked over to the toilet flushing the alcohol and tiny bits of what looked like fries down into the sewers.

"Come on," I said lifting her to her feet. I moved her towards the sink and turned on the cold water. "Rinse."

She began drinking handfuls of water and spitting most of it out. I popped open the medicine cabinet but found nothing of value. I turned to a cabinet door, opened and the mouthwash was sitting in front of me.

"Thanks Drew." She lifted herself up too fast and lost balance falling into my arms, she was near passed out.

"Let's find a place for you to lie down," I carried her slowly out of the bathroom and Mike was starring down the hall.

"Come on, man, you don't have to do this. She's young and innocent and you're not that desperate," Mike joked. "You need a hand?"

"No, thanks," I thought a moment, "actually, remember Jenny?"

"The white blonde girl?"

"Yeah."

"Yeah, Drew, that's like half the girls here."

"She was the one who was doing body shots off of the other blonde."

"The one with the perky breasts."

"They're all nineteen, Mike, they all have perky breasts."

"Ass you could ride for days? You could bounce a quarter off of it?"

"Sure, that's her."

"She also--"

"Damn it, Mike, just get Jenny and bring her into the room." Mike winked and headed away. I cracked open an already slightly ajar door and peeked in. There was a couple getting hot and heavy with one another on a futon. I decided not to say a word and close the door but my sight caught familiarity and I did a double take. It looked like Chelsea and, as I squinted my eyes, I became positive it was her. I felt dejected and sober. I looked away but still had her in my sights, Chelsea and her companion had yet to notice the hall light spill into the room. All the hurt and all the pain from last summer flooded back in. One year of life had disappeared and I was the scared, slumped-shouldered kid from before. I stood frozen for a second until Kathryn moved again. I lifted her back up and turned once more to see in the dark who she was with but I couldn't tell. I closed the door. Personally witnessing Chelsea with another man was the nightmare coming to life. Kathryn groaned and I forced myself to continue taking care of the girl I barely knew in high school but was increasingly creating a connection with.

I opened up a door across the hall and the room was empty. I carried Kathryn in and placed her gently on the bed, her stomach facing down. I leaned next to her face as she began to breathe heavily.

"Alright Kathryn, Jenny will be in here to watch over you in a while."

"Thanks Drew."

I nodded and my mind shifted back onto Chelsea. It was a heartbreaking image, even though I knew there were others after me, to witness it was the end of any denial that covered my heart.

"Drew," Kathryn whispered and I moved in close.

"Yes, Kathryn."

"Thanks," and she lifted her hand towards my cheek and moved in. It was a kiss. A very small and forgettable kiss that I backed away from. She lowered her head and passed out. Mike and Jenny entered the room.

"This her?" Mike asked standing behind Jenny motioning his hand up and down so I could verify it was the fantastically built girl I sent him to find. I nodded.

I left the room and went into the hallway. Kathryn had already forgotten our kiss. It wasn't anything sexual, I think she wanted to kiss somebody and so she went for her knight who saved her from the evil throes of the toilet. Chelsea, however, was an image I wouldn't soon let go of no matter how hard I tried.

"You ready to go stumble out of here in the rain and head back home?" Mike asked.

"Yes I am. You see Brad anywhere?"

Mike twisted his head around a quick second then shrugged his shoulders.

I opened my cell and scrolled down to his number. I heard the ring and as I lowered the phone from my ear my eyes gazed toward the closed door, the one that concealed Chelsea. I hung up and looked at Mike.

"Screw it. He knows how to get back to his place."

We left the party and walked in the rain; both of us stopped twice to relieve our filled bladders onto unsuspecting trees.

As I was laying on my couch/bed and Mike was getting comfortable on a comforter on the floor he relished in the old times and let out a hardy bubble that had been resting inside his body for the better part of a half an hour. It was loud and juicy and I cringed as he laughed. The laughter turning into sympathy as the odor reached his nose first and he began wafting over into my direction. I was laughing with my face buried in my pillow. I thunderously hiccupped and nearly brought up some alcohol causing Mike to just about lose it. I sat up in the dark as we both settled down and he assured me there was nothing else on the horizon but if there were I would be the first to know. I chuckled and, often times as you come down from the high that is generated by a good laugh, reality set in.

"I think Chelsea and Brad were making out at the party tonight."

There was silence. Mike rushed for consoling words but didn't produce any. There was nothing he could say to alleviate this pain.

"Maybe you're just seeing things. You did do like three shots of Jack." I didn't say anything and he continued, "But you're not seeing things, so let's not pretend. Look at the bright side, maybe they aren't dating, they just hooked up."

"Yeah, let's hope," I stated over-sarcastically.

"Wow, there is absolutely nothing that I can say," he spoke defeated. "I'm sorry, dude."

I positioned myself onto my back with an arm behind my head for support. The room was near pitch black and I could sense it spinning a little bit. Then I heard Mike fart again.

"By the way, I have to fart."

I counter-balanced by lifting my own leg and fought fire with fire.

For the rest of the time that Mike was in town I was a bit off my usual boisterous track. He noticed and was always trying to bring me into a good mood but no matter how funny things got I constantly had the image of Chelsea with an unknown figure in my head, the figure slowly resembling a clearer form. The side of Brad's neck, his hairline. I pictured their lips closing in on one another's. Their mouth's parting and their tongues slipping around. I know how she kissed, and now so did my best friend of nearly fifteen years. It's times like these when you wish you could speed up the wound healer known as time but it still goes by at sixty slow seconds per minute. Everyone has been through the emotional pain and yet it plagues the earth like the common cold, nobody knows the cure. I wanted hindsight. I wanted a future version of myself to appear and reassure me that these feelings of betrayal and anger and sadness would subside. I wanted the answers that the future held. The ones that were impossible to know in the present.

"You can't get rid of an image you've seen that you never wanted to see. You can repress it but that just means it will come back at some inopportune time like in a campaign speech or during sex," Mike said when I brought it up for the fifty-seventh time how unbelievable it was for this action to have occurred.

"I'm sorry to keep on bitching about all this, but..." I trailed off because there was no excuse for it yet no excuse not to talk about it. I tried to shove Claire into my mind but that only momentarily diverted my mental path.

Mike left on a Wednesday night. I drove him to the airport, we said our goodbyes and I promised him that I would make it to Chicago earlier than the original plan had entailed. The summer was pushing along quickly as summers often do and before you knew it you were back at school sitting in a required class you cared very little for and reminiscing about how nice it was to stay in bed until the afternoon and watch TV until the evening. We shook hands and even held out our arms like good buddies who wouldn't see each other for a long time and hugged.

"Maybe I'll come out here that weekend after your bros wedding if Claire's still around, you know, instead of August. I can sleep on the floor in the basement again and take pictures of you two humping like a pair of monkeys at the zoo," Mike said as we approached the security. "Hey, we should go to the Lincoln Park Zoo when you're in town."

I smiled, "That sounds lovely. We can piss off the orangutans by shouting obscenities and they can fling poo at us."

He stepped into the barrier between airport travel and the

real world and I slowly walked away. Right before he reached the metal detectors he turned around and gave a wave.

"You're better than her!" Mike screamed from thirty feet away. "Don't ever forget it and don't let her get to you." I smiled at him, appreciating the very public gesture of expelling his advice. "Never!" He screamed with hands in the air like a battle cry before a knight took his men into battle. He lowered them, smiled and nodded.

I was in a pretty damn good mood because of Mike. On the drive home my pocket began to vibrate and I reached in for my cell phone. Brad was displayed and I contemplated answering for the few seconds between ring and voice mail that the time allotted. I put the phone down onto the passenger seat and spent the next forty-five seconds turning my head to wait for the voice mail indicator to appear. It eventually did but I refused to open the cell phone, dial my number, put in my password and listen to what Brad had to say. Considering we hadn't spoken since the party, and this was the first the other had tried to contact the other, he probably suspected that I knew something. I knew his message would be one of general conversation in attempts to slowly figure out if I indeed knew what had happened. I pondered if the happenings of that was a one time fluke or an ongoing affair.

The unwritten rules of friendship specifically indicate that you must first ask your best friend, or any friend you have known for a time in which said friend was dating the "pursued", and/or has close contact with a friend, i.e. third party, if you could indeed pursue the "pursued". Brad violated this rule and therefore was going to actively inquire if he had gotten away with his crime or was witnessed and therefore guilty.

I had waited for nearly four hours to listen to his voice mail constantly checking my phone to see if any new calls had come through. Perhaps it was a way to see how relevant he deemed our friendship and that, considering the days that had passed, how much damage control there was to be done. I wondered for hours how much trust would remain between us if I accepted an apology; how much trust there really was in our relationship now. I would always be afraid to introduce him to a girlfriend. I had known Brad for decades and to have something like this happen, to have your best friend since Elementary school make out, or worse, have sex, with your ex-girlfriend who you cared for deeply for three-plus years and still found feelings for, well, it was just a shitty feeling.

I analyzed the outcome of a falling out and its effects on my social life. I could find friendship at work, at least to hold me over for the summer, and then I would leave the state and travel back across country to school. My needs for returning would be dramatically diminished as I assumed Claire would remain in my life much, much longer. Mike, although I considered him a great friend of mine but hadn't yet placed him into a best friend status due to Brad's seniority, was now claiming the top spot. With the approaching school year I would be turning twenty, a new decade in my life, and I could turn my back on my teenage years and all the pain that seemed to be packed into them. It would be a spring cleaning of my life. I was optimistic and even smiled at the hopeful and now inspiring voice mail that lay on my cell phone. If he apologized or came forward with his guilty plea I could shun it off as a horrible act and then debate if it were worth returning his phone call.

That asshole, my thoughts suddenly flipped into an opposing direction, and I told myself that I didn't need Brad or Chelsea in my life. I picked up my cell phone and with the three signal bars and four battery blocks I pressed my thumb against the number one, moved it forward to send and waited for the time to press the pound button and dial in my password. I stood tall and stern; I couldn't wait to hear what Brad had to say. His betrayal and how he would cower behind technology; to hear his relief, albeit for a half second, in his voice when he realized that my voice mail picked up and he didn't have to face me and my tone.

"You have one new message. To hear your message, press one." I did. "First new message, sent today at three-oh-three p-m."

"Hey Drew, Brad here. What's going on? Haven't talked to you in a couple days, I know Mike was in town, I think you said he was leaving today. Anyway, if he's still here, tell him goodbye for me and that it was nice meeting him. If not, well...crap, maybe next time. Anyway, just wondering what you have going on tonight. If you don't have anything going on give me a call, let's go see a movie or something. I think, don't quote me on this, but I think Boris might be having a poker game. Pizza and no beer because his parents are in town. That might be tomorrow night. I'm rambling. Give me a call, ya wicked bastard."

"To save this message press two, to erase it press three."

I deleted the message. I was almost insulted that his message was so friendly and sounded authentic; that he didn't think I knew and that he could continue this friendship. Wasn't there always that loyalty in movies that a best friend says to the girl as she tries to sleep with him that he couldn't. Her response being that the man would never know. The best friend then says that it didn't matter because he would know. For a half second I wondered if maybe with the alcohol on my breath that night, I saw things, heard things. I considered the real possibility that the cell phone ringing in the room with Chelsea may have been somebody else's; that Chelsea herself was making out with somebody else. I was scared to be wrong instead of being scared to be right. Perhaps this is what I truly desired.

But ignorance is bliss. He knew I knew. Chelsea probably knew that I knew. And I wish I didn't know.

As I stood behind the register at the front of the bookstore I surveyed a few of the browsers. I tried to classify them in certain categories. It was a game to help the time move on. I should be reading a book creating the illusion that I not only worked at a bookstore for the paycheck but also liked reading books. As someone would enter I would size them up and figure out where they would go and what books they sought. This only worked about three percent of the time. The lady with a few extra pounds for her short height went straight to history, I guessed romance, and the ultra-skinny goth teen who hated the world opted to browse the best sellers before moving on to true crime, I figured he was a horror or straight-to-music young lad.

Angie strolled by every once in a while or glanced over and smiled when taking a customer to their destination. She passed by three times while helping the same soccer Mom who was dragging her four year old across the carpet. After the soccer Mom left without purchasing anything Angie came up and I ducked beneath the register in fear that her aggression would be misrepresented onto me.

"I swear, Drew. I swear. If it weren't for the great money, the benefits, and the killer discount, I would kill someone."

"I've seen your paycheck and we don't get benefits. Could you give me a little warning before you bring in a knife and start hacking away at the unsuspecting customers and employees? That seems like a good day to take off."

"You'll be the first to know." She looked on me with a caring motherly gaze. "You're not you. What's wrong?"

"How much time do you have?"

"Ah, girlfriend?"

"No," I started to confess. "You know Brad, right? My friend who came with us to that stupid mid-summer indie flick that Jon recommended." She nodded. I continued, "I caught him making out with a girl." Her eyebrow rose. "That girl was my ex-girlfriend." Angie sucked her face in and cringed. "Who I was with for three years." Her face squished tighter as if she was sucking sours after a root canal. "We broke up last year." She un-cringed her face.

"That's not the most horrid thing in the world."

"Are you serious?"

"What did he have to say about it?"

I relayed the story anticipating the advice of someone a few years older but certainly much wiser in the language of relationships. The early twenties are prime growing time for a love life.

"Is it all worth losing a friendship over? You two have been friends for a long time, right? Is it worth getting dramatic over an ex-girlfriend especially when you have a girlfriend?" Angie advised like I knew she would.

"This constitutes peak dramatic times," I argued, "your best friend feeling up your ex."

"Drew, it happens," Angie reassured me and with a small amount of pressure she spoke of her own fate. "Let's just say, since it happened to me, I haven't been able to get along well with my younger sister. It sucks twice as hard when she heard all your never-ending 'he's an asshole' stories and then proceeds to live them herself. She expects me to listen to her whine and cry? I don't think so."

"Is this a recent event?"

"Four years ago. What a bitch. It makes Thanksgiving and Christmas really hard." She waved both her hands in the air, "Drama."

"You can't help where the heart goes," I offered generically.

"Bullshit, yes you can. Don't believe the crap you hear on television or read in four hundred year old plays." Angie walked away towards a confused older man scratching his head and reading the signs above the different sections. She turned her head back to me, "At least it's your best friend and not your sister."

My cell phone vibrated, I checked out the text message. It was from Brad. "Where have you been?"

Time was not friendly with me. He knew where I worked and there was a fifty-fifty chance I was here if he came in. I was stuck at a register, the only one. There was no hiding even if I wanted to. I was trapped in my prison with only a laser barcode reader as protection.

I had an audience. I didn't want one but they wouldn't let me go without asking questions and following me to my car like paparazzi on a coked out Hollywood celebrity. Page, Angie, Bill, Jon, and Tricia all crowded me in our break room. The shifts were over and the store was closed. Innocently, Angie had approached me and asked if I had talked to Brad. I nodded which garnered interest in Bill who had to meet a few pals at a restaurant where the waiters wore suspenders and had drinks named "The Ultimate Margarita" and "The Lemonade Shocker", names that Bill would tell me his friends turned into sexual terms. Three's a crowd and if three were to stand in any line then others would approach and inquire further. As Page typed in her code in the time clock she leaned back listening to me begin the story and refused to leave as well. When Tricia came in to grab the Tupperware she brought her daily lunch in she held the small plastic in one hand and placed another on the counter. Jon pretended not to care but used the excuse of exclusion to stick around.

"Okay, go on. His car was parked in the driveway when you got home," Angie started. She was the only one who I had told the story to the other day.

"Was he in your house?" Tricia asked.

It was starting to sound like a horror story and I opted to leave out the fictitious detail of Brad holding a rusty axe in one hand and displaying a decapitated head in the other.

"He was getting there when I got there. Had I come home one minute later I would suspect that he would be sharing a soft drink with my soon to be sister-in-law. Keep in mind it had been a week and a half since the incident," I held up my fingers and displayed quotation marks. "He opened the car door as I was pulling into the driveway. He waved and I put the car in park. I was pretty sure he saw the blood drain from my face and my heart beating twice as fast to compensate for the lack of blood. I attempted to lick my lips but my mouth had become dry. I got out of my car and he held his arms out."

"Did you hug that son of a bitch?" Angie asked. The others interest peaked. This story had a 'son of a bitch' as the antagonist.

"Not that kind of arms open. More like he was surprised to see I was alive. He immediately asked where I had been and I didn't have the time or the energy to create an appropriate response that didn't involve an alien abduction or witness protection program. I figured that if we were going to have this conversation we might as well have it in the privacy of my driveway where anyone could walk by, drive by, or overhear; of course, my parents and brother and his girlfriend and the baby were home, so they could hear this as well.

"I took in a deep breath of air and looked right into his eyes and straight out said..."

"So, you and Chelsea, huh? How long has that been going on?"

Brad's mouth dropped down to the driveway bounced up and fell down again. He was speechless and there was neither hiding nor denying it. His actions couldn't dictate anything to the contrary. There was nearly three straight minutes of 'ums'.

When he finally spoke his first question was how I knew and I explained what I had witnessed and heard at the party. His shoulders slumped, this wasn't an isolated incident. I asked a second time how long.

"Just a couple weeks."

"Christ, Brad, when were you going to tell me? When were you going to ask me if I'd be okay with my best friend messing around with my ex-girlfriend?" I wasn't a confrontational man but this situation required it. The choice was man or mouse and I probably could have gone through the rest of my life waiting until they came out and told me their situation before I said anything. I could find a personal and private way to get through it, I was leaving town again in two months. I could have claimed to still be friends with regret for sixty days. I chose not to.

"I'm sorry," Brad said.

"For what? For fucking Chelsea or for me finding out?" He was silent, embarrassed and off balance.

"I don't know," he replied firmly. "It just sort of happened, you know? I was drunk, she was drunk, we talked and, it just happened."

"Dare I ask when it started? When you were drunk and she was drunk and you two looked into each other's eyes and decided to lock lips?"

He could only reply with stutters and half words.

"It doesn't matter. You'll probably lie to me." I spun around and started walking to the front door. I wanted to close my eyes, re-open them and see that this was all make believe, that none of it happened.

"I really am sorry, Drew."

I didn't turn around, I couldn't turn around. I reached my porch step and reached in my pocket for my keys. I looked down shifting through my pants.

"I kind of started to like her. I think I like her." Brad's voice pleaded for me to turn around and give some sign that all this was going to be okay. "We've been friends for fifteen years, come on!"

My keys were still sitting in the ignition, in my car, which was conveniently placed next to Brad in my driveway. I tested the door and it was locked. So much for miracles.

"So, what happened?" Page asked me.

I didn't want to tell her that as I stared down at myself on the porch that the stress and the aggravation caused tears to form and that my nose began to run just enough where I had to do my best to hide the loudest sniffle from the world. It became hard to swallow like taking a large piece of bread from the basket at a restaurant and shoving it down my throat while expecting it to go down without a problem. My pride had sunken with the idiocies of forgetting the car and house keys. This I couldn't tell my co-workers.

"I told him to leave," I started. "I told him to leave and that when and if I was ready to talk to him I'd call him. Don't expect that to happen tomorrow, I said."

"Dude, I would have knocked him on his ass. Throw him to the ground," Bill began to mimic, "and just stomp on his ass. And his balls."

"How graphic, thank you," Jon said. "I don't think you can remain friends with such a betrayer. In the interest of all parties, I would say cut your ties and be ready for one of them to come to you in the near future all up in arms about how the other did the other wrong."

"Unless they get married and live happily ever after," Tricia said.

"Don't be so pessimistic," Jon shot back.

"How is happily ever after pessimism?"

"Because it's happening against Drew. If he were in Brad's shoes, then happily ever after would be optimistic," Jon concluded with a nod.

"There are enough sad songs out there, I'm sure you can find one that relates," Page started for the door. "Good luck with your problems and remember that suicide is merely a permanent end to temporary problems. But, ya know, population control is best for everyone."

"I'm not going to kill myself."

"All I'm saying is if you do, try to take some people out with you, preferably the ones who hurt you." Page left. Behind her back, I thanked her for her advice.

Angie asked, "So how did it all end?"

"He left and I waited to hear his car leave before I went to my car and got my keys."

"Well that was quite dull," Jon said. "I waited around for this. Goodnight one and all." Jon left and in his wake went Bill and Tricia. Angie shrugged her shoulders and asked if I was going to be okay before she opted for the drive home.

The road was nearly empty the entire way home. I picked up my cell phone and scrolled down to Claire. There wasn't much for us to talk about and the conversation had awkward silences and more than a few "so"s. I felt different. She felt different. Before I knew it I was pulling into my driveway and walking to the front door double checking to make sure I had my keys. We spoke a few more minutes as I threw myself down onto the couch and closed my eyes. She confirmed her excitement to see me in just two weeks and I apologized for sounding like I had been ran over by a car before being ran over by a semi.

"Don't worry about it," she reassured me. "We all have our days."

My brother sat at the kitchen table with the Saturday morning paper wide open under his bowl of cereal. He was engrossed in an article as I came upstairs. It was a big change from the previous years when he would be dressed like hell and stoned or hungover.

"What's in the news?" I asked David. He flipped through a few pages and tossed aside the front page section.

"I don't know. I'm trying to find a movie to see. Mom said she was going to take care of Theodore for us tonight."

"Nicole feeling good enough to go out?" David answered with his silence and I opted for a question that would produce a verbal response. "How's the job?"

"Job's fine." David said monotonously.

"Am I bothering you?"

David shot his head up toward me. "What? No." He folded the paper closed. "What's new in your life? How's Claire?"

"She's good." I hesitated. I hadn't shared the Brad/Chelsea

incident with any family members. They sensed something was hovering around in the air over my head. I started telling David the story. He sat patiently eating his cereal and soaking the whole incident in until I ended my speech.

"Huh. Interesting." To the whole crisis of my summer he had two words to spurt out and neither was helpful in either way. "That certainly does suck."

"Please tell me there is more you can offer than that?" I begged.

"What do you want? Is everything going to be okay? Yes. But you already know that. Is it all going to suck for a while? You bet. But you already knew that too. You have a chick, and based on the pictures I've seen, a damn fine looking chick that is traveling across this great land to see you and attend your beyond awesome brother's wedding. This all went down last weekend, right? And you saw Brad two days ago?"

I affirmed.

"You feel like you're in a better place now than you were twelve days ago?"

"A little."

"You want brotherly advice? Here you go. Take note, young peasant, because you'll never get any better counsel than this. Are you ready, I mean, are you mentally prepared to handle what I, David Meade, will expel onto you?"

"If you fart I'm going to be really upset."

David stood up grabbing the newspaper and came over to me. He put his arm on my shoulder and held out the weather page. "It's supposed to be sunny tomorrow and the next day, clouds and that looks like pm showers on Tuesday. There's even a ten-day weather report. Can you believe it?" He squeezed me into his body for quick brotherly gesture and patted me on the shoulder.

"That's your advice? The ten-day forecast."

"Think about it."

"Can you throw a little more wisdom on me than the back

of a newspaper? Just so I know you haven't completely lost your mind. Elaborate maybe? Elaboration would certainly be a plus."

He changed his tone to overly sarcastic to a lower serious expressive nature so I was guaranteed to pay attention and take his advice to heart. "The weather report, Drew. It's all in the weather report," he let go and started toward the stairs.

"That's bullshit. If you tell me what the ten-day forecast means I'll probably get through this a little easier."

He stepped on the bottom step and looked back at me.

"I can't. You need to figure it out. I'm serious." He disappeared and I was left by myself with the entire Saturday paper and a mostly consumed bowl of cereal.

"Thanks Confucius," I said aloud.

The ten-day weather report. I stood in the kitchen for a few minutes staring down at the newspaper. The USA was covered with multiple colors indicating storm patterns and highs and lows. There was a quick reference lower on the page informing me of the temperatures in major cities across the nation. New York, high eighty-seven. Los Angeles, ninety-one. Atlanta, ninety. Dallas, one-hundred. Juneau, sixty-two. David was messing with me. The time I really could have used some quality advice and sympathy he jumbles my head with the weather going through next week.

"Put your bowl in the dishwasher," my Mom said entering the kitchen. She was in a hurry.

"It's David's," I responded.

"Fine, put his bowl in the dishwasher."

"Oh, that's fair," I belted back sarcastically.

"I never said it was. Come on, Drew. It's no big deal; he has a child upstairs to take care of. He has a wedding in less than two weeks. The least you could is put his bowl in the dishwasher. Do you work today?"

"No," I said picking up David's bowl. I surrendered under the powers of my mother. "I work tomorrow though."

"There's a book I would like you to get for me, okay?" It

wasn't a question as whatever Mom says usually goes, denying her request would merely bring forth the motherly guilt of when I was six and wanted a toy to the point I busted into tears in the middle of the store until she tried to trick me into believing she would leave me there. Her threat had been empty for two reasons; the first was I was six and being trapped in a toy store would have been a blessing. Eighteen rows of action figures, bicycles, and games, not to mention the candy strategically placed near the register. The second reason was she was my Mom and you have to be messed up beyond all reasoning to leave your kid anywhere in public alone. I still cried and she still ended up buying me one of the two toys I wanted. I could buy her a book with my discount.

"Write it down and I'll get it," I told her.

She thanked me and gave me a peck on the cheek before grabbing her purse off of the kitchen counter. "I'll see you later. Love you."

Claire was coming in tomorrow. I had just hung up the phone after talking to her for nearly an hour and a half, I had her flight information on hand and I was ready to follow the take-off insuring her determined arrival so I could meet her at the baggage claim with a big smile and open arms, ready to embrace for the first time in months. I'd kiss her in front of everyone and she would kiss back harder throwing me off balance. We would block people trying to get through the gate and into their respective family member's arms. I knew I wasn't going to be able to sleep that night and as far as the next I hoped I wouldn't be able to fall asleep. The rest of my family had the thrill and excitement of an approaching wedding, but I had Claire. They could have matrimonial bliss; I just wanted to see my girlfriend.

Nicole sat in the living room with the baby silently lying with its stomach against her chest with a spit up rag on her shoulder. She held Theodore like a mother instinctively knows how to hold their child. I couldn't imagine ever being that small but I'm sure Theodore couldn't imagine being as big as everyone who surrounded him.

"You excited? You and me, we're going to be relatives. That means you have to love me no matter how drunk and belligerent I get."

"And you get to love Theodore no matter how much he spits up on your shoulder or how many times he pees on your face when you're trying to change him. Truth be told I really don't care about the wedding," Nicole started but I didn't believe her, "I have a girlfriend who paid upwards of thirty-grand for her day. I was a bridesmaid. This was four years ago. Ya know what? Last week she celebrated her two year anniversary of being divorced. Thirty thousand dollars. You might as well stress over buying a car for six months and after five hours just throw it off a cliff."

"We're optimistic about this, I see. Does David know how you feel about the institution of marriage?"

"Of course. We're getting married on our terms with a ceremony that we can afford, well, we can't afford it but we're not going to be broke and in debt because of it. By the way, that girl's parents are still paying off the wedding. We both agree that we don't need the big theatrics to prove that we love each other. Love isn't a giant party or signing a legal document."

"Yeah, but you're a little excited."

"(Fuck) yeah I am. It's my big day." She refused to swear aloud in front of her baby and anyone who did was sure to get a smack above the neck. Theodore shook a little bit awakening from a short sleep. He nudged against his mother and yawned. I couldn't help but gawk mentally over this. It was pretty damn cute.

Claire's flight was taking off at nine in the morning and she was scheduled to arrive at four-thirty in the afternoon, an easy non-stop over the Rockies, the plains, the Mississippi and into the

Detroit metro area. I only knew that the more I wanted to see her, the more likely that her flight was going to be delayed. Even though it was clear skies in both cities there was bound to be something mechanical or a late arrival, a late departure, anything that would prevent this airplane from landing on time. My cell phone rang at eleven (eight Los Angeles time). It was Claire. She was at the airport.

"Hello." It was more than just a greeting; I had a giant smile on my face.

"Hi." There was something wrong. The bearer of bad news, the flight was cancelled, the flight was delayed. She sniffled.

"Claire? Everything okay?" It took a second for her response as I listened to the hustling of businessmen and families; fathers and mothers grabbing their child's hand as they rushed to catch their flight. "Claire?"

"I can't come."

"Why? What's wrong?"

"I can't fly." She sniffled again louder. She wiped her eyes, I could hear it. "I've only flown once before and I just, I..." She trailed off.

"Claire, it's completely safe. It's the safest form of travel ever in the history of travel. You can do it."

"No." We were both silent. I had to convince her to board the airplane; I had to get her to where I was for my own selfish reasons. She had to come because I wanted her to. I couldn't speak though. I wanted to remedy the situation but had nothing to say.

"Claire."

"I can't." If only I visited her and we flew back together, I thought. I wanted to play the role of the protective gentleman who could hold her hand and tell her that the noise she heard was just the flaps, the bump was just a small bit of turbulence, the humming and the noise that sounded like a drill was just the baggage handlers closing up the bottom compartment. I was thousands of miles away. "I'm so sorry, Drew. I thought maybe if

I came to the airport then I would be able to go through security and if I did that I could get on the plane. I even told my Dad to leave so it would make it harder for me to stay here, but..."

I opened my mouth to tell her that it was all okay, but silence. I stood in the middle of the basement for a few moments collecting my thoughts, the one thing I wanted more than anything this summer was falling through the cracks and there wasn't a way to control it.

"Why are you afraid to get on the airplane?" I asked as softly as possible, trying to be the psychologist who comforted his patient in hopes for a final breakthrough. "Twenty-five thousand commercial airliners take off every day even if one crashed the odds of it being yours is one in twenty-five thousand. How often does one go down?"

"But, Drew," more tears fell down her cheeks and were wiped away by a sleeve.

Logic was gone. "For me then? Please." I begged of her. I heard a little whimper and crack of a phone hitting the terminal carpet.

"Hello?" Claire asked.

"I'm here."

"Sorry, Drew. I dropped the phone." She was silent again, all I could hear was a nervous cry and I pictured her trembling outside the 'I Love L.A.' souvenir shop. My attempts at sympathy and guilt to make her board the airplane and fly four and a half hours to me where I can see her and hug her and congratulate her on conquering her biggest fear failed. "I need to go. I have to call my Dad. I'll talk to you later."

"Claire, wait!" It was too late. The conversation ended, our communication was gone. My chest tightened and the lump in my throat had returned from a long dormant rest. I felt rejected. I felt scared. I felt alone. I looked down at my cell phone in hopes that it would vibrate in my hand, a call from the west coast with Claire on the other side saying she had mustered the courage to board that airplane and fly to me. That call never came and I spent the next few hours upon the couch staring at a television that remained on the same channel. The door creaked open upstairs and my mother asked when I planned on leaving to pick up Claire. I didn't answer and she called my name to see if I was even downstairs. The TV was on and the volume was up so she came into my underground room and looked at me. My red eyes and stone face told her every fact a mother needed to know; something disastrous was occurring.

"Honey? What is it?"

"She's not coming, Mom." I said in hopes that she would leave it be. I needed comfort but no talking. I needed a dog. Some creature to rest it's head on my lap and let me pet; an animal that would rise up and yawn before lying back down and sleeping. I needed something that wouldn't ask questions and therefore I wouldn't have to tell any tales.

"What happened?"

I repeated solemnly. "She's not coming."

"Is everything okay?"

"Oh, everything's fine, Mom, with the exception of one minuscule overlooked issue that I didn't see coming." I paused waiting for her to inquire but she stood at the bottom of the steps looking ever more concerned and needing an answer. "She's scared shitless to fly."

"Oh." Her voice declared doubt and it wouldn't surprise me if she thought Claire hadn't even bought a plane ticket. This was the easiest and greatest break up in the history of any break up in the Meade family. Fake a fear to fly and it all ends.

I groaned loudly and put my hands to my head. "This is gonna suck," I started. "Having to live through this is bad enough but now everyone who is here this weekend for David and Nicole's wedding are going to ask 'where's this Claire we've been hearing about? Why isn't she here? What happened?' And then they will all want to give their condolences and I'll be that jerk that ruins his brother's wedding because my girlfriend who I saw for a month before moving away for four months decided to have a big fear of boarding an airplane, an act literally millions of people do everyday, and not come." I noticed my sadness had switched back to anger. It was steadily bouncing back and forth for the past two hours. Your mind gets to thinking which becomes the end-all-be-all of blessings and curses. I wanted to scream and punch the innocent pillow that Claire's head would have been laying on later tonight. I wanted to kick something. My anger rose higher as I thought how stupid it would be to physically abuse the pillow or go outside and kick the side of the house. It was all buried inside and I clenched my fists.

My Mom remained nearby remaining silent.

"First Chelsea and Brad and now this. What a great month this is turning out to be."

"What happened with Chelsea and Brad?" I closed my eyes, upset at myself for letting the secret spill. More explanation. More bitter reminiscing. Another story to tell that ends in me getting royally screwed by life's trials. Just leave me alone, I wanted to say. She sensed my problems were best to let settle and not forcing a conversation just yet. She wished me well and reminded me of her motherly presence if I needed to talk things out. I couldn't blame her for being worried; nobody wants to see their child upset.

She departed and I took the pillow from the edge of the couch and placed it upright in my lap. I squeezed it, hugging a little at first but then choking it against my chest out of anger. Out of an absent girlfriend. Out of projected anger from the lost friendships of Brad and Chelsea. Out of fear of being alone. My muscles were tense and my arms became sore. I released the pillow from my emotional clutches and cursed at nothing in particular.

As the company my family had hired began setting up the small decor of chairs, tables, and altar in the backyard for the wedding I stepped away for a fresh breath of air. I approached a movie theater and wished I was drunk. I even acted as if I was occasionally tripping over myself in attempts to act like I had spent the past few hours in a bar drinking my problems away. No one seemed to mind. The teenagers screamed at each other about useless high school problems, swearing too loudly in front of innocent children and families. There were families trying to keep their kids in line and couples holding each other's hands. A group of twenty-something's were staring down the marquee. Another group of older folks, in their fifties, were struggling to recall the lead actor in the movie they wished to see. Another group spoke in a foreign language I didn't understand and were dressed too high class for an evening at a movie theater.

That's how the world was. One man's bad day was another's day in paradise; for the man with the white shirt who had pasta sauce spilled on him at dinner it was a different degree of a bad day. I kept looking at the people around me and lost myself in a day dream of Claire being at my side in this very spot debating on which summer blockbuster to spend money on. The movie was irrelevant. We would spend a good part of it holding each other in the back of the theater and kissing, the kissing leading to a second base depending on the capacity of the theater.

I went to the box office and bought a ticket to the next available show for any movie which was fifteen minutes away. It was an action movie. Something guaranteed to be low on quality and high on special effects. No romance. I wanted to escape. As I sat in my aisle seat having to occasionally lift my legs for a twenty year old girl to pass with her twenty year old poser boyfriend or the forty year old lady I had to stand up for because she was too wide to squeeze between my legs and the seat in front of me without causing much discomfort to anyone, I was constantly being queried on whether the seat next to me was available. The first two people to ask I rejected telling them that it was taken up and envisioned that a buddy of mine was in the lobby buying overpriced popcorn. The third time it was two middle-aged couples and I told them it was free. They sat down and immediately commented to each other on how busy the show was tonight which lead them to talk about how often they attended the show. It had been nearly three weeks for the two gentlemen but only four days for the two ladies. The last movie the two ladies saw was a romantic comedy, the kind released in mid-June opposite a sequel to a superhero film to try and make money on the non-comic book theater-going audience. It starred two overpriced and under-talented actresses, one who according to the lady had just won an Academy Award for an art film last year in which she bared her breasts for nearly ninety minutes of the one-hundred-thirty-five minute film. I tried to overhear the title but couldn't quite make it out. The summer rom-com was about two girls who make a pact after they both have a hard break-up to not date any men for one year. To their surprise, surely not the surprise of the audience, these two meet a pair of brothers, twins, and the shenanigans roll from there. The comedy coming in with the twins being identical and the two leading ladies often confused on which one is which. I had no desire to sit through that movie and, if I did, it was ruined by one of the lady's spilling out the ending. "Of course everything gets squared away at the end and they get married on the same day. February second," the lady said with a squeal to her voice as her excitement grew. I thought about how sleeping with this lady, an unfortunate event that her husband had to probably partake in at least once a week, would drive me insane. Neither of us would be able to climax because I would punch her in the mouth within a minute and a half. Whatever statistic thrown out yearly about how much men think about sex didn't necessarily mean all of that time they were thinking about good sex. Like the chickpea in the carrot bowl at a salad bar, some things entered that weren't welcome.

"Groundhog's Day," her husband claimed to the February second wedding date in the film.

"That and two, two. They picked it because there was two of each getting married. Isn't that clever?"

I was upset for myself for choosing this specific seat and

letting these two couples sit next to me. It only seemed to add to the bad day.

The house lights dimmed and the movie previews began. As each preview came on the lady next to me announced individually to each of the other three folks that she has seen or heard about this movie. Four out of the six previews ended with her leaning over again saying they should see it. I considered moving but the theater was full and I wanted to play it safe. Safe and annoyed with unsolved anger issues.

The movie ran on and I kept checking my cell phone in hopes I would receive a call from Claire. If she hadn't phoned me by movie's end I decided I would give her a call just to make sure everything was okay. I also hoped that she would claim to be sitting at in the airport baggage wondering where I was. An hour and thirty-eight minutes later I still had no call and thought of how much of the movie I missed due to more day dreaming. I walked down the steps pensively catching sound bites from the everyday critics and how they thought, based on the newspaper critic's review, that the movie would have actually been good.

When I arrived home I parked my car in the street, the large truck carrying all the necessary equipment for the wedding was still in the driveway. I pulled the key out of the ignition and opened the door. My cell phone vibrated. It was about three minutes prior to when I was going to call Claire and thought this to be a good sign, we were on the same level of thought. It was Mike.

"Am I interrupting happy sex time?" He asked enthusiastically.

"Oh dude, do I have a story for you." I told him the whole scenario and he constantly interrupted after every other sentence stating 'bullshit'. He also was sorry and sad. He gave advice and passed on an outsider's optimism.

"Look. Fear is a bitch. She was paralyzed by fear and the very fact that she did spend money on a plane ticket and did go to the airport shows you how much this little lady cares for you.

We'll drive back early, alright? Our apartment lease begins on September first so we'll just head out a week earlier than planned. We'll move some stuff in, build some furniture, we'll start with your bed. You can then have sex in said bed while I'm out doing what I do. I'll come back, we'll set more stuff up, I'll leave, you'll have naked time and all this will go away."

I smiled as I sat in the dark car, the porch lights cutting a sharp shadow across my lap and steering wheel. He was right, or at least, I hoped he was. It made sense but it still didn't take away how upset I was that I even had to have this conversation. Nothing bad happened to the flight; I checked on the airline's website earlier in the day and saw that the flight she was supposed to be on landed safely and on time. My mood was no longer angry or bitter; I was now partially filled with positive encouragement.

"Just remember, my friend, no matter what happens, you will always have this," Mike said and there was a pause in the conversation followed by what sounded like a small balloon deflating. "Prepared just for you, just the way you like it. Crisp with a little nutty flavoring."

I laughed for the first time in which seemed like decades although could be traced back to the early morning.

"You're missing the best part too," he added. "Woo! That has a musky odor that would take down a pride of lions."

"Yes, well. You just give me a day's notice before you're out here. I'll need a good eighteen-to-twenty-four hours to drink a gallon of milk and let that goodness settle," I responded as a friendly threat.

"You can bet it's all about Mexican food before and during the drive out there."

"Looking forward to it, bitch."

"Bet you are, douche bag."

We hung up and I was beginning to feel a little better about my day. Mike slapped some sense into me and I started to think for a moment, before I called Claire and after four rings was sent to her voice mail, that everything was going to be fine. I heard her voice and attempted to gauge her feelings based on a cheerful outgoing message she left months ago. I held on for as long as I could, listening to her sweet voice, embracing every syllable. Upon the beep I pressed my teeth hard together, wanting to hear her longer but knowing I couldn't call back anytime in the near future.

I felt restless all night but probably got more sleep than everyone else in my family. The last night of my brother's bachelorhood was spent lying upon my couch in the dark damp basement listening to a distant dog bark. By one in the morning I gave up hope that Claire would call, at least as little hope as I could muster. I never lost hope because of naive optimism and blind faith. I slept on my side where I would be able to see my cell phone light up with Claire's name on the display if she chose to ring back.

The guest list for the wedding was near forty. Mostly aunts and uncles, nieces and nephews, distant cousins and friends. They were the people who only gathered at family gatherings and called one another when they needed a favor. Uncle Leonard who worked in the court system received phone calls when someone was mailed an affidavit to serve on a jury; they wanted to know the best way to avoid it. Then there was my cousin Kevin. He was a police officer and never received too many calls but whenever there were family gatherings the kids asked if he had ever shot anybody and anyone over the age of eighteen offered their latest criticism on the local police department and the state of downtown even though Kevin was one of eight officers in a town two hundred miles to the north. He found solace in anyone who wouldn't talk shop with him.

My mother had three siblings and my father had four. Considering that of all the aunts and uncles had no more than three kids, it seems that folks didn't get as busy in modern times as they did fifty years ago. Maybe there were less forms of contraception, I personally think without as many television options people had more time and opted to spend that time as busy bees and having lots of sex in parked cars atop hills called 'Make-Out Point'. Either way, my biggest fears of the day were Aunt Meg and Aunt Missy, both who loved gossip and would certainly ask and constantly harp on myself and Claire. I hoped the newly born Theodore would take away most of the attention from me, however, general courtesy towards family members, and with the fact that only so many could surround a baby at one time, placed me as a target. I prepared my answers for the two questions I expected to hear the most:

"Where's Claire?"

And.

"What do you think of your new nephew?"

At eight in the morning I was awake and alert. I woke up thinking of my girlfriend and blessed the opportunity to have a day with incalculable amounts of business so I could divert my mind elsewhere. There was rustling upstairs and I decided to start this long day. The sunlight beamed into the kitchen as I came out of the basement. There were a few catering plates coming in full of turkey, salami, ham, and all kinds of meats to throw on a sandwich. It was a glorified graduation party. My mother donning jeans and a t-shirt barked orders at the caterers and anyone within earshot who was working to keep this ceremony on course to a two o'clock start. Once my Mom, the General, saw me she pointed to me and ordered me to grab the remaining chairs on the back of the truck in the driveway and place them neatly in the backyard. Six to a row and make sure there was an aisle for the bride. I reached under the plastic for a piece of turkey and my mother shunned me for doing so.

"Is this stuff going to keep all day?" I asked still hovering over the deli tray.

"Oh, better yet. Forget the chairs; we got most of them last night," my Mom said as she opened our nearly empty refrigerator, "try to consolidate all this stuff onto one shelf so we can put the food in here until game time."

"Game time?" I laughed at her attempt to make this whole day into an epic sporting event, "can we call it H-Hour instead?"

"Ya know, pardon me for being in mental overload on my oldest son's wedding day. Wait until yours," she leaned in close to me so that nobody near could overhear her words. "Do me a favor, Drew. Give me a big wedding, okay? This is nice and intimate but I want chicken options, seating arrangements and maybe an ice sculpture, not deli meat and thirty dollars of gas station ice bags. Oh shit!" She screamed grabbing everyone's attention.

"Just give me the money and I'll go get the ice." I offered. My bladder sent a message to my brain stating it's at full capacity and as my Mom went for her purse, I dashed for the bathroom.

Within a half hour I was back in my basement, my hands still defrosting from lifting deli trays and maneuvering old mustard bottles and bread in a thirty-eight degree metal box. Instinctively, I went to check my cell phone even though the chances of a missed call at eight-thirty in the morning had a low probability.

I looked down at the partially lit display screen astounded I had missed a phone call. Before I picked it up, it lit up again and started to vibrate indicating that I had a new voice mail. I was frozen debating whether or not I should check who called first or go straight to the message and be surprised. On a day such as this, it seemed real trivial but I found this to be a major decision.

I picked up my phone, flipped it open and looked at the missed call log. Claire. My heart beat started into double time and my stomach did a somersault and dropped ten feet if it dropped an inch. Why would she call me at five o'clock in the morning California time? I wondered. I dialed into my voice mail. My breathing became heavy and my heart which was already beating fast increased in speed, my face was warm. I closed my eyes and listened for the awaiting message.

"Hey Drew. It's Claire. I, um, thought I should give you a

call. It's your brother's wedding day and I know you're busy and you might even be sleeping so I'm sorry if I woke you up. Um, anyway, I guess if you want to, give me a call but you don't have to, I'd understand and everything. Tell your brother congratulations and good luck, well not good luck but, yeah. Um, bye."

I saved the message. Not sure what to think but over-analyzing everything. Every tone change, every word, every sentence. I decided to call her back. There was a crash upstairs. I pretended not to hear it.

"Drew! I need you, come up here." My Mom yelled down.

"Drew, hurry up," now my Dad was in the picture.

I cursed to myself, put the phone down before pressing the send button, and spun on my heels towards the basement stairs.

Two o'clock was the deadline. I hopped into the kitchen to find both my parents putting one of the deli trays on the kitchen counter. The refrigerator door was open and what remained of the eggs on the bottom shelf were splattered and oozing its yellowy substance around on the shelf that fell on top of it.

"Looks like we need a plan B," my Dad said. "God damn shelves. Piece of shit." I feared I would be to blame. My Dad started barking orders to the family with the same fury as a commander in the midst of an uphill battle. He looked at me first, "okay, we need ice. Now! Get dressed and head to the gas station, better yet, the grocery store. If we need something then that's a good place to be. My wallet's upstairs, just..." I interrupted and held up the cash that Mom had already given me. He then shifted his gaze to my mother. "You and I, we're gonna find some way to put all of this back into that." He eyed the open refrigerator door.

"Deli meat on the bottom, we can get away with that being a bit crushed but the fruit should go on top," my Mom said.

"What a waste of electricity," my father responded scratching his head for a moment staring at the open refrigerator.

"Screw the ozone?" I offered as a sarcastic remark about the wide open door.

"What?" My Dad didn't pick up on the joke.

"I'll head to the store."

I skipped every other step on my way upstairs where my brother was exiting the bathroom.

"What's all the commotion?" David asked as his son started crying and he slumped his shoulders down, "Aw Christ. Nicole!" He turned and went into my old room, the baby's room. Through all of the happenings thus far and occasionally throughout the summer I forgot and instinctively went into my old bedroom to retrieve items that were no longer there. I spun around and almost ran into Nicole. She was exiting her and David's bedroom. She looked like hell. She looked like a Mom of a one month old who was trying to be ready for a wedding in five hours.

"What did David want?" She asked me.

"Don't know. Theodore's crying." I jumped every three steps until I hit the bottom. A quick change of clothes and a ball cap atop my head and I was out the door.

As I pulled out onto the main road which put me one and a half miles from the grocery store I reached into my pants pocket. I wanted to talk to Claire. I shuffled around the right pocket, the left pocket, then as if I actually believed there was a possibility of missing an object the size of a cell phone in a pocket like someone would miss Shaq in a room full of auditioning Wizard of Oz munchkins, I moved back to my right. I blasted my hands against the harmless steering wheel and yelled a few obscenities that would offend a sailor at having forgotten my only form of communication.

I grabbed the first grocery cart I could find and went inside the store. I hit the frozen food section in hopes of finding an end freezer with bags of ice. I was indeed lucky and began throwing twenty pound bags of ice into the cart which garnered the attention of a handful of fellow patrons even garnering a comment from a senior citizen.

"That's a lot of ice for such a young man," she said leaning against her cart with coupons in one hand. I twisted around to acknowledge her remark.

"Got to keep the body cold," I wanted to say and even smiled as if I had. "It's for a party," I told her and continued throwing bags of ice into the cart.

When I completed my task I pushed the cart and slammed my stomach into the bar. I hadn't anticipated the hundreds of pounds now weighing down the thinly manufactured cage on wheels. I had to put my back into the cart and it started to move. It was going to take a lot of muscle to stop this freight train once it started going. I slid it into an empty fifteen item or less lane; my logic being I had one item, just a lot of that one particular item.

I tossed one bag onto the conveyor belt and relayed to the bored redhead that there were nineteen more sitting in the cart.

When I was back in the car I checked on the time and so far this entire trip had racked in eighteen minutes. The possibility of Claire calling back or my parents having a dire emergency I placed at nil on a good day, thirty percent today. I raced out of the parking lot.

I tapped the steering wheel as if I was in a hurry. I couldn't listen to any music. I flipped through the radio stations in hope of finding the perfect song but ended up on a station playing a commercial about discounted cosmetic surgery. I was almost relieved. My time inside this automobile was limited and I didn't want the pressure of committing to a song and having it play past the time I was getting home. That wasn't fair to me, to the artist, or to the melting ice.

Back in the basement I stood above my cell phone which lay on the coffee table next to my couch. I looked down at it and it at me.

"Here we go," I motivated myself and lifted the phone. I hopped, like a boxer jumping rope, but only a quick couple of jumps. I was itching to start this conversation.

"Drew!" My Dad screamed. I tossed my hands in the air, giving in to the necessities of helping my family on our big day

161

and with it went the phone landing safely and softly onto one of my pillows on the couch.

The minutes went on faster and faster and each time I thought I had a moment to breathe, to relax a millisecond, to be able to pick up the phone, I would be called upon to one more task and one more chore. At high noon some extra help had arrived. Kevin the cop showed up as requested to help with the finishing touches as the family went into their respective bathrooms for preparation. Half an hour later I strolled upstairs dressed in a sharp suit looking damn sexy with my tie and jacket. I should have made the phone call before but a second's lapse in judgment took me towards Kevin and a few other early arrivers. As I shook hands, gave hugs, and received kisses on the cheek, I thought how much easier it would be to tell the story of Drew and Claire if I could advance to the next chapter to know what happens after the scene where Claire doesn't fly in. At one o'clock, Aunt Meg showed up with Uncle Rich.

"Hiya, kiddo," my Uncle Rich said tossing his hands in the air as if it had been eons since our last encounter. We hugged and Aunt Meg pulled me in for a kiss on the cheek following up with a thumb smearing her lipstick off.

"Look at you, you are so handsome. Are you excited? Best man. Brother's getting married. An uncle now." She stated each event as if reading off a long laundry list and I felt the allusion of having more responsibility than what was truly upon me. She looked around with a giant smirk on her face, all roads leading to this next question. "So, where is she? Where's this Claire you've been bragging about?"

I put my best face forward and answered truthfully. "She actually couldn't make it."

Aunt Meg put her hand to her heart and gasped loudly. I couldn't imagine this news as any cause for a massive coronary and didn't play into the theatrics.

"Something came up."

"What came up? What could possibly come up?" Aunt Meg

leaned in close. "Did she break up with you, Drew? You can tell me."

"It's just..." I tried to think up a good excuse, one I could use over and over. I wasn't about to confide in my Aunt when it was in regards to my romantic life. "I just. We didn't break up and there was some emergency, she couldn't fly in." It was close enough to the truth.

"Well, I'm thirsty," my Uncle Rich announced bee-lining to the alcohol display upon the kitchen counter. "No bartender?" He twisted his neck and looked at me. "You know how to pour?"

"Oh, Rich, don't make Drew mix your drinks for you."

"Blah!" He retorted and eyed me, "Being in college is like getting a certificate in mix-ology." He lifted the whiskey and started pouring.

After a few minutes of the constant attention my mother and father gracefully made their entrance and the whole party now in the double digits turned and ogled over the groom's parents. They all huddled around my parents, refusing them air to breathe. I finally had the chance to escape. I decided to check on my brother.

I knocked on the door expecting an immediate response. I turned my head to look at my old bedroom door. I knocked a second time and opened the door slightly.

"David." I entered. He was staring at himself in the mirror carefully poking at his tie to make sure it looked perfect.

"How is this?"

"It's fine."

He squinted his eyes and moved his head closer to the mirror. "Yeah, I think you're right. Fine will have to do."

He walked over to the window and surveyed the yard. He could see the altar, the chairs, and the aisle he was soon going to be walking down. Years ago it was a yard he criss-crossed hundreds of times, ran with footballs and baseballs, and chased me down with water balloons. He had fallen asleep on that grass and built snowmen in the winter. We were both silent and I could see in his eyes and the expression on his face, the way his mouth curved slightly upward, that he was proud of this day. His mood changed within a second and he shifted his look to me now tense and scared.

"I can't do this. I can't get married." He claimed.

"What?" My last job was getting my brother's ass down that aisle whether he wanted to or not. He was the last thing on this day of overwhelming jobs to be completed. After they say their "I do"s then I could sit back, relax and slip some rum into my drink. David's eyes bored into mine until he could no longer hold in his laughter.

"I'm kidding, Drew. I'm fine. I'm excited for this."

"Jesus Christ," I gasped grabbing my chest in the same fashion as my Aunt and faking a massive coronary.

"I've never actually seen someone's blood just drain from their face. Can't really say that anymore. I thought you were going to piss your pants."

"That's because I was about to piss my pants. You're a douche bag." I reminded him, even though he didn't need one. He chuckled a bit. I had to rest my wobbly legs and took a seat on the bed. "Are you nervous about anything?"

"Nah, I pretty much figure she's got to say yes. Are her parents here?"

"Yeah, they arrived as I was coming up."

"The deal is once I head downstairs you have to knock on the bathroom door and let her and her entourage know I'm gone. Then do that again when we all go outside."

I accepted my duties.

"You going to tap one of the bridesmaids?" David questioned turning back towards the mirror fixing his tie one final time.

"I wasn't aware there were any bridesmaids."

"Not technically bridesmaids because I don't have any groomsmen, but any of her friends are tap-able. Might be a nice

164

reliever considering the previous..." he waved his arms around attempting to think up the right words. "You know."

"I do know."

"I'd hit one of them if I wasn't getting married today," he turned to look at the beautifully prepared backyard. "Lawn looks good."

"I know it does."

David crossed his arms and watched as a few of the relatives on both sides of the family and a handful of friends congregated.

"I hope I don't have to fart while I'm up there."

"I think that would be a nice touch."

"I'd blame it on you."

"What are best men for?"

Forty-five minutes later my older brother was married and we were at T-plus one and ascending. The very thought of the completed ceremony was inconceivable; it was so unreal that I almost wrote it off as a dream. I now had new relatives including an incredible looking cousin-in-law that I could never make out with. Somehow as I reached across the fruit plate for a slice of watermelon I couldn't help but think it would've been okay to steal that kiss this very morning. I put the piece in my mouth and watched as David and Nicole posed for pictures and I wondered if I was some sick weirdo for thinking what I just thought. I shrugged my shoulders and thought it was probably okay, either way I wasn't about to share it with anyone.

"Hi Katie," I said to my seventeen year old cousin who decided to smash the hell out of her parents, my Aunt Missy and Uncle Brett's, Jaguar three weeks ago. A stupid mistake really, she was dialing her boyfriend when she parked and got out somehow forgetting the final steps before exiting a car: putting the car into park and removing the key. Removing the key I could relate to but how one forgets to put the car in park is beside me. As she started walking away the horns honking drew her attention away and she froze as her parent's Jag rolled into traffic.

"Hi Drew. Oh my God, Aunt Meg told me about Claire and you and how she dumped you a few days ago. I am so sorry. That totally sucks."

"We're not broken up," I stated firmly.

"But she dumped you at the airport, right? I mean, she's not here. Why wouldn't she be here?"

I shook my head, annoyed. "I'll have to get back to you on that."

"That's just totally shady, right? Do you think she's cheating on you? Maybe she met another guy in California. If I lived there, I couldn't help myself. There are so many hot guys out there. I'd be at the beach every day. How can you do anything out there when the sun is shining all the time? I'd spend every day lying on the beach."

I wasn't sure which were questions and which were statements. I tried to nod my head up and down or left and right accordingly.

"It's a rough life out there."

"Have you ever been to Orange County? I'd want to live in Orange County. The OC."

I had to get away; I had never felt a headache settle in so quickly.

"I've been there, yes. A couple times. Nothing really exciting."

"Oh, there are. There seems to be a lot of exciting things going on. Trust me. I bet you've seen like tons of famous people out there. Isn't it strange to just see them doing normal people things like going to Starbucks and, like, at a restaurant?"

"Excuse me," I started. "I have to go inside for a minute." I turned and walked away fearing if I looked back she would be right behind me wanting to tell me more about hot guys, beaches, and where I could run into some teen celebrity I never heard of who graced the cover of Teen People.

I opened the sliding glass door and entered. A rush of cool

air batted the small beads of sweat on my forehead. I was alone, if only for a second, I had a chance to let the day soak in. Even as I closed the door I was staring out at David and Nicole holding their son as the flash of four cameras temporarily blinded them. A few older people, I suspected Nicole's relatives, were making their way toward the house and I decided to duck back into a room just out of reach of the kitchen. I felt like a child trapped in his parent's closet as they discussed financial burdens or a sibling. I had no reason to hide other than the need to be a voyeur with my ears.

"It's pretty nice."

"Yeah, I don't know. How long do you think it will last?"

"Are we starting a pool?"

"I'm thinking we should."

"If we do, put me down for next March, what is that? Nine months?"

"I'll give them two years."

"Two years? Are you out of your God damn mind?"

"Everyone wants to make it to at least the first year."

"I'll say October of next year. Put me down for October twentieth. If they're still living here then hell, it'll be..." Whoever was talking stopped for a second, "...yeah, October twentieth."

"Now is this a full on divorce or separation?"

"Divorce," two of them said simultaneously.

"Just think if that happens, Nicole is moving back in with you. Imagine a baby next door to your room."

"Christ."

The bottles had finished clanking and the voices were becoming distant as the three gentlemen headed back outdoors.

"They better not get divorced until I move out for school."

The door slid open and slammed shut. I stepped out from the other room and opted to fill a party cup with a steady mixture of soda and alcohol. Regardless of age, it was still my brother's wedding. I sipped and then turned the sip into a gulp. I followed up with a couple more gulps and my cup was a quarter full. I looked out the kitchen window into the backyard and saw my cousin Katie chewing the ear off of her brother, Kevin. I looked across the yard to my Aunt Meg and Aunt Missy chatting away and at my father and mother posing with their son and daughter-in-law. My Mom started deliberately looking around the yard, lifting onto her toes to get a better view of everyone. I felt as if she was looking for me. Prior to rejoining the festivities I took down the remaining quarter of mostly rum and shook my head in evil tasting bliss. I re-filled my cup part way and walked outside.

The sun was still high and the party was still going fairly strong as we entered the early evening. Everyone was socializing and the deli tray was nearing empty. I had done my best to help my Mom carry the lovely dessert trays into the backyard. When she told me to carry a side of the wedding cake I refused and said I would retrieve Dad. I could live with spilling a few brownies and cookies onto the nicely manicured lawn but after a few drinks I wasn't about to dare to even think about carrying a wedding cake further than three inches from the table it sat on.

I approached my Dad and told him that Mom wanted to see him. My parents knew I was drinking a bit but it didn't matter to them, I was in the right and Kevin wasn't about to arrest any family members on a wedding day. They figured I had a cocktail or two at parties and trusted me to not throw a lampshade on my head and dance the "sprinkler" on the thin plastic party chairs.

I was able to leave Claire in the distance for a while until another family member interrogated me further on the situation. They either asked me privately like I was revealing an ATM password or aloud in front of a minimum of four other guests in which I would be too embarrassed to shy away. Only twice did it get extremely bad when they told me how sweet Chelsea and I used to be.

I watched as my brother shoved cake into his wife's face and vice versa. I wished Claire was here to share this moment with me. Maybe it was time to actively make a move to call her. Three drinks plus maybe one on the way into my private underground lair and it could be a full on drunk dial, I had had trouble walking a straight line for quite some time. At the very thought I hopped out of my seat and went inside as Uncle Rich took it upon himself to start slicing and handing out pieces of white wedding cake.

My eyes were droopy. I had a hard time determining if I was acting inebriated or actually was. I placed my mostly filled mixed drink onto the table and picked up my cell phone. No new calls. No new messages. The time was six-twenty-two and the realization of how early Claire had actually called me was sinking in. I lifted my shoulders and smiled drunkenly thinking that it takes a special kind of girl to be awake and call me at that hour. Maybe guilt kept her tossing and turning all night. I scrolled to her name and before I pressed send I tilted my head and awaited someone to holler my name from the floor above requiring my assistance. There was nothing and I pressed the send button.

The rings stopped after two times and I heard her voice, live and in person, for the first time in a few days.

"Hello?"

"Hey." I belted, probably a little too loudly, I tried my best to compose myself in a manner that didn't obviously state that I've killed off a good chunk of a bottle of rum. I failed.

"Well, you're drunk," Claire giggled. I wasn't going to make this awkward by pining over what didn't happen and she wished for the same.

"That depends on your definition of the word."

"Can you walk a straight line?"

I laughed and told her no way.

"Hold up your hand. How many fingers do you see?"

"I can't see, it's above my head," I giggled.

"Good party?"

"Yeah, as far as backyard weddings are concerned. This is the first one I've been to in about ten years so I have a little different perception on how it's all supposed to go. I don't think I'll be throwing up from eating too much cake from the dessert table this time."

"You'll just throw up for a whole other reason." We both laughed but mine was more of an impending doom laugh and I followed up with a half hiccup slash dangerous burp.

There was silence for a few seconds. We were both considering our next words and if the giant elephant the size of ten states would be mentioned. I chose to talk first but only a half-second prior to her and we both stopped talking immediately and followed with telling one another to speak first. My reacting skills were slow and she re-started.

"Drew, I'm really sorry."

I was too drunk to not forgive her and with the constant replenishing of alcohol I had a steady stream of confidence-boosting rum and a little bit of vodka filtering through my system. I thought of her dressed in black lingerie, I had yet to actually see such a marvelous sight. I looked over at my couch and thought how if she were laying down on top of it at this very moment I wouldn't hesitate to ravish her.

"I really wanted to be there and I really wanted to see you, but I was just—"

"Claire. I get it," the fantasy was put on hold, "you left me with a lot of uncomfortable explaining to do but, ya know, it's okay."

"I just don't want you to think that it has anything to do with you or something out here. I'm just really embarrassed by it all. I feel so bad. There isn't another guy or anything. This whole summer all I could do was think of you."

I smiled to myself silently and replayed her words over and over in my head.

"Why would you think that I would think there was another guy?" I asked Claire. It was an awfully random question to pose.

"Oh, come on. Anybody who is anybody would think that. If you were going to come out here and suddenly cancel, that's one of the first things I would think was going on. It's a pretty human thought process."

"Well, maybe for you." I sarcastically pointed but an absence of dialogue made my clouded head think that she didn't see it as facetiously as I had hoped to portray. "That was a joke."

"Oh, it was?" She quietly said back. My heart sank and I nearly crapped my pants. In the midst of our closure I messed up big time. "I know it was a joke," she screamed back at me having put me at the butt of a joke.

"You can't do that. I'm not in the most mentally clear place right now and my brother already nearly scared the shit out of me earlier. I can't handle that sort of pressure."

"Which makes it all the more fun."

We continued talking for another ten or fifteen minutes. It seemed longer than that due to the forty-plus people at the party above me. I didn't want to keep guests at my brother's wedding unattended. Claire was the one who told me to get back to the party and we both agreed that we were incredibly happy with our conversation and that, despite the circumstances, we were as happy as could be. When I put the phone down and lifted up my drink I toasted myself for a job well done. It seemed that July wasn't the worst month of my life. I may have lost two friends but at least I still had hope when I went back out west.

With a skip in my step and a grin on my face I went into the backyard and joined in on a conversation. I stood next to my father. My Dad put his arm around me and David, who stood on the other side, and continued boasting about how proud he was of us. I think it was part of the overall mood and general spirits circulating the party. Either way today was a good day and tonight I was going to sleep like I did the day after finals.

6

I slowly slide my boxers up and put on my pitch black socks rolling them high like an old man in khaki shorts in the middle of summer. As I look in the mirror I wish momentarily that I had put forth the effort to drop just five or ten more pounds. I shake my bulging stomach knowing that my fittest days were behind me but these days aren't too bad. I let go and realize that everyone thinks they are fat. I just have a minor spare tire.

The moment I hesitate thinking about the next part of my life is the second I begin to think about it. David was right and I knew that my life didn't begin at nineteen, it started at birth, before birth, for everything that preceded my birth was merely the prologue. I sniffle. I can only be so sad at this moment. I remember staring into a mirror years ago filled with the same longing and same dread. I wanted my best friend to be my best man but the world doesn't work out the way you always want it to. I look outside and see the overcast sky and smell the drizzle in the air. Sometimes the meteorologist has to predict storms even though he would prefer not to.

I sit at the edge of my bed and scratch my right calf. The hair on my legs and the nerves on the skin aren't used to socks at this level and I push them down slightly. I beg myself not to think of my life and I turn on the news to relinquish the urge to let my mind wander into dangerous territory. I was too late. An afternoon movie on cable won't help me now. I'm hours away from marriage, minutes even, and they melt away all the same.

Sad. I've never felt this way. No one ever expects to feel this way. If we chose this path and constantly strived for it the world would be doomed. Pain is necessary though. I'm not sure why but it's something that we all need to feel. I hate feeling this way.

It started only a few hours ago as I was punching out of work. I looked at my watch and my excitement was overwhelming. I had a lot of time to hang out with my usual bookstore friends but none had struck me as great friends, they weren't the ones you depended on or thought you'd be playing cards with in a retirement home talking about the good old days when prices were low and kids didn't go around getting drunk all the time. Aging isn't only about losing your memory, its forgetting about the day-to-day.

Moments later I was sitting in the living room watching TV; flipping through the stations in hopes of finding something worth watching and indeed I found a movie that I hadn't watched in years, one that I remember enjoying but hadn't thought about since the last time I had seen it.

My cell phone buzzed. It vibrated on the carpet near the wall shaking the cord around. I hadn't checked it since I plugged it in, I'm sure the battery was back to four cells. It was a number I didn't recognize, one from an area code I couldn't pinpoint although I still darted my eyes to the right side of my brain in hopes of memory retrieval. I answered and my world changed forever.

I was young. Nineteen years old seems like a high number when you're that age. You think you know the world, but you don't know the green in the grass from the blue in the sky. I didn't know what to say, how to respond, or the proper actions required. They understood my position and let me go quickly. I hung up expecting my alarm clock to sound but it never happened. The movie kept running and the wind kept blowing. I stood in shock until the rug was swept from under me and I sat with my legs crossed. My eyes stayed fixed where the carpet met the wall. I don't know how long I was there for and I didn't hear anybody enter or leave the room.

The door leading into the garage opened and I was whisked back into reality. They were all home now. My Mom, my Dad, my brother, my sister-in-law, and my nephew. They were chatting but none of it registered. They silenced as they saw me on the living room floor. The TV still on, my cell phone still in my hand, still plugged into the wall. I turned my head slowly and looked up at them. They all looked at me, even Theodore. No one had to inquire; they waited for me to speak. My mother shifted forward in front of everyone else and her lower lip dipped slightly.

"Mike's dead."

My vision blurred and the lump in my throat grew to the size of a boulder. My teeth started chattering and my stomach would reject anything I offered it. I said it for the first time and it became true.

I started to cry.

It was the middle of August and the wind blew into Chicago. I stood amongst family members and their friends, people I have never met. I was alone at my best friend's funeral. I had no support as the only ones who could help me out were the ones who were grieving the hardest. I heard Jerry, his Dad, on more than one occasion point me out and say I was Mike's friend from college.

My parents bought me a plane ticket to Chicago, driving would have just been too hard. I had a hotel room even though Mike's parents offered their house to me. One of his uncles picked me up and we made idle conversation asking about my situation at school. We had a lease on an apartment that started soon and I was minus one roommate. I couldn't afford the two-bedroom in

Westwood on my own so it was either find a new roommate or find a new living situation. I just looked out at the Illinois suburbs, the trees passing and the group of kids playing in the front yard. I hated the children who got to live their sunny summer day. They ran towards the sprinkler and shifted when they were hit expelling a shriek one makes when un-expecting cold water touches the warm flesh. Their parents made them peanut butter and jelly sandwiches. They didn't have the opportunities to play in any of life's card games; they were never dealt a bad hand they could fold out of. I was jealous of them and their ability to smile.

I wish I could remember more of the experience but it was all blurred together. Just bits and pieces in a memory that is better left repressed. There was hardly another option other than lethargy as a way for me to cope. I remember his family at a reception at their house afterwards. They cried and I saw old photos of Mike as an eight-year-old little league player. Another photo was him at graduation. Others were prom, friends, family, and Halloween ten years ago when he went as Dracula. I didn't know this Mike, I knew a different Mike. A UCLA Mike. A constant opponent in the war for supremacy in the Dutch Oven; who had more built up in their bowels, him or me? The Mike who advised me that Claire and I were fine, the kind that listened to me and knew who Brad and Chelsea were and what they had done. The Mike that flew to Michigan on a delayed flight and decided to drive out the next time. The Mike that died fifteen miles from home in a thirty car pile-up due to bad weather conditions. He was one of four to have their lives taken as national news networks lamented on how the traffic behind this "freeway mess" was an "annoyance" to deal with but the cars would be cleared soon so "remain patient and use the surface streets".

He died on his way to see me and I felt guilty about it. Four had to die that day in that traffic accident, one of them had to be Mike. I'll never know why it happened; I just know that I wish it hadn't.

* * *

175

The next day I was at the airport again. Sitting slouched in a leather chair staring out at the nose of a 747, listening to the faint hum of its engines and occasionally hearing another airplane roar skyward. I checked my watch for the tenth time in a half an hour. I wanted to get to the airport early, there was no use sticking around and nothing I could do to remedy the situation. I was uncomfortable and, in this case, preferred to sulk alone. My aura told others to stay away and I got annoyed when I heard a gentleman on his cell phone on the opposite side of the leather couches of me blab on about how horrible life was because he showed up five minutes prior to his flight and they refused to let him on board. What an asshole, I thought. If he only knew what people in the real world went through. He probably never had his best friend killed. My mental images of everyone around became more than I could bear, I saw them as a lesser than what they really were. The world wasn't bad; it just reflects your mood. I felt that my experience allowed my social standing to elevate; no others could share this pain. I didn't want to share my horrible circumstances; I wanted it all for my own.

I hopped off the seat, grabbed my carry-on and began roaming the terminal. Back and forth, back and forth, until a mother asked her little boy if he wanted milk or orange juice. When the boy responded milk I chuckled to myself and then the lump in my throat returned. I darted for the bathroom closing the stall door. I hesitated as best I could but I couldn't stop the tears from forming. The sniffling and the whimpering I was able to contain and within a few moments the feeling subsided. I wondered how long it would be until I got over this feeling and part of me hoped I never would. Mike's death deserved to be grieved forever for the only reason that he was my friend.

As I glanced at the gate monitor and saw my flight was delayed an hour, I decided to flip my phone open and give Claire a call. There was no reason to other than just to talk. There was no ring, just a straight shot to the voice mail and I hung up without leaving word. We hadn't talked since the day Mike died and she started to cry on the phone. I did my best to remain composed but failed.

Fifty minutes later I was on the airplane. Forty-five minutes later I was landing in Detroit. My window seat allowed me the luxury of seeing Lake Michigan and the open lands that lay between the Windy City and the Motor City.

I expected an open arm when I crossed into the baggage claim area; a family member's embrace which I would accept. They would provide these arms with the personal knowledge of knowing how terrible and miserable life is when you lose someone, a conversation that would create boredom for the listener as everybody knows the feeling, and an outlet for me.

My breath was stolen from my chest. Her shoulders hunched up and the look of partial "oops" and "gotchya". I hugged her and spun her around. I held her so tight and felt that I should never let go because if I did this time she would never return. I was speechless and my eyes fixed onto hers.

"I thought...but you're afraid..." I couldn't complete sentences.

"Now seemed like a good time to conquer that fear. I don't know. You seemed like you could need someone and I thought maybe I could be that someone. I wanted to be here for you."

I hugged her. Three and a half months of missing her being squeezed in the middle of a terminal at Detroit Metro Airport and we didn't let go of one another for fifteen minutes. She said she was sorry about Mike and I didn't feel words were appropriate to express any return thoughts. All I could do was thank her repeatedly for doing this for me; for standing up to her biggest phobia at my expense. For a few moments that week I had finally been able to take my mind off of my best friend. I was finally able to be happy.

Claire had never been further east than Las Vegas or further north than San Francisco so I wanted to make her trip to see me

177

the best that I could possibly make it. She had an open-ended ticket and decided to keep extending her stay until it was time for me to drive across the great open country and back into Los Angeles.

"Just because I flew doesn't mean I keep wanting to do it," she said. I never got tired of her and we were around one another for nearly three weeks straight. When I was at work, she was at my house sleeping in late or laying out in the sun. She played babysitter to my nephew and caught up on books, which I seemed to be buying a new one for her every two days, in the sun. On my days off we would go to movies, roam the suburban streets, and travel a few miles out to visit key areas of interest. We took in a Tigers game one day and she asked how far Canada was from us. A light bulb the size of the sun was lit above my head.

"We should go over to Canada. It's only a few minutes from here." She smiled at the idea and began to glow mischievously when I informed her that the drinking age was only nineteen.

"Oh, it is?" She lifted her hand to her face and started tapping her chin, "You bring this up now?"

It was settled and after the game we drove across the bridge into Windsor, Ontario where we spent the better part of the night at the bars getting sloshed on all the legal drinking we could handle. We found a hotel room near the row of bars where we would make all the noise we wanted with out fear of a parents overhearing or a baby's cry ruining the mood and when the morning sunrise burned its way into the room we woke up in each other's arms with smiles on our faces, disheveled hair, and breath that stank like a sewer truck crashed into a sulfur mine. We didn't care. When you like, or as this seemed to be slowly turning into, love someone, nothing will stop you from that show of affection, not even the taste of alcohol and nachos that had been stirring in your stomach for twelve hours.

Two days later I left the bookstore saying my goodbyes to Tricia and Jon and Page and Angie. They wished me good luck and I promised them that the next summer I would come back, throw on the name tag and shelve books. Page preferred not to see me leave but she didn't admit it. She wrapped her arms around me and told me to not get shot and not to get tattooed, at least in Los Angeles; she wanted to be there when it happened. I reassured her that permanent skin ink would not be near my body and she said she has the whole next summer to convince me otherwise.

"Slowly I'll wear you down and make your life miserable until you give in. Either way," she said sisterly, "don't stay in LA next year for Claire, you make sure to come back."

"She has you for eight months, we get you for four," Tricia said.

"Good bye, you bastard," Angie said giving me a big friendly hug.

"Here," Jon handed me a list, "whatever you do don't listen to the man and pick up these books. You'll be taking another English Lit class and I can't bear the thought of you having to suffer through the drivel they consider a classic."

I grabbed the list and took a quick glance at it.

"I read half of these in high school. 'Of Mice and Men'? I read that four years ago it was really good."

"Quit acting like the modern classrooms consideration of classic and quality literature is actually a decent read."

"I'll miss you, Jon," I turned to Angie, "I look forward to making fun of Jon behind his back with you."

"Of course," Angie held a strong smiling face but she was sad. Her mouth curved upward, her eyebrows downward; there was no hiding it.

"I'll be back before you know it." We embraced once again and they let me go. As I pulled out of the parking lot they all waved goodbye, turned around and went back inside the bookstore. The issues in my life weren't about to stop the flow of customers needing coffee, recommendations, customer service and paying for their merchandise. The skies were dark but the local news meteorologist didn't predict rain this evening.

The next morning my parents treated Claire and I to an early breakfast and I watched as Nicole held a wailing Theodore outside so the fellow patrons would not be disturbed. My mother assured me that she would visit me in California this year and my father promised to join her. David stoically rested his arm on the table and cut his French toast with his fork.

"Don't expect me to come out and see you. I've got shit to do here."

"David. Don't use that language at the table in a restaurant."

"Sorry, Mom," he muffled with an abnormally large piece of French toast in his mouth.

"Haha, you got in trouble," I said harassing my brother for what would be the last time of the summer.

Outside, Nicole was waving over to David who nodded and excused himself.

"Fatherhood calls." We quietly watched the exchange of words and Nicole handed Theodore over. She came into the restaurant and stood at our table.

"He's cranky so I'm going to take him home." Nicole held out her arms for a hug and I jumped out of the seat and embraced her. "Have a good drive out there. I'll miss you and all that crap."

"Right, Nicole. I'll miss you too."

She turned to Claire.

"Lovely meeting you, Claire. You keep this guy in line, okay? Remember that nerve in the arm," Nicole made a fist, "don't be afraid to hit it."

She promised there was no fear when it came to physical abuse.

They hugged and we both walked out of the restaurant and I playfully told my nephew goodbye. By the end of the day the very thought of having an uncle will have subsided him and the next time our paths crossed I would be a stranger. We came back into the restaurant and sat down. In less than an hour I was saying my farewells to my parents. A repeat scenario of one year ago and a tree blowing by a light wind in the distance brought to my attention all the changes that had transpired since the last time, with my wandering gaze into nowhere I realized the major, and even somewhat subtle, differences were uncanny. As Claire and I merged onto I-94 heading west I made her aware of how much things have changed in the past year and how I would prefer to keep this next year a little less dramatic. The freeway sign confirmed that we were en route to Chicago and I cared little for the constant reminder for the next four hours that I would be passing by where my best friend had died.

I rekindled a friendship with an estranged ex-girlfriend only to have my good friend Brad sleep with her. I became an uncle and watched my family grow. My grandfather died. There was a balance of good and bad. Opportunities that were taken and others taken for granted. The synopsis of one year was read out in my mind almost month-to-month. It kept me quiet as Claire watched the farmlands pass by and sang a few of the songs that were picked up on radio stations still close enough for us to pick up the signal.

"I remember when that song came out, I was interning at a station in Boston," the deejay started and continued meandering for a minute about a memory long since passed. "Now we'll go to Meteorologist Lucas Hasselmeyer for the weather report". The local weatherman told his listeners about an incoming cold front in the evening and the light showers that will arrive with it. He then went into the ten-day weather report and I chuckled to myself. Claire looked over at me.

"What?" She asked.

"Ten-day weather report. My brother insists there is a key life lesson to be learned from it and its just one of those things I think about every once in a while and then conveniently forget about until times like these. Now I'm stuck pondering the meaning."

She found it compelling enough to consider the hidden message but neither one of us discussed it further. Just the hum of the road and the radio stations play list filled the background as we headed towards the Pacific Ocean at an average of seventy-five miles for every hour that passed.

"Huh," she replied, "I wonder what the relevance is."

As we entered the Los Angeles city limits a couple days later my speedometer hovered near fifteen miles per hour. It was the city's way of welcoming its citizens back as if bad traffic at off-peak hours was the way of life and an immediate reminder of what you missed most. I dropped Claire off at her house and followed my Internet directions to the apartment. I was nervous as I knocked on the landlord's door. She handed me two sets of keys and inquired about when my roommate was expected to arrive. I shrugged my shoulders and turned away.

The apartment had the fresh paint and clean carpet smell one anticipated on their first review of their new living situation. I walked inside my desolate new home and dropped my backpack onto the floor. I looked into the bathroom; the kitchen was attached to the living room and then entered both bedrooms. I wasn't sure which one was supposed to be mine so I took the one closest to the main road so I could look out of the window at the passing Bruins and hear the yells of drunken classmates in the middle of the night; a comfort which would toss any feelings of still being in Michigan in my parent's basement away.

Within an hour, everything I had crammed into the trunk of my car and backseat took up a tiny corner in the living room. There was no TV set up. I only had the couch that came with the place along with two beds and a refrigerator. I sat down and listened to the rustling of a palm tree right outside the window. It was quiet in a way where you couldn't concentrate; it was similar to sitting in a library during finals and the paranoia that someone is looking at you from across the room. I was restless and had to move around.

I walked around the campus taking in the air and the views of the Santa Monica Mountains and the tall corporate buildings of nearby Westwood. I thought I could see the ocean from atop the tallest hill but it was too hazy and my best landmark ahead was the track stadium.

It was lonely and would remain so for the next week until all the freshmen I knew of the previous year would gather around campus as sophomores and once again we would talk of the summer over an alcoholic mix prepared in a giant garbage bin. I called Claire but there was no answer. I called my parents to let them know of my safe arrival. I scrolled through the phone to see who else I could contact. I passed Brad and Chelsea, Claire and David, finally I stopped at Mike. Whether it was on purpose or some subconscious desire to hold on to his memory, I had yet to delete Mike's number from my phone. Maybe if I pressed send his father Jerry would answer and I would have to explain why my name had graced the incoming call list. Maybe I would be calling a stranger; somebody who picked up this fallen number when and if the account was closed and the ten digits recycled. I didn't delete it. Not yet.

I ate. I went into an electronics store to check on the price of a television. Back at my apartment I opened up a couple of boxes and started putting clothes into my closet. I closed the door to the other bedroom. I busied myself with moving-in tasks. I went to the grocery store and bought $45.18 in groceries. I read a chapter in a book that wasn't on Jon's recommendation list. My eyes scanned the words but my mind did not pick up on a single sentence. I opened up a bag of chips and stood next to the kitchen sink eating tortilla triangle after tortilla triangle. I put the sheets on my bed and at a quarter to ten I fell on my back with one arm behind my head staring up at the ceiling. A new ceiling. One I had never looked up at. I sent a text message to Claire claiming that I wished she was here; she had to work really early the next morning. I continued watching the headlights from cars coming down the street making strange shapes through the street lamp and trees outside my apartment. I went to sleep. Woke up. Fell back asleep. Woke back up. Fell back asleep. Woke up one more time and my body was through resting. I was standing in my apartment before the sun shone in. It was early in the morning and I had nothing to do all day.

September felt like a daze. I couldn't figure out my mood and whenever I was around Claire she could see that I was very different. She stuck around because she cared for me. I cared for her too. Even as classes started I would hazily attend lectures and sit in my apartment alone working on a paper or reading whatever was required. I nearly failed my first test and I didn't know why. I had studied long and hard, I knew the information through and through. I reviewed the incorrect answers and shook my head knowing that I had put the wrong answer and struggled to figure out how I could make so many stupid mistakes. I was frustrated.

A couple of old pals from last year ran into me a few days before the semester and invited Mike and I out to a party just off campus in a house. I declined the offer. I felt out of place.

"What's wrong?"

I shrugged my shoulders, "I don't know," I told Claire as we sat next to one another at a sushi bar just having put our order sheet on top of the glass. Three of the chefs thanked us and began our order.

I continued. "I feel like I don't belong here."

"Is it because of Mike?"

"I don't know, I think maybe the more I think about it the more I think he is just part of the problem." I caught my words and looked over at Claire. "I didn't mean that to sound the way it sounded. I like you, Claire. You're my red rose in a field of dead flowers."

She didn't respond and we sat in uncomfortable silence for the remainder of the meal. It had been a bearer of bad news that left two people in their own thoughts with the inability to look into each other's eyes for fear of what might be said. If we spoke it would only be to speak of the problems which neither one of us wanted to address; the ones we wanted to ignore in hopes they would go away.

The roaring car engine flying by outside caught my attention and I looked toward the Westwood street. This scenario was increasingly feeling like an inescapable dream and one morning I would wake up and everything that happened upon arriving for the second year at the University of California - Los Angeles would disappear with a morning shower. I saw my reflection bouncing off the glass and next to me was the back of Claire. I felt the urge to run. I envisioned opening the door and starting into a light jog, my speed would ascend until I was sprinting. I saw myself taking off at high speeds yet I was at no specific destination and no idea where I was headed.

I turned back around and my eyes bored down upon a display of dead and tasty seafood. Claire and I remained silent, her hand slipped onto mine which sat on my leg. I held it. I looked at a television which had the news on. A good looking gentleman with a stage name was standing in front of a seven-day weather report. Claire chuckled.

"The weather report," she said matter-of-fact.

Sunny and hot for the next seven days but I couldn't look beyond the evening's lows.

I pulled the checkbook out from the kitchen drawer. The balance would more than cover the amount needed for October's rent. I filled out the date. I filled out the recipient and the amount in cursive and signed my name. As I tore the check out, I looked up and around my nearly empty apartment. After almost a month I still didn't have a TV. My kitchen table was my work desk which had books and papers piled in odd angles. I went into my bedroom which was still rather void of anything other than a bed and clothes I was too lazy to pick up. A framed 5x7 photo of Claire and me at a park back home sat on an overturned plastic crate next to my alarm clock. Back at home, I had thought to myself, this wasn't home. I picked up the photo frame and carried it with me into the living room. The emptiness of the apartment was equivalent to the void in my life. I had trouble believing this was all associated with Mike. I thought that maybe this nothingness had been here all along but it was the people I was around, the Mike, the Brad, the Chelsea; they were the ones who kept it hidden and it worried me that Claire wasn't able to help be rid of it. Something had to change, I thought. I didn't want to feel this way anymore. My emotions just weren't playing fair; it was a scratched CD on a long road trip. That first track played fantastically, that was Claire, that was the thing that made sense. Nothing else did. I became scared and I didn't know why. With the picture frame in hand, I paced throughout my apartment looking for answers that I didn't have. I was sad and hurt for no other reason than because I couldn't break being sad or hurt. I must have looked down at this picture for nearly fifteen minutes hunched over the kitchen counter.

I slid down to the floor leaving the silver frame next to my rent check. For the first time since I moved back I let all the stress and tension get the better of me.

It was inevitable and I cried.

7

I'm refusing to sit down. I think I'm afraid that there is some random piece of chocolate or somebody had rested a pet on the chair when they weren't supposed to and I'd have white cat hair all over my ass. I walk from the door to the window, looking out. The water is calm and the clouds are still only moderately spilling small light drops of rain.

There is a knock at the door. I see my brother standing on the opposite side of the peephole looking down the hallway. I open up and he comes in patting me on the shoulder.

"Let's do this."

"How many people are downstairs?"

"No clue. Haven't gone down yet."

"What about Nicole?"

"She just went down there with Mom, Dad, and the kids."

I nod my head.

"What part of life are you on now?" My brother asks.

"Hmm?"

"Your whole life review thing you were talking about earlier. What chapter are you on?"

"Oh right. After Los Angeles. I'm on the magazine, Rose, that stuff."

"Haha, right. That was a barrel of monkeys."

"A good chunk I'm scanning. It's all some hazy blur. Ever look back on your life and have it all mesh together and not really make sense."

"All the time," David patted my arm. "All the God damn time. Let's go."

5 YEARS AFTER LOS ANGELES

I looked at the clock at the bottom right hand corner of my computer screen. It's 3:17pm. The afternoons always drag on, the body's way of making up for the quick mornings. You come in at nine in the morning and before you know it noon comes around and you think half the day is over. At twelve o'clock, I slump down thinking to myself that there are still six more hours to go. My stomach bulges out under my shirt; my lunch at the nearby galleria sits undigested. I have gained a few pounds over the last few years. Slowly but surely I'd step onto a scale like a small child afraid of that first step in the shallow end of a pool. The number hops up one pound and I tell myself that one pound is no big deal, probably fluctuation from the water I just drank. I think back to my high school days when everything either looked so much better or so much worse in hindsight. I used to look good, I remember. I was twenty pounds lighter and I could have sworn I had more hair, although David and my father constantly tell me it is merely a skewed vision because everything looks better when you look at it from the future. Your clothes are the things that look worse. I belted out a loud sigh and grabbed my stomach, shaking it a bit and remembering when I couldn't do this. I don't think I'm fat, I'm sure I'm not, but I figure it's best for me to get onto a treadmill before a doctor tells me that my life depends on it.

A picture of my wife and I sit at the end of the desk. I turn it around. I'm a little tired of looking at her and I feel guilty for feeling so. What they don't tell you is, just because you love them when you marry them doesn't mean you can't get sick of them eventually. I think about our courtship and how I probably should have waited a little longer to see if I could spend the next fifty years with this woman I only knew for a couple. I believe in marriage and I think it's good for the individual as well as society but it shouldn't be entered lightly. You can't impulse buy marriage, it should be treated like any other serious contract you consider signing. Just because her friends were getting married and having babies and her parents were pressuring her as well as your own doesn't mean you should give in. I think about the divorce rate for men and women and I wonder what it would be like if it were friends. I think about Brad and our friendship; that didn't work out after fifteen years. Mike and my friendship, I'd be a widower. Chelsea, we would have divorced in three years. Friends are easier to let go of than a spouse and usually a little cheaper.

"I can just feel that we're going to be happy forever," she told me the day after the proposal. For better or worse; no one wants to think of the 'or worse'. It's always easier to believe in a fairy tale. We wanted to believe it, I occasionally wonder if we were duped.

"Drew." I twisted around in my chair and stare up at an older man named Lee. Leonard actually, but he has always gone by Lee. "They're moving the water," he informed me.

"Oh?"

"Yeah, God damn prima donnas throw a fit and we got to walk to the other side of the office for water."

It's a menial complaint which I wished I no longer had to listen to. The editors and the reporters are the hot shit which leaves us salesmen and saleswomen to have to fend on our own. At least if I get fired I get a severance package, I think. I spend a lot of my time tracking down possible advertisers to contact and once found I report them to my boss so he can create a sales plan, or have me create most of a sales plan. Finally he edits it then contacts the prospect. It's a little slow but it works for what it is. I also get a health plan and tell people I work for a magazine.

"It's really not that much further than where it was," I assured Lee observing the ten feet it had moved.

"That's not the point. They're yelling jump and leaving us in the backyard (the back of the office where accountants and sales-folk jockey the desks) to fend for ourselves".

"I'm not sure what that means. I think we should let them have this win."

"We don't have a choice," Lee says looking up and away. He scratches his moustache and looks back down. "What do you have going on this weekend?"

"Not sure. The missus and I will probably visit my family."

Lee's phone rang and he shot over to his desk to answer. He stood at his desk and I watch him speak to whoever had called and think to myself that nobody ever wants to become an accountant. Nobody really wants to be a salesman either. It just sort of happens.

I pulled my four door, four year old sedan next to my wife's similar model vehicle under the tiny carport provided for tenant parking at our complex and headed inside. The sun was still shining heavily as the dog days of summer continued to drag on.

"This is it," she says to me, anger flooding my wife's eyes.

"Put the knife down," I respond a little too calmly.

"I've had enough of the bullshit, okay. This is it," she doesn't scream back at me, it was an interesting choice. I thought she would have screamed at me.

"Sweetheart." I'm cut off.

"Don't call me sweetheart, don't you dare ever call me sweetheart again. I'm sick of you. I'm sick of this life and there is only one way I see out of it." There are tears in her eyes. I'm impressed as I usually am but I see the knife close to her wrists.

"Honey, the knife is really close to your wrist," I say in a concerned manner, my eyes stuck on the sharp blade which seems inches from an artery. She holds it up for me.

"It's fake, don't worry."

"Jeez, that looks really real. Is that what you'll be using?"

She smiles at me.

"It's good," I tell her. "I can't wait to see it."

"We're not done yet. The show opens next weekend and I really need to learn my lines in the last act."

"The ghost scene?"

"The ghost scene."

She tilts her head to the side and playfully sticks her tongue out through a small crack in her teeth. I chuckle and give her a kiss.

"Gosh darn it," I start, acting like an innocent mid-twentieth-century baby boomer, "it's times like these when I realize why I fell in love with you." We kiss again and she backs away, lovingly tapping me on the nose with her index finger. "Make dinner, bring in, or dine out?"

She walked to the window and looks towards the sun as it descends backlighting her and creating a silhouette.

"It's early. I'm all about an All-American restaurant." She said.

"And ice cream," I throw out like an excited little kid.

"Not for me," she pats her stomach, "I've got to be on stage." She passes me and pats my stomach heading into the bedroom. "And maybe you should hold off."

"Thanks for the self-esteem boost."

"You're married, you have no more self-esteem."

I nod to myself in agreement.

I was excited when I walked in the door and she mentioned that she wanted to rehearse lines for her play. That usually meant she was in a good mood. Some of the best sex we've had was during or after we rehearsed her lines. A customer service representative at an insurance company by day and a local community theater actress by night, I first saw and fell in love with Rose when Angie from the bookstore took me as a date to see the show. I think it was all a ploy to introduce me to her friend's single friend Rose, the actress. The plan worked swimmingly. Her latest theater show was opening soon, written by the playhouse theater director, Hans Smith, this latest tale was about a woman who ends her life and the ghost lives on in the apartment in which she committed suicide in to see others deal with whatever issues they were struggling with. She attempts to help them. It was an average play, I enjoyed going over lines with Rose, but I've seen better, much better. The very thought scared me as the bad plays often provided weeks, if not months, of very intolerable mood swings. Reassurances from Hans remedied her manic/depression. We've had some bad fights and bad times when there were bad shows.

I scanned my eyes across the apartment feeling varying degrees of un-believability. I was married. I was living with someone. I was getting regular sex. We had shared bank accounts and I had someone to always hang out with. It was all good and yet part of me felt it was bad. I remembered the times I sat in a one bedroom apartment and flipped TV stations at my own will without wondering if the person sitting next to me would mind because there was no person sitting next to me. When the phone rang it was for me. When I left I could go where I wanted to and not have to explain myself when I came back. There was nobody to explain myself to.

I loved Rose but there was a recent internal struggle where I was asking myself if I made the right choice. I would shake my head to get such an evil thought out and assure myself that I did, of course, make the correct decision. It was all a matter of getting used to this. It had been two years; I should be used to this. She exited the bathroom rubbing her hands together soaking up the lotion. She came over to me, grabbed my right hand and rubbed the remaining moisturizer onto my hand. I didn't mind, it was a display of affection.

"Walk or drive?" She asked.

"It's nice out, let's walk," I said grabbing my stomach, "I can get some exercise."

* * *

Rose and I had a lot in common. We both had grown up in the suburbs and, like most people who lived near each other, when we first met we started asking if the other knew of people who went to the same high school. We hung out at a lot of the same places, but who in their high school teens didn't frequent a mall? Rose had two brothers, one older and one younger, and a sister that was six years older. When I met Rose, the older sister Jacqueline, was four months away from walking down the aisle. She was the maid-of-honor and I watched her hold arms with the groom's best man as they made their way ahead of the bride.

She went to college for two years for the sole reason that that is what everyone was doing. She wanted to get married because that's what everyone was doing and the typical family question leading up to Jacqueline's nuptials was, "So, when are you getting married?"

Rose was typical. Her mother worked part-time at a bank and her father worked for one of the Big Three working his way from the factory floor up to the corporate offices. His blood was in auto-making and he rested on Sundays with the Lions, cheered on the Red Wings, and fell asleep to the Tigers. He had half-season tickets to the Pistons which was where I first had bonded with him between time-outs or quarters. It was an icy cold winter night when we headed to the Palace and as the game ended triumphantly against the Lakers, he always invited me to Laker games due to my one year stint on the west coast; I had asked if I could have his blessing to marry his daughter. He loved the idea and was proud I had been so respectful and chivalrous.

The small stint of Rose's college career remained a mystery, she refused to tell me what she had done or who she was with. It worried me at first but I soon stepped away from the issue and she promised me she would hide her photo albums. Upon review one boring winter night with glasses of wine in our hands she started reminiscing. There were multiple guys in the photos along with bleached-blonde college roommates and brunettes dressed scantily. We never asked for each other's numbers, whether out of respect or fear. I accepted her wild days and figured that not every new guy who appeared in eight picture sets she had slept with, I didn't dismiss it either. I let it slide off my conscious and that night we made love in a way that told her she cared for me.

Her brothers played football in high school and football in college. One became a teacher and the other a police officer. I found it ironic how the two authority figures known for ridicule and prone to teenage assault were the jobs chosen by the two who did just that.

I loved Rose and she loved me. We were married on a spring day in late May. We took our vows and promised to be there for one another. Six months later reality hit and, although we loved each other, we realized that just as the youth aren't immortal despite their thinking, marriage wasn't a fairy tale. We worked and cultivated it. We had celebrated two years very recently and wished to continue further. David told us that we were the third longest lasting married couple her knew besides himself and a co-worker.

Angie called Rose Friday morning to discuss going out at some point on the weekend. She agreed and emailed me at work to inform me that plans were created.

There were four of us: Angie, her boyfriend Eddie, Rose and myself. I stood outside with Rose and Angie holding the pager conversing and trying our best to not look at our watches to see if the estimated twenty-five minute wait had passed. Eddie was inside at the bar watching a baseball game. I didn't feel like standing next to Eddie. The only way we would talk is during a commercial and I preferred to not get a stiff neck staring up at the screen above the bar.

Angie picked Mitchell's because it was across the parking lot from the bookstore. She still worked there but now as a full time manager. I received bits of news about the dwindling staff members that I once shared shifts. Tricia was long gone and living somewhere in the southwest, Jon was fired my second summer working there, and Page fell off the face of the earth. Eddie was in his forties now and still working his forty hours five days a week. I figured Chelsea didn't work at Mitchell's anymore but that still didn't erase the idea of seeing her from my head. Every time we ate here I thought of her. I pondered where she was and what her life had amounted to thus far.

At the table we ordered appetizers and drinks meanwhile Eddie, a different Eddie from the one that worked at the bookstore, was constantly looking away from the table to watch the game. In the bottom of the seventh inning he clapped his hands together loudly when the first baseman slammed a three run homer to push a ten run lead. I didn't mind sports enthusiasts but ten runs in baseball was pretty much a game clenching lead so looking back every minute seemed futile. To each their own.

Angie would occasionally glare at us from across the table with eyes screaming their relationship was so going to be over by Labor Day. Rose and Angie shared their gossip and I remained out of the loop, hunched on the inner side of the booth, and staying quiet. The food came. The game ended and Eddie started telling everyone about his work week. We all paid as much attention as we could stand. Angie's eyes glazed over first and I held in a chuckle when I first noticed it. Eddie was shooting at break neck speeds into law and Angie was learning the life lesson that just because you may have money it doesn't make you interesting. My cell phone rang and I reached into my pocket and glanced at the caller ID. I excused myself as I answered shoving my face away from the table as not to disturb their meal.

"Yes?" I whispered telling my brother that I was most likely at dinner or in a movie theater prior to its start. "Uh huh," I responded. "Okay." I hung up and looked at Rose who was looking back at me waiting for me to reveal the details of the quick secret conversation.

"Your lover?" She asked.

"Yes. Threesome's in. Tying up is out. And Spanking is preferred but not required." I looked up to see the waitress a few feet from the table. And whispered embarrassingly, "shit", to myself.

"More drinks?" She inquired awkwardly.

"Please. 'Nother one," Eddie said holding up his near empty beer glass.

"No thanks," I replied. Angie and Rose had their faces down biting their lip. The waitress departed and they laughed. I shook my head in an attempt to conceal embarrassment.

"Now we're going to have to tip her big," Rose said.

"I'm not going to give her a big tip, she's hardly done anything," Eddie shot back not picking up the sarcasm. We ignored his comment.

"Maybe I should write a phone number and see if she's interested?" Angie asked.

"Gee honey, your ears are really red." Rose said rubbing her thumb across my left earlobe. I didn't respond, my quick remark made me speechless. A couple moments passed and I looked up at Rose.

"Barbeque tomorrow at my parents," I was finally able to say.

"It's supposed to rain."

"Let's hope it doesn't."

The waitress returned with Eddie's beer. We sat silently, like a child just scolded in public by their parent, until she left.

A cell phone blasted a modern hip hop tune and Eddie reached into his pocket, taking his time answering the phone making sure the restaurant knew he had an incoming call.

"Yeah?" He screamed as if modern technology had yet to solve the volume crisis on phones. He looked at all of us who were staring back, he dropped his head putting his hand up and rubbing his temple in serious business-like thought and continued talking oblivious to his surrounding. Angie leaned into us.

"He drives a really nice car," she said to us mocking the gold digger types.

"That makes it all worth it then," Rose replied.

* * *

"UNCLE DREW!!!!" Theodore came busting out of his room and rushed down the stairs. Every subtle creek in the wooden staircase rang familiar. I knew them all by heart. He leapt from the last step and flew through the air nearly knocking me over and giving me a big hug.

"Hey bud, you keep growing up you won't be able to jump into me like this, you'll be liable to give me a hernia."

"Dad told me to."

"Don't listen to everything your Dad says."

"Grandpa said I should do it too," he yelled back at me. I put him down as David came downstairs.

"Dad! Uncle Drew's here."

"Oh good, he can help grandpa out." He looked at me, "Drew. Help Dad with the barbeque. Where's Rose?"

"Outside on the phone."

Nicole came down holding my little niece in her arms.

"Mom, Uncle Drew is going to help Dad with the barbeque," Theodore bursted out jumping up and down.

"Quiet Teddy, your sister is sleeping." Nicole who was still slowly working off the weight from baby number two looked fatigued and dressed as if fashion was no longer honorable. "Bro." She said acknowledging me.

"Sis," I replied. "How's number two?"

"Properly named, that's all she does."

I approached the little gal and nestled my index finger against her cheek. Half her face was buried in a pleasant slumber against her mother's upper chest. "Hello Layla," I said childishly. She yawned.

"Uncle Drew, wanna come see my room? I got a new poster." I looked at my brother thinking I needed an okay and he shrugged his shoulders.

"Yeah, let's see the continuous butcher job you and your parents inflict on my old room." I looked at my brother. "David, go help Grandpa with the barbeque."

As Teddy opened the door I was struck by the small bed in

the corner with the bright red headboard, the amount of toys strewn about on the floor under a race track rug and the cartoon poster above his bed.

"Wow, is that the poster?"

"Yeah!" Theodore leaped on the bed and started jumping. I looked at the poster and couldn't recognize the cartoon character. Something modern and Saturday morning-ish.

"That sure isn't Bugs Bunny," I said under my breath. "When do you start back at school?"

"I don't know."

"Soon?"

"Sure." He didn't stop jumping.

"What grade are you going to be in?"

"Um?" He stopped hopping. "Kin-da-garden." And the jumping continued.

"Wow, Kindergarten. So, it all begins." I got on my knees and lifted up part of the sheet covering the mattress. The faded scribbled lettering of D+C was still visible. I chuckled to myself. "This used to be my bed."

"Really?"

"Yes, for a long, long time. Pretty much until you were born. Then I moved in the basement. I had a lot of good times in this bed." I smiled at a reference that Theodore wouldn't understand for another seven or eight years.

"I have good times in this bed too." Theodore bragged.

"Not as good as the ones I had."

"Did you ever build a fort?"

"Yep."

"Did you ever jump on the bed like this?" Theodore shot high in the air almost touching the ceiling and bringing his legs up high as well. Another few inches on his height and he's going to knock his head through the ceiling.

"Oh. I jumped. I bounced." I felt wrong for toying with his young mind, but they were only dirty if taken out of context and a five-year-old didn't know to take it that way.

I stood back up and held out my hand.

"Come on, let's go get some food." Theodore grabbed my hand and leapt off the bed crashing his feet down hard onto the floor.

I caught up with my parents and my brother during dinner. My parents bought new patio furniture at the beginning of the year and desired to have as many meals on it as possible for the reasons of the price tag that accompanied it and the weather. Rose mentioned her play and they assured her they would be at her opening the following weekend. My brother boasted about a promotion at work and Nicole mentioned that she was officially on leave until she wanted to go back to work.

"I'll wait until both of these two are in school and find something." She said to her children.

After dinner, Theodore and my Dad threw a Frisbee around which was either my Dad having to constantly chase the disc around the whole yard or him yelling for us to duck at an incoming saucer. My Mom, Rose and Nicole sat around talking about whatever those three liked to talk about and my brother and I, along with a beer bottle in our hands, stood over a crib looking down at Layla.

"She's cute," I assured him.

"She's my little heartbreaker. Another eighteen years and I'll have to let her date."

I laughed. "Please, David how old was the girl you lost your virginity to?"

"I don't remember." He did.

"She was fifteen and she wasn't a virgin." We both were silent for a moment. "She going to get her own room or is she losing her virginity on the same bed you did?"

He countered. "For your information we got rid of that mattress."

"You guys planning on moving out?"

David shook his head.

"Don't really see the point in it."

"You're, what, twenty-nine with two kids still living at home?"

"Yes. Yes I am." He twisted his head at me with a stern and serious look in his eyes. "I like this home. I like living with my family and being close to them. It's not for everyone, Drew, but you know what? I can't imagine living somewhere else besides home."

"Isn't this..." I couldn't find the right words.

"I know what you're talking about. Nicole and I talked about moving out of here a long time ago. Living maybe somewhere between her parents and my parents, but we like this house. Like I said, I couldn't imagine...I don't want to imagine living somewhere else."

His words struck me in an unintended way and I suddenly felt excluded from my family. It resonated that I could never go home because where I grew up and the place I called mine could not be the same place.

"I'll probably turn one of the rooms downstairs into a bedroom; build a bathroom. As Mom and Dad get older they won't want to climb a flight of stairs too often. Layla will end up in this room and we'll get the master bedroom. I don't want to not live with Mom and Dad."

I wanted to be a part of it but the very thought was all so unsettling. It wasn't like Rose would actually consider moving here. I excused myself and strolled out the front door, down the driveway, and into the street. I started walking down the block I grew up on and turned on the path through the park I was so familiar with. I could have done it with my eyes closed. I wanted to think about life on my own. I let the buzz from the alcohol sit in my system and looked at the new families in the neighborhood. They were hesitant on waving at me and I didn't think about raising my hand to them. My neighborhood grew up and moved out, now a whole new set of Moms and Dads, boys and girls, dogs and cats, and minivans and SUVs moved in. I felt like a stranger everywhere I went.

I wasn't gone long enough to be missed, but my brother reflected on his words in his slight alcohol-induced buzz and apologized if it came out too harshly. He was tired of defending his reasons for why he still lived at home. I told him it struck a chord within me that made me think of those old-time New York families that all lived together in a brownstone in a neighborhood where kids were always in the streets. It was a nice thought, but one I didn't think would have been associated with my family. I liked it and regretted that I couldn't be a part of it. He understood.

When I stepped back into the backyard my father was resting on a chair despite Theodore's constant insistence that they continue playing. He tried pawning it to one of the ladies but they refused as well. It was either David or I who would have to take over bending over to pick up the Frisbee.

"What do you feed this kid? He doesn't stop." I asked David as I tossed the disc towards my nephew but somehow it flipped to the side and went rolling past him.

"Sugar by the spoonful. Should we not do that?" David said facetiously.

"I don't ever remember having that much energy." We watched as Theodore picked up the Frisbee ran a few feet toward us, planted himself and tossed the disc awkwardly back in the incorrect manner.

"Heads up!" David and I hollered at the rest of the family. It bounced off the sliding glass door and once there was confirmation that the glass remained intact we all breathed a sigh of relief. Nobody moved.

"Theodore, if you want to keep playing you're going to have to go get it," David told his son and the kid shot off towards the house. "When are you two having a baby?" David asked nonchalantly.

"No clue. Rose doesn't want to get pregnant anytime soon

because of the acting. She loves it too much to give it up and I don't know if we can afford it."

"You can afford it."

"I don't know."

"Come on, bro. I don't have that great of a job and Nicole doesn't work and we're doing fine. If there's one thing I've learned it's that you don't need money to raise a child, you just need the desire and the drive to want to give them everything you can possibly give them. No one can buy the world."

I glanced over at Rose who was leaning back in the chair away from Nicole and little Layla who was in her arms. Theodore was standing next to her. I had only seen her hold the baby once and she never picked up Theodore. She liked them but she preferred to have them at a distance.

"Come play, Aunt Rose," I heard the little guy beg. She shook her head and denied him.

"Do you want children?" David asked nudging my arm with his.

"Yes," I replied. I watched Theodore plea with Rose until Nicole told him to stop bugging her. I had felt a pang a handful of times in the last few years. It was a small shock to my stomach that something was wrong or my world was not balanced. I couldn't figure out why it happened when it did. I began to recognize that it occurred more frequently.

"Did I tell you I ran into Amy?"

"Who's Amy?

He reminded me with three words: "High school. Bitch."

"Right. Amy. Broke your heart into a million pieces and I had to comfort your depressed ass all summer when you weren't smoking pot."

"Yeah," he said gritting his teeth annoyed by my sarcastic candor.

"We were at Mitchell's last night and I kept thinking about running into Chelsea. I haven't seen her in years and I'm married,"

I added extra emphasis on the last part. "It was odd, to say the least."

"My heart skipped a beat. A rush of all those feelings. The love. The pain. Christ, Drew, I've been married for five years and I'm crazy about Nicole but seeing Amy..." he faded off and looked over at Nicole and his son, Teddy. His eyes lifted to the open window on the second floor where his baby girl slept night after night. His mouth curved, smiling, and his eyes became wet with the remnants of held back tears. "I actually missed her, but honestly, I don't want to know where I'd be if she hadn't broken my heart. I would suffer that heartache a hundred times over if I knew it led to this."

We walked over to the family and huddled around. I watched David pick up his son and lean over to kiss his wife on the forehead.

"Give Mommy a kiss," he told Teddy.

All I could do was watch my brother's interaction with his family. He knelt down and kissed Nicole passionately on the lips. I wanted David's life. I was jealous, the grass seemed greener.

When we got home that night we fell into our general nighttime routines. Any annoying occurrences from the evening were discussed on the ride home and usually brought up by Rose.

"Nicole really needs to take care of herself. She looks like a train wreck."

"I think she looked fine."

"She wasn't wearing any make-up, her hair wasn't done at all, and she was wearing sweat-shorts. I don't know. It didn't seem like she even cared that there was company."

I tossed my keys onto the kitchen counter and they clanked off the side and fell to the floor. Rose put her purse on the kitchen table next to the empty flower vase and piled up mail. I bent over with a groan and picked up my car keys and placed them next to the newspaper we never read but still felt obligated to subscribe to. By the time I turned around Rose was already in the bedroom. She exited minus her sandals and plus one cell phone against her ear. It was Hans she was talking to which was the equivalent of an important business call over international affairs that required strict silence from any nearby parties. I being the only party sat down at the table and started sifting through the mail.

I overheard new rehearsal schedules, possible understudies for other cast members, and development talk for Hans' next great community theater project. As owner and operator, he had free reign on productions and actors. He was president, director, writer, producer, and made sure all those around them knew their local acting careers depended on how much ass kissing you had done. Rose admitted that when she was eighteen she had a three month affair with Hans who was two-and-a-half times her age then at forty-five years old. She thought that bit of knowledge would upset me but I remained calm as best I could explaining that it wasn't really an affair because neither of you were married or in relationships. Her argument was that anyone older than twenty years with no long term ambitions was an affair. Out of fear of losing sanity I had placed it in my head that whatever Hans and Rose had years and years ago was over and done with and never likely to reappear. I may not be a realist but if I couldn't trust my wife then who could I trust?

They talked for over an hour and a half. After tossing away the junk mail and paying as many bills as I could with the amount of money in the checking account I went into the bedroom and picked up a novel I had started three weeks ago. I read the first page, the new chapter page which took longer than it should have; the distant sound of one-side of a conversation broke my concentration every other sentence. When I finished the second page I tried to remember what was on the previous one and a half pages I conquered and when I couldn't, for the life of me, think of it, I tossed the book onto the night-stand and placed the back of my head on my pillow on my side of the bed.

I wanted to leave. There was no where to go. I wanted my

wife to come in here and slowly strip down to nothing while I did the same and make love to her before collapsing in sexual ecstasy and falling asleep until one of the tenants in a nearby apartment let out their dog at eight the next morning. A desire that rarely seemed granted. Instead I closed my eyes and wished I had drunk a little more and let Rose drive home. As I studied the inside of my eyelids I listened to my wife talk about Holly cutting off her lines in the second act. Rose didn't have one strong scene, the whole show was a strong scene made specifically for her. She threatened that if Holly couldn't get her shit together she would leave the play and offer Hans the option to cancel the shows or find an understudy. Rose refused to work with an understudy exhibiting her flawless attendance record. Hans trusted Rose. Rose trusted Hans to do the right thing.

I fell asleep and dreamt that I was walking down a street I had never seen and had never been on. The world was slanted. Everyone was used to walking at an angle except me. I kept tripping over my leg as I continued forward on the road. It was a country road, the kind in the great American open where your nearest neighbor is a ten acre farm away. I couldn't get my balance and everyone who passed greeted me with a tip of their circa 1920's style bowler hat and the women politely smiled and nodded their head. I neither gestured nor spoke back, I was flustered and unsure.

At three in the morning I awoke with a partially numb arm under my head and my wife breathing heavily next to me. I pulled the covers off, which always find a way across a man's body when they fall asleep in the presence of a woman, and went into the kitchen for a drink of water. I leaned on the counter, my elbows creating two equal lines meeting at my crossed hands which held my chin. I was awake and didn't think lying back in bed would produce the desired results of another few hours of sleep. I situated myself down on the couch and put my feet up on the coffee table with a cup of water in one hand and the other hand draped across my lap.

I was determined to sit here until I figured out what was wrong. After three minutes I was frustrated and turned on the television hoping to find some late night cable movie that played for the two others in the world awake at this hour searching for an action flick. I saw the explosion and tossed the remote down next to me. Whatever I was watching had things blowing up and that's really all one needs in life.

"Huh, I haven't seen this movie in like ten years," a bit of an exaggeration. I continued watching. A commercial shot on within five minutes: an SUV, a mortgage lender, a local ceiling fan company, the station then offered their latest program as the final TV spot prior to returning to the late-night car crash extravaganza.

"Premiering this Sunday," the low toned announcer began, "when the world is on the brink of destruction, one psychic man and his doctor," the commercial continued with sound bites, action sequences and two actor's names I had never heard of. "Premiering, August ninth."

Ninth, that made yesterday the eighth. I leaned back on the couch and slumped down. Mike died five years ago yesterday and I totally forgot. I felt a stabbing sensation in the pit of my stomach. Every year I had made it a point to contact Mike's parents just to let them know how things were and to see how they were doing. I had done this for five straight years, never forgetting. I would schedule a one hour time slot some time around the early evening and dial in the number that never had changed. Same house, same phone. Same Jerry picking up excited to hear from me. I would tell myself I should call more often but the days and weeks rolled on and life continued, the everyday becoming a procrastinator. I had been one of their connections that promised to always be there, after so many of Mike's friends continued with life or found it difficult to just say hello, I had vowed to not become that person. They enjoyed the hour conversation I would have and through the years I heard the family grow and become better situated. This was wrong. I was wrong. I had to correct this whether for my sake or the sake of the still grieving family.

I went into my bedroom quietly and pulled a pair of jeans off of a chair in the corner. I silently opened drawers and the closet to retrieve various clothing items. I left a note on the counter telling Rose that I had gone away for the day and might be back at night. I told her to call me when she read this.

I drove out onto the empty main road heading for the freeway. I didn't know where Mike's family lived, a mere small challenge I told myself, there was Internet all over the area and any one website map could provide me with accurate directions to the tenth of a mile to reach their home. I turned on the freeway and began my journey west to a family I hardly knew but was forever connected with. As my odometer clicked past the first mile I began to think that this was a stupid idea that a phone call would have been sufficient yet I refused to turn around.

After two hours of flipping through radio stations and the boredom that an open road at night can bring I had begun to wonder if Rose was awake. Had she leaned over and felt an empty void where a warm body should be? Did she walk around the apartment and inquire in her own mind where I was? I looked at my cell phone, there were no missed calls.

Another hour passed and in my rearview mirror I saw the first hint of the sunrise. It was a clear night leading into a sunny morning, the black of pre-dawn was being cut by a yellow ball, turning the sky behind me into an ironically named midnight blue. I stopped at a gas station to fill up my car. I picked up an orange juice and continued my journey. As I opened the bottle a spit of the liquid dripped onto my pants. I swore to myself and placed the beverage in the beverage holder determining the amount of area on my pants soiled by the accident. I rubbed it away and there was only a small dark spot of wet OJ.

A couple miles into Indiana my cell phone rang.

"Hello?"

"Where the hell are you?" Rose screamed into the phone, my

first thought being that if I were mad at her this was no way to get into her good graces.

"Just entered Indiana," I replied shyly.

"Indiana!"

"What the hell are you doing in Indiana?" It was hard to explain. It was a situation that the only person involved in the act knew the reason and it was near impossible for most people to grasp the concept. I told her such and she insisted I try.

"Okay," my mind raced for the answer. "I'm seeing Mike's family."

"Who's Mike?"

"You know, Mike. My friend from Chicago."

"Your dead friend?" It was an unnecessary and probably unintentional punch to the sternum.

"Yes."

She sighed dramatically. "When were you going to tell me? How long has this been planned?"

"Well, honey, I kind of came up with the idea to do this at around three in the morning. See, yesterday was—"

"Three in the morning. Most people decide to go to the bathroom at three in the morning. Most people get a drink of water at three in the morning. The rest are sleeping. You're acting stupid, Drew."

"Rose."

"No, Drew. Come back home. You just don't leave at three in the morning and leave a note telling your wife to call you." I apologized to her. She shouted back, "Sorry doesn't even cut it."

I looked out at the road holding the phone to my ear. I was still westbound and I refused to turn around.

"Rose, yesterday was—"

"I don't give a shit what yesterday was."

"Will you let me explain?" I tried to remain calm. I didn't like raising my voice and I hit a bump in the road that knocked the small container of orange juice resulting in a little spilling out and onto the console. I felt weak like Rose was the controlling master and I was the puppet. I really felt married.

"You can explain when you get back."

I sighed the kind of sigh before you face a big challenge. The kind of sigh before you make an important life-changing decision. The kind of sigh before doing something stupid like telling your wife you will indeed explain when you get back with no intention of telling her it won't be for another twelve hours. I put the phone down onto the passenger seat and grabbed my drink, the side sticky from drying citrus.

"I'll explain when I get home...tonight." I said aloud to myself.

Within two hours I was in Mike's neighborhood. I knew the general direction just not the exact freeway exit, street, or address. I stopped at a nearby copying center that provided access to the Internet at a phenomenally inflated cost. I plugged in Mike's address and grabbed a business card to get the location of my area. I was four miles away. I looked at my watch and it seemed too early to go knocking on somebody's door unexpectedly. I opted for some breakfast.

I was alone in Pancake Palace. I sat in a two person booth by myself and the waitress who was older than dirt itself occasionally refilled my water. I looked straight at her face and thanked myself for not starting an addiction to cigarettes. She was one of those day-to-day folks you take a good look at and realize how bad some of the vices in the world can be.

I spent the whole time wondering how I was going to introduce myself to his family. I started to worry that they would be out of town and I'd be left on their porch steps for twelve hours before giving up. I would hang out until I got hungry and left for something to eat. I would come back and have to go to the bathroom and would leave again. I would spend all day there and after I left to go home, after an unsuccessful trip, they would show up five minutes later never realizing I had arrived to annually apologize for the loss of their son.

I rubbed the morning out of my eyes and prepared to face the unknown by breathing in a few quick successions of air.

I recognized their house. It changed very little with the exception of a fresh coat of paint and different car in the driveway. I stopped at the curb which was past my point of no return. I should have stopped further back; nothing would be worse than if one of the family members saw me sitting here contemplating whether or not I should go through with this. My cell phone buzzed, it was Rose. It was an odd confirmation that I should leave the present confusion for the clarity of the past. I tossed the phone onto the seat and exited the car.

I walked up the driveway and went right to the door. Knocking or ringing the doorbell seemed to be a massive decision. I rang the bell. This wasn't a movie or television show where within three seconds the door is opened. I waited for what seemed like five minutes but was probably not even thirty seconds and debated whether or not to ring the doorbell a second time. I did. I turned my head and looked out at my car. The sprinklers on the yard across the street shot up and started spraying the lawn. I heard a bolt unlock and I turned my head.

"Drew?"

"Hi."

"Oh my, come on in," Lorraine, Mike's Mom, told me opening the door wide. I entered and she gave me a hug. She was dressed comfortably in a tank top and jeans. "What are you doing here?"

"Who's at the door," a deep voice bellowed from the top of the stairs and footsteps pounded down.

"Jerry, it's Drew."

Jerry reached the bottom steps and saw me standing near the door, my hands shuffling on my jeans and in my pocket like a scared five year old. I thought he was coming in for a handshake but threw his arms around me instead. I looked at Lorraine who put her hand to her mouth on the brink of genuinely happy tears. I knew I had made the right decision.

"What are you doing here?" He asked releasing his grip and staring at me fatherly.

"I just asked him that," Lorraine snapped back. "What are you doing here?"

I opened my mouth but no words came out. I suddenly visualized my cell phone vibrating up and down my passenger seat.

"I don't really know, I guess." They both looked at me in an attempt to figure out my logic.

"When did you get in to Chicago?" Jerry asked.

"A few minutes ago."

"You drove? All night?" Lorraine asked and I answered by shrugging my shoulders.

"Lorraine, excuse us for a moment." Lorraine nodded and headed upstairs. Jerry put his arm around me and led me into the kitchen. He was in gym shorts and a dark blue tank top. It was obvious my doorbell ringing awoke him from his slumber. He sat at the kitchen table and I felt obliged to do the same. I could sense that he sensed something was amiss.

"Everything okay?"

"Yeah," I responded, slightly confused by the question.

"Drew. What the hell are you doing driving all the way out here in the middle of the night?"

"I didn't call you guys yesterday."

"Yes, we know," he didn't sound upset.

I sat in silence trying to look everywhere I could but into Mike's father's eyes. He refused to converse unless I was the one who initiated it. I hadn't really poured my feelings out in a long time, now seemed to be a good time to start.

"It totally slipped my mind yesterday that yesterday was the day that," I hesitated saying his name or the event in the presence of his father, "um, well you know. I remembered at three o'clock this morning and I just felt the urge to come out here and...I don't know. I didn't like the fact that I forgot it. It didn't feel right. There are a lot of things that don't feel right."

"How do you like your job?"

"It's good."

"Your wife?"

"She's good too."

"Your family?"

"Good," I said laughing a bit, trying to release the nervous tension within my body that was filling up from the interrogation. "Everything is just good, not anything beyond that."

"Life has its ups and downs."

"Things could be better," I added, "for me, at least. There is something eating away at me and I can't figure out what it is. It's like when Mike died," I couldn't believe I said that aloud, it still felt strange after five years, "he took away something in me." That sounded gay. That sounded too gay for a mid-western boy talking to a mid-western father. I had to continue, "That was the tipping point. Everything from that point on has been a slow decline and I don't think I realized that until really recently. The very idea of me forgetting my best friend's death date told me that things were headed down a dark road."

"Your generation, mine too, but it seems to be with the younger folks, seem to give up too easily. You're confused with the way it's supposed to go instead of seeing the way it is. Richer or poorer. Better or worse. Sound familiar?"

I nodded.

"Sometimes it doesn't work out, I'll give it that. But once it goes south we aren't inclined to wait for it to go back up." Jerry shifted in his seat and held his hand up like he was in front of a conference room about to make a point to a prospective client. "Marriage is like the stock market, it's like the Dow Jones Industrial average. Some years you make money, some years you don't. The overall lesson that no one learns is that when it's going down you don't sell, when you hit rock bottom, that's when you put all your money into it because," his hand started an elevator like ascension, "it goes up," he started to descend, "then it goes back down." He moved his hand back up and smiled, "then up." He lowered both hands to his side for a moment before raising one up to scratch his head and became silent.

"Thanks," I said sincerely.

"Things I was never able to tell my own son." He patted me on the shoulder. I felt the urge to apologize and did so. "You want to go see him?" He asked.

"Who? Mike?"

"Yeah." He lifted himself out of the chair. "We were going to go see a movie today, you're welcome to join us, but yeah, we should go see Mike too."

I sat uncomfortably, shifting my legs, re-crossing them and sitting up straighter, I was obligated to say yes and hesitantly did so.

I looked back at Mike's family. His mother. His father. His sister. Jerry nodded his head at me and I turned back to face Mike's grave. They were out of earshot in case I decided to speak to my friend aloud.

"Hey Mike. What's up? I'm married." I wasn't sure what to say to him. I kicked a little rock nearby. He wouldn't want me to give the synopsis of my life, would he? I looked to my sides and saw the row of graves, the nearest person speaking to their loved one was an old lady being held up by a cane and her son behind her was typing on his phone.

"So, the stories you hear around this place. Ever find it ironic how most people want to believe they go to heaven when they die but they will hang around a graveyard and talk to someone thinking they can hear them? Do they call you down like you're in jail? Tap on the bars and say you have a visitor and you fly down from above to listen to someone yammer on graveside about life. They think you're around too, only conveniently like closing a bedroom door as they ponder whether or not they should re-arrange the living room couch. If we were both dead we'd probably just go around and fart on people's pillows and then watch them sleep on them. It's funny; I actually think you're around too. I hope you can hear this.

"I'm married, dude. And no, I haven't Dutch ovened the little lady although some nights she's really asking for it." I laughed, my shoulder convulsing with each chuckle. "Oh shit, remember the time that you and I went to...crap, what was that guy's name? We went to a party at some frat house. The guy in my Lit class. That drunken slut was trying to hit on any guy with a Greek letter on the front of their sweater until she went to talk to a friend and forgot who she was trying to screw." I couldn't contain my laughter and started naming all the things we were saying we would do to her. "Fill her out like an application. Stuff her like a Thanksgiving turkey. Bang her like a drum in the San Francisco Philharmonic. Bend her like a river. Pound it like a baker's bread. Tap it like a keg."

I laughed a little more trying to contain the noise, biting my lip. I sensed his presence and pictured him nodding and rolling over on the grass unable to stand up because he was laughing so hard. I shook my head, sadness consumed me. I thought how different my life might have been. I probably would never have met Rose in the context that I did. The times were good with her but I'd give her up to hang out with Mike for another day. I started talking to him again.

"I really have to quit dwelling on the past. It's not like you and I are going drinking anytime soon. Your father assures me this sinking feeling will pass. I don't love her like I used to, I feel bad about that. I'm not divorcing her or anything, I mean, come on, that's the road everyone takes. Shit, you don't even know her and I'm talking bad about her. She's a pretty good actress; we go back and forth on lines whenever she has a play coming up. She's not one of those Hollywood whores we always saw in Santa

Monica, she works at an insurance company. Acting is a hobby. She's pretty. Nice set of boobs. You'd like her."

I turned around and saw a family who let their son's best friend from five years take his time talking. I looked back at Mike. I felt confident and more self-assured.

"You got a good family that really misses you. I miss you too, dude. Every time I let out some gas I do it in your honor. Like raising a glass at the bar."

I hugged Jerry and Lorraine and they told me I was welcome inside their home anytime I wanted. They appreciated me spending the day with them and wished me luck for when I faced the wife. A day full of ignoring phone calls was going to equal a night full of berating and screaming. I'm sure I deserved what I had coming to me. I was sad when I pulled away from the curb of my best friend's house and watched in my rearview mirror as they waved goodbye. I pulled out my cell phone not wanting to talk to Rose but sending her a message: On my way home. Please don't be mad until I have a chance to explain. I love you.

Two minutes later I got a response: Fine. I quivered as a chill ran down my spine from the icy tone of her response.

Before getting on the freeway I stopped at the gas station to buy a drink for the road. I scanned the fountain drinks and smiled to myself as I turned my head to the refrigerators. I paid for the quart of milk and within a few moments I was on the road eastbound. I lifted the carton toasting my spontaneous adventure.

"Here's to wishing you were sitting here next to me," I said to Mike wherever he was and drank the first sips of the two percent milk.

I had a heart to heart with a dead guy and felt that no matter the consequences that faced me beyond the front door the trip was worth it all. I left with a sense that I can begin the ascension from the valley and up the mountain to the next great thing. My petty issues with Rose were going to be brushed aside. I would ask for forgiveness and begin anew with the woman I married, with the woman I loved. My watch read 12:24. I had been awake now for twenty-two hours and drove over six-hundred miles; perhaps my body and mind didn't know how to react anymore and that brought on my sense of elation. Please just hug me, I thought.

I opened the front door. It was quiet and the lights were on. Rose was on the couch. She turned off the TV, stood up and tossed the remote control onto the cushion. I didn't have a chance to speak.

"I want a divorce." It was a sledgehammer to my chest, I didn't believe her. I wouldn't let it happen.

"What?"

"I. Want. A. Divorce."

"No."

"What do you mean no?" She shot back at me. "You left at three o'clock in the fucking morning. Didn't tell me why you left or where you were going. I was worried. I thought you probably went out to find some girl to mess around with behind me. Even if you didn't, what you did was pretty shitty."

"Can I explain? Please?"

"What's there to explain? You left while at your parent's house and didn't tell anyone where you were going. You've been distant for weeks now and progressively getting worse and you don't seem to care at all about anything I do."

"That's not true. You know that's not true. I go over lines with you. I..."

"You?"

"I...come on, Rose, you're just upset, I'm sorry."

"Sorry? You don't even know sorry. I was talking to Christy, I was talking to Jennifer, and I was talking to Hans. They all say the same thing. They all think this was just one big mistake. Deep down you and I needed someone so badly, we saw some friends get married, we settled for each other, and didn't think it through and you know what, Drew, the more I think about the more I think they're right. I had just gotten out of that relationship and you were looking for a companion. I'm not saying it was bad or anything, but maybe we should have just been a couple instead of a married couple."

"That's devastating, Rose. How could you think like that? Do you really think like that?"

Tears finally came to her eyes. Maybe she was tired too. Maybe my absence and lack of communication in the past day created the opposite effect of what I projected.

"I just think that if you and I were boyfriend and girlfriend we probably would have broken up a while ago. We were just so in love with the idea of marriage, with the idea of love, that we never stepped back to examine whether or not we truly were."

"Rose, I love you." I think I meant it. I could look in her eyes and see that this was the woman for me. She was the girl I could spend the rest...she wasn't. We stood feet apart and looked into each other's soul. Like a ton of bricks I was seeing what she was trying to relay. For the first time in our marriage I stared at my wife and realized that I never saw us in an old folk's home together holding hands.

"Rose," I continued, "I don't want to give up on this. Let's give each other another chance to fall back in love, to find that point where you and I were so clouded with affection for one another that all judgments were irrational and silly." I offered my plea and awaited her response. I refused to become another divorce statistic so easily.

She wiped her eyes and nodded her head. "Okay, Drew. Okay."

"Take two."

She chuckled and we closed the gap between us and hugged each other. As we both lay down on the bed we began kissing which grew in intensity. The passion for continuing was batted away by both of our exhaustion after the day's events and we ended up falling asleep in each other's arms and eventually through the twists and turns that occur in the nighttime our butts pointed at one another's.

* * *

Rose's play opened to a packed house the first night. All of the actor's family and friends showed up and cheered loudly at the show-ending bow. Angie and I waited on the outside of the actor's stage entrance for Rose to exit. My flowers were still in hand after sitting across my lap for two plus hours. With a numb ass and plastic wrapped flowers any shift in my seat became a show unto itself. When Rose appeared I handed her the flowers and gave her a kiss telling her she did a wonderful job. Angie hugged her. My family, her family, and some of her friends stood behind us all. Her sister congratulated her and her sister's boyfriend said the play was great; a total lie as I counted at least eleven times that he checked his watch on top of his lack of hesitancy to share his low opinion not one minute ago. His critique was shared by many as when the play ran in its entirety it lacked a definitive story, character development, and interest. We all kept our thoughts to ourselves and contemplated what we were going to have to say on Sunday when the local paper tore it to shreds.

"No, honey, it was good. This is just some critic who feels the need to destroy other people's work to compensate for his lack of talent and inability to write anything worth reading including this review." I had planned that out in the second act.

As was customary the cast went to a local friendly and group-oriented restaurant to brag about how great they all were as their loved ones sat in the shadows. My parents knew better and claimed age would keep them from attending and David had a wife and two kids to go see. I had no choice but to go and when I looked at Angie for comfort she shrugged her shoulders and told Rose she had to get into work very early the next morning, a shift she had planned out the second she heard the date of the play.

"I'll probably end up turning it into a screenplay and have those monsters in Holly-Weird take a look at it. I already have a producer interested," Hans boasted before the waitress had a chance to approach the table of twenty-four.

"Oh my God, I can totally see it as a movie," Holly,

the community college actress and bane of Rose's existence, confirmed. "I still get to reprise my role, right Hans?"

"Of course, my sweet. No girl could play the suicidal teenage runaway, the sheer image of the great Rose Devereux's character, like you," he winked at the actress and looked at Rose, "and my dearest Rose, I hear the west coast calling your name."

Rose smiled feigning embarrassment. She liked keeping her maiden name for her acting work, it sounded more actress-like she told me.

"Yours truly at the helm and Sir Thomas Hanks as the lead," he dramatically told the table who all gasped in excitement as if the ink was still wet on this fictitious contract. I leaned close to Rose.

"I didn't know he was knighted." Rose nudged her elbow playfully at me and shushed. "I didn't know he was now going by Thomas either."

Rose turned her gaze to me holding back a laughter that was surely mocking her director if she let it go. "Stop it," she said smiling through clenched teeth.

As the actors conversed I was reminiscent of my time in Los Angeles. Sitting in a restaurant or a coffee shop I overheard actors (waiters) on their cell phones talking to their agents about auditions loudly in case a casting director or producer was stopping by to dine. A group would sip their specialty coffee and all talk shop, discussing those who were making it in the "biz" and what work they were getting and their featured (extra) roles which allotted them mass amounts of screen time (five seconds behind the guy behind the day player) and big-name directors knocking down their doors for work.

I smiled at the excitement and occasionally diverted my eyes toward the TV screen a full room away to peek at the news. I ordered and ate silently doing my best not to stare at my watch. By the time Rose and I got home we were too tired for anything more than falling asleep, back-to-back, and comfortable.

8

Sweaty palms. Weak hands. Bear hugs. Hugs. Kisses. Smeared lipstick. Constant sighs of impatience.

"Congratulations. I've never seen you happier." I wasn't sure who he was or how he was related to me, if he was. His grin produced the sight of dark spots around the edge of his teeth and I pinned his age in the late-seventies range. "They don't make these places like they used to. Up and down, this way and that way. My missus and I went on a cruise for our honeymoon forty-six years ago and I spent half that time vomiting buffet food in the stateroom." He grins again and moves along towards the bar. My Mom approaches me.

"Mom, who the hell was that guy?"

"Oh, he's your father's cousin."

"Honestly, he creeps the shit out of me."

"I know," my Mom said patting me on the shoulder as if I was a five-year-old boy shying away from a birthday clown. "He creeps the shit out of everybody."

The cruise ship was my bride-to-be's idea. What better way to start our lives together than on the sea. Metaphorically speaking, it was a great unknown abyss filled with opportunities. We also got an incredible rate. Most guests stayed on the mainland until a few hours before the ceremony and would leave soon after the reception. We would pull out to see for a few hours and the guests would be shuttled back on small, covered boats. It was a nice idea although I preferred something more manageable on land.

I wave with excitement at Jerry and Lorraine. They both gave me a hug with big smiles, even though I had seen them the previous night. I hadn't visited Chicago since that one time but found myself in contact more with Mike's parents. Jerry was proud of me and saw in my eyes that a good lot of this happiness fell upon his shoulders and advice.

My second marriage, her first. I let her decide her dream wedding as if I really had any choice in the matter. I shake a few more guests' hands. I can't escape the onslaught of mostly unfamiliar faces who glance at me suspiciously at being so young and being on marriage numero dos. The other looks were from my side of the family who recalled changing my diaper when I was a baby, the same faces I hadn't seen since the first time I walked down the aisle.

That Monday was the day I pinpointed as the beginning of the end. Fate had set in motion a series of events that eventually caused the final downfall of our relationship. It began with a late-morning meeting with the advertising executive who had a meeting with the chief editor who decided to extend the sponsorship nationally. The magazine was slowly rising in readership and the monthly audience interested in everything Michigan from tourism to sports to hunting to general news increased. I joked with Lee that there must be more doctor's offices opening up. The twenty-percent increase in subscriptions was proof enough to start a nationwide tour of businesses looking to gain a niche in the mid-western marketplace.

"We are looking at sending you to a few small markets and a few big markets and we are in the process of setting up meetings with some major corporations. I need you and Lee to create proposals and sales pitches. We will most likely take this style magazine to Ohio by the beginning of next year and within two years we will extend to Indiana or Pennsylvania. Our goal is to make the Standard the leading monthly print news source state-to-state." The editor spoke excitedly, over-enthusiastically, and seriously.

"Like a regional version of Time." I stated with my yellow legal pad with a couple chicken scratches in front of me on the conference table. The editor leaned back with a smile on his lips and nodding his head.

"I like it, Drew. That's an appealing viewpoint."

"I'll write it down."

At my desk I started on my proposals and mixed it with researching companies that would consider advertising in our little circulation. I had working price plans and a few worthy companies that were scattered across the nation. Most would be phone calls, the others I would see face-to-face and get travel time. Lee came over to my desk with his arms crossed, upset.

"Hi Lee," I started.

"Listen, Drew. They threw down an interesting offer. I know the idea of this place going all national is appetizing but I need you to keep focused on the small picture, the reality. A twenty percent increase in subscriptions is barely much to brag about in the scheme of things. A waitress getting that tipping percentage on a cup of coffee doesn't add up on the bill. Our subscribers are doctors and dentists and since people are moving out of the state the amount of offices will be decreasing meaning subscription numbers are going to peak sooner most likely rather than later. They will have a meeting with accounting, fumble the numbers, and by Friday we will be back to cold calling gun ranges and sports stores in Midland." Lee was out of breath after his pessimistic mini-lecture.

"Come on, that's not an optimistic look at the picture."

"It's the realistic one. I just don't want you getting your hopes up of more money and buying a new car you can't afford. I made that mistake when I was your age and it ended up with debt and lots of pasta dinners".

"I will heed your warnings." The thought of overeating pasta caused my eyes to gaze at Lee's bulging, middle-aged stomach line.

Lee nodded and walked away. His argument for world peace would be that with no militaries the economy would tank. I decided to put his theory in the back of my head and continue working strongly towards being the one to grab that big corporation and, with it, a rising paycheck.

I wanted to relay the good news to Rose that night but I opened the apartment door to no one. I made dinner for two and waited another half hour until the meal was at the point of needing to be re-heated. Rose wasn't answering her cell phone. I was worried and hungry so I ate my portion, part of hers, and threw the rest into the refrigerator. At eight-thirty she entered, stumbling over her feet.

"Where were you?" I asked.

"Happy. Hour." She slurred back.

"You could've called. I would've met up with you. There's dinner in the fridge."

She nodded. "I ate. Half off appetizers. Mozzarella sticks. Mmm. Fried cheese."

"Healthy. I called you like four times, why didn't you answer?"

She shrugged her shoulders. "Didn't really feel like it."

"Oh. Are we in a fight that I'm unaware of?"

"No." She responded and I was confused.

"Did you drive home?"

"It wasn't that far."

"Rose, you're drunk. Not like a little drunk, full on drunk and you drove home?"

"Shh. You're shouting. It wasn't that far." Her heavy eyes drew upon my look of concern and disarray. "Everything is..." she gave me a thumbs up, "...grand."

I suspected something. Her actions dictated she was hiding

a major issue from me. She stood at the door for a few seconds and took in a deep breath. Her expulsion of two full lungs of air ended with a whimper of sadness or worry. She went into the bathroom and closed the door. I heard it lock and the bath water began to run. I listened carefully for signs or a definite cry for help. After a few minutes I went to the bathroom door and put my ear against it.

"Rose?"

A moment passed. "Yes?"

"Just making sure everything is okay."

"I told you. Everything is fine." It was commanding and harsh and I didn't know if it was directed exactly to me.

"Well, if you need anything..."

I didn't get any response and I went back to the couch and tried to wrap my consciousness around network programming. Canned laughter in half-hour doses or dramatic prose in one-hour time spans? One-hour, I decided. It kept me moderately entertained and around the second commercial of the ten o'clock cop show, a time slot that allows a little more controversy, the bathroom door opened and Rose came out in a towel. I heard her sift through the dresser drawer and within a minute the bedroom light went dark. I turned off the television and flipped the light switch down. By moonlight and familiarity I made my way across the living room and into the bedroom. I slowly approached the bed and crawled in wearing my clothes. I spoke to Rose in a low almost romantic tone and inquired about her problem. She remained silent but appreciated the gesture of concern. I told her all the usual, how she could speak to me about anything and I would listen. She stayed facing away from me and responded with only a plea for me to leave her alone. It wasn't malicious, merely letting me know that she wasn't ready to talk. I accepted her request and slept the night with my body facing hers in case she turned over and needed an arm around her or a body closer. No such demand was made and the morning started as they all did. I woke up forty-five minutes before she did. I had coffee made for both of us when she woke up. This morning she thanked me for it and we kissed goodbye. I could tell she had a slight hangover and was still not prepared to talk.

Within two weeks Lee and I completed our sales pitches and performed for the suits above. They jotted notes and gave us a report. We began revising. The previous weekend Rose came home from her performance upset and went to the freezer to dig out a bottle of vodka and combined it with tonic. She had been quiet and upset and still wouldn't provide me a hint on the problem.

A week later the bosses liked our revised pitch and requested a list of potential clients to get to advertise; a week after that our business trips would be planned. I would head off to the southwest for six days while Lee would handle twice the time in New York, Chicago, Philadelphia and a hot spot in Tennessee.

It was a Friday and I not only had two days to rest and relax I was now able to relay my good news to Rose. She wasn't home and I refused to let my news sit in the pit of my stomach. I went to the playhouse to watch her performance and afterwards share a drink and the excitement. The parking lot was empty and dark as I pulled in. Showtime was minutes away; a light mist filled the air. My flowers sat still in the passenger seat. I parked at the curb and walked to the door, the car remained on. I pulled on the handle. Locked. I peeked in. Dark. I turned around expecting an answer to stand there in the form of a prophet but received only the sound of traffic on the main road and my idly parked car.

When I called Rose I was confronted with her voice mail, the upbeat words telling her missed callers to leave a brief message at the beep. I asked where she was and told her my current location. I dropped the phone next to the grocery store bouquet of flowers I bought her and placed my hands on the steering wheel as if I was looking for an address or was pulled over by a suspicious cop. Through the windshield I prayed for an answer and ultimately decided to head home. I called David and sensing my worry assured me that Rose had not called and I would be the first to know if she did.

"The playhouse is dark," I told him.

After some consideration, David replied. "I think you have the beginnings of the problem in front of you. I say you head to two places. The bar near your apartment where she has spent so many a happy hour the last couple weeks and if she's not there, go home and wait."

I waited in silence for a moment with my mind twisting between states of denial and lunacy. I decided to ask David a question he wouldn't know the answer to and any response would merit my concern further. "Is she cheating on me?"

"I don't know," David said low and serious.

"You're supposed to say 'of course not'. What kind of brother are you?" My attempt to add a small semblance of comic relief rolled off both our shoulders with no effect.

"Drew. I don't know."

We hung up and his refusal for a definite answer ate at me. If David had posed the question regarding Nicole I would have shot back with the 'of course not' I desired in my present situation. I instead had confirmation that the possibility of infidelity was looming on my shaky marriage.

A giant five, a giant zero and giant percentage mark hung in my mind floating like a maestro's wand. If my brother was in the happy marriage statistically I wasn't. Based on the numbers one of us would end up in a divorce and as more moments flashed by as I sat in my car I was realizing that I was the more likely candidate.

I went to the bar looking over heads and walked by mingling couples and singles. Rose was not present. When I pulled into my parking spot I saw the empty one next to mine and knew Rose was still not around. I called her again and requested a call back as soon as possible even asking for a text message, some sign that she was okay. My last resort was Angie.

"Angie, is Rose with you?"

"No she isn't Drew. She's acting tonight, remember?" I responded with what I had seen at the playhouse.

"Don't be so dramatic, Drew, it's not your style."

"Angie, she's been coming home drunk almost every night."

"Is she becoming an alcoholic?"

"Well, no." Wait, was she? "Well, I don't think so. Why wouldn't she tell me her play got cancelled?"

"Who says it was? For all you know there was some mishap at the playhouse, they went dark for the night, and they all went out to party the night away."

"Bullshit."

"I know."

"So?"

"So, what?"

I pleaded. "Come on, help me out here."

"Okay, here's what I think. Her play is cancelled and she didn't want people to know. I don't know why she's drinking every night but the cancelled play might be a big first clue."

"It's not every night!"

"Four out of seven?" Angie asked to get a rough estimate.

"Five."

"I haven't talked to her in over a week. Tell her to call me and maybe I can get back to you with some information."

"Angie, this isn't good. We're husband and wife; she should be sharing stuff with me."

"Unless it's about you." Angie said and the quick lack of further speaking was scary. She had wished she didn't say what she just said. My heart beat faster and my selfish cares increased ever higher. "I'm sorry," she continued but I stopped her.

"You're right."

"I'm not, I was kidding. A mere facetious statement to lighten your dark mood." I didn't respond and her cover-up failed. "I'm at the bookstore. Let's talk about this."

I left a note for Rose begging her to call me the moment she stepped through the door and I drove through the now light rain towards my former house of employment.

"I would tell you if I knew anything," Angie swore to me. We sat in the back office, a place I was familiar with whether it was asking for time off, more work time, or the general chatting with Tricia.

"Is she cheating on me?" I needed the definitive answer but I only got the raising of shoulders of indifference. "I just wish I knew more."

"Why? Isn't ignorance bliss?" She quoted. Angie was the second person in under an hour to silently add merit to my fears.

"There's a difference between being ignorant and then knowing that you're ignorant. Choice A equals bliss. I'm on this ying-yang of life right now. I just wish I knew."

"Is that all?" Angie asked and I expressed clarification. "Let me ask you this. Do you even care?"

"Of course."

Angie raised an eyebrow and I dug deeper into my soul for the correct answer, the one she didn't want to hear, the one I needed to realize.

"I care about her," I started, "I love her and she's my wife. I don't want her to be cheating on me and if she was..."

"That's the question. Did I ever tell you the time I cheated on my boyfriend?"

"Which one?"

"There haven't been that many and only one I cheated on. Joseph. He was smothering me, I couldn't breathe and I was creating ways to avoid him. That's why I initially got promoted was because of him. I increased my hours and refused to leave, corporate saw it as initiative and gave me a promotion. I wasn't happy but I didn't want to break his heart. I couldn't find an escape and I ultimately ended up cheating on him, uch, with some sleazy guy too." Her vision from the past caused goose-bumps to form on her arms and a shiver to shoot through her body. "I felt like complete shit for the longest time to the point where I started to cry as we were having sex, me and Joseph. Eventually I had to end for the sake of his self-esteem, how would you feel if the woman you were with was suffering emotional problems every time you thrust your manhood into her womanly parts? He never knew I cheated on him and I never wanted to tell him."

"So, Rose wants out."

"I'm not saying that," Angie hesitated a minute, "but I'm not not saying that either."

"Maybe I should call Hans."

"The director, producer, writer, thespian, center of the world? What would that do?"

"Maybe she talks to him. They're close."

"And they've been close," Angie spouted out and I shot her an icy look.

"There is such a thing as not saying everything you're thinking."

"Yes and I use that frequently. I'm blunt, but I also have a conscious."

"Okay, miss blunt, straight up, what should I do?" I braced myself for the worst critique and the most horrible suggestion. I used the pause in the room to think of all options she would say minus first degree murder.

"You're riding a dead horse." She hesitated and tilted her head and rephrased her words, "you're riding a horse with two broken legs, a busted kidney, that's been beaten and bruised...and has hepatitis. If horses can get hepatitis. Point being you're not at the glue factory but that seems like the only option."

"Your optimism towards the romantic is uncanny." I responded sarcastically.

"If you want romance go to fiction. I'm giving you current events."

"Wouldn't I go to the romance section?"

"Don't be a smart ass, I have that right in this conversation, not you."

"Shit," I slumped my shoulders, "I wanted this to work. It could've worked."

"Eh, what the hell do I know anyway?"

"Oh don't pull that with me." I had elevated quickly from acceptance to anger.

"Hey, you wanted honesty. I can go a little deeper and say you two should have never been married; you both were in love with the idea. You two should have been that couple that stayed together for four or five years and instead of getting married two years ago, broken up six months ago."

"Funny how everyone excludes this from conversations prior to the nuptials," I sighed, frustrated, "Christ, Angie are you planting this shit in Rose's head or vice versa? She said the same thing after my Chicago trip and I tried convincing her otherwise."

"It's not our place to say these things."

"Yes it is. You're my friend. You're her friend."

"And you two would've disowned me for saying such. Come on, Drew. You're smart; you know exactly how you would have reacted; how anyone would've reacted."

"I don't want to give this up."

"No one ever does," Angie started leaning in close to me, lowering her voice as a psychologist would before expelling breakthrough advice. "If you want to try to work through it then work through it but do it because you think you should and not because you feel the need to prove something to yourself. Don't kill yourself or Rose because you want to convince Drew that this was the right decision when it wasn't. There is a time when you just need to accept it."

"None of this would have ever happened if you didn't introduce us," I told Angie hoping that my partial blame would roll off her, "I personally place all responsibility on you."

She leaned back and threw her hands in the air. "What can

I say, I'm no matchmaker. Both of you just needed to get laid, I didn't think it was going to go much further than that."

I wanted to prove to myself that this was the right decision; that our vows, rings, and wedding photos weren't all in vain. I was slowly pondering that I would rather be miserable than wrong.

I found a lone rock sitting on the ground when I exited the bookstore. I kicked it a few feet ahead of me and walked leisurely up to it again and kicked it into the street. I continued until my aim was off and the rock skipped to the right further than I was willing to go to retrieve it. I looked up at Mitchell's and a flash of Chelsea popped into my head. I remembered her donning her serving uniform walking through an open door while I was resting my elbows behind the register at work. I replaced the conversation we had with one that never took place and never will. She asked about my life and I summarized it using her image as my own mental therapist. I opened up to her and told her I didn't want a divorce because it was too trendy and expected. I didn't want to leave Rose but Angie was right that we should have broken up already. I can't remember the last time I saw her as the woman of my dreams and, as Chelsea leaned against the counter in my mind and I was a couple years younger, I told her that it was only a phase and she disappeared. I was home without any clear recollection of driving there. Rose's car was still absent and the apartment windows were dark.

We held out a little longer. It was our Hail Mary pass in the last quarter. Both of us hoped that we would look into each other's eyes and find something in them that made us smile again. We acted like roommates. I confided in my father one night over a cup of coffee at home. Nicole, David and my mother wanted to go out and see a movie, eat some dinner at a restaurant where the meal was served by someone in a uniform, and talk. My Dad was a little under the weather. He noticed my problem and heard the continuing saga of distance forming between myself and my bride. I inquired if he and my mother were ever like this.

"Sure we were. But we always saw that we loved each other. Even the worst bad time, and it was bad, we just knew."

"How does it work for so many people who are older?" I asked like a boy begging his Dad to tell him how the drill on the wall in a garage works.

"I don't know. I'm sure there are lots of schools of thought on it but I never put much into it. It's a little more expected these days, which is sad, maybe a grander sense of individualism. But it does let a lot of people go back on their mistakes."

"Dad. Rose and I might..." I didn't want to place the word divorce in front of my own father. It would have been a shameful thing to say.

"Hmm," he sniffled his cold further into his nose and drank another sip of his Earl Grey tea. He didn't respond which I estimated was neither a negative nor a positive sign. He thought hard about his reaction avoiding eye contact and staring down the last bit of liquid in his UCLA mug. Before he had a chance to respond I fired a question.

"Dad, did you ever doubt we were wrong for one another? That this was all a blunder from the start?"

"No. I never thought that," his words forced back at me quickly, "not once, not ever." I believed him.

"Angie said this was something that never should have materialized."

"Drew, I know you're good friends with her and that you value her opinions but often times people portray their wishes over fact. They get clouded in their own reality and impress those desires on others. Maybe she never saw you two together forever because she never wanted to see you two together forever. I also am projecting. I saw you two in love and always in love because as a father, that's what I want to see. Anyone can guide you but ultimately it's you that makes the decision."

My father stood up and put some more boiling water from

the teapot into his mug. I followed him around, twisting my body towards his direction.

"Nobody really knows what's right and wrong except you. Unless I'm more right. Always listen to your father...and your mother. You can gather all the advice in the world but deep down the decision is only up to one person." He motioned the mug at me and nodded his head slightly. "That's you."

"Can you tell me if I loved my wife, Dad?" My father looked at me and shook his head. He was unable to provide an answer to the most important question I ever asked him.

"I'm sorry, Drew," he said, heartbroken for letting down his youngest son. "I just don't know."

"Are you drinking so much because of the play?" I asked Rose in part concern and in hopes that after these few weeks I could finally get an answer. I wanted her to confide in her husband.

"What?" She responded. Her faded thoughts were continually corrupted by alcohol and it took her a moment for the question to resonate.

"Ever since then you've become a different person. You're not you and..." I shook my head looking at her profile as she refused to turn her head. I could see the tears forming in her eyes, seeping out slowly and falling down her cheek. She wiped the residue with the side of her hand.

We made eye contact, true eye contact, with our thoughts and feelings ready to test one another's souls.

"We did okay the first weekend. The second weekend was a catastrophe. We only sold thirty tickets on four shows. We usually do ten times that, minimum. At least one near show at capacity. Hans was depressed and he took it out on me."

I moved in closer and put my arm around her, she leaned in close. I remained silent.

"He told me my acting wasn't up to caliber and he was putting serious thought into dropping me from future shows.

Not just for this one, but never using me again. He was using it as leverage."

"Leverage. What do you mean?"

"He wanted to sleep with me again. He poured me a glass and we shared a drink." My heart beat quickly and my breathing became heavy through clenched teeth. I was sure she could feel it through my chest. She continued. "I didn't. I couldn't. But I almost did. He wanted a reason to keep me around and if I wasn't up to par acting-wise then he said there were other useful performances I could give. He said that, verbatim. I was nervous, so I backed up and started unbuttoning my shirt. I took it off."

It took all my power to not jump off the couch and leave. Leave her everything and walk away forever. I held my composure.

"I stood there and he smiled at me. It was evil. It was just like a movie where the villain is perched half in dark with a malicious smile because he was going to get what he wanted. I picked up my shirt and told him no. He stood up and approached me, came real close to my face and told me that I will never be seen on this stage ever again unless I gained some sense of how the real world worked and told me to leave."

She lifted off of me and looked me dead in the eyes.

"I did not cheat on you." Her lips quivered. She wasn't done telling me all that I needed to hear. "But, Drew, I didn't cheat on you for the purposes of fidelity. I didn't cheat on you because I didn't want to sleep with him."

I leaned back, the wind nearly knocked out of me. I had listened carefully and we discussed further. The urge was there but it was the wrong person. She didn't see us as right for one another and I was overtaken by a flurry of emotions, mostly confusion. Confusion brought on by me not caring so much that she had the urge to cheat on me. Tears were streaming down her face. I'm sure my own were splashing down from my eyes. All we did was look at each other and we couldn't place the signal that had long since been evacuated from each other's eyes. We had once existed but faded away slowly and gradually, creeping away steadily like the fog as the sun warmed the morning sky. One day a long, long time ago we said "I do" and meant those words. Time took its toll, however, and stole our passion for one another until one morning, years later, we woke up next to the stranger we knew everything about but had lost all emotional connection with; the only thing that had kept us together.

"So, this is it then?"

There was a difference between love and being in love. We both cared deeply for one another and once we separated and once we filed the papers and once her maiden name became her last name again we would still keep in touch and wonder where each other's lives took us. There was no malice, there was no hate. We accepted the fate that had been set upon our plates and engrossed our lives.

Rose was an actress at heart, a passionate hobby that graciously manipulated her life, and her heart was taken away. With it came an unintended self-evaluation at a time I was searching for my own meaning. Once upon a time we were lovers but that was once upon a time.

I asked if she wanted another drink and she declined. That night we slept in the same bed our giant elephant now absent, the weight lifted from our shoulders, whether it was out of routine or comfort or our subconscious way to prove that there were no hard feelings. On the last night we ever shared the same mattress we faced one another and the last thing we saw before we closed our eyes was each other's face.

I threw my bag on the floor and put my hands on my hips. This time it will be very temporary. Surrounding me, as if I had never left, was my TV, my table and my couch in the dark cool basement of my parent's house. Theodore stomped down the stairs screaming my name in childlike excitement and I thought that I needed to go apartment hunting as soon as humanly possible.

9

I check my watch for the fifteenth time in as many minutes. It was under an hour; under a half an hour actually. I had hid from the guests. My brother and I are in a side room designated for the groom and his party. In my case, it was my brother and my cousin Kevin. The other groomsmen, who consisted of my bride-to-be's cousin, was somewhere not here. I met him for the first time only last night at the rehearsal dinner and we spoke very little to one another.

"Why does everyone insist on interviewing me? I don't know how to get you out of a traffic ticket for Christ's sake," Kevin said annoyed and partially inebriated. David and I didn't answer. "If you're under the age of sixteen you want to see my badge and gun. Why would I bring a gun to a wedding? If you're between sixteen and twenty-five, you see me as some authority figure who hassles you because of how you look and think I'm going to bust you for possession of an illegal narcotic. Again, I'm not interested in arresting anybody at a wedding, and ya shouldn't be smoking up when you're going to be near a cop. Everyone over that age pesters you about bullshit. About shitty laws in states I have no jurisdiction in." Kevin sighs loudly, pulls a flask from his inside coat jacket, spins the top open and takes a swig. "That broad I'm walking down the aisle, is she do-able?"

"I think she might be. I don't know. She's 'the friend'." I respond not caring for my cousin's problems, I have my own concerns. As always, I'm constantly wiping my palms onto my pants to dry them;

my nerves have popped open whatever sweat glands lie in the entire body. I check the thermostat and the claimed sixty-two degrees didn't seem cold enough. I go over to the window and see a steady rainfall hit the deck and the water. The late-afternoon clouds darkened the skies.

The time is one minute past the last time I checked.

"Those minutes add up," David says. "You'll check your watch here, and then at the head of the aisle, and then you'll want to as you're waiting for your broad to come down. All that time."

"I should take a piss then," Kevin says standing up and heading into the bathroom. "Hey, this is classy," he screams from the other side of the door.

I pace silently, uncomfortably. I look at myself in the mirror as I feel the beads of perspiration form at the hairline of my forehead. I don't see any water markings above my brow.

David stands up and walks towards the thermostat.

"It's colder than a witch's tit in January," he flips the temperature up a few degrees.

"Are you kidding me? I'm sweating like a whore in a Phoenix church." I change the temperature my brother messed up. I remember stepping off the plane in Phoenix, the heat that punched you like a chair to the face in a bar fight.

Phoenix. It was hot. Ninety-five in the middle of October. We landed five minutes ahead of schedule. I love the feeling of exiting an airplane. The sounds of travelers and the looks on a handful of people staring at the door as you smell the fresh air for the first time in hours. They glanced up with their headphones on or pausing mid-sentence out of the same curiosity that one senses when they see two people meet up in the middle of the restaurant. I increased my pace and headed straight for baggage claim. I re-adjusted the bag that was slung over my shoulder and entered the land of giant conveyor belts connected to metal slides and an opening that would spew out your suitcase in a manner that respected very little of the precious contents inside. After seven minutes of waiting and watching my fellow plane-folk cross their arms and complain of the wait the belt moved and our belongings were revealed. No one collected the first bag as no one ever does, mine was tenth down and I fought the crowd that gathered shoulder to shoulder in tight formation to reach it. I was at a hotel downtown so without a rental car, and only the instructions to take a shuttle to a nearby hotel, I stepped out into the dry Arizona heat and waited for the small bus to roll up.

I embraced my on-time arrival and thanked whoever it was that allowed me to have most of an afternoon and an entire night to myself. I unpacked everything required for the following day's three meetings in office towers that surrounded my hotel and headed down to walk the streets of downtown Phoenix.

I roamed for an hour gathering the atmosphere and opted to check out a movie. Alone, I stood in the middle of the lobby, my eyes glued at films I hardly heard of, the box office cashier waiting impatiently for me to decide so he could go back to his homework. I surveyed the open area around me and figured if I was only holding up one guy, and his job was to cater to my needs, then I won't let his frown and stare bother me.

I was one of four people in the theater. It was an autumn thriller based on a book I vaguely remembered selling a couple years ago at the bookstore. Generic in theme, heavy on story, and weak on character development and acting, I first looked at my watch forty minutes in. The ending was eventful; a fantastic chase scene through downtown Vancouver doubling as downtown Boston. I've never been to Boston and personally didn't think it played the part too strongly.

The sun was just setting and my eyes didn't need to adjust to a bright glowing ball in the sky. I walked back to the hotel and decided for a drink at the bar. Myself and two other businessmen, who remained at a table and talked about their co-workers behind their backs, were the only patrons. I could play the role of the out-of-town businessman nursing a drink and seeking out idle conversation about our respective lines of work and family members waiting back home. I decided against it and was in my room by seven catching up on syndicated television, by nine I was restless. With the air conditioning blasting, I lied in my bed, my arms resting behind my head. I closed my eyes and spent the next ninety minutes trying to fall asleep.

The next day I held one blow off meeting that my bosses thought I should try because I had an open time slot, and two heavy considerations in advertising in the magazine. My prized and most likely catch was the Phoenix Tourism Board.

"Michiganders love golfing and in the wintertime they love getting the hell out of the state. Florida isn't holding its sway and people find the southwest intriguing," I told them. I used a similar argument on my other likely candidate, a real estate development firm with seventy-five homes being built in Chandler with half of them one-story. Again I exploited the elderly, informed them that doctor's offices loved our magazine and asked them who visits doctor's more than retired senior citizens who flee cold weather.

The Phoenix-based airline company lacked enthusiasm. They were the third and final meeting; the blow-off meeting.

I landed in Los Angeles the next day. It was my first time back in nearly four and a half years. I had a rental car waiting and a knowledge of the city and a memory of a few places that required an I.D. bragging of twenty-one years or older for entry. I had two days of business and muscled the office into letting me stay the weekend before flying to Texas for my final day of meetings on Monday and Tuesday.

They shacked me up in the center of the San Fernando Valley, an area I was not too familiar with but knew I was a stone's throw over the hill from my old school and only a few miles from Hollywood and the bar scene on Sunset. I had used the eighty-five minute flight in to plan my weekend. It was going to be part nostalgia and part complete-tourist.

I stepped outside of LAX to await my ride and hesitated taking in a deep breath of the smoggy, dirty air accumulated under the enclosed terminals. Buses and taxis burped their pollution onto the innocent bystanders. Two young blondes who stood with their parents double took when they thought they saw a star of a network reality program cross the street to the center parking garage.

I spent a long time in traffic with a smile on my face before I reached my hotel. The window was rolled down and I grinned at every recognizable street sign. Horns honked and people were cut off. Others sped and used the shoulder to get one car length further ahead as they merged. I missed this dump. I saw the UCLA exit and my stomach knotted up. A flood of faces and experiences splashed around my head. Mike and Abigail. Dave and Denise. I recalled the infamous Dutch Oven and laughed remembering Mike and my last visit to Chicago. I promised myself I would go back to visit more often. Had it really been as long as it has been? It was yesterday and four years ago at the same time.

Claire. I gripped the steering wheel and leaned back. I hadn't thought of Claire in quite some time now. Her face and her smile. I could smell the scent of her lotion and remembered the time her head rested on my chest that morning we woke up in Windsor, Canada. I looked upwards at the Getty Center and remembered an afternoon we shared observing the artwork on the inside and the gardens and view of the world on the outside. I touched my pocket and incurred the phenomenon known as phantom ring tone. I considered calling her but I didn't remember her number and it hadn't been stored in a cell phone of mine in years. She was probably married. She probably had kids. Who knew if she even lived in Los Angeles. California. The United States. She was on my mind until I reached my exit and had to occupy myself with directions and impossible left turns.

It was annoying having her walk around my head again but I found myself seriously missing her. My stomach tightened up and my heart twisted in remembered loss. I unpacked in my hotel room, without a view, on the third floor of a ten-story hotel at the bottom of the hill. I looked at the street and saw stationary vehicles and lots of drivers on their cell phone. I was hungry and thirsty. My stomach growled and my body begged for nourishment. As the elevators door opened to the lobby I grew nervous that I was going to see Claire which was ridiculous in theory. She wouldn't notice me if I were standing right in front of her but I cautiously left the hotel and walked down the street to a nearby outdoor mall to spend my per diem on a moderately priced dinner.

My first meeting the next morning was a personal disaster. The man I was selling to did not care and thought of my presence as a nuisance. He used our time to tell me more of his clientele and magazines he advertised in claiming there wasn't money for a small time Michigan based forty-pager. He mentioned having dinner in West Hollywood the previous night with his girlfriend, an aspiring actress, and Danny Glover. I translated it to mean that he went to dinner last night with his girlfriend and saw Danny Glover, probably from the complete opposite side of the restaurant and tried to spy on what he was eating. He saw me as some kid who couldn't sell his way out of a wet paper bag. He was condescending. I thanked him and left.

The next one was a little tamer and relaxed. When I arrived, the woman I was meeting with was yelling into her headset to her child saying that she was busy and to call her father to pick her up. She switched from Mom mode to business mode and professionally greeted me. Although she denied my proposals she originated from Ohio and was interested in meeting another Mid-Westerner. I mentioned our possible ventures into the Ohio region and her eyebrow raised; she welcomed me to call upon her if that started up.

* * *

241

Once again, I had merged onto the freeway at the beginning of rush hour and was doomed to live over an hour of my time never exceeding fifteen miles per hour. I used this time to check in with my boss who took the news of the two meetings lightly. With a heavy sigh he placed hope on the possibilities of tomorrow. When I entered my hotel room I added up the time difference between where I was and where my family was. I called my brother.

"Hey, how's Cali?" David asked. "A giant blast from the past?"

"Sort of. It's good. I'm thinking of contacting Claire." I threw it out not meaning to or expecting it to land anywhere.

"Yeah? She some chick from college?"

"David, she was the one who flew in Michigan when Mike died and spent like three weeks there."

"Oh yeah. Nice ass. You should call her," the speaker rubbed against his shirt and his voice was directed elsewhere. "Oh honey, you know your ass is the only the ass for me." He lifted the phone back up. "Sorry."

"What the hell am I going to say? Hi remember when I dumped you years ago and moved away because I was a freakin' wreck? Well, I'm back and want to give it the old twirl in the sack."

"That could work. Unless she's married, but that's Los Angeles, so there's probably still a good chance that would work. Call her and just tell her you're in town and wanted to catch up. If she's married or fat you just say you wanted to rekindle the memories of yesteryear and if she's single, well, ravish it like a pack of wild coyotes."

"Thanks. I don't know."

"Be a wussy little girl, that's good too."

"Come on, David. Help me out here."

"Fine. The world doesn't revolve around you, okay, there's still the ten day forecast. Quit acting like your life is a big amendment to the constitution and try it. Worst case? Ya hook up and get syphilis. Or you wake up in a bathtub full of ice minus a kidney, but that only happens on TV and in Asian countries. You know what I always say, better a kidney than your soul." My brother refused to cater to my fear and within minutes I was no further ahead on the advice I wanted and hung up.

I lifted the white pages onto the bed and thumbed through for Claire's name. I recognized her father's first name and the address was familiar but no Claire. I swallowed hard and slammed the book shut shoving it under the night stand, my search hit a roadblock. I opted for blind luck and decided to visit my old stomping ground. I pulled out of the hotel parking lot and headed south for UCLA and Westwood Village in hopes that she would still like reading at the coffee shop we always frequented.

I loved the view near the Powell Library Building overlooking the stadium with the Santa Monica Mountains in the background. The fog was beginning to roll in and the enormous white lights bounced off of the low clouds softly. I strolled back down the hill and noticed all the current students. I felt so much older in the more realistic world that post-collegiate life offered. School pride burst off of everyone's clothes, a light blue sweatshirt with a bruin in the middle, dark blue with yellow lettering; even light gray and black letters boasting where your priorities during football season lay.

I grabbed an ice cream sandwich at my favorite cookie shop and sat down at the old Starbucks. Nothing changed except the co-eds that studied there. No Claire to be found, I waited for a half hour before giving up. I remembered where her father's office was located and toyed with the idea of "pretending" to be lost and "accidentally" going in for directions in the unrealistic hopes of not being recognized. Her image and possibilities clouded my foolish, post-separation mind.

* * *

The next morning I woke up thirty minutes early to spend the extra time priming and making myself look the best I could in my lifetime. I spent only an extra five minutes on grooming and watched the news for the remaining twenty-five minutes sitting at the corner of my bed. I floated through my morning meeting and rushed excitedly into Westwood. I tightened my tie and checked my hair in the rearview mirror. I tried to pump myself up hoping the added adrenaline would create a flattering, self-confidence effect rather than presenting a stuttering stalker. In the lobby I noticed her surname on the display board and, with a deep breath, smiled. I pressed the up button on the elevator as my palms began to sweat wondering what I would say if she so happened to be stepping out of the elevator. Every step closer increased the chances of our meeting prior to my desired time. I reviewed conversation after conversation in my head trying to cover as many bases as possible for as many reactions imaginable. I tapped the up button one more time expecting the elevator doors to open sooner; the computerized operator recognizing that someone had to be somewhere in a hurry. The light above the elevator flashed and dinged and the doors opened seconds afterward. It was empty and I recognized the odor upon entering of that of any doctor's waiting room. I climbed higher and higher, my destination and destiny mere moments away. My palms felt more perspired than normal and I dreaded a handshake. I considered finding a doctor in the building capable of ridding palm sweat as it was constantly bothering me in stressful and unnerving situations. When the doors opened I descended down the hallway to the office and stood outside rubbing my hand from the top of my tie down, extracting any creases.

My hand crept slowly to the handle and my world stood still. I felt my fingertips touch the metallic handle and dreamt of Claire sitting behind the desk. The door opened inward widely and I stepped in. I looked to the receptionist's desk and saw a young lady, brunette, her head resting on her left hand, her right hand motioning a computer mouse. Click. She lifted her head and I twisted my head away to a lingering patient with a magazine in his lap who raised his head as well.

"Sorry, I think I'm in the wrong office." I told the unfamiliar face and slowly stepped backwards to the door wondering if I waited a few more seconds if Claire would pop her head from around a corner. I smiled shyly and left.

"Shit." I said aloud disappointedly in the hallway. My search ended. I expelled all the resources I knew. The option was available to ask for her father but his reaction was too much of an uncontrolled factor for me to risk. I was too negative. I pictured him smiling mischievously as he told me to hold on one moment as he dug out his daughter's phone number only to return with a loaded sawed-off shotgun. "I've been waiting for this moment, sonny," he would bark as I shit my pants and begged for my life. Instead I let the soles of my shoes drag along the light green carpeted hallway. There was nothing more to do but go back to my hotel room and garner up a plan for the following days in Los Angeles alone. I unfortunately no longer thought about reminiscing in the city that directly followed high school graduation and my first adventure as an adult. I sat in traffic heading north and was inclined to find a new adventure in a new city. I didn't even want to go home, not back to Michigan. Not the basement I had put up temporary quarters in. Awaiting me were family and an apartment search, paperwork and an explanation of the good and poor meetings I intended. Collaboration and life.

Sunday afternoon I drove my rental car south to the Los Angeles International Airport and jumped on the shuttle to my terminal. I arrived early. Three hours early partially due to the little amount of traffic and partially due to my enthusiasm for leaving. Coming here had left me feeling the same voids that are visible upon leaving home and returning months later to find that life moved on without you. Buildings were razed and raised. Familiar faces left their usual spots in search of new places to frequent in places far away. I breezed through security, the final portal of near guaranteed departure from your destination. An airport terminal is the median between where you are going and where you came from. Its purgatory and I wanted the happiness of leaving my previous life behind.

With plenty of time before my flight, I sat at the bar and ordered a burger and a double-shot rum and Coke. I sipped my beverage slowly on my empty stomach awaiting my order along with the fries I was craving more than the sandwich. My eyes fixed on one of the three televisions conveniently within visual range. I had World Series Playoffs on one screen, a soccer game on another, and news on the third. I soaked in the sports bar atmosphere vibe and watched Game Four from the fifth inning to the end. The Yankees clinched the playoff spot once again against the Angels and would face the Mets in a much anticipated subway series similar to years before. I imagined Lee across the country wandering a city at riot's edge over the victory. I lamented the fact that every meeting would begin with baseball and could very well be determined upon my co-worker's opinion.

When my plate was empty and my drink was down to melted ice cubes sticking to one another I looked around the bar; my attention falling to an older lady. I figured she was in her early fifties, vacationing perhaps but definitely not on business. There was a familiarity about her that I embraced and when she looked up from her airport bookstore novel I smiled and said hello. She placed a bookmark between the pages and closed the book.

"Where ya headed?" I asked. It could have been the affects of the strong drink I just polished off but I was not in a mood to sit on a bar stool and watch the highlight show of the game I just watched.

"Kansas City. Yourself?" She was friendly and warm.

"Dallas."

"Business?" She asked and I nodded. The bartender pointed

to my empty glass and inquired if I wanted a refill. I responded favorably but opted for the single shot.

"Are you from Kansas City?"

"Yes. I was visiting Los Angeles. It's nice out here. Can't beat the weather."

"I used to live here. I went to school for a little over a year. I'm originally from Michigan."

"And you're wheeling and dealing on the west coast?" She was amused by the responsibility I projected considering my age.

"Yes I am. Peddling my goods." I chuckled and hoped that the reference I intended did not shadow a sexual innuendo.

"Why did you only stay out here for a year? Are you really smart and finished school in a year?"

"No, nothing like that. It's complicated."

"Yeah?" She shifted out of her seat and moved closer to me. She checked out her watch and her boarding pass. "My flight is delayed for another forty-five minutes so tell me."

"Um," I started. I was being pressured by a lady twice my age to reveal the biggest secrets and mistakes in my life. "Well, what do you want to know?"

"Why did you move out here?"

"School."

"That's it?" I lifted my arms and shrugged my shoulders. "Didn't like it?"

"It was fine."

"Girl troubles?"

I smiled and shook my head. "No. In fact I had a pretty good deal. I had a great girl."

"Handsome man like you I would expect so. So?"

"My best friend died the summer between freshman and sophomore year." She lifted her hand to her mouth attempting to catch the air she gasped out of her lungs. She apologized.

I looked away from her and down at the drink the bartender tossed down on a new cocktail napkin. "I had a really hard time coming back, we had an apartment which I couldn't afford and couldn't find a roommate. I didn't want to find another roommate. I didn't want to replace him, ya know. It would've been weird having someone split the rent and I couldn't find another place." I lifted my drink and carefully placed it to my lips sipping the top of the glass trying not to spill. It was strong, the bartender was kind. "This girl was really supportive."

"What was her name?"

"Claire."

"Pretty."

I nodded; it wasn't just her name that was. "Anyway, I was having a hard time adjusting," I waved my hands as drunken visual gesture. "So, I left."

"Did she come with you?"

I shook my head.

"Why not? Did you ask her?"

I thought about the question posed and asked myself why I didn't ask, but the idea felt ridiculous. "No."

"Well, why not?"

"We were only going out for like six months and almost four of those we were apart. It would've been weird."

"You were leaving anyway; did you not want her to come with you?"

I shrugged my shoulders. "I guess I would have but that's all hindsight. It was three or four years ago and the situation always looks different from the future. Hindsight. It's a bitch."

"Was she tied down here? Would she have come with you?"

I spent a mental hour which is often immeasurable in real time pondering the answer and I couldn't produce one. Claire may have come with me. I thought of my return home and moving back into the basement. Leaving and finding an apartment and working at the bookstore. I remembered Angie sitting next to me at the play and me spying out of the corner of my eye her gaze directed at me while I mentally undressed her friend's friend on stage. Her joy and optimism of Rose and I getting together. My wedding and how beautiful Rose looked. I pictured myself on a street and slowly Claire was drifting into the background, clear at first, now a blur, and eventually disappearing. She reappeared when I shifted the destination to Wilshire Boulevard; her and I standing outside a movie theater. I was my true age and she still looked years younger. I had no intention of thinking about Claire again. If I never returned to Los Angeles, I may not have felt the regret now stirring in my rum-soaked brain.

"I don't know," I replied. "That's all in the past and there's no use visiting something that isn't going to happen, right?"

"No."

"No?"

"Visit."

"I tried to find her and I couldn't. She's probably married. She probably has two kids and living with some guy in Montana."

"Or maybe she's waiting for you."

I smiled at the absurdity.

"Aren't you waiting for her?"

"Not, um. Well, what do you mean?"

"Wouldn't you be the happiest boy in all the land if she walked through the door right now?"

"Yeah. But I was married. It's not like I was waiting for her then. I wasn't dwelling on her at the altar."

"You're not at the altar. You're in an airport bar in Los Angeles?"

I tilted my head accepting her logic.

"Look Mister, you're not going to get her by not trying and if she was in love with you once then there's a chance those feelings will bubble up to the top again upon hearing from you".

"There is a difference between this world and that," I concluded tapping my finger on the closed novel she was reading.

"You're right," she said standing up and shaking her book, "the end of this has already been determined." She held out her hand and we shook.

I chuckled at her response feeling like this was a scene written by Mike, it was too unreal. "Who are you?"

"Just some old hopeless romantic," she said smiling picking up her purse and carry-on bag. "Good luck." She threw a few dollars onto the bar for her drink and left.

I was sitting at my desk at work. It was Wednesday. Instead of checking on the news or the weather I surfed for Claire. I started by simply typing her name in a search engine. Millions of different pages were available all having some connection with Claire. She was an attendee at a real estate sales conference in Las Vegas, an old lady who had done her part in the Second World War; she had even been arrested on drug charges in Chicago fifteen years ago. The name never matched the age. The time periods were wrong. She had died eighty-two years ago. I toyed with the idea of contacting her family, telling them I was a fellow high school student and acquaintance of Claire's. The scenario scrolled along in my head never with appealing results. I imagined myself stuttering and eventually hanging up the phone only to be reverse-dialed and a restraining order being placed on my head.

When I asked David for advice he offered off-the-wall options and insisted I had to know someone who worked for the government, or preferably the I.R.S, who could easily look up the information.

"If you're not going to put a billboard on a Los Angeles freeway then there are only three options I see for you but you won't really like the third one. You can check out dating websites, how many twenty-somethings are on that thing anyway? Option two is one of those lame look-at-all-my-friends places, the ones where everyone becomes friends with bands and, get this, spy on exes. Not that I've ever done that." David sarcastically turned his head as if he was evading authorities; or Nicole.

"Okay, the second choice could work. I'll give that a try. What's the third one?"

"The third one," he started leaning in closer, "the third one is sneaking into the I.R.S. and finding her tax forms thereby giving you a legitimate work address and home telephone number. You can even see if she's paying fewer taxes because she's married."

"That sounds easy. Gee, why didn't I think of that? If only I actually had the balls to commit a major federal crime."

"Come on, let's go check I'm-cool-look-at-my-friends dot com." David shot out of his chair and raced to the computer room. He plopped down into the chair and rolled the mouse. The screen lit up and he typed in a website.

"Don't you need a profile?"

David answered by plugging a user name and password without turning his head and partially embarrassed. "I can't believe you haven't set one of these things up, what's the matter with you?"

I shrugged off the comment. "Guess I'm not up with the times."

"What's her name?"

"Claire. Are you serious?"

"Her last name shit-for-brains."

"Cox."

David laughed a gargled throat chuckle and typed in the letters C-O-C-K-S.

"That's not how you spell it."

"Oh yeah, that's how I spell it."

"C-O-X. Douche bag. You have kids, act like it."

"Is her middle name Likes?" He said childishly.

"Don't make me teach Theodore an embarrassing word. Next time you're at the toy store I'll have him run around asking you to help him find a clitoris. Of course, you won't be able to and he will cry and start screaming really loud, Daddy why can't you find the clitoris."

David deleted his version of Claire's last name and typed in the accurate one. "Using a man's children against him, you're low, man." He tapped down the enter button and a list of possibilities popped up. He scrolled to the first profile available for viewing.

251

"That her?" He asked in an unenthusiastic monotone. It was.

"Yes. Holy shit. Open the profile."

"Alright, calm down ya little freak ball."

Her profile came up. It matched up. Her age, her face, everything. I found Claire. David clicked on the pictures which opened a window revealing five other photos. She was standing with her family on a boat. Another one she was surrounded by friends at a bar. A couple close-ups. I was entranced. She was beautiful, more than I remembered.

"She lives in...Delaware. Who the hell lives in Delaware? Probably with a boyfriend."

"She's got a boyfriend?" I was hurt and already felt rejected.

David looked at me in disgust of lack of intelligence. "Are you serious? Can you name me one reason why anyone in their right mind would move from Los Angeles, the land of sun and beautiful fake breasts, to Delaware? People just don't do that unless there is a good reason for it." He scrolled down the page. "She doesn't have a boyfriend."

"How do you know?" I asked leaning in close to the monitor scanning the page.

David pointed to the screen. "See, genius. Single." David leaned back in his chair and put his hands behind his head.

I grabbed the mouse and voyeuristically delved into Claire's life. There was little she decided to reveal. I scanned up and down, left and right, for any information but ultimately settled on her being single and living in Delaware. The other details were minuscule.

"So, you going to see her?" I shifted my head and faced my brother. He looked into my eyes and smiled. "Yeah you are you crazy bastard. You have to if for the only reason that you live in an age when you technologically spy on ex-lovers. Mom and Dad could never do this."

"That's true," and I nodded. It was my generational duty to do this.

* * *

I busted into my boss's office the next morning and asked him if I could have the upcoming Friday off. He saw that I was on the brink of begging and inquired why I wanted to leave so soon after coming back. I did the only thing I could think of: lie like a whore in a confessional. To him I was worn down from the business trip all around the southwest and needed an extra day to have the time catch up to me. He complied under the condition that I work an extra hour everyday the following week. I agreed. I wanted to leave that very moment but had to settle for shaking my leg at my desk in heart pounding nervousness and excitement. I had a missed call on my cell phone which was on the floor having vibrated off the desk. It was Rose. She was checking in, an old habit that had yet to die. You just can't be with someone for so many years and shut them off. I had parallel feelings and felt obligated to call her back omitting the latest Claire addition in my life. To Rose, Claire was a mere faded memory of the ladies I courted before she came along; an adventure that vanquished at the start of my affection for my Rose.

I buried myself in as much work as I could. I called David and begged for his login and password so I could spy once again on Claire. He harassed me for a little while and eventually negotiated me babysitting for the pertinent information that he held. A flood of memories poured in as I studied all five pictures she had placed on her web page. I shunned my cowardice, my stupidity from the previous years. I closed the window on the screen and felt a lump form in the back of my throat.

At three in the afternoon there was a general office meeting in the conference room in which all employees were required to attend. There was idle-chit chat before the chief editor, Doctor B as he liked to be called amongst friends stemming decades ago when he aspired for a career in the medical profession, entered. What started as harassment when he failed out even before applying had now become a standard nickname. I had yet to adopt the nickname and called him Benjamin. "Good afternoon one and all," he shouted rushing himself into the room. "My sincerest apologies for the tardiness." Everyone in the room collectively checked the clock hanging on the wall to see the minute hand drop to 3:02 and then respectively glance at their watches. "If you're not early you're late, you know I always say that." He smacked his hands together with enthusiasm and backed up toward the wall. A giant white board with permanent blue and green and red residue from pesky markers that refused to be wiped away stopped his momentum backward and he sprung forward again, he always liked moving in front of a crowd.

"How many people have ever been to Ohio?" He asked business-professionally.

Everyone in the room raised their hand.

"We have been prospecting down there. Most of you know that I have considered opening a second magazine displaying all of the state's wonders and small hide-a-ways. Secrets for tourists and citizens alike to visit, to vacation, to spend a weekend at. To learn more about your fellow state-folk. The Up-North piece on the ten best hiking trails north of Midland was not only the most viewed article of last fall on our website but we have continued to seasonally provide Michiganders and surrounding states with the best locations to view nature's pastures in accordance to the time of year. Thank you, James." Benjamin announced clapping his hands in James' direction. He nodded and smiled. The others, myself included, felt obligated to applaud.

"We're opening in Ohio starting March first next year. I will be asking some of you to set up residence as we open our branch to the south. I would like to keep it close, in Toledo, so those who do go won't have to go far but I was contemplating going further into the state to really soak up the culture from all angles. Possibly Columbus."

Doctor B's overzealous attitude mustered fear of more hours but excitement of more money in most of the room. I pondered whether I would be one of the lucky ones to leave town. I lacked the seniority but had a decent sales trip behind me which could thrust me into a new and better paying position. I glanced over at Lee who looked to be chewing on his own tongue or sucking in his cheeks. I spun my head around and felt that Lee had roots in southern Michigan. I had a couch in my parent's basement. Financially and professionally, it all depended on how much business I brought in from the west.

"What's wrong?" I asked Theodore, his head resting on the palm of his hand as he gazed upon his plate of spaghetti. "Don't you like spaghetti?"

"Yeah," he whimpered.

"Come on, tell Uncle Drew."

He hesitated, lifting his fork and twirling the long strings around and plopping them back onto the plate. He lifted the utensil again and watched the sauce drip down.

"Let it out, little man. Don't keep your feelings bottled up, you'll end up bitter and alone, I'm living through both and let me tell ya, it's not a pretty sight."

"There's this girl at school. I'm in love with her but I don't think she loves me."

"Are you serious? How old are you? Five?"

"Six."

"No you're not."

"I'll be six soon."

"Soon in eight months. Aren't you a little too young to be in love?"

"The heart wants what the hearts wants, Uncle Drew."

I lifted a fork full of my pasta. "Touché," I responded shoving a mouthful of food into my face. "What's her name?"

"Lisa."

"Lisa," I said back softly and smiling. "No shit."

Theodore's eyes opened wide at my curse and he put his hands over his mouth.

"Let's keep that little slip between you, me and the wallpaper. Lisa was the name of my first love."

"What did you do?"

"I kissed her."

"Really?" He leaned in close. I was his mentor in the game of love now and he was all ears.

"Didn't really go so well after that though. The thing about that first love is it's not really love. Love is complicated, remember when we got the new TV and Grandpa couldn't figure out how it worked, it's something like that."

"Go on," he said.

"Um, go on. Okay. How about more metaphors? Love is like the wind, at first it takes your breath away, the next it's blowing dirt in your eyes, and it's never good when the wind breaks, that stinks." I chuckled at my flatulence reference which went right over Theodore's head.

"I'm confused." Theodore confessed. "What should I do? I want to marry her."

I was amused by the innocence and ignorance bellowing out of my nephew. I had been there before; I had been in love before I even knew what love was.

"I'll tell you what, bud. This worked for me," I stood up and headed toward the cabinet and pulled out a handful of chocolate chip cookies. I placed them on the table in front of Theodore. I then dug into my pocket and pulled out a one dollar bill and tossed that down too. "Go up to her tomorrow and kiss her."

"Where?"

"On the cheek. Or on the lips. Lips would be weird though, you are only six. You do that and no matter what, you'll feel proud. If she rejects you, you gave it a shot, you come back here tomorrow night and you get these four cookies and a dollar. I didn't even do something like this until I was eight so you're peaking before your uncle."

Theodore stared at the cookies and thought. He remained silent for a few moments and I reminisced back to the childhood wager I took part in.

"How will you know?"

"Oh, I'll know."

He still looked down at the cookies and I stood above him. He scratched his head and continued thinking. Something was wrong and I picked up a cookie and ate it. He shot a look at me.

"It's a silly bet," I said. My attempts to conjure up an old victory from the past fell flat. I was happy that it did. Theodore wasn't Brad and I wasn't eight.

"But," he started but didn't have a vocabulary to continue.

"Look, kiddo," I rested a knee on the ground and sincerely looked into his eyes, "you need to do this when you're ready. No pressure and no," I looked over my shoulder, making sure my brother wasn't about to walk into the room unexpectedly, "no bullshit. This whole love thing is hard to control and it's even harder to let someone fall in love with you. Sometimes putting yourself out there and giving it all you got isn't good enough. You can try and try and nothing will ever happen, or if it does it may not last long. You're almost six years old, trust me when I say life is bigger than you realize. I'm almost twenty years older than you and I still have to learn the very thing I just told you. You go to school tomorrow and you go up to Lisa and tell her how you feel and if she says anything contradictory to your thoughts then you know what, there is always the day after tomorrow. Here." I stood up again and went over to our kitchen counter and grabbed the newspaper. It didn't strike me until I opened the page and laid out the whole section in front of Theodore that I realized what David was trying to tell me years ago. I had figured it out and I was prepared to share my wisdom with my little nephew.

"You see this?" I pointed down at the paper. "It's a map of the United States. You have highs and lows across the country, but focus on this part right here," I told him placing my finger at the beginning of the ten day outlook. "What do you see?"

"A sun."

"Very good. And here?" I placed my finger on the next day.

"A sun with a small cloud over it."

257

"Yep. Here?" I moved my finger into next week, next Monday, where the meteorologist for the Detroit Free Press was predicting a cloudy day with a thirty percent chance of precipitation. The low was projected to be thirty-six; the high was fifty-two. Theodore told me there was a cloud and I smiled.

"You know I was thinking about going out of town for the weekend, right?"

He nodded.

"Well, I'm about to take on something like your Lisa but on a much grander scale than you can imagine. The risk, oh boy, I wish all I had to do was cross that playground again and kiss Lisa." I paused and smiled at my dramatic adventures from yesterday. I held my tongue for a moment and thought for a second if she ever remembered my gutsy kiss. I continued. "We both face these challenges in our lives, Theodore. It's what they call a crossroads. But whatever happens to you tomorrow or to me this weekend," I tapped my finger on Monday, "the world will still be here on Monday. It's right here in front of us, there is no stopping it. If it's good we embrace it, if it's bad, well, we will just have to move on, won't we? I mean, they're already making plans for later dates, right?"

"Yeah," Theodore said smiling at my smile. My enthusiasm rubbed off on him. His heart was racing with the same adrenaline as mine and I held up my hand for a high five and he smacked it with all his might. I grabbed another cookie and he grabbed one too. I tapped the cookie into his and said: "Cheers."

It was just after two o'clock in the afternoon as I stood across the street from East Coast Cruises. I was in Delaware and prepared to give it my all. I had very little sleep and had been driving for hours on end. There was no hotel room. There was no game plan. Her online profile mentioned where she was employed and I found the closest East Coast Cruises to her city that was listed. I only prayed that it was all accurate. I actually prayed for more than accuracy. The sheer lunacy of this act was spilling all over my sleep deprived brain. I had more than a horse's share of coffee and wished for my bladder to not fill up again before I had a few minutes with Claire. My cell phone buzzed.

"Don't Be a Bitch!" The message read from David. I closed my eyes and took in the biggest breath of air that my lungs would allow and expelled slowly opening my eyes. The skies were overcast and a slight drizzle patted my nose and the top of my head. The last look in the reflective glass only made this adventure more difficult to take. The bags under my eyes could carry an elephant across the Serengeti. I looked both ways when the light turned and took my first step into destiny.

A bell above the door announced my arrival and upon first glance I didn't see Claire. An older lady spun toward the door in her chair. She had the look of three kids all under the age of ten and had accumulated the same amount of sleep I had.

"Can I help you?" The place was empty. The small office housed a handful of cubicles toward the back, a counter up front, and posters of the trees, leaves, and old towns New England had to offer. I poked my head up and around to get a better glimpse of anybody else in East Coast Cruises other than the mother of three.

"Um, is Claire around?" I asked shyly subconsciously putting my hands in my pockets. A truck roared by outside and I spun curiously catching a glimpse of myself off the reflection of the window. My dark jeans, my green shirt under an unzipped jacket. When I turned back around the lady was shifting her gaze toward one of the back cubicles as the back of a rolling chair popped out, leaning back was Claire. An unsuspecting face froze, she didn't move a muscle but everything seemed to change. Her eyes widened and she slowly raised, her mouth dropping slightly. She looked just like before but aged a few years; more mature, probably the same image I portrayed back.

"Drew?" She asked me, trying to confirm whether or not her mind was playing tricks. I bit my lower lip and shrugged my shoulders. "What are you doing here?" She asked.

I had no answer, not one that made sense at least. We just looked into each other's eyes until the older lady stood up and told us she was going to go into the break room. We were silent; not knowing whether to shake hands, hug, or have wild and crazy sex right in the middle of East Coast Cruises in Dover, Delaware. She started walking slowly and accelerated the closer she got and our arms wrapped around one another's. We embraced. The smell of her hair was indefinable and lovely; the scents had changed but could still be individualized as Claire's.

"What the hell are you doing here?" She asked again backing away.

"The whole story?"

"Hey, it's not like we're busy right now," she responded lifting her arms as if she made everyone in the world disappear. As I stood in front of Claire I thought of all the different stories I could tell, how a divorce and a business trip had led me to Delaware in a desperate attempt to find a woman I had loved eons ago. "So? What are you doing here?" She asked again in partial amusement of my presence.

"I'm here for you." I told her and continued on to the story of my life. From the time I walked away from her knowing I was making the wrong decision, to my long drive home alone in a car that had started making a funny noise when I entered Colorado. I told her about swallowing my pride and hanging my head low as I moved back in with my family, shutting myself off from the realities of life. I told her at first I was thinking of calling her but how useless it felt, the heartache of holding a phone in my hand with nine numbers dialed in and struggling for the tenth; how futile it seemed and a complete lack of knowledge on how to deal with this particular problem. There was nothing for me to say with the exception of long distance relationships never work unless they know exactly when they will be able to see each other and stay with one another again. The longer I hesitated the more obtuse it seemed like time was creating the distance, and not the actual miles, until one morning I had woken up and she was no longer on my mind. I confessed that I was just too scared. I started again at the bookstore and hung out with Angie and Page, even twice with Jon. I told her about Rose and how enamored I had become. I told her that I proposed one night during a thunderstorm. The constant streaks of lightning across the sky building electricity within our bodies and how I feared not her reaction but what if the single bolt of lightning became attracted to her ring. I told her we were married and soon after the regret that sunk in. I called it buyer's remorse. We just didn't work. We divorced and I went on a business trip to Los Angeles and when I saw UCLA all I could do was think of her. "You popped into my mind and I couldn't shake you. You're that song that's stuck in your head, it just so happens I like this song. Good or bad, I just had to try," I concluded.

She wiped the tears from her eyes. Her older co-worker had leaned out from the break room to hear all that I had to say.

"I traveled all this way; I left at two o'clock in the morning and drove over eleven hours on chance. When you don't have much to lose it's easy to risk everything." I stopped mid-thought and looked into Claire, into her soul. "Actually, I have a lot to lose now that I think about it." I stopped again and fought to find better words, the kind that doesn't exist to explain such feelings in moments such as this. "I lost you before by my own fault." I felt defeated, "I don't even know what I'm expecting and the more I think about it the easier it would have been to call you and just say hello. Something in me had to make this trip. I'd like to try and love you once again, Claire."

I waited for her response and I looked over to her co-worker who ducked away. Claire stood in front of me frustrated and the tension in the room was thick.

"Bet when you woke up this morning you didn't expect

your day to go like this, huh?" I said poorly trying to break the tension.

She smiled and chuckled and sniffled.

"Drew, I'm seeing someone. I'm sorry."

"Oh." I made a mistake. What could have easily been discovered over a phone call was found out six hundred miles from home. I nodded. "Well," I said backing away toward the door, "I guess this is goodbye." Again. I felt myself being sucked out the door by a foreign wind-like force. I was outside before I even realized it.

She didn't say a word or confirmed her gratitude of my appearance, at least not aloud. I was something to tell her co-workers later on. I zipped up my jacket. The drizzle fell steadier, not quite rain but certainly getting there. I took my time walking to the car hoping to hear Claire bust out of the East Coast Cruises door and run down the street. I waited for her to tell me that my drive to Delaware wasn't made for nothing, that she cared for me, and we belonged together. I opened my car door and sat inside, my eyes diverting towards the office. She wasn't in the window seeing me off. The only thing left of her in my life was that which was in my mind. I had a long drive home and lots of time to create an explanation on why I undertook this silly adventure and how good the failure was for my character. I had hours to invent my bullshit story to whoever knew prior that I was going after the girl who I should've gone after a long time ago when the percentages were in my favor.

I was hungry but judged best that I shouldn't stick around to eat. Fast food was my friend; a cheeseburger loaded with calories topped with mushrooms to give those who cherished a little health in their food some false hope. The fries would be greasy and loaded with salt. My drink would barely fit in the cup holder but I still took it with me.

Within a few hours I was stuck on I-76 with a full bladder

and a traffic jam, a sea of cars on a still freeway. I was finding contentment when the speedometer passed the ten mile per hour threshold. I felt like I was flying until the hundreds of red lights stayed steady and I was parked on the freeway. It was a time to reflect on everything I had just been through. It was a time to muster a new plan on life. Where was I headed? Right now, home. The only real home I ever knew. I thought that going into the office Monday morning and requesting an assignment to the new office in Ohio would be a spectacular idea. I didn't want familiarity. I hated familiarity. I wanted change. A half hour, or five miles, later I was shaking my leg and eyeing the freeway exit. I had a change of heart and now craved structure and the familiarity I had thought I loathed moments ago. Hell, I wanted to release the near forty ounces of beverage I idiotically drank.

I knew nothing of the area and very well could be exiting the freeway into a demilitarized zone. I stepped into the gas station to use their bathroom and caught a news story on the television of a series of accidents along I-76 and the expected hours of gridlock. Two middle-aged gentlemen stood at the register.

"What a mess. If I have to sit in this crap all I know is somebody better be dead."

"No shit," the second man said as the cashier dumped eighty-nine cents in change into his hand. That dead man causing an annoyance could be someone's best friend, I wanted to say, but all I could think of is how they wouldn't understand the same way I did.

As I tossed a few bucks down for some gasoline I took in the surrounding scenery. I walked outside to the cool evening air and eyed the freeway which still barely moved. As I filled the tank I weighed my options. I needed a hangout and a bookstore across the street seemed like the best option, that way I could keep tabs on the road conditions.

After browsing the fiction and literature section for a few moments I turned my attention to the mystery/thrillers and pulled one of the short-chapter easy-reads about global terrorism and assassination plots directed towards our government with corruption stemming from the highest levels. I plopped down onto one of the conveniently provided puffy chairs and opened to page one. By page two my eyes blurred and the lack of rest was catching up. The last thing I remembered prior to my slumber was how it was weird when people fell asleep on these chairs, especially towards the end of the night, and you had to shake them awake and escort them to the door. I slipped into a dream about being stuck in traffic.

I shook awake, the blinding florescent light burned black dots into my dilated pupils. I wondered if I was snoring, which I assumed no, and checked my chin for drool. There appeared to be none. The sun had dropped below the horizon a long time ago; I could see the parking lot lights reflect off the wet tar. I checked my cell phone for the time and as I did it vibrated. A 609 number I didn't recognize was displayed and I considered whether or not I should answer. It could be a calling card or a telemarketer. I flipped open the phone and pressed send.

"Hello?"

"Drew?"

"Yes," I answered suspiciously.

"It's Claire."

Now I was awake, the grogginess shooting out of me like a circus acrobat from a cannon. I sat up straight and looked around thinking she was near even though the possibility was remote; I even went so far to pat down my hair that I feared stuck straight up in the back.

"I still had your number in my address book. Kind of silly, I guess, I don't even know why I didn't just not add it when I got a new one." I yawned as she continued. She was nervous, her volume dropped steadily and faded away. I had no response. I was ten seconds out of a deep sleep in the middle of a bookstore, my synapses weren't striking off one another as quickly as I preferred, and I only hoped she didn't take my silence as contempt. "You still there?"

"I am," I replied expecting the question.

"Well," she hesitated again. Whether or not the news was good or bad I wanted to encourage her to continue but it was at that moment a loud and random dong blasted into my ear and I took the phone away. A low battery light flickered.

"Claire, my phone could very well die at any moment," I started standing up and walking toward the door, toward my car, toward the cell phone wall charger I brought along. I was bee-lining through the store dodging bargain tables and paperback bestsellers.

"Oh, well, maybe I should let you go," she said without a hint of truth to that statement.

"No, no. Just need to get my charger and we're good as new. Well, not new, but..." The door was opened by an employee who smiled and looked me in the eyes.

"Have a good night, sir. Thanks for stopping by."

"Wait, what?" My heels almost squeaked as I broke hard and turned toward the employee.

"Have a good night." He still smiled and I eyed the hours even though my concept of time was on the edge of oblivion.

"You're closing?"

"Actually, closed."

"Drew, I can call you back, it's no big deal."

"No." I shouted into the phone. Dong! My cell phone told me once again that I should charge it or risk losing my call and any possibility to talk in the immediate future. "Shit."

I darted out into the light rain and darkness of a city, town, or village I was occupying. My car sat alone in the middle of the lot under a bright light.

"Look, Claire, if my battery dies I'm going to plug it in and call you back, okay?"

"Drew, we can talk another time." She was giving up. She thought I was brushing her off, that maybe I was closer to home than her and her voice was causing more harm. I only need a bunched up piece of paper to crunch near the phone to emulate a dying signal.

"Claire, let me get my charger."

"Where are you?"

"No idea." I shouted lifting my arm in the abyss and I started running toward my car. I hopped in and turned it on. The engine roared to life and I looked around at the closed restaurants. Dong! I swore to myself, gritting my teeth then biting my lip. "So, what's up, Claire?" I didn't want the last bit of conversation prior to the death of my battery to be my heavy breathing.

"Well, I wanted to talk to you about earlier."

"Okay." Keep her talking I told myself, like a hostage taker.

"Remember I told you I was seeing someone?"

"Have yet to get it out of my mind." I threw back to her as I pulled out of the parking lot. No place was open and a gas station, I couldn't imagine having a plug conveniently placed for cell phone use, was the only place boasting an open sign.

"Well, it was sort of true."

"What do you mean sort of?"

I saw a hotel down the road and gunned it. A lobby was a sure bet and, after the call, get a room for the night, I figured I was too many hours away on too little sleep to make it home this Friday night.

It took her a moment as she collected her thoughts and placed them in an order to make sense when spat out. "Okay…"

That was all she said and as I felt my cell phone vibrate in my hand. I looked at the inside display to see it powering down.

"Shit!" I barked as I hit a red light and saw the hotel entrance only feet away. "Shit!" I screamed a second time as if the heaven's above declined to hear my first curse. I tapped my fingers on the steering wheel and shook my left foot in anticipation. The light didn't turn. I was on the short end of a major intersection. "Come on," I begged at the yellow box hanging from the wires fifteen feet above the street. I saw the light flash to yellow for the opposing traffic, then red. I looked on my side. Green. I floored it toward the hotel parking lot entrance and gunned it up the ramp.

I found a parking spot near the lobby entrance and jumped out of my car. I threw open the trunk and dug into my bag for the cell phone charger. My trunk was slowly turning into a laundry basket as I flipped my bag inside out. I grabbed the charger and raced for the revolving door.

I entered the hotel and twisted and turned in search for the two little sockets on a wall. They were hidden. I continued my search where four well cushioned chairs and a long couch sat surrounding a glass table. There was one on the ground and I jammed the plug in and put the other end of the cord in my cell phone. I held down the power-on button and watched in delight as the screen blinked on. Directing my hand to the send button, the call list popped up and staring me down was the unrecognizable number. I pressed send again. I heard ringing.

"How much did you hear?" Claire answered.

"Huh?" I was caught off guard expecting a commonplace greeting.

"What was the last thing I said?"

"I think the last thing I heard was 'okay'."

"Oh, okay." She started as I collapsed onto the nearest chair. "Well, I was kind of not telling the whole truth when I told you I was seeing someone. See, you threw me off and it was the first thing that popped in my head. I went out on this date last Saturday night with this cute guy I met at a coffee place near work. Not a corporate place or anything, just some organic one that I heard of and wanted to try out, but I realized I was one chapter away from finishing my book so I had to go to the bookstore and buy a new one which, if you remember anything about me is like asking a kid to walk in a candy store and telling him he can only have one candy bar and two minutes to choose. I'm rambling."

"I noticed."

She giggled back embarrassed and now thrown off track.

"Where was I?"

"Cute Coffee guy."

"Right. So, I asked what he was studying because he had a laptop out and was typing and looking at notes and he said he was working on some sort of thesis. I felt weird and didn't want to bother him but we got to talking and then he said he really needed to continue and I gave him my number. So, he called. We talked. He took me out."

I sensed there was more to the story, at least hoping there was because it was really anti-climatic and not heading in a direction that favored a happy ending for me, but I tend to believe life is all about average anti-climatic stories mixed in with the occasional bit of drama and excitement. I prayed for more detail.

"And?" I asked.

"I'm waiting for him to call me."

"Did you call him?"

"Yes," she said shyly low. "On Wednesday. I don't think he's interested."

"That makes him an idiot then." I opened my mouth to continue and took notice of my remark. It could be construed as flattering and I hoped it was taken that way. Her small laughter had me believe it was understood appropriately.

"Thanks." There was a moment of pondering silence before she continued, "Drew, I'm not seeing anyone. If he isn't going to call six days after a date then the smart money is on me getting dropped like a morning deuce after a nighttime alcohol binge."

I was taken aback, very far aback. "Claire, Jesus Christ."

She laughed and gasped simultaneously. "I can't believe I actually just said that. That was disgusting, I'm so sorry."

"Actually, I'm kind of turned on." I could sense her concern that the unladylike comment would be the deal breaker. I offered a comedic, sarcastic remark in hopes to alleviate any worries. "No, you're right. That was disturbing on multiple levels. You didn't say things like that on your date, did you? 'Cause that certainly would explain the no return call."

"Of course not." I could hear her pacing her apartment and

imagined her hand against her head, even squeezing her hand into a tight little fist scared that whatever message she wants to relay got lost in a joke. "I just had this strange moment of familiarity with you."

"Yeah," I responded softly, understanding.

"You're not in Delaware, are you?"

"I honestly have no idea where I am. I want to say Pennsylvania."

"Can you do me a favor?" My silence gave the green light to ask. "Find out where you are and let me know. I'll drive to meet you. If that's not too weird."

I smiled to myself, placed the phone down onto the chair and walked to the front desk. After inquiring about my exact location I strolled back to Claire and told her where I was. I let her know that the unknown amount of nap time I ingested at the bookstore probably would only hold me over for so long. Claire told me to sit tight and said, with my permission, she would like to see me. I accepted her offer with a renewed sense of energy, my eighteenth wind of the day, I believe.

I approached the front desk a second time and was able to get a room for the night placing it on a credit card I knew was near its limit. In a matter of minutes I fell upon the hard mattress and stiff comforter that a hotel room offers and closed my eyes. After a few seconds I reopened them frustrated on not being able to fall asleep immediately. I closed my eyes a second time and thought about Claire and me meeting up a second time. My legs dangled off the edge of the bed, an arm resting behind my head, the other on my chest. The cell phone vibrated on the dresser next to the TV and I jolted upwards. It was Claire telling me she was at the hotel in the lobby and couldn't find me. I groggily told her my location and she was on her way up. The last three hours had blinked by and I hoped I would be able to hold on to being awake a little longer.

There was a soft knock at the door and I quickly gave myself a once-over in the mirror.

"Hi," Claire said smiling when I opened the door.

"Hi," I responded moving backwards, "come on in."

She nodded and entered. She carried only a small purse and was dressed more casual than before. An army green tank top under a matching green long-sleeve shirt. She tossed her spring jacket on a chair in the corner. We both stood in silence awkwardly with the same burning question of 'now what?'

"You came all the way to Delaware to see me." It was stated as an unbelievable fact as if she had to read it in a textbook to find it correct and satisfying.

"I did."

"And now you're driving back."

"I was. There was bad traffic and this is where I stopped."

"That's pretty crazy."

"I know." I put my hands in my pocket as a way to hide the shame of seeing myself as a stalker or a general run-of-the-mill psycho.

"I didn't really expect it."

"I didn't think you would. I was thinking of calling you but..." I trailed off. I could feel my palms begin to sweat and I wanted to rush over to the air conditioner and blast it, anything to relieve the sudden heat wave that has taken over the hotel room.

"So, you're divorced." She started.

"Yes, I sure am. I am part of the statistic."

"I don't know what I'm expecting out of this, ya know? You kind of threw a curve-ball at me today. Now I'm in Pennsylvania." We were having trouble keeping eye contact. We created false images in a corner or on the floor, something to help divert our eyes. "The last thing I expected to see was Drew Meade walk into the Delaware office of East Coast Cruises."

This scenario was beyond idiotic. She stood in front of me having been so angry that she was blown off by a date from last week that she craved familiarity, even if it had to be a painful familiarity from years ago. I was the guy who drove hundreds of miles for the chance to rekindle a romance and hope my gesture would melt her heart and sweep her off her feet.

It was awkward but still felt right. Her and I being together was ultimately my goal for the weekend, it was scary and ballsy. This was supposed to be different though. Meeting in Pennsylvania shouldn't have happened, I thought to myself, we should have been with one another in California, or Michigan, the location was irrelevant, we shouldn't be in this position because we should have always been together.

"What did you want from me? Why did you drive all the way?" She finally asked me.

I shook my head and honestly told her, "I just wanted to see you."

"You understand how crazy that is? I mean, isn't there a good chance you'll end up hacking me up into a hundred pieces and bury me along Lake Erie?"

"Well, there isn't a good chance in that; I don't even own an axe." I tried to lighten the situation as best I could.

"We're crazy. You and I. We're mentally unbalanced."

I couldn't help smiling at the accusations and the many forms that insanity comes in. Neither of us was mentally unfit nor did we require straightjackets but I was positive our friends and relatives would think differently at this point.

"You know what I wanted out of all this?" I asked myself the question knowing that now was my time to strike the iron and tell her exactly where I stand. "I wanted to see you and have you so excited to see me that you jumped into my arms. It was conveniently raining outside so it would've made for a perfect movie scene. I have been in love a few times in my life and for one reason or another they didn't work, but you, Claire. You and me. That worked. I think I'm different now. I hope I'm different now." This was all coming clear in my head. I was my own therapist and patient, this was my breakthrough. The whole trip was characterized and my feelings for Claire were defined in perfect saturated color for me now and I went right to the edge of the bed that she had sat down on, her arms and hands behind her holding her steady. I got to one knee and was able to look into her eyes.

"Claire, maybe I didn't know how to fight before for what I wanted. I know I loved you and a part of me I think still does. You're worth fighting for. That's why I drove out here. I want your love and if you didn't come here tonight, I probably would've driven back to Delaware tomorrow and find you again." Love at first sight is the only thing I could think of as I looked at her biting her bottom lip, her eyes that began to water, her smile.

I didn't want to leave this. I was beginning to feel that my whole life led me to this make or break point. I had looked into Rose's eyes and pictured us old and together, a quick mental snapshot. But with Claire I could see our lives. I didn't see us old and wrinkled playing shuffle board on senior cruises, I felt it. I connected fifty years in the future to this moment. When our kids asked how we met, she was sitting there next to me. I was scared that she might be scared too. My stomach tightened at the prospect of loss.

"You hurt me, Drew. Badly. I loved you." She doubted herself as the flood of remembering the pain overwhelmed her.

"I don't know how to explain my actions. I was so...I don't know how to explain it. I broke your heart and my own. My pain of being there overshadowed my love for you." I was afraid she was ready to bolt out the door, that she wouldn't accept my ignorance or situation as valid from all those years ago. "It's not an easy thing to ask after what I did to you. I'm afraid that now I'll have to accept those circumstances. They are only my fault. But I did love you, Claire."

"So, do you love me?"

"I don't know if it's love but all those feelings I felt for you years ago have smacked me in the face a hundred times more intensely."

A tear spilled down her cheek and she wiped it away and lowered her hand taking mine.

"You're the best thing that ever happened to me." I commented.

She chuckled, "That's the sweetest thing anyone's ever said to me. Christ." She said wiping away more tears. "Making me get all emotional," she said quietly.

It just may have been the sweetest but I made a promise to myself that I'd try to be even sweeter.

I apologized and she accepted it.

We were silent and had suddenly had a hard time looking at one another again. I looked down at her hand in mine and she was staring off toward the wall. I tried to judge what she was thinking on the faint heartbeat I felt in her fingertips and how tight she was holding onto my hand. A flurry of thoughts rummaged along in her mind. She was analyzing and I was the defendant awaiting the verdict. I hoped for good but feared a life sentence away from her. Out of the corner of my mind I saw her head move and her eyes faced me. I looked up.

"What are you still doing on the ground?"

I smiled and lifted myself onto the bed next to her and we leaned in close to each other and held both our hands. We slowly moved our lips close and kissed.

There are weekends that were good and then there are the ones that are worth remembering for the rest of your life. Most people remember the weekend of their twenty-first birthday, that is, if they didn't overindulge in the possibilities of truly being of legal drinking age. You spend it in Las Vegas or at a nearby bar or club with everyone you know who is over twenty-one. A honeymoon, a wedding, a child's first birthday party; events that can take place over that forty-eight hours that never pop out of your head; the stories that start with the same words of "There was this one weekend."

* * *

273

There was this one weekend back when I was twenty-four. I had recently been divorced and on a business trip to Los Angeles when the girl of my dreams re-entered my life albeit only mentally. I chased from one ocean to another in search of her and found her in the most unlikely of places near the Atlantic Ocean. At first we weren't sure what to expect or how to handle this new speed bump in our life but we took it as best as we could. That first night we made love countless times and I drove back into Delaware to spend that second night at her place. We watched the sunset and had breakfast at two in the afternoon. We held each other for hours and talked about what had happened back in Los Angeles all those years ago. We spoke about an uncertain future not knowing where our careers were headed or what we really wanted in the end. I told her that no one knows what the future brings but I'd sure like to spend it with her. She concurred and we made the promises that naive couples make at the beginning of a relationship. This one was different, but they always are.

"Long distance relationships only work when they know exactly when they're going to see each other again. And when they see each other, they know they won't be leaving. I don't know when I'll be seeing you again and I don't know how long we will be together then."

"Somehow we're going to have to make this all work because I don't usually go this far on a first date."

I left Delaware for the second time that weekend only this time under better circumstances. I hoped that my drive would take place mostly in my mind as I daydreamed about Claire, the weekend we shared, and the future that followed. This was a safe bet for the first half hour, by then I was halfway through a CD, and did my best to sing as loud and poorly as possible for the remainder of the disc. I would be arriving home at two in the morning at the earliest and even if I was healthy enough to attend work the next day, I honestly wanted one more day. A day to reflect, to sleep, to do nothing but sit on the couch in my parent's basement and have time dedicated to my own self. The more I felt the urge to play hooky the louder I sang. A sore-sounding, hoarse voice would do the trick to tell my boss I was ill.

I set my alarm for seven-thirty and upon waking up I rubbed the sleep out of my eyes and rehearsed my sick call a handful of times. Luckily I hit the boss's voice mail and explained that I was feeling under the weather and was staying in today. I would call later to confirm that I was feeling better and he could expect me in bright and early Tuesday morning. I crashed my body back onto the couch and fell right back asleep, not opening my eyes until around noon when my body told me to get my lazy ass up and my bladder was hinting that if I didn't drain it, it would drain itself.

Hair a mess and still donning a pair of sweat-pants and a T-shirt I plopped down onto the computer chair and started a search for east coast jobs. I was in a position for a second risk, if that meant leaving behind a good paying job in Michigan for a not-so-hot one in Delaware, then so be it. I wanted to dedicate my life now to fixing the mistake I made in the past. There was something about Claire, a feeling emitting from her that I had never detected in anyone I ever met. Perhaps she was the one. When I married Rose I was certainly in love but in hindsight I recognize I lacked enamor. I couldn't find the point where I was so punch-drunk in love with her that nothing else mattered; a connection that was there with Claire and I shuddered with the possibility of a similar idea. As I scrolled marketing positions in the Dover area my stomach made a straight shot upwards and plummeted back down. For the first time I was bordering on an idea that maybe Claire didn't feel the same way. We hadn't seen each other in over five years and the near-sixty-plus months can create a lot of energy that may have been released too quickly. I doubted. I was scared again as I toyed with the incredible idea that the memorable weekend was just a fluke. My story changed from "There was this one weekend that was too good to be true".

I scrolled down sales jobs and the prospects were shaky. I entertained the idea of asking Claire to come out to Michigan or maybe Ohio with me, if I did get the transfer. Life was starting to rear its ugly head into this fantasy. My worst case scenario was working retail and bringing home a small amount of bread until the right job threw itself upon me. I played with figures; numbers, savings, I looked at apartments in Delaware and was worried about what I would do if it didn't work. I would crawl home once again having gotten a knockout punch one more harsh time. I would show God my plan and he would laugh and say "Yeah, right".

"Good weekend?" I spun around in my chair and saw my no-make-up wearing, quick showered and tired sister-in-law standing a few feet away squinting at the screen. "Sales rep in Delaware, huh?"

"Good morning, Nicole."

"I'm assuming life offered the handful of aces considering you got home after I went to sleep last night and I didn't see your car outside when Layla started crying at one-thirty."

I relayed the story. The first time I told the tale and she got a kick out of it, saying they should make a movie about it. I then used her as the only woman who could offer me unbiased advice on the whole situation. I told her how I felt about Claire and how I feared having to come back, my tail between my legs, and burdening the family by crashing on the couch in the place I called home many times in my life.

"First off, Drew. Whether you believe it or not, we like having you here. You're a good babysitter and we don't have to pay you. Your brother knocked me up and we decided to get married, you know what? Best thing that ever happened. We love each other so much. Maybe you didn't understand that with Rose, but I can see you get it now. I'll be out with my girlfriends, one of which is now divorced if it makes you feel any better, and I'll see their struggle to find true love to the point where they will fool themselves into thinking they're in love. With Claire, I can tell you love her. You should never have to try and be in love, it happens. You move to Delaware, she moves here, you both move to Egypt; nothing should stop you from pursuing the one you love. It's better than sitting around wondering what could have been."

"So, you're saying I should go for it." I responded facetiously, understanding her point.

"I'm saying you should go to a strip club and empty your wallet in a pathetic pursuit to buy your true love."

"Thanks, Nicole."

"No problem." She said turning and walking away. "Oh, you're babysitting on Saturday," she added.

My cell phone was buzzing on the coffee table next to the couch. I leaned over and saw Claire's name pop up. I told her I was faking sick in an attempt to recover from the weekend. She was on a lunch break.

We discussed in our short amount of time the overall plan which was still nearly impossible to figure out.

"I'm a little apprehensive about moving for a guy. I did that once and got stuck in Delaware indefinitely." Claire told me.

"A good reason to get out then."

"I can handle moving. Dealing with the change of addresses and getting my wardrobe to a location hundreds of miles away isn't the biggest challenge. I'll tell you, Drew, I'm afraid."

"Of what?"

"Of the unknown," she started her debate, "who's to say that this isn't some sad attempt on both our parts to make up for being hurt recently? We were great together, but that was years ago and I know I've changed a ton and I can tell you have too. It didn't work then, why should I move to you? Or you to me?"

The question gnawed at the surface of my brain. I struggled, like a man does, for a comforting answer. Chicks say they dig honesty, so I opted to go with that.

"I don't know," I stated as monotone as possible.

"I mean, we're talking pretty much moving in together and starting a new life together without really knowing one another. This doesn't make sense". She sighed heavily on the other side of the phone, the bearer of bad news, horrible news, the kind a doctor expels prior to telling the next of kin that they have to bury a family member. "I'm just thinking that maybe we should leave it to this past weekend and call it a day."

"No." I stopped and tried to think if my inner voice said that or it was spoken aloud. "No." I said firmly. "I'll move to Delaware. I'll get an apartment and if we end up moving in together and it doesn't work, well shit, I waste a ton of money on a risk. I could put the money into a stock that's drowning. My life? What do I have? I have my family and a job. Something is missing and, maybe you're right, maybe you are just the gravel to fill in the void, but maybe you're not. I'd like to gamble on it being more. You're more to me than that girl I got to sleep with again."

It was settled, at least for the meantime. I had stood my ground and told Claire that, like it or not, she was going to be mine. Her concerns began to resonate as the day continued and I felt the unsure beats of my heart. There were more reasons surfacing on why I shouldn't take the plunge, the cons began out-weighting the pros. I did have to find a new job. I did have to move all my clothes, books, DVDs, and magazine subscriptions. What if it was all another one of life's elaborate set ups, another failure? I sat safely on the couch with the TV on as I had many times before with the background soundtrack blaring as I crisscrossed excitement and nervousness. My deep thoughts falling further into a hole I may not get out of. I was scared shitless. Not heartbreak, I begged. Not another move away that boomeranged me right back to the basement.

My parents were even hesitant on accepting my decision. They felt that constantly chasing a dream had only caused pain in the past. A dream to California lead to a series of down-spiraling events which ultimately guided me into a marriage that couldn't last two years. Their intervention on settling down, concentrating on work, and getting my life into a semblance of order wasn't working, I told them. I pleaded with them to accept my actions. They were my Mom and Dad, my brother and sister-in-law, I was their relative and by the very nature and laws of the universe they had to let me back in if it all went belly up. But it wasn't about me coming back; I had to convince them that this wasn't another way to chase down a mirage. Perhaps I craved life's chaos too much. They wanted order. I wanted Claire.

"One last dream," I said. Nicole already believing in me and her persuasion over her husband brought the score to a tie. "Don't let me go through the rest of my life asking 'what if'."

"Drew," my Dad started, "that argument is relevant in the other direction. What if you would have just stayed instead of what if you went? You'll never know the opposite answer in the choices you make. The girl of your dreams could be waiting for you as you drive to Delaware."

"Or when I go to that girl the real girl of my dreams could be waiting in Delaware."

"Or South Carolina." David added and everyone turned to him curiously. "I'll just keep my mouth shut," he said looking at Nicole.

"Please, honey." Nicole patted his knee.

My father sighed loudly and looked to my mother, connecting, bonding. They were having a whole conversation with one another without saying a single word out loud. My father turned to me again. "At least pick a time when we can drive out with you this time, okay? We really wanted to go with you to California."

I smiled and assured them I would move at their convenience with my mother adding she wanted to go prior to the winter in order to avoid hazardous driving.

10

What if those back doors open and all I see is a view to the Atlantic Ocean? What happens if she's not there? I remember feeling this way only a handful of years ago when Rose was walking down the aisle. I look over my shoulder at David who is smiling and looking back at me. He nods his head as if it would alleviate all fears and concerns. I've become nervous. I look at everyone in this room and take notice of my Mom, my Dad, Jerry and Lorraine, Kevin, my fiancé's father and step-mother. I remember asking her father for permission to marry with hands convulsing anticipating that he was going to inquire about my previous failed marriage. Aunt Missy and Aunt Meg are here. There are about forty on-lookers but they seem like a thousand staring down at me. Each bead of sweat on my forehead is the size of a quarter-sized mole and seems just as obvious. The boat seems to be rocking more than ever. Stabilizers my ass, I'm thinking. The world was just so unbalanced and I had absolutely no control over the future. Weather forecast, I remember, looking at my brother. It's all fine and good to have a ten-day weather report unless the world ends today.

I face the doors leading down the aisle and out the altar and close my eyes taking in a deep breath of air. When I re-open my eyes everyone is beginning to stand up taking one last look at me then they all look at the opening doors. My brother leans in to me.

"How does it feel to have a whole room of people cheering on your life?"

And so it was officially set in stone. With butterflies floating in the stomachs and heads fogged in a sea of uncertainty, one month later to the day we packed as much stuff as humanly possible into two cars and began our trek east. I smiled as we drove past the Pennsylvania stop that held the memories of that one weekend. What was going to take two days we decided to make in one arriving at the hotel a little early and preparing for an arduous day of apartment hunting. Claire had the day off and joined us; an awkward first meeting with the last time being the very last time my parents thought they would see my college sweetheart.

I settled for an apartment on Baytree Road in Dover near where Claire resided. I joked telling her that things might get awkward if we broke up again. The lack of laughter made me look away in embarrassment assuring her that it was merely a quip at the tension that was mounting. The manager hesitantly let me sign the lease as my parents vouched that I was a good kid. A decent credit score and just enough in the bank to pay a deposit and the first and last month's rent helped.

When all was said and done I stood looking out onto a neatly manicured lawn in my new home. It was dreamlike as if I were floating in the abyss of a clean, empty room and that the alarm would buzz and I would hop awake shoving the covers over to Rose as I started my day. It was a haunting image as I truly was overcome by fear that all this was a concocted scheme in my mind to play out while I breathed heavily in a slumber. I never needed to wake up. Claire was the first one to knock on my new door exclaiming that my father wanted me at the car to help bring the boxes up.

"Third story," he cried as he hauled another box into my apartment. I apologized. I relayed my concern of his heart giving out and he brushed it off letting me know that he may be getting older but he could still carry a box up a flight of stairs.

"It's not the flight of stairs I'm concerned about, it's the three

281

flights." I told him. Claire helped with a few boxes as my mother stayed near the cars reading a chick-lit novel, one that I bought on my last trip to the bookstore; Angie saying her final goodbye, again, and giving me the employee discount. She thought I was insane with a side of misguided guts. I stood outside the bookstore for five minutes staring down Mitchell's wondering if I would see Chelsea, my first real, real true love, my high school sweetheart, ever again. She's here somewhere in this small world, I thought and with my luck, probably Dover, Delaware.

I suddenly recalled the day many summers ago that we had her house to ourselves. I saw her face again, this time the way I wanted to always remember it. We woke up in each other's arms. The tired eyes were the result of an uncomfortable night's rest and having no clue how poorly two people can sleep in a bed when they weren't used to it. The way she said "good morning" and yawned in a way that melted my heart. I smiled at this memory and quickly but vocally told her goodbye across the parking lot and silently thanked her for the memories we shared.

After an extremely long second day of lifting and opening boxes my parents opted to go back to the hotel and crash for the next twelve hours. The door closed behind Claire and me. I went to the window and watched my Mom and Dad get into their car and swerve onto the street and away. Claire came up to me from behind, placing her arms around me and her chin rested on the back of my shoulder.

"So. Where should we do it first?" I turned around and saw her mischievous smile and we kissed passionately.

"I feel bad for the people below us," I said as we went to the floor, I was on top of her and we began kissing harder as if each one wasn't enough and we craved to be even closer. My leg kicked a box full of books and she shifted, moving her arm, hitting another box full of clothes. We rolled over one another and continued our battle of locking onto each other's lips until the stripping process began. Her shirt. My shirt. Her bra. Her pants. We cared very little about removing our socks; that would only bring more time apart.

Afterwards as we were lying upon the floor looking up at the ceiling, her head resting on my arm, our hair disheveled and our breathing labored, Claire said to me, "This apartment has been christened in the name of Drew and Claire".

We chuckled and I added, "Just this room. There are plenty of other places around here that require christening. There's the bathroom, the kitchen, can't forget the parking lot."

"The closet," she added.

"Over there," I said nodding into a corner of the living room.

"The front closet."

"Once I get a kitchen table we should do it under the kitchen table."

I brought her closer to me arching my arm so she would lean over and fall upon my chest. I shifted my neck uncomfortably to look down at her and smiled.

Dover treated me a little harsher than I anticipated; perhaps it was just the circumstances. My car needed maintenance; a new belt, fuel filters, and replacing an unplug-able flat tire depleted a chunk of my savings and I was in desperate need to hand out my resume like flyers on a college campus. I settled for a retail gig at a department store ringing up pants and shirts that would clear shelves once put on sale. Retail was bulking up its staff for the holiday season and I decided to take advantage as I scanned the internet in the evenings. To cut back on a few costs Claire and I decided to split our bills as best we could. She held on to cable at her place as I purchased the most affordable internet service. We ate more like college students than most others in their mid-twenties.

It certainly wasn't easy especially with Claire having befriended an array of girls and guys by drinking at some of the local bars with her ex who, I found out earlier than I had hoped, had broken up with her in late-August, my eyebrow rising when one of her pals brought over two drinks, one for her and one for Danny who I apparently resembled. My shock plus her shock equaled a trip to the exterior cold for an explanation. I not only found out that he still lived nearby but if Danny decided to go for alcohol there's a hefty chance that I would meet him at the bar we now frequented.

I was jealous at first and she explained that there was nothing to worry about mentioning that he had dumped her, I overreacted exclaiming that if he wants her back it's more likely to happen. I feared that I would end up like Claire; being in a relationship that brought me to an unknown territory and eventually finding myself alone with the ever building tension of seeing Claire at a bar with another guy.

"I saw him here like a week before you came out here and he was with someone," she did her best to relieve my fear but I couldn't shake it. Knowing from experience, I knew that you don't travel across the country for someone and get over them too quickly, I was working with a timetable not in my favor.

She wanted a girl's night out around Thanksgiving and she sensed my overwhelming hesitation, of all nights when her friends were trying to hook up, she was the one in the relationship who would end up seeing her ex-boyfriend. They would get to talking as she would be there as company to her friends and not on the prowl. I couldn't help pacing around my apartment with my cell phone in hand awaiting a call. I tried to tell myself I was over-reacting but that did about as much good as wrestling a bear with bare hands and expecting to win.

My cell phone rang. Claire was indeed at the bar with her friends, there were four total and three had met another trio of men when I had a panic-stricken scenario play out in my head, lo and behold, a few blocks away, the nightmare was coming to life. I answered the phone.

"Hey," I started.

Claire's speech was slurred and filled with anxiety. She begged that I came down to meet her. "Girls night is over, Drew." She told me.

I threw on a sweatshirt, a jacket, and rushed out the door. I was at the door to the bar in ten minutes waiting in a small line. A man with a bucket of gel in his hair, yammering on his cell phone and reeking of the men's cologne section stood in front of me making sure he got an over-exaggerated look at every girl's ass that walked by. Twice he lifted an eyebrow with a giant grin on his face hoping I would concur with his choices.

The girl behind me constantly told her friend how cold she was and when I saw her in a mini-skirt, boots, and a low cut white shirt and a pitch black bra underneath I could understand her dilemma. Her friend would critique every skank that the guy in front of me would check out.

Five more minutes passed and I was inside with blood rushing to my dark red ears. I found Claire, our eyes met simultaneously, and we kissed pathetically.

"What's wrong?" I asked and her head tilted back to a tall gentleman by the bar licking the neck of a skinny blonde with awkward, unnatural breasts the size of watermelons. I immediately knew the answer and brushed my arm down Claire's towards her hand.

"He didn't say hello, didn't even acknowledge me, and after two strike-outs he landed that slut." Claire was bitter.

"Let's go."

She shook her head and told me we couldn't. She had to stay a little longer for the sake of the oldest friend in the group who was losing her man's interest and would need a drinking buddy within ten minutes. Out of friendship and kindness she was trapped in a flood of hellfire. A pain that was purely emotional and impossible to fight off. Unintended jealousy crossed through her and flashing in my head was the comparison of the Chelsea and Brad incident of long ago. I sympathized squeezing her hand harder telling her I understood and a desperate reminder that I was here too and wasn't going to leave. I, myself, was consumed with the pain of possibly losing Claire and had this gentleman approached her she may have caved as Chelsea did that one summer. We were two people in love with one another yet had trouble releasing the past's grip from our conscious.

"How could I mean so much to someone and then they ditch me and then a couple months later they do this in front of me?" Claire asked and I had no answer. She meant a lot to me once and I had ditched her too. I felt my body tense up in fear. "I don't even know what I'm upset about, Drew." She looked at me, nervously, "It's like I never even mattered." She turned back to Danny who not only had his tongue down the slut's throat but was eyeing Claire. He was too tall and too built for me to pick a fight. "Who would do that to someone? What kind of person breaks your heart then shoves it in your face?"

"Claire." I said very low, almost impossible to hear in a packed bar. She turned and looked at me with tears forming in her eyes. I did the only thing that came to my mind.

I kissed her. I kissed her so hard that she knew that she mattered to me, and in our world, that suddenly became all that mattered. I kissed her so that she knew I was going to be there. I kissed her in a way that expressed how my heart belonged to her. The world disappeared and there were only two people: Claire and myself. We got lost inside the emotion that stirred within our bodies, a confusing and incredible sensation that told each other how connected we were. We parted and, at that point, she was able to let go of her past and I became the only person that mattered to her and her to me.

It was indescribable, incredible, and to me, it was the beginning of an undying love I felt for Claire. The last bridge as two separate entities had been crossed and we crossed it together. I understood what it meant to become one with somebody else. It was more than a cookie, more than a dollar. It was more than chocolate milk or the satisfaction of proving to Brad that I could do it. Just like the previous dares I had to triumph, what a cookie is to a fourth grader was what Claire was to me. Everything. The world.

In a dive bar in the heart of Dover, Delaware I had lost my virginity. There are many ways of making love for the first time and for the first time I had created true love with my true love.

11

My knees buckle and I nearly collapse to the marble floor. Perhaps it was a lone wave from Poseidon himself striking the side of the ship in an evil attempt to thwart the big day. Staring back at my bride-to-be my heart sank and met the pit of my stomach. Her white dress flows behind her and the bouquet of white, purple and dark red flowers match perfectly with the dark red trimming. She holds them in her hands inches below the prettiest smile I have ever seen in my entire life. Her bright eyes are fixed on mine. My vision narrows and all I can see is my bride-to-be. I feel a shiver from my spine tingle through my body and up my arm. I clench my teeth to fight back the tears welling in my eyes. I feel the slight tingle of sweat on my palms and still hope for a cure for moments like these. I'm overjoyed, happier than I had ever been in my entire life.

We were together on our honeymoon traveling up the east coast of the United States. We watched the leaves on the trees as they changed from a dark green to a brown, red, and gold slowly falling from their homes onto the manicured lawns. We couldn't help stare at the cloudless nights as I stood behind her with my arms wrapped around her waist holding her tightly. I felt a shiver and only held onto her tighter as she smiled. I told her how much I loved her and how I was so happy we were in each other's lives again. When our first child was born, a son, we named him Mike. My parents gathered around and my brother was the one holding the camera. My favorite picture was David and I smiling tapping cigars like toasting a drink. Nicole wiped away all the color so it was in black and white. I always would say that we were Frankie and Dean, if just for that moment. Claire and I had two more children who played with my brother's kids.

I was starting to grow gray hair and Claire called it salt and pepper to add a generosity to my aging. We left Delaware and took up residence in my home state. Where I was employed mattered little to me. Claire eventually became a dentist; that made her father happy. We provided and spoiled our children as best as we could.

When they were all grown up we refused to leave our little home. It was where all the memories came from. Our wedding picture above the mantle was only touched when dusted. It was our constant reminder to occasionally look into the past if you ever wanted to know how you arrived at where you are.

My three beautiful full-grown kids gave me an amazing retirement dinner. The meat on the ribs was falling off the bone and the bread that was served had the correct amount of too much delicious garlic and butter. I held Claire's hand as we sat on the front porch staring out into the neighborhood that we had watched change over the years, she leaned her head on my shoulder and we didn't talk. There was nothing to say and, if there was, we already knew because when you know someone for that long you already know what they're thinking.

"I do." I vowed to Claire.

Countless times I knew I would fall madly and deeply in love with her. My bride. My Claire. Meteorologists gave us the next ten days of weather, I decided to predict the next fifty years in hopes of greater accuracy.

CPSIA information can be obtained at www.ICGtesting.com
Printed in the USA
BVOW07s1938300713

327272BV00001B/2/P

9 781440 156991